Not a Chance

Cover Design by Silver @ Bitter Sage Designs

Interior Formatting: We Got You Covered Book Design

Edited by: Jennifer Herrington, Fresh Look Editorial

Line Editing & Proofreading: One Love Editing

Alpha Edits & Beta Reader: Made Me Blush Books

Epitaph Poem: Sian Wilmot, swrpoetry (Instagram: @swrpoetry)

WWW.VIOLETKAVERY.COM

Not a Chance

VIOLET K. AVERY

A Note For Readers

The city of Amado and Almaden University are both fictional locations. For geographical reference purposes, Amado is located approximately forty minutes drive south-west of San Jose, California.

A word about hockey in this book: The heart of this book is relationships. This means that the focus of the narrative happens *off* the ice. My goal was to capture the dedication, team spirit, camaraderie (read: banter) and rigorous schedule of a team of professional hockey players.

There have been a few alterations to NHL deadlines to accommodate the narrative (i.e. the trade deadline which occurs in March, but Theo is traded in September and still eligible to play regular season games.)

If you would prefer to read the Content Information first, it is provided on the next page.

(If you would like to jump into the book spoiler-free, you can skip ahead here.)

This book has been professionally edited and proofread. Every effort has been made to make it typo-free. But sometimes, despite our best efforts, typos happen. If you spot a typo, please email me at **info@ violetkavery.com**. It is the best way to ensure it gets corrected.

Content Warnings

This book is intended for an 18+ audience only. It contains material that may not be suitable for some and is intended for a mature, adult audience. It contains adult situations and explicit sexual content.

The following topics are present in the book: Childhood emotional neglect (off page but the effects in adulthood are mentioned), death of a parent (past, off page), parental estrangement, personal life and financial/career manipulation by parents.

Your well-being is so important to me. Please feel free to contact me at **info@violetkavery.com** if you are uncertain about the suitability of any of the subjects mentioned. I would be happy to provide additional information.

do you think
a bolt of lightning
doubts her worth
before she lights
up the sky?

SWRPOETRY

This book is dedicated to those trying
to reparent their inner child as an adult.
They failed you by making you feel unworthy.
Be kind to that young soul inside you.
You can be the one to give yourself the
patience and care you've always needed.

You are easy to love.

One

INDIE

"At twenty-five, I would have thought you'd be over your need to embarrass this family at every turn, but now I know I need to take matters into my own hands." Frustration laced every word my father spoke.

As business mogul and much put-upon father, Gerald Layne's face was a mottled red since he had been ranting for over twenty minutes. I sat in my usual chair in his study, enduring my quarterly "scolding," as Emery liked to call it. It was my parents' chance to review every detail of my life that didn't fit into their opulent and ruthlessly managed world—which to say was all of it.

They could make time in their busy schedules to tell me what a disappointment I was.

Lavished with such loving support, it was a wonder I did everything I could to fight back against taking my allotted place in the Layne family dynasty.

But this was a new threat.

Like a searing electrical current had been pressed to the base of my spine, my posture went rigid, despite the way my father's visitor's chair attempted to suck me into its depth.

Death by upholstery sounded less horrifying than whatever commands he was about to deliver.

I had expected this "visit" to be a repeat of the same lecture he'd given me ever since I moved out of the family home for college. Each conversation had the same objective: to show me what a disappointment or disgrace I was to the family name.

"Indigo, are you listening to me?" my father snapped, making me realize I hadn't acknowledged his statement.

"Absolutely. I am a stain on the good name of Layne." Was I rhyming now? "I'm not fulfilling my obligation to this family by making a name for myself in this world. Or, at the very least, using the considerable privilege that has been afforded to me my entire life to contribute to the collection of companies that have supported the Layne name for so many generations. I will strive to do better, Father. So, if that is all…" Maybe I could get out of there before he laid down whatever scheme he'd been cooking up to finally fix me, once and for all.

"Sit," he spat.

I sat. His tone had changed from the exasperated tone of a man forced to acknowledge the disappointment he had for a daughter to the ice-cold one he reserved for corporate mergers where he ripped people's livelihoods apart for profit.

"You've had four years to do better, and not a single thing has changed. That stops now." He pinned me to the spot with a livid gaze, a predator daring its prey to move.

I had truly arrived at the end of my leash.

"I'm sure I don't understand?" I kept any trace of nerves out of my tone. I didn't want him thinking I was afraid of anything he was about to do, even if wariness had flooded my bloodstream.

I peered at my mother scrolling intensely through what was no doubt a very urgent email from her legal practice partners. That or some juicy gossip from the country club their circle belonged to. Both happenings warranted the same level of concentration.

"Mother?" My voice was almost hushed, hoping she would hear the plea in my tone and, for once, come to my rescue.

The weakest throb of hope passed through what was left of the mother-daughter attachment in my heart. She had to know what this was about. Catherine Layne let nothing in this house get past her.

A quick glance up from her phone was all I got as an acknowledgment, causing a cascade of hurt to rush into my chest.

I had felt alone in so many moments of my life, but that second of optimism that she'd act like a real mom for once made the sting of abandonment worse than I'd grown used to.

"Indigo, your mother is not going to save you. She agrees you need to be brought into line."

A familiar numbness crept out from where it made its home in each of my body's cells, knowing I had no recourse but to sit through whatever he was going to tell me. The pain in my chest lessened to a dull ache. My face was frozen in a placid expression.

I would get through this moment and then deal with the fallout once I was back in the safety of my apartment.

"Do not pretend that there isn't at least a modicum of common sense in that brain of yours, Indigo. You did not earn a double degree by being an idiot. Stop being obtuse. It doesn't become you."

He was good at pretending silence meant tacit agreement, so he continued without regard to any answer I might have.

"Watching you insist on working a job outside our family's corporations with absolutely no advancement, despite being vastly overqualified, has shown me you can't be trusted to know what's right for you. I refuse to allow you to embarrass our family any further." He pressed his lips together in a firm line.

"But, Father, I told you. I wanted to earn my way in the world, not have things handed to me." Why I thought it was a good idea to contradict him, I wasn't sure.

"Oh yes, I am very aware of your well-practiced speech about 'pulling yourself up by your bootstraps.' That excuse has grown tired and flimsy, a mere disguise for the rebellious nature you seem to think we have forgotten wreaked havoc on our lives during your teenage years."

I stared at him, no rehearsed reply at the ready this time. Had he seen through me so easily all these years? I'd believed my anti-nepotism speech had appealed to his sense of work ethic.

Had I been wrong?

"Here is what is going to happen next. You will resign from your current 'position' at that second-rate advertising company. I know the CEO of the highest-valued sports and media company in North America from my Yale days. He is going to do me the favor of taking you on board as a communication team assistant. With you working for the Tempests, unlike your current agency, it will at least spare your mother and I the humiliation of having our only child working at a firm with no chance at advancement. You're going to get a trial period to prove that you can be useful to this family in some capacity. He's going to ensure I'm kept apprised of your performance. There will be no allowance for simply taking up space in a multibillion-dollar enterprise." He raised an eyebrow, his expression daring me to argue.

I sucked in a painful breath, choking on the shock that he was about to upend my entire life that I'd built in the last few years.

"Wait, wait. I'm trying to catch up here. What do you mean *quit* my job? I can't just quit." I couldn't stop my hand from pressing against my stomach, trying to relieve the sudden ache that formed.

"You can and you will. Unless you want me to put the full weight of the legal resources I have at my disposal to challenge your grandmother's will. I know you used the money she left you at eighteen for school but have otherwise left the remaining token amount untouched. I have the ability to drag this out for years. Do you think you can win if I take you to court?"

Had he somehow found out about my plans to start a nonprofit for children in Amado? I hadn't even started any of the formalized paperwork! I'd only gotten some initial legal advice so far.

Fear pushed through the thick blanket of emotional numbness that had settled over me.

As much as I liked to think that he would be more afraid for the reputation of the family, there was a part of me that believed he would actually do this. He could probably get the courts to seal the proceedings and figure out how to come out on top somehow.

I hadn't played this game with them for many years to walk away with nothing. I wanted to make a real change with this money. I was eleven months away from properly getting started.

It physically pained me to admit he'd won this round. The consolation prize would be that I could be free of their control this time next year.

Just do this one last thing. Then you'll be free.

"Fine. I understand. Where am I going?" I managed to force out the words between my lips, despite how my jaw wanted to lock around my clenched molars.

I hunched back in my chair with my arms crossed, waiting to hear my father's plan that would put my life on hold for however long he demanded.

Two

INDIE

TORONTO

It wasn't enough to send me across the country. They'd put an international border between us. Not to mention sending me more than 2,600 miles from the home that I'd made for myself in Amado, CA.

I stepped out of Union Station with my too-heavy bags and into the muggy late-September day.

Beads of sweat dotted my forehead with the change in humidity from inside the city's main transit hub. I wondered where this so-called Canadian "fall" weather had escaped to.

I'd been here only once before as a child, not that I remembered anything of the city other than the smell of the sewers outside the subway. My nose wrinkled as I became aware of the scents surrounding me.

Yep, that still smelled the same.

My parents had come to see the premiere of a movie at the Toronto International Film Festival. I couldn't recall the name of the famous actor they were wooing to work with one of their firms at the time. I'd spent the few days we were here in a suite in the Royal York with a nanny, reading at the windowsill, watching groups of people as they smiled and laughed on their way to the Rogers Centre for some sort of sports event.

I hadn't even gotten to see the CN Tower while it was the tallest building in the world. I supposed I would have a whole year to see it now.

Pulling up Maps, I tried to orient myself as to the direction of my hotel. My father had pulled some strings to get me a furnished apartment in one of the buildings Layne Holdings owned in the Financial District, but it wouldn't be ready for a few more days.

I wished I knew someone who could check it for listening devices. I wouldn't put it past my father to stoop to a new low and bug my apartment so that he could have someone listen to my comings and goings at all times. He was ruthless when it came to getting what he wanted.

Though that idea made me shiver despite the heat, I chastised myself for considering it.

The reality was Father's concern went as far as my effect on the family's reputation and had nothing to do with me personally.

I rubbed my sternum at the thought. The keening pain of being unlovable had long dulled to a ghost-limb-type ache after resigning myself to the truth that I was a simple pawn, not a daughter, for my parents to move around at their will.

Since I had a relocation budget, I'd splurged on a hotel within walking distance of the south end of Bay St. I hadn't thought about walking distance dragging two large suitcases along uneven sidewalks, however. Contemplating a cab while sweat dampened the back of my shirt didn't seem like something worth bothering with at this moment. I wanted out of this unexpected heat and into a shower as soon as possible.

After pulling my hair into a hasty ponytail that would normally have me cringing, I headed eastward, still fueled by frustration at how I'd ended up here.

The twelve-minute walk gave me time to ruminate on all my decisions leading up to this point. I grimaced at the thought of leaving Abbie and Emery behind after so many years in each other's pockets. I'd waited a week before telling them I had to leave for this new job. I'd spent seven days thinking over every option and ultimately discarded any idea of trying to work out a compromise with my parents, knowing from experience they wouldn't budge.

A glance at the lock screen on my phone had a selfie of the three of us squished together around the table at our final girls' night before I left Amado.

We were sitting in a café after work. Emery had come from the university after her office hours to meet us around the corner from Appeal, where Abbie and I worked together.

Since it was Emery's turn to pick our Friday night meeting spot, the coffees we had in front of us were ultra-fair-trade-eco-conscious masterpieces made with magic beans picked by woodland sprites and brewed with the freely shed tears of angels. I hoped the sprites were enjoying their $8.50 coffee profits.

Looking across the table at my two friends, I noted the marked difference in their mood. Abbie, the perpetual worrier of the group, looked as if she needed to be tethered to the table leg so she wouldn't float away on a cloud of happiness.

Emery was usually extra chipper on days where she got to choose our girls' night restaurant, but tonight, her whole vibe was dimmed, like she was weighed down by something. Her outlook was naturally a glass-

half-full kind of deal. Worry fizzed in my chest at what kind of thing would have her looking so worn and tired.

Concerned, and not ready to jump into my own bad news, I wanted to know what was up with her first.

"Babe, we're in your happy caffeine place. Did something happen in one of your classes today?"

Emery, who had been spinning her ceramic coffee cup in circles, looked up at me. I couldn't blame Abbie for blinking a few times as if she was looking at Emery for the first time since sitting down. Being so loved up seemed to be heady stuff.

"No. They're fine, I guess," she sighed. "It's just not what I thought it would be, but whatever." She waved away her troubles, refocusing on me.

Emery was determined to honor her mother, who had passed away when we were twelve. She wasn't letting anything get in the way of becoming Prof. Yao, even her own happiness, it seemed.

My heart hurt with the realization that I couldn't even try to fix her mood for her because I wasn't going to be around for this semester or the next, even. Not only that, but here I was about to pile more bad news on her shoulders, unavoidably breaking apart the only family I had ever known.

Taking a deep breath, I just wanted to get this over with now.

"My parents are making me quit Appeal. I gave my notice last week. I'm being banished to Toronto to work for a company of my father's choice."

I'd shocked them into silence. Twin expressions of disbelief looked back at me. Abbie opened and closed her mouth a few times. Emery found her voice first.

"Wha... how... Can he do that?"

Sighing, I tried to think about how to explain it to them. I'd never disclosed the amount of money that my grandmother had left me in her will. I knew they assumed it was a lot because my family owned more companies than I could keep track of.

"Yeah, he'd probably pay off some judge to declare me legally incompetent or something and take my inheritance. I couldn't afford to fight him in court. You know I have plans for that money. I'm so, so close."

Abbie looked at me sadly.

"I know you wanted to do community outreach with it. But do you really need to give up your life here for it? There's lots of other ways to help kids," Abbie suggested gently.

"How much money are we talking here, girl? I know it's rude to ask, but it must be a lot more than you've let on all these years." Emery flushed with embarrassment at asking, but we'd always stuck together all these years.

Separating like this was a big deal.

"Ten million. It'll take every cent to get the nonprofit up and running before donations even become part of the equation." My volume was just above a whisper.

This time, it was twin expressions of shock looking back at me. If the wind changed, they'd be frozen like that.

"Well, damn, I'll move to Toronto for you," Emery breathed. "Two birds with one stone. You get your money, and I'll get to avoid my undergraduates. Think they need an artist and wannabe academic with no business skills?"

"I wish they did, babe." Her enthusiasm had me smiling for the first time since my father made his demands known.

Arriving at the hotel, sweaty and tired, I waited in the line at reception, looking forward to the best shower of my life to wash away this day.

My phone vibrated with a notification, bringing a smile to my face. It was just like Abbie or Emery to check on me, but when I scanned the screen, my stomach clenched.

Father

**You have one chance, Indigo. Proving
that you can make yourself an asset
in the Tempests organization will
help convince me you are ready for
the financial responsibility of your
inheritance.**

As much as I wanted to ignore him, I knew choosing pettiness now would only push me further away from my objectives.

Indie

**Yes, Father. Thank you for this
opportunity.**

Even if I gagged a little as I typed, I hoped he took my words at face value.

I needed a distraction from my father's pleasant reminder that he controlled my life. I texted the girls to let them know I'd arrived safely.

Indie

**Made it to the Great White North. (maple
leaf emoji)**

Abbie

Is it snowing?!! (snowman emoji)

Emery

Glad you got there safe, eh!

They both contained a vast reservoir of ridiculousness. For all the disgruntled masks I might wear sometimes with them, I secretly adored it.

Indie

**I can't tell if you are being serious about
the snow, it's been a couple years
since college and none of us studied**

> geography, but do you think I'm in Antarctica?

> And don't even get me started on the "eh." I will not succumb. You are the one with dual citizenship.

Abbie

> Okay, okay. No snow yet. You still have time to buy a proper winter coat. Do you remember our pre-graduation trip to Vancouver and Whistler in January? So naive.

I did remember. We were idiots thinking that we could get away with our version of a northern California winter wear with an extra hoodie underneath. After all, we'd decided we "wouldn't be outside the chalet that much" while in Whistler. I could still remember my eyelashes freezing my top and bottom eyelids together.

Emery

> Ha! We'll see. You'll be oot and aboot too much to avoid picking up the slang.

Abbie

> Ooooh. What about moose and polar bears! Seen any of those yet? Or Mounties?

Indie

> I can't with you two. I hope you can feel me rolling my eyes all the way back in Amado. Now I know you're joking because you're just typing every Canadian stereotype you can think of. Where have we ever seen a bear in BC

> other than the one behind a fence on Grouse Mountain?
>
> It's the biggest city in Canada. Think Vancouver with no mountain view and endless condo buildings along the lakeshore. Though the lake itself looked cool from the plane window.

Abbie

> Don't pretend that you didn't just look that up on Wikipedia on the plane.

Abbie was correct. I had done that exact thing, not wanting to land with zero information about my temporary home.

Emery

> Fine. We will cease and desist. But I expect daily reports. And the phone number of whatever cute Mountie you might happen to meet. With two passports, I have options, you know. I will relocate for love. (dreamy love.gif)

Indie

> Gross. No, just no. I'm turning off my phone now, ladies. You'll need to find some other poor soul to torment. xo

Abbie

> (heart emoji)

Emery

> Good luck on your first day, eh?

Three

THEO

*G*etting called into Coach's office after practice was never a good sign. I couldn't think of one good moment in my thirteen-year career in the NHL that was preceded by a meeting within these four walls.

It was even worse to see the GM in the meeting, sitting in one of the two guest chairs. It usually meant one of two things, and my reputation was spotless, so I knew I wasn't in trouble.

I knew how to keep any unwise decisions under wraps. And since I was out of my twenties, my life was far too routine compared to my younger teammates.

The only other thing it could be was something I'd managed to avoid by being one of the most in-demand goalies in the league. They'd traded me.

I closed the door behind me with a soft click and resigned myself to the conversation about to unfold.

I had one year left in my contract, so while it wasn't impossible, I had really thought that I'd be one of the rare players to make it through my whole career playing for the same team.

My body was ready to retire, not that I had let anyone on the team or the organization's staff know that.

Coach allowed me to get settled in my seat, always content to let us settle into tough conversations. He gave me a nod in greeting.

"Theo. Thanks for coming in. I know it was a rough one this afternoon, so I'm sure you're eager to head home."

Not particularly. The only thing that waited in my condo was a kick-ass view and a fridge with questionable takeout and some expired condiments.

And a severe case of "what's next?" because you know your knees can't take much more. This is what you get for pushing everyone and everything away for hockey all these years.

The GM, Marco DeLuca, however, did not seem to share the same laid-back approach. He was newer to the team, having been hired the season before. He'd seemed fair in my experience with him, if a bit abrupt in his delivery. He chose to cut to the chase.

"Theo, listen. There's no easy way to say this, so I'm just going to come out with it. You've been traded to Toronto."

Even knowing such news was coming, my body still rocked back as if his words were a physical blow. It was like having a bench press with too many weights dropped onto my chest. I struggled under the weight of a decision that changed my whole life without any input from me.

Shit. If this is what being traded felt like, having years of contributions to an organization washed away with a few words, then I'd been an asshole all these years to not lend more support to teammates who experienced this situation throughout their careers.

We'd been so close to winning the Stanley Cup last year. The hunger in my teammates' eyes told me that this was going to be the season it happened for the Frost, and I would be thousands of miles away playing for strangers.

Winning the Cup wasn't the reason I played hockey, but I'd be lying if I didn't hold some deep belief that achieving the pinnacle of hockey success wouldn't validate my choices all these years.

I was going to Toronto. The destination didn't really matter other than being across the fucking country, which put me even further from my family, who I already didn't see often enough.

DeLuca didn't give me any more time to process the bomb he'd dropped in my lap before he barreled on while Coach watched me carefully.

"I know you probably don't want to hear this. The higher-ups are looking ahead with a specific vision for the team, and it's my job to make that happen. I'm sorry."

I'd yet to speak in this meeting. I cleared my throat and forced the words out of my mouth.

"Thanks, Marco, I understand." That was it. That was all I could give him. We didn't have any history together. It was just business, and I was an asset to move around as they pleased.

I guess I'd just been lucky so far. My thoughts turned sour. It hurt to think about being a line on a salary cap spreadsheet. This team had been my whole life since the day I'd left home.

Yeah? And what do you have to show for it other than a bunch of zeros in your bank account? Does a full bank account and an empty condo make a life?

He walked toward the office door, clapping my shoulder lightly as he passed my chair.

"I truly appreciate your dedication to this team, Theo. The younger guys have had an excellent role model all these years. Just know you'll be missed, eh?"

I'm sure he meant those words, but he hadn't been here to really see what I had given to this team every day for years. Marcus only knew what had been written about me before he took over. He took my nod of acknowledgment as a goodbye and closed the door behind him.

I turned back around to face Coach James. The shock was keeping me from saying anything further. Coach took the burden off my shoulders.

"Well, shit, kid. This fucking sucks." Coach's words hung in the air between us. Now, here was a man who'd gone through the highs and lows of the last several seasons with his team.

His accurate assessment of the situation dragged a chuckle up from my chest. I dragged both hands down my face, scrubbing my skin in an effort to get my blood flowing again.

"Yeah, Coach, it really does. Nothing against Toronto—I'd have felt this way about any team." I was quick to clarify the source of my disappointment.

James had been my coach for more than half my time with Vancouver.

My primary motivation for accepting a contract with Vancouver when I had been drafted had been to stay as close to my family as possible. That I'd gotten an offer just hours from San Jose meant I didn't even need to think about my decision.

I'd wanted to be close enough to home to support my two younger brothers and baby sister. Our mom had died from cancer when Emery was twelve years old, just a few months before my eighteenth birthday. All of my brothers' wild sixteen-year-old twin antics came to a halt, leaving the house in a perpetual state of shocked silence. I'd felt guilty as shit entering the draft when all of us were still reeling from the loss of Mom.

My dad had been a shadow of himself, and I'd considered waiting a year, but it came with too many risks. Injury, for one, but more than that, watching my family grieve had locked me in a place where I'd nearly given up the NHL altogether. I'd had to get myself out of that house, even if it cost me so much pain in leaving my siblings behind.

Back then, I'd been naïve enough to believe that I would follow through on staying in their lives to truly be there when they needed me. More than a decade later revealed that my record of actually showing up for them was abysmal.

The sound of Coach James's voice shook me out of my pity spiral.

"Kid, let's talk off the record. You've gotta report within seventy-two hours anyway. As far as I'm concerned, you left my office right after DeLuca." I got a kick out of the fact that he called me "kid" when I was the second oldest player on his team. I guess all of us were kids when held up to his years of experience.

"You've got one more season left in that body of yours. I know this isn't the way you wanted to go out, but you can make it another nine months, even if you have to go to Toronto to do it. They've got just as much a chance at the Cup this year as we do. You might just be the player to push them to greatness, bum knees and all."

I was humbled by his kind words, even if they were accompanied by such a brutal assessment of my physical condition.

Shit. Had I been showing my aches and pains more than I thought? I'd been militant in my PT and conditioning, trying to mitigate the pain in my knees. I knew my left MCL was fucked. The right knee was heading in the same direction. I'd need surgery sooner than later, but I'd wanted time to decide if I'd renew my contract first.

"I've been working toward the Cup for my whole career, Coach. I've got a couple more seasons in me, at least." I aimed for humor, hoping to turn the conversation from his accurate assessment.

"That's horseshit, Yao, and you know it. There's more to hockey than the Cup. You've already made yourself the poster boy for clean living and dedication all these years. Shit, your legacy is cemented in the history books with your charity work alone. You have a lot to be proud of, son. Take the win."

Flattening my lips, I let my shoulders drop in defeat. My heart buoyed before sinking at him calling me "son." There was a paternal pride there that I hadn't known how desperately I needed to hear until just now. Was my dad proud of me too?

Maybe you should get your head out of your ass and ask him? It's not like he doesn't have thirty years' experience with elite athletes to give some advice on your next steps.

But while I could sit in this office and take whatever truth bombs Coach James threw at me with gratitude, I didn't know if I could take hearing my dad not express the same pride in my hard work that Coach did.

"Yeah, maybe, Coach." A deep sigh escaped me. I trusted Coach enough to be honest. "My knees are going to shit. I gotta retire before I'm walking like my seventy-five-year-old grandfather used to before he had his knees replaced. I don't want to spend my thirties in pain."

"You sure as shit don't, kid. I got enough aches and pains to fill a medical textbook. I wouldn't be surprised if my wife doesn't donate my body to science when I go, only for them to find out it's been held together with hockey tape and chewing gum all these years."

I nodded my agreement. I may not know what my next steps were, but I wanted to be physically able to take them.

"You've given this team everything you had all these years. I hope Toronto appreciates the caliber of player they are getting from me unwillingly."

"Aw, Coach. I knew you loved me after all." I offered him a magazine-worthy smile.

"That's it. Toronto can have you. Get out of here, Yao." His eyes warmed with affection despite his gruff words.

I shook his hand and took my leave.

My chest ached with the knowledge I wouldn't even need the full seventy-two hours to pack up my whole life here in Vancouver.

Four

INDIE

A little over a month into my new job with the Tempests, I finally felt like I was getting into a routine where I didn't feel like an absolute idiot at all times.

I could see that my father had specifically chosen to push me into a communications role. With my job being dedicated to liaising between the team and the media on an almost daily basis, I was sure he imagined me coming home and taking on spokesperson duties for the family.

Right under his thumb, where he could keep me in control.

With the extent of my team sport experience peaking in high school track and field with a third-place ribbon at regionals, I was sorely unprepared in understanding the world of sports communications.

I spent my days learning the tasks under the communications manager. I was lucky to have been paired with a saint in the form of Jermaine Kenton.

He also happened to be married to the love of his life for the past thirty years. The expression on his face every time he spoke about his wife suggested that a certain kind of love could last a lifetime.

They'd also already had me over for dinner twice since I'd started with the Tempests, making me feel welcome in ways I wasn't ready for. Warm and gooey feelings were not my default setting, even if their adorable little Morkie wasted no time in claiming my lap each time I visited.

On top of being so nice, Jermaine was an excellent boss who understood I had come into this role completely devoid of any useful sports knowledge. I was one of those people who only watched the Superbowl for the commercials and the half-time show.

After receiving a summons to his office, I gave the open door a quick knock to alert him to my presence.

Looking up from his computer, he waved me into the seat in front of his desk with a smile.

"Indie! How's my favorite junior communications assistant?"

"Pretty good. Considering I'm the only junior communications assistant here."

"Only a technicality, Ms. Layne," he assured me, as smooth and charming as ever. "It turns out you're about to move into the eye of the storm, or even a *tempest*, if you will." He winked.

God, even his terrible dad jokes were more tolerable than most.

"What do you mean?" Between learning a new job and the complexities of hockey itself, my plate felt pretty full already. I wasn't sure I was prepared to take on anything more without humiliating myself and having it get back to my father.

Failure wasn't an option here. My stomach churned with nerves.

"It turns out Cadence, our team member who works on special features with national and international magazines, has to fly home to Montreal for a month or so to deal with a family situation. So, my dear, that means you're going to need to step up and take over a couple of her away-game duties." He lifted an eyebrow, his gaze assessing.

"Okay. No problem. I can do that." I nodded, hoping I looked more capable than I felt.

Each team in the league had an in-house communications team dedicated to preparing game notes for the media, stats, and info for social media, creating posts, and so many more tasks that I hadn't ever fathomed before.

A quick nod of approval from Jermaine was my cue to leave his office and head back to my desk.

It was a far cry from the repetitive reception job I'd left behind in California.

My phone lit up with a text from Abbie. She and Emery had been amazing about checking in on me regularly and keeping me updated with their news back home.

Abbie was just a week away from moving in with Aiden. He'd been stockpiling expensive treats to win over Mew, Abbie's cat, in his new home. Mew was my boy since I'd taken care of him a couple of times this past year when Abbie was out of town. An avid anime fan, I'd sewn Mew a dozen or so cute outfits that he hated wearing, but he'd gone viral as a grumpy Pikachu and now had his very own Instagram account where his judginess could entertain the masses. Passing the torch of his account to Abbie was another thing I'd left behind.

Abbie

So I sort of did a thing.

Indie

Oh God. What does that mean? You're not changing your mind about moving in with Aiden are you? Did you paint all the rooms in his house black without telling him? Did you cut yourself bangs and you

are filled with immediate regret?

Abbie

No of course not! And no. If anything, it would be anime murals on all the walls. Could you imagine! And no. The Great Bang Experiment of sophomore year in high school cured me of bangs for the rest of my life.

When you use those examples, my "thing" might not be so bad. Promise you won't be mad...

Indie

Geez. Never has any message in the history of messages ended well with those words.

Abbie

Okay, so I was on Instagram looking at all things Toronto. I wanted to find out some cool stuff for Emery and me to do if we are able to visit. And you know how I got Mew from a cat rescue out here? Well, there's an awesome group in Hamilton, ON who rescues small dogs from Texas and brings them up to Canada for adoption. I checked it out and it's less than an hour from you.

Indie

Okay, so you're a sucker for animals. We knew this already. What did you do?

Abbie

Wellllll, I may or may not have filled out a foster dog application on your behalf. And before you start, remember, I know your number one secret wish is for a pet. You definitely don't hide the fact that you turn to mush whenever you see a puppy of any size.

Indie

Excuse me, what? I definitely don't go all heart-eyed over puppies. What are you talking about?

Abbie

Wait. Did you actually think you were hiding all the gooey-goodness on your face all these years?

I absolutely had. I was mortified. Even more so with the heat that filled my cheeks as I imagined what I looked like with a mopey expression whenever I saw someone out with their new puppy.

Abbie correctly interprets my silence as agreement.

Abbie

OMG, you did! Too funny. I promise I won't tease you about it if you forgive me for what I've done. There's a crazy amount of puppies being abandoned right now. Anyway, older dogs aren't as easily adoptable, and when I saw a post for this little one on Instagram.

(She sends a picture of a small gray animal that might have been a dog. Except it's bald with overly large ears. Its little lips are turned up in a kind of curl on one side. Not quite a snarl, maybe a sneer?

Unfortunately for me, it's damn adorable.)

Indie

Wtf is that?

Abbie

Isn't she super cute?! Her name is, unfortunately, Gizmo. They leaned hard into the whole Gremlins 80s vibe. And yeah, the bald thing. She has alopecia because of her specific coloring. It can be a thing.

Indie

Why would I foster this little creature exactly?

Abbie

Because she's been waiting in Texas for months and people are picking the puppies. But more than that, you are going to go through caregiver withdrawals soon and this will give you something to look after.

Indie

I have no idea what you are talking about.

Abbie

Riiiiiight. So it's not like you take it upon yourself to smooth over situations when shit hits the fan for me or Emery. And you definitely weren't the one to tell Aiden off, risking your job, when he had his head up his ass. Nor did you single-handedly annoy the shit out of every independent gallery

**owner to get them to give Emery her
first showcase when we were 18?**

I had done those things. What was so wrong with wanting my friends to be happy? It filled the vast chasm of emptiness inside me for a little while. I only loved two people in this world, and I would be damned if they were unhappy, and I could do something about it.

Abbie

Do I need to keep going?

Indie

**No. Please, don't. FINE. I will do it if you
just stop talking about it.**

Abbie

**Great! I knew you'd think it was a good
idea. It'll be fun. You'll get to buy her
a whole bunch of cute stuff. That dog
is going to need a whole wardrobe for
winter! (heart eye emoji)**

Indie

**OMFG. You are the worst. How are we
friends, again?**

And that's how I'd ended up at not one but two pet stores on the way home from work, going completely out of my way for a dog I hadn't even met.

After I'd carried too many bags up the steps of my apartment building, feeling too edgy to wait for the elevator, I reached my apartment door. With both arms full, I dug blindly through my purse for my keys.

It wasn't until I heard the footsteps coming my way down the hall that I realized someone else was in the hallway with me. Other than a couple of people in the mailroom downstairs, I hadn't seen another soul since I'd moved in.

If I had a new neighbor, I wasn't in the mood to make nice. My mind still spun with nerves and excitement about getting a dog, even a temporary one.

In my rushed effort to get into my unit, my key jammed because I hadn't put it fully in the lock before I started turning.

The footsteps halted at the door diagonally across from mine. Shit. I was going to have to say hello or risk looking like a jerk.

I braced myself to force some sort of cordial expression on my face. I pushed the too-heavy bags against the door for support before I angled my body in a way that allowed me to catch a glimpse of the person who stood about ten feet down the hall from me.

"Rocky?" A voice choked on what might have been a surprised cough.

Five

THEO

Arriving at Pearson Airport from Vancouver this morning hadn't felt different from any other away game I'd played in Toronto.

My mind had not yet accepted the fact that this city was going to be my new home now, for the next year at least.

The ride from the airport flew by as I tried to imagine what actually living here was going to be like. I packed up my condo and said goodbye to my teammates, still in a haze of disbelief. I hadn't really allowed it to hit me how much my life was about to be turned upside down.

Toronto's team services manager, Christine Goode, had hooked me up with a furnished rental for the season, so I'd been able to arrange the larger stuff in my condo to be put in storage in Vancouver for now. I didn't know where I'd be next June, so I didn't want to send anything home to San Jose just to ship it somewhere else in nine months' time.

I'd had two big bags worth of luggage to my name at this point, with the hope that one of the team services assistants would take pity on me and grab any essentials missing while I was integrating myself into training camp.

After I tipped my driver, I looked up at the refurbished warehouse that was now a set of what looked like twenty or more units. I wasn't big on style or design, like my brother Chase, who'd gone into architecture, but I could appreciate the cool vibe of the building.

There wasn't much of a view to be had, though I knew Lake Ontario was only a few blocks away, hidden by the multitude of skyscrapers in the downtown core.

It was hotter here than in Vancouver, even though it was technically fall. I knew from experience with Toronto that this was just a blip at the start of the autumn weather to lure the city into a false sense of complacency, and then the temperature would drop 10°C from one day to the next. Vancouver got a lot of rain, but I couldn't remember an entire sunny day while in Toronto during October and November over the past couple years. It could get pretty gray here too.

Mom had always just said to enjoy these brief hiatuses from seasonally appropriate temperatures because winter was long in Canada, whether it was raining, snowing, or you were just plain freezing your ass off.

Plus, I'd found since moving to Canada permanently, Canadians really did love talking about the weather. So temperatures going wacky were always a good way to fill awkward silences.

Thankfully, there was an elevator in this building because I could feel my muscles tightening up from all the travel and lugging these heavy bags around. Maybe I'd try to find out from Christine if I could get into the gym to loosen up before the official training camp started.

I guessed the direction of my new apartment when I got off the elevator into a central foyer area on my floor. At the end of the hallway, I could see a young woman with dark hair overloaded with bags while trying to open her door.

If I'd been on my game and not weighed down by heavy luggage, I'd have offered to help her. Both my parents had deeply impressed upon all us kids that we should offer help when we could.

Except I felt a bit like death warmed over from travel fatigue and the stress of the last few days, so I gave myself a pass on being a good neighbor for the moment. Mixed with a hefty dose of self-pity at being traded away from a team I'd worked so hard for to a city where I literally knew no one, I wasn't in any shape to be making small talk.

Instead, I tried to be as quiet as possible as I checked the unit numbers on the way to what I hoped was my front door.

With her back to me, I couldn't tell much about her other than she was tall and lithe. At six feet, I stood taller than most but based on where her head reached compared to her front door, I'd have put her at five nine or five ten. As I got closer, I could see her hair was the same shade of warm brown, and it fell in a thick, shiny waterfall down her back.

She was murmuring softly to herself, likely frustrated with the lock when all she wanted to do was get inside. As I reached my door about ten or so feet away from hers, she tilted her head in a way that brushed her hair off the right side of her face.

I was shocked still, with my keys frozen in my hand.

Indigo Layne. In Toronto.

Here. Now.

Theo, Age 15

"Mom, I'm ready to go to practice!" I called up the stairs, hoping to be heard through the music filtering through the door of my mom's office.

"Okay, Theo! Get your bag in the trunk, and I'll be down in a couple minutes."

By a couple minutes, I knew she meant about ten. I decided to wander out into the backyard to see what my siblings were doing. I hoped the twins weren't planning anything that was going to piss Dad off when he got home. At eleven, they were tall and strong enough to get into more trouble than ever before but had yet to understand not every moment of the day was the right moment for a prank.

They had a habit of constructing elaborate "traps" and "defenses" around the front and backyard that usually ended up with an adult swearing with some sort of minor injury.

Opening the sliding kitchen door, I peered out around our deck to make sure there were no swinging obstacles about to knock me out before we left. I'd already had a couple of concussions since starting rep hockey six years ago, and I didn't need my father to have any ammunition to dislike hockey. The only thing he'd ever mentioned to me about hockey was that he worried about head injuries. I'd taken that to mean that he'd wished I'd played football instead.

Though, as the head football coach at San Jose State, I didn't know how he could justify his sport over mine. Football had the highest rate of concussions of all sports—thank you, Google—but maybe he thought football injuries were more worthy in some way.

My survey of the area deemed it safe to exit the house; no sign of projectiles from the twin masterminds. I walked out to the edge of the deck and heard giggling coming from the tree house.

My baby sister, Emery, and her best friend, Indie, were either up there cooking up elaborate revenge on the twins for some prank, gossiping, or planning world domination. It was anyone's guess.

I was glad they had each other. The only thing that had made me nervous about starting high school was leaving my baby sister behind.

Emery was all sunshine and rainbows, a sweetheart through and through. Her feelings were easily hurt, and she forgave too easily, something my brothers took too much for granted.

I never worried about the twins. They had each other, and they were the tallest and strongest kids in their grade, thanks to genetics and their years in peewee football. If anything, I thought more about the well-being of those around them.

"Just grabbing my laptop, Theo. Be right there," my mom called out the window. We were a step closer to leaving now that she was actually packing up.

Leaning against the porch railing, I played Snake on my phone while I waited.

"Come on, Indie! You can do it!" My sister's voice drifted across the yard.

The tree house I'd helped my dad build sat in the huge tree that dominated the yard. Emery, being tiny and agile, had been climbing down the branches and trunk for a couple of years now, despite knowing the house rules stated she needed to use the rope ladder.

The tree house was built into the biggest two limbs of the tree, which were about twelve to fourteen feet off the ground. If one of us fell out of the tree house, the fall could easily break a bone or our heads.

Emery was already three-quarters of the way down the tree, having gripped onto some of the newer shoots that grew out of the base of the tree.

"Hey, Em! You know you're not supposed to…"

I didn't get to finish what I was saying before I was racing across the yard because Indie had decided to take Emery up on her dare of climbing down the branches.

Indie had about six inches on Emery, despite being just as scrawny in stature. Still, I knew from experience that growth spurts made you clumsy.

"Indie! Wait! Just let me…" I called out too late.

Her little brow was furrowed in concentration, her bottom lip caught beneath her teeth. My voice yelling her name must have shocked her because she looked up at me instead of where she was putting her foot next.

I could see the next seconds unfolding at rapid speed. She was going to step on a branch that couldn't hold her and fall. Visions of blood and tears clouded my mind.

I had to get to her.

Somehow, the haze of fear cleared from my eyes, and I managed to get underneath her just as the branch she was balancing on one foot on snapped.

Her shrill scream echoed through the yard as she fell. It was less than a ten-foot fall from where she'd slipped, but it felt like a hundred before she hit my arms with a thud that jolted my whole body.

Still panicking from the fall, Indie flailed her arms and legs as if she were in a fighting ring. She clocked me above the eye with the side of her fist or her elbow. Either way, she'd rung my bell good.

Too upset, she hadn't noticed my head getting knocked back. Her breathing was ragged, and choppy sobs escaped her mouth.

I tightened my grip on her, my arms easily wrapped around her back and legs.

"Easy, Rocky. I've got you." The nickname fell from my lips before I'd even consciously thought it.

Her movements slowed as she realized that she was no longer falling. Just like a spider monkey, she righted herself by throwing her arms and legs around me. She held on so tightly I loosened my grip around her slightly. She started crying in earnest.

I walked over to the edge of the deck and sat down with her in my arms and looked over at Emery. She, too, had tears in her eyes, no doubt in fear for her friend but also knowing she was going to catch shit from Mom and Dad for not being careful.

"Em, go inside and get Mom, okay?" I tried to keep my voice level.

Nodding, Emery raced into the house.

Turning my attention back to Indie, I awkwardly shushed her to help her calm down. Despite being attached at the hip to Emery since kindergarten, I didn't know her that well.

She was the most well-behaved kid I'd ever seen. Reserved to a point that almost seemed like an adult in a way I couldn't understand. It was definitely eye-opening to see her this upset.

It had taken a year for me to hear her laugh. She, Mom, and Emery had been baking some sort of catastrophe in the kitchen, and the bag of flour had burst when the girls had tried to pull it open and absolutely coated the three of them. A giggle had burst from Indie, and I'd seen the joy in my mom's eyes witnessing that. I'd raced into the living room for the camera, keen to show Dad the disaster later.

That photo sat proudly on our mantle, the three of them grinning like loons.

Her tears were slowing, and she pulled back, suddenly realizing she was stuck to me like a barnacle. A flurry of limbs and a much gentler elbow to the chin for me had her sitting beside me.

Geez, at this rate, I'd have to tell the guys at practice I'd got hurt playing road hockey with the twins for all the bruises I'd have.

"Thanks, Theo." Her little voice was barely above a whisper.

"No problem, little Rocky. Maybe keep those feet on the ground for the rest of the day, okay?"

She blushed and nodded, embarrassed.

Mom came racing out the door and pulled Indie into a hug. Mom gave the kind of hugs you could just melt into, knowing that she wouldn't let go until you were solid.

"I'm glad you're okay, sweetie." She looked at me over Indie's shoulders and mouthed, "Thank you."

I shrugged. It was no big deal. I was just glad she was okay.

"Here's what we'll do. How about you girls come with me to the rink, and you can watch Theo's training this afternoon?" Mom smiled warmly at them both.

Even though Mom would have a safety talk with Emery later, Mom's talks were always delivered with a big dose of comfort.

Both girls nodded eagerly, knowing an afternoon at the rink meant a carload of snacks and playing hide-and-seek around the empty stands.

"Come on, Indie! I'll race you to the car!"

Potential disaster averted, Emery took off into the house. Indie, who was poised to take off after her, turned back to me and smiled gratefully before heading inside.

Mom came and wrapped her arms around me. "My hero," she whispered in my ear before giving me a peck on the cheek.

I shook the memory off; the nostalgia was bittersweet. My brain refocused on the very grown woman in front of me.

Her naturally golden skin was sun-kissed from what I imagined was soaking up the gorgeous months of California summer weather. Even scrunched in frustration and only half-visible, her face was perfection. Emery, with her artist's eye and hands, could not have rendered a more beautiful woman.

Without my permission, my eyes swept down her body. She had a slight, athletic build that reminded me of a dancer or runner. The back of my mind tickled with a memory of her running track fairly competitively in high school.

Simply, she was gorgeous. She could have been on any runway or graced any magazine cover. The back of my neck heated with the realization of how inappropriate it was to be checking her out.

I could not be looking at Indie like this. She was my sister's best friend, despite us not seeing each other for six or so years (Christ, had it really been that long?). My mind flipped back to the last time I'd snuffed out my attraction toward Indie. I'd spent my time avoiding temptation when Indie had turned eighteen and I'd been home for an extended summer visit because of a concussion recovery. It was not okay then, and it wasn't okay now.

The conflicting feelings inside me had an awkwardness I rarely felt settled in my chest, making it hard to think. I cleared my throat to say something.

"Rocky?"

My long-ago nickname for Indie fell from my lips, and she whirled around, eyes wide.

Six

INDIE

The voice of the man I'd steadfastly avoided for six years rang out behind me.

I had exactly 2.4 seconds to school my face into a cool, impassive mask after Theo Yao-Miller shocked me into turning around.

The term of endearment exclusive to him was still echoing in my ears.

My arms still overloaded with pet supplies and my huge tote for the office, I slowly turned to face my former teenage crush.

"Theo?" I put some confusion into my tone, despite knowing exactly who was standing in front of me.

I'd recognize Theo anywhere, anytime. Aside from being a media darling, every bit of his essence was burned into my brain.

Theo, however, didn't need to know that.

At one point, I'd been so obsessed with him that if I were given the right magical powers, I could conjure him from thin air. It seemed too much to hope that he was a figment of my overworked brain.

I wanted to blink and wish him back into my now smothered

38

daydreams. But he really stood in front of me after all these years.

"Merry Christmas, Rocky. What are you doing up?" Theo stood in their family kitchen after an early gym workout.

I made myself answer him, trying to come off casual, but my voice betrayed a slight tremor.

"Dunno. Just couldn't sleep." I shrugged, as if I hadn't planned the next few minutes for years.

"Yeah, strange bed and all that. I know how hard it is for me to sleep during away games in all those hotels. I don't blame you."

That was Theo, always trying to make others feel at ease around him. He turned his back to me to get the coffee maker started. I took the opportunity to silently erase the distance between us.

I laid my trembling hand in the middle of his back. And he swung around, his eyes widening at the physical closeness between us. I'd avoided the hello and goodbye hugs over the years, finding that touching him in even a platonic way made my heart hurt.

"Indigo? What are you doing?" There was a hesitation in his tone that I couldn't heed.

I quickly opened the palm of my left hand and revealed the beat-up sprig of mistletoe that had left sharp imprints on my hand from my strangling grip. Before I lost my nerve, I closed the distance between our mouths, brushing my lips lightly over his before immediately kissing him more firmly.

My brain must have short-circuited in those few short seconds as I felt his soft lips on mine. When his hands came up to gently grip my hips, my first thought was "Yes! He wants me too."

It took another few seconds to realize that his lips were not moving under mine, and his light hold on me was to hold me back from pressing into him further.

Horrified, I took a big step back, dropped the sad little sprig on the floor, and covered my mouth with both hands.

His expression looked shocked. I had seen that kind of expression on people's faces before. It was the kind that meant bad news was coming and the person was sorry to have to say it out loud.

"Oh my god," I whispered. "I'm so sorry." I wanted the ground to open up and swallow me whole. I couldn't ever look at him ever again.

I had experienced my share of painful moments in my life, but the excruciating pain of his rejection coupled with a feeling of humiliation so acute I thought I might pass out if I didn't get out of there.

"Indie. I... ugh, we... can't. You're way too young for me. I'm flattered. You're a great girl." His voice got quieter as I bolted out of the room, needing to get out of that house as fast as possible.

I cataloged the changes in him since that fateful Christmas morning in his family's kitchen while I attempted to offer a bland but not rude smile.

If the years of dread at facing this moment turned my efforts into a grimace, then so be it. It was the best I could do being caught so off guard running into him this way.

He was just as handsome as the last time I saw him. His height and frame still commanded notice. His hair was a little longer, still so dark brown it was almost black. Now, its waves flopped down over his forehead, covering the side of one of his espresso-colored brown eyes.

At twenty-five, his face had been clean-shaven. Now, at thirty-one, his sharp cheekbones and jaw were accented by enough dark scruff that it was nearing beard qualification status. I could see a few tiny laugh lines creasing his eyes and near his full lips. His olive skin was deeply tanned after the summer months. He wore a plain white T-shirt under a gray hoodie, neither of which hid the work he put into his arms and chest. I didn't let myself think about the abs that were hiding under that shirt. His look was rounded out by a pair of worn jeans that hugged his powerful thighs. Thank god I hadn't seen him from behind.

My heart, which I had locked away the exact moment I'd realized Theo didn't want me back, thumped pathetically in my chest. Though I'd tried dating in college, not one person had ever caught a glimpse of my heart since I'd offered it to Theo like a hastily wrapped Christmas gift.

All those feelings I'd built around my one-sided love for Theo ached to come back to life.

Instead, I imagined a hydraulic press crushing them back into the back of my brain where they belonged.

The last thing I was going to do was let Theo have any power over my feelings ever again. To do that, I had to get away from him now.

He stared back at me intently. I was so caught up in my swirling emotions I couldn't decipher the look on his face.

Nor was I going to stick around to find out. He seemed at a loss for what to say next. I was going to take advantage of his inaction and make my escape.

I got my key unstuck and knocked the door open with my hip.

"Hope you're doing well, Theo. I'll see you around."

There had been some talk among the senior team members about a new starting goalie. Since it hadn't come across my desk yet, I'd put it to the back of my mind.

Why did it have to be Theo?

I shut and locked the door behind me, gently setting all the bags in my arms on the ground. Before I could do something like peek out the peephole to check if he was still in the hall, I kicked off my boots and headed for my bedroom.

I wasn't going to feel bad about avoiding him. I'd just learn his schedule and adjust my own accordingly. There was no way I was going to erase this distance between us just to make him feel better.

I didn't owe Theo Yao-Miller anything.

Seven

THEO

Still standing in the hallway, I stared at her closed door.

Had Indie just given me the brush-off as if I were some stranger? As if I hadn't spent countless afternoons of her childhood and my youth with her as practically a surrogate member of my family? What the hell had just happened?

Torn between irritation and disbelief, and maybe more than a little hurt in there somewhere, I unlocked my door and dragged my duffle inside.

I could concede that the last time I saw her would have been pretty embarrassing, but I'd chalked it up to one of those crazy things we all did as teenagers.

At the time, I'd just put the moment aside, keen not to let on to my family that I'd had anything to do with Indie's unexpected departure from our Christmas Day celebrations.

Had she been that affected by what I'd thought was a gentle letdown that she'd been upset with me all these years?

Goddamn. Was I the reason she hadn't come to spend Christmas with us since? Fuck.

Emery had said that Indie had family obligations. But god, what if she'd been alone instead?

That idea didn't sit well with me at all, causing a burning sensation in my chest.

I needed to fix things with Indie. I couldn't bear the thought of being the source of her pain.

My mind was too riled up to take in what I'm sure was a very nice condo that the team had provided. I caught a glimpse of some wrought-iron details and some large wooden beams on my way to the dark gray sectional in the living room.

Allowing myself to fall backward onto the cushions, I leaned my head against the back of the couch. My eyes fell shut as I scrubbed my hands over my face.

I couldn't stop the memories of Indie flooding my brain.

As a girl and teen, she had always been reserved, to put it mildly. Rocky could have won a medal for the best poker face for all her facial expression gave away.

So it wasn't new to me that I'd need to puzzle out the interaction, but what was new was the abrupt, borderline dismissive attitude that she had shown me.

The Indie I knew took a long, long time to warm up to others. Her family was mega-wealthy. They owned a whole legion of businesses that I never paid attention to. While our house growing up had been on the larger side, Indie had grown up in a literal mansion.

When she first started coming over to our place, she hadn't even acted like a kid. She was like some mini adult that her parents had ordered out of a catalog. Always perfectly polite and never a hair out of place.

She'd warmed to Emery almost immediately. My baby sister had that effect on people, and over time, she had become comfortable with the rest of us, especially my mom.

My phone buzzed, drawing my attention away from Indie. I unlocked my screen to see that our sibling group chat was buzzing.

Emery

WTF Theo! Why do I have to find out you're in Toronto from Indie?!?!

Chase

Bruh?

Liam

What's going on? I just woke up.

Emery

Our long-lost brother was just about to tell us why he's in Toronto and not getting ready for training camp in Vancouver.

Shit. Everything had moved so quickly since the meeting in Coach's office I hadn't told my family about my trade.

I had to bite the bullet and apologize. Em was going to be pissed at me for keeping this from them.

Theo

I got traded two days ago.

Emery

WHAT DO YOU MEAN YOU GOT TRADED?!?

You moved to the other side of North America without telling us? But you told Indie?!?!

Liam

Not cool, man. I mean, we're not your

**keepers or anything. But you could
have at least texted us.**

Liam has left the chat.

Fuck. Liam was the more sensitive of my two brothers. I had really screwed up here. I owed them more than this.

Theo

I'm sorry. It's been hectic. They sprung this on me two days before camp was due to start. I've been up to my ears in logistics for 48 hours. But that's no excuse. I'll do better, I promise.

I didn't tell Indie anything. I just literally ran into her. What's she doing here?

Chase

Those are only words, T. Thanks a lot. Now I'm going to have a pissed off wingman at the bar tonight. Neither of us are going to be able to hook up.

Emery

Am I the only one who cares that we are going to be seeing Theo even less than we already are?!

For someone with such a sunny disposition, she knew how to aim guilt trips for maximum effect.

Chase

Yes, Emery. You're the only one. He hasn't cared what's been going on with us for years. Why should now be any different?

Emery

Chase! That's not fair. He's our brother.

Chase

Yeah, well. Maybe he should act like it once in a while rather than only coming home when he absolutely can't avoid it.

Chase has left the chat.

Theo

At least they have each other's backs.

Emery

***sigh* I'll talk to them.**

Theo

Em, it's okay. This is my fault. I'll fix it with them. You don't need to take this on.

Emery

Fine. But if you need my help, the offer is there.

Theo

You're too good to me, sis.

Emery

Damn right, I am.

And you still have to tell Dad!

Theo

Fuck.

Emery

Yeah, good luck with that. I've gotta get to class. Freshmen to corral and all that. Even though I'm mad at you, I still love you, Theo.

Theo

Love you too.

I chucked my phone onto the couch beside me.

Great. I had three pissed-off siblings, and I hadn't even unpacked my suitcase yet. I'd have to make an extra trip home during the first break in the team's schedule.

There were things I should have done to get ready for my first practice with my new team tomorrow. I could have been making use of the cell numbers of the captain or alternate captain of the Tempests, watching old game tape, or even reaching out to team services about the arrival of the rest of my stuff.

Instead, the weight of the last few days hit me all at once. A tsunami of shock, now tinged with guilt over my siblings, rolled over me and sank deep in my gut. My body was trapped by the overwhelming sense of powerlessness to fix all the ways I'd apparently screwed up.

I'd spent too many years while playing in Vancouver so deep in the mindset that I needed to give every ounce of myself to hockey so that I could prove I deserved to be there. That reaching the NHL and my career as a professional hockey player was somehow the mark that I had "made it" in a way.

Looking down the line a year, however, with knee surgery on the horizon, suddenly seemed a lot more daunting with my brothers and sister angry with me. There would be no blaming my schedule for the distance in our relationship anymore.

My mind quickly pushed that thought aside. Coming back to my immediate issue of the mystery of Indie as my new neighbor.

Being on the receiving end of the brush-off was new to me. I was used to people wanting my attention, whether it was the media, fans, fans who were looking to hook up, or other industry professionals.

I couldn't imagine Indie still feeling awkward because of our last encounter on that Christmas morning.

A strange sensation ran through me as my mind merged the nineteen-year-old Indie hesitantly pressing her soft lips to mine with the distant woman in the hallway just now.

Before I realized who she was, the visceral attraction I'd felt approaching her still churned in my gut. I could never consider acting on it because of Emery, but that didn't change the fact that I was drawn to Indie in a way I couldn't remember feeling before.

She had always been stunning. Back then, I hadn't even considered her in that light because I'd automatically connected her to Emery. They were so much younger; my protective big brother instincts had always extended to both of them.

At twenty-five, I'd had my head so far up my own ass it wasn't funny. I'd been working hard and playing harder. I was out every night with the other guys on the Frost. I hadn't gone at it as hard as some of the others, but I had still had enough nights that I was lucky social media wasn't the way it was now.

I scrubbed my hands over my face with the frustrated realization of how much of a wall I'd put up around myself.

I was a guy who didn't like things up in the air. I needed to think of a way to prove to my siblings that I wanted to reconnect after allowing my career to come between us.

I rolled my neck and shoulder muscles like I was shaking off a bad hit on the ice, way back in my minor hockey days before I found my niche as a goalie. But this time, I was shaking off an emotional hit rather than a physical one.

It was time to make amends. And I'd start with the woman across the hall.

Eight

THEO

I hadn't been the new kid in class in a very long time. Despite being a long way from my childhood, the feeling of walking into an established group dynamic was still daunting.

The captain and alternate captain on this team were a well-known dynamic duo in the league. Every team had a rhythm. I had a feeling that Reese Michaels and Ryan Campbell set the tone for the Tempests.

I'd had a brief welcome-to-the-team call with Toronto's head coach, Jacob Reyes, before I left Vancouver. Everything else I had learned from the team services manager, Christine. She'd helped me arrange everything from a place to stay while I settled into the city to moving my belongings across the country to getting an assistant to stock my fridge so I wouldn't have to worry about starving when I arrived in my temporary condo.

I walked into the arena for my first practice, wondering what the vibe was going to be like. Already off-kilter from my run-in with Indie the day before, I needed this first introduction to the team to go well.

Christine, the angel, had also prearranged all of my security clearance, so I breezed through the check-in area with several minutes to spare before I needed to find Coach Reyes.

My phone ringing was the last thing I expected.

Worry spiked in my gut as I saw Emery's name on my phone. Was it Dad? My brothers? Was she in trouble? Ever since my mom passed away, I couldn't shake the sliver of fear that chilled my blood every time my phone rang.

"Em, you okay?" I picked up, apprehension making my voice a little hoarse.

She must have heard the concern in my tone since she was quick to reassure me rather than remind me that she was still mad at me for the trade lack of communication debacle.

"Whoa, Theo. Everything's fine. Why would you think something's wrong?"

Since I couldn't tell her the truth, I opted for teasing. Emery didn't need to carry my issues too. I'd left my siblings behind to flee from my own problems.

"Well, considering you're allergic to phone calls, you can imagine why I'm surprised." I forced as much humor into my tone as I could. If my joke landed a little flat, Emery was kind enough not to push me for what was really going on.

That was Emery in a nutshell. The sweetest, kindest person I knew. A literal ray of sunshine.

"Ha ha. Very funny. I'll have you know, I make phone calls on a regular basis. Some of these tenured professors have a moral imperative to keep us frozen in the 1900s."

Her graduate studies in fine arts came with teaching assignments for a variety of academic personalities. I'd been so wrapped up in my own worries about my knee injuries and what it meant for my NHL career that I didn't even know what she was teaching this term.

Emery was on her way to becoming a professor, just like our mom had been. Though I'd had my doubts about her choice—she'd been so passionately dedicated to *creating* art throughout her childhood and teenage years—she'd insisted on pursuing her master's and PhD. She had been 100 percent adamant at eighteen that this was what she wanted to do.

"I'm going to be Professor Yao one day, T. That way, I can honor Mom's memory the way you have."

I'd chosen to wear Mom's name only on my jersey from the moment I'd been drafted, even before we'd lost her. She'd been my number one supporter and fan. I was only here because of her unwavering commitment to my childhood dreams.

"Ouch, sis. Don't say the 1900s like it was all Gold Rush fever and fur traders when I was a kid." I felt ancient now that the internet had made that a thing.

"It was… close, I'd say. Anyway, I'm not committing Gen Z blasphemy by picking up the phone for nothing, T. I wanted to wish you good luck with your new team on your first day of practice."

Well, shit. She'd hit me right in the chest with that one. Even fifty pounds of goalie gear wouldn't have shielded my heart from her thoughtfulness.

"Em…" I paused, not having the words to convey how much she meant to me. "Thank you. You have no idea how much I needed to hear that today."

She was quiet on the other end of the line for a moment.

"I'm glad I called, then." Her tone was bright. "But you know I'm still mad at you, though, right?" She punctuated her statement with a laugh.

The sentimentality that had pressure forming behind my eyes receded to a bearable level when her inability to resist needling me took over once again. Sibling rivalry ran strong among the four of us.

"Yeah, I'm really sorry I let you down, Em." Even though her tone was teasing, she had every right to still be mad at me.

The distance the earlier years of my career created between me and my siblings had helped me survive those first seasons without Mom. I'd panicked at the thought of coping with my siblings' grief on top of my own. When I essentially ran away from home and made hockey my entire personality, I only hurt our connection further.

I'd stopped reaching out to them, only making a few half-hearted offers to have them up to see me play. Whether they consciously or unconsciously understood the wall I'd put up between myself and the family, they stopped mentioning coming to any of the Vancouver home games.

Instead, I gathered passive news about their lives via social media and when they'd text me anything they wanted to share. Each time I'd shut them out created a layer of regret I'd worked hard to push to the back of my mind. With Mom gone, a part of me got stuck as the eighteen-year-old rookie who didn't know how to relate to anyone.

Emery's sigh was deep enough to carry across the line.

I wasn't in the running for brother of the year, that was certain.

"I'd say having one of the best goalies in the NHL for a brother isn't a letdown by anyone's imagination." There she went again, trying to give me the benefit of the doubt.

"It's the 'brother' part I've let you down on, Em. This trade shook up everything inside me that I'd been pushing away for so long. I want to do better."

She didn't say anything in return, which told me all I needed to know. The guilt that had been growing year after year was a lead weight in my stomach.

The bang of a heavy metal door brought my awareness back to

my surroundings. I'd ducked into a random hallway just inside the practice facility when Emery's call came through. But now, I heard distant voices echoing down the hall. As loath as I was to end this long overdue conversation with my sister, I didn't need my new team all up in my business on the first day.

"Listen, I don't want to go, but I feel like a couple dozen hockey players are about to invade the area where I'm standing. Let's talk again soon, okay? I want to hear about your worst students and have you tell me they can't even compete with the twins. And make sure to tell me when your next exhibition is so that I can see if I can make something work."

If I was going to be a better brother, it meant showing up. For a start.

"I'd really love that, Theo." Her voice was quiet. She only did that when she really wanted something but was too scared to ask for it.

My gut clenched again. When was the last time I'd seen any of her work in person?

Too long.

We only had time for a quick goodbye before two familiar faces came around the corner toward where I was standing.

Granted, I was used to seeing them in a helmet on the ice. But it was easy enough to recognize Michaels and Campbell from their easy camaraderie on or off the ice.

Despite playing against them several times a year, I'd barely given more than a cursory greeting to either of them over the years.

Even though I was older than nearly everyone on this team, I was way out of my comfort zone.

"Well, well, well. If it isn't Mr. Vezina Award winner two years running. I'm still not over that wrist shot you blocked in game six." Campbell wasted no time in eyeing me like he planned to hold that against me for the foreseeable future.

"Easy, man. Yao's not used to your shenanigans yet. You could do him the courtesy of letting him settle in before you start needling him." Michaels gave me an easy smile. He held out his hand and stopped in front of me. "Welcome to the team. Things happened pretty quick, eh?"

I took his hand, returning his firm shake. The three of us stepped to the side to let some of the other players pass on their way to the locker room. I nodded as a couple of groups passed us by.

"Thank you. It's how things go, I know. It's just different when it happens to you, you know?"

"I hear ya. Three seasons ago, I was in your place. That's how I got stuck with this guy." The captain jerked his thumb at Campbell, who feigned an insulted expression. "Unfortunately, the powers that be seem to think we 'complement' each other."

"I can tell you right now that's not true," Campbell chimed in. "I haven't said a single nice thing to your face in all the years we've known each other." He bumped Michaels with his shoulder, his antics drawing a chuckle from both of us.

Michaels just rolled his eyes in response, clearly used to his alternate captain's brand of humor.

It was clear these two had each other's backs, despite all the ribbing. No wonder they led such a powerhouse of an offensive line.

"I'm sure you need to see Coach before long." Michaels checked his phone. "But we've still got an hour before we need to be on the ice. We'll show you your locker."

"You'll love it. I blackmailed Lapointe with last year's holiday party photos to switch spots so you could be right next to me." Campbell gave me an exaggerated wink.

I had a feeling that the defenseman to whom he was referring was just being nice to the new guy. But all the same, Campbell struck me as a man who liked to keep people on their toes.

"I even talked him into leaving you last season's lucky socks." He snickered as he put his arm around my neck to guide me toward the locker room and whatever biohazard awaited me.

On second thought, maybe this wasn't so much a "welcome" as an initiation ritual.

Nine

INDIE

I'd spent the rest of the evening after seeing Theo steadfastly ignoring his entire existence.

I told myself that I was long over him, and while, yes, it had been a shock seeing him so unexpectedly, I had been able to keep my cool.

I was no longer the impressionable nineteen-year-old looking for someone to love her. My early years consistently taught me that others only looked after themselves. My parents looked after their own interests first, as did everyone in their circle.

I was an afterthought, if they thought about me at all. I'd spent my childhood convinced that the only reason my parents acknowledged my existence was because one or more of their admin assistants sent them an email reminding them there was an event I should attend to show what a perfect family we were.

It was Angelina, our housekeeper, who had come to all of my ballet and piano recitals because my parents were "away on business."

I'd gotten things mixed up spending time at the Yao-Miller house. It was like walking into a Hallmark special. Lots of excitement and inevitable drama, but the love of family always overcame any obstacle.

My walls had come down around Emery and her family. And then Abbie joined our little crew too. Her ability to hold on to the joy in simple things had further thawed me to the idea that I could trust someone with my heart.

That Christmas morning had shattered any delusions about opening my heart to anyone other than the slivers I gave to Abbie and Emery. It jolted me back into the reality I should have learned when Alice passed away. Love doesn't stop bad things from happening.

Theo's rejection cemented the lessons I'd learned from my parents' neglect year after year. Love wasn't in the cards for everyone. At this point, I had no desire to involve myself with anyone other than the short flings I'd had since starting college.

I didn't want to need anyone so much that they had the power to devastate me. Watching Abbie go through her struggles with Aiden had made me vicariously ill. They'd had so much power to make each other miserable.

I busied myself filling out the detailed foster application for Gizmo. Now that I'd been talked into it, I was kind of looking forward to having a little company in this apartment.

Plus, I was keen to keep chipping away at what I called my "Learn to Do Normal Stuff" list. Each year, I chose one thing to learn that a regular kid might have experienced growing up. It was written on a cheesy piece of Abbie's kawaii stationery from a rare drunken night in college. Now more wrinkles and coffee stains than paper and ink, it held an ever-growing list of things I wanted to try.

I'd enjoyed learning to bake from Alice. Emery had taught me how to climb trees. Chase and Liam had shown me how to ride a bike in a rare moment of patience.

Once I left for college, I'd continued the tradition by continually seeking something I'd missed out on.

With my unplanned relocation, I'd added tourist attractions as my goal for the remainder of this year and until I returned home. It always made me sad when I thought about all the business trips in North America and Europe that I'd gone on during my childhood years, but I never got to experience any of those cities.

Now, I was going to find out what Toronto was all about.

Even better, I'd get to live the life of a pet owner, at least for a little while. On the plane, I'd read that it sometimes got to -20°C during January and February in Toronto, which was freaking cold when Google converted it to F. I'd be buying two new winter coats, one human and one canine.

I liked the challenge of not being able to do something and then learning how. I was lucky that the office was pet-friendly, so I'd be able to take her to work with me if she was chill enough.

We'd hang out while she waited for adoption. Then, she'd be off enjoying her new life as a Canadian canine.

Simple.

Just as I was starting to get into a daily routine at work, I was summoned to my boss's office on a random game night.

The moment Jermaine gave me a big smile when I arrived in his office two hours before the Saturday night game was due to begin, I knew something was up.

"Indie! Come in and have a seat."

Apprehension crept up on me as I settled into one of my boss's extra comfy chairs. I idly wondered if he'd chosen these cloudlike chairs to lull unsuspecting employees into a false sense of security before he fired them.

Was that what was about to happen to me? Jermaine was a positive person, but I doubt even he would fire someone with a smile on his face. So I was probably safe.

"So how has your first month been?" Jermaine's expression remained pleasant.

Was I here for chitchat? My fingertips embedded themselves into the plush cushion where I sat.

"Fine. If by fine, I mean I'm now dreaming of columns and columns of hockey stats," I joked, trying to shake off my own nerves.

Oh shit! These chairs were inhibition lowering. Was I at the joking comfort level with my boss? I zipped my lips lest anything else unprofessional slip out.

Jermaine just laughed in response. "I'm glad to see you settling in. I can tell you're not one for small talk. Truth be told, neither am I, despite appearances to the contrary."

He was so good-natured it seemed that he would actually like talking to people. But as I knew well, appearances were deceiving.

"On to why I called you in here. Now that you've had a month to acclimate yourself to the organization, I'm about to assign you to assist me on a fairly big project. With Cadence away, I'm going to need an extra set of hands. I've been impressed by your ability to hit the ground running, so to speak. Now, you're going to learn to wrangle athletes." He chuckled to himself.

Why did he make them sound like feral toddlers? How hard could it be to get grown men to fulfill their contractual obligations? Was I missing something?

"Thank you?" I didn't know what else to say. I wasn't used to being complimented on my work. At my last job, I had avoided applying for any promotion opportunities. I'd been focused on learning as much as I could in a midsized company but didn't feel right standing in the way of another employee's career advancement when I knew my time at Appeal Media had a set end date.

I'd also been mistaken in my belief that holding a steady job was going to keep me off my father's radar. My relocation to Toronto had shown me I was wrong.

"We've been contacted by one of the country's rapidly growing and widely read online sports publications, *The 49th*. They want to do a feature on a few of the players."

A sense of foreboding filled my veins, flooding my system head to toe.

Jermaine glanced down at his notes. "They want Andrews, Campbell…"

I knew what was coming.

"And Yao, of course. The Rookie, the Showman, and the Veteran."

My stomach sank. Maybe getting fired wouldn't have been so bad. I could have been on a plane back to Amado by the afternoon. My life plan would crumble, but I wouldn't have to spend any time with Theo.

Was the opportunity to avoid further mortification worth my ten-million-dollar inheritance if I was fired?

Realizing my career dreams with a nonprofit versus losing ten million dollars but never having to face the most horrifyingly embarrassing moment of my life?

I was still on the fence.

Totally oblivious to my internal teenage-crush existential crisis, Jermaine barreled on with the explanation.

"When I said 'assist' me, I meant you're going to have to shoulder most of this, I'm afraid. The powers that be are pulling me in too many directions to do it justice. We need good PR to keep the investors happy. And I need someone to micromanage the crap out of these boys to make sure this goes smoothly. I'm talking about Campbell specifically. That kid is as predictable as a hyena on cocaine."

It was a struggle not to smile when he called twenty-one, twenty-six, and thirty-one-year-old men kids. I just nodded along instead of commenting.

"You're lucky in one respect, though. They're going to start with Andrews first. He'll be the easiest one for you to tackle, figuratively speaking. He's like an overgrown puppy. He won't give you any trouble. He just needs a review of the media protocol of what to say and what not to say. We don't want to censor them."

"Okay. I can do that." There was a media relations package that I'd practically memorized to prepare for game night posts. Hell, I'd had media training myself at my parents' insistence before the age of ten.

My life had been one big show-and-tell when it came to the media. That's why I'd always tried to remain as unremarkable as possible in public. The paparazzi would salivate over catching the "Heiress to the Layne Fortune" in a compromising position.

I could teach a college class on media relations at this point. I didn't say any of that, though. The last thing I wanted to do was ever draw attention to my background. I couldn't help who my family was. I absolutely did not want to draw attention to the fact that I was here because of nepotism.

"On second thought, you're going to need to censor Campbell. Make sure you reiterate that they are obligated to give us final approval on the article. You never know what that wildebeest will say."

"No problem. You can count on me." And he could. Letting my bosses down was not something conceivable in my world. I may not have wanted to stand out at my last job, but my work was always well done. I wouldn't let this first big assignment be any different.

Even if my father had thrown me into this new position, I had my pride. I wouldn't succeed for him; I'd do a great job in spite of him turning my life upside down.

With no new updates required outside of the norm after Saturday's game, Monday found me waiting outside the Tempests' locker room after their morning skate. There was no way I was going into that changeroom full of half-naked, hungry athletes who expected to go home for food and their pregame naps.

It was less about a sense of propriety and more about a self-serving approach. None of them wanted to see a member of the communications team there to interrupt their day. Instead, if I stood just outside the door, I could catch an unsuspecting Connor Andrews rather than facing a cacophony of hangry groans.

Plus, it was kind of nice listening to the muffled sounds of the team ribbing each other good-naturedly. I couldn't make out what was being said exactly, but their boisterous tone, punctuated by various amounts of laughter, made it seem like they had a genuine sense of camaraderie with each other.

A few efficient players started exiting the changeroom, notably avoiding eye contact with me. The alternate captain, Campbell, seemingly a lone wolf in his lack of reticence, offered me a charming smile as he slowed down to pass by me. When it became clear that I wasn't there for him, he gave me a wink and made his fingers into the signal for a phone and mouthed, "Call me," much to the amusement of the two third (or fourth?) line players walking with him.

I wonder how Theo has settled in? Does he feel welcome in that room?

I shook those thoughts from my mind. I didn't have time or inclination to dedicate space in my head to Theo. He was a big boy and could handle himself.

But what if he misses home as you do? Did he have best friends like Emery and Abbie that he left behind too?

Thankfully, Andrews finally made his way out the door of the changeroom, offering me a small wave. He seemed like a sweetheart. I felt a little bad about disrupting his routine.

"Hey, Connor. Can I borrow you for a sec?" I waved him over, using his first name.

Campbell, who apparently was not far enough out of earshot, turned around at the end of the hall. "Indie! You wound me, darlin'. What does the rookie have that I don't?"

He was endearingly incorrigible. I couldn't stop the smile that I directed his way. I tried and failed to put a haughty look on my face.

"Well, if you were half as charming as you think you are, we'd have something to talk about… darlin'." I parroted his cheeky endearment back to him. "For now, it's Andrews I'm after."

"Dammmmmn, Campbell. She put you in your place," one of his teammates called out as he slapped him on the back.

A faint redness tinged Connor's ears. I'd bet most of his feelings, especially embarrassment or anger, showed on his pale, freckled skin. It was pretty cute.

Despite his size of six foot two—it was decidedly weird knowing the personal health statistics of most of my "coworkers"—Connor was deceptively stealthy as he appeared by my side while I was distracted by episode 1000 of The Ryan Campbell Show.

"Oh! Wow, how'd you do that?" I asked, commenting on his ability to sneak up on me.

"I have three older sisters. It came in handy when I used to sneak up behind them at unsuspecting moments." Connor offered me a warm smile.

Damn. Once this guy relaxed a bit, he was almost drool-worthy. The media and fans were going to eat him up.

As someone nearly five years his senior, I gave him what I thought was a pretty good impression of a mock stern tone. "My goodness, Mr. Andrews. I can't imagine a consummately professional young man such as yourself stooping to such antics."

"I take it you're an only child." He laughed. "My favorite pastime is annoying the hell outta my sisters."

"You got me there," I admitted. "I'm sure you're wondering why I'm here."

"You mean, you didn't come looking for me so we could spend some time getting to know one another." Connor widened his beautiful blue eyes in some sort of deadly kicked-puppy expression.

Caught in some sort of trance by his cute pout voodoo, I heard the locker room door swing open and shut again in the background. I sensed more players passing by us, but I didn't turn to acknowledge them.

Jesus, his adorableness factor skyrocketed. I bet he could get out of trouble with anyone with that look.

I tried to think of an appropriate non-flirty response—I wasn't here to hook up, only do my job— as my gaze slid to the side.

To Theo, of course. Theo was taking his sweet time in leaving the locker room. He made no secret of glancing between Connor and me pointedly.

I offered him a dismissive nod before turning back to the reason I was standing here.

"You are dangerous. Save those pretty eyes for someone they'll work on."

Oops. So much for not flirting.

"Well, I think they might be working on you just a little." Connor winked. I heard Theo choke in the background.

God, Theo. Just keep moving. This is none of your business.

"That's neither here nor there." The truth was it would take a lot more than a pretty face to get me interested in someone, though I appreciated Connor's commitment to his game, both on and off the ice.

Finally, after what seemed like forever, Theo moved far enough down the hallway to be out of earshot.

"Okay. Enough fun and games. We're going to be serious. I've got a date—" Connor's face fell comically as I slipped my phone from my back pocket to check the time. "—with the CN Tower in about three hours. And I'm not going to miss it." It was on my "list."

I barreled on, keen to get us back on track. "So here's what's happening. Jermaine has made me the messenger of all things media today. You, Mr. Andrews, are going to have your first major feature in a magazine since joining the Tempests. We need to spend the next hour going over some pre-interview prep."

"Wow. Okay. I'm not going to pretend that isn't pretty fucking cool. My mom will love it. She's made a hobby of collecting my hockey stuff since my first 'rookie' card when I played Timbits hockey at the age of four." His eyes sparkled with excitement.

"Aw. That's sweet. Well, we can make sure to showcase how important your family's support has been during your career. Give her a shoutout for being such an amazing mom. That would be a nice surprise, right?" I threw out the suggestion.

Truth be told, I didn't know what the hell a person could do to make their mom happy. I hadn't been able to make my mother happy or proud a single moment in my life. But it seemed like the sort of thing that would've been really meaningful to Theo's mom, Alice.

His eyes softened. "Yeah. She would love that."

I had to swallow against the very real pain in my chest. Moments like these always brought up how much of a relationship I didn't have with my parents. The gaping void of that parental bond was a never-healing wound. I could ignore the pain for a while until life ripped the scab off again and left me bleeding inside.

Connor narrowed his eyes briefly, his gaze scanning my face. I wonder what he saw there. Was my mask of forced confidence slipping?

"You know what would make my afternoon?" He smiled.

"I can imagine."

"If a certain someone would let me join her at the CN Tower after she wraps up at work. Just think of all that extra media prep time we could get in. Besides, no one has eyes for the second-line center rookie anyway. I want to do as much stuff as possible before I have to think about privacy and all that." He didn't bat his eyelashes, but it was close.

Now I was desperate for a distraction. So, even knowing I probably shouldn't agree without thinking it through first, I found myself not wanting to go see one of the landmarks I'd missed out on as a kid alone.

And I could understand wanting to seize a moment of calm while we both could. I was working on anonymity while he was a rising star.

"Sure, Connor. That sounds good. We can meet there. You can climb the stairs. I'll take the elevator," I agreed.

"Deal. How many stairs does it have? I never got to go as a kid living way up north. Being from Northern Ontario, I just haven't made the time to play tourist since hockey always had to come first," he explained.

"Not too many for a fit NHL athlete such as yourself. Piece of cake." I snickered, all of a sudden even more excited to see his face when he realized the actual number.

Ten

THEO

I should have been concentrating on the earnest questions flying at me from defensemen Young and Lavoie, both sitting across the table from me. Riding high on Saturday night's win, they were both keen to pick my brain.

I sipped my beer distractedly. They were trying to build a rapport. If I had been able to pay them proper attention, it would have probably been endearing. They'd taken the philosophy that defense/goalie relationships were essential to the team's success to heart.

I appreciated a good hustle. They wanted to grind their way off the fourth line. I respected that. It paid to figure out that there was no way around putting in the hard work for the thing you wanted most.

Tonight was not the night for me to play mentor, though. I'd agreed to come out to an informal gathering at the team's favorite post-game bar at our captain's request. They'd been so welcoming to me, and I was trying to make the effort to get to know my teammates.

The problem was one of my teammates had chosen this bar for his hangout spot as well. So instead of listening to the two keen defensemen trying to hold my attention, my eyes were glued to the high-top table across the bar on Andrews and Indie.

I was sitting at the far end of the team's table. On either side of me were Michaels and Campbell, team captain and alternate captain, respectively. It was a bit like being under the welcome wagon microscope or being held captive. I wasn't sure which yet.

They were doing what good leaders should, trying to help me integrate into my new team, especially after a surprise trade like mine was.

It might have even been nice, except I couldn't concentrate for shit. The only thing I saw was my sister's best friend sitting with my teammate across the bar.

They might as well have been the only other people in the room, seeing as I had already cataloged every detail of their interaction.

Were they on a fucking date? Just the thought of it had the back of my neck heating with the effort of suppressing my shock and protective instincts.

The kid was twenty-one years old and about as wide-eyed innocent as they came.

Indie, on the other hand, was the definition of beauty and grace. Her espresso-colored hair fell like a sheet of water down her back. Her perfect facial features were mostly hidden from me as she focused her attention on Andrews.

And that was just what you could see from the outside. Did Andrews know that she was the smartest person I knew? I may or may not have created a LinkedIn profile just so I could see what she'd been up to over the past six years. My mom had been a brilliant woman and would have been so impressed with all that Indie had accomplished.

I was trying very hard not to think about where that landed me on the cringe scale.

She could have easily pursued a career in academics with her dual degrees: one in Business Administration and the other in Social Welfare. She'd been a Presidential Scholar recipient, for Christ's sake.

So what in the hell could Andrews have to say that would hold her interest like that? Her eyebrows scrunched adorably as she listened carefully to whatever that little doofus was saying.

I mean, he had an inch of height on me, so he wasn't that little, but he was just a baby. He wouldn't know how to handle a woman like Indie.

Not the way I could.

Shit. Where had that thought come from?

My forearm tightened on the tabletop as I squeezed the beer bottle in my grip, watching him slide his hand across the table and cover hers. That sweet smile that she hid from everyone appeared on her face.

People had to work for that smile. Most people saw the snark Indie had developed in her mid-teens and took her at face value. I remembered her when it took me a year to coax a genuine smile from her face when Emery had first invited her over.

So what the fuck had Andrews done to be rewarded with it?

I forced my eyes back to my beer, and I spun the half-full bottle between my hands. I had to stop looking at them before someone misunderstood my instinct to look out for Indie as something else.

"Yao?"

I looked up and saw Michaels and Campbell staring at me with expectation on their faces.

"I'm sorry, what?" Clearly, they knew I hadn't been paying attention.

They chuckled good-naturedly at my lapse in attention, probably chalking it up to post-practice fatigue. Coach Reyes did not pull punches, no matter how we performed in our last game. Win or lose, he kicked our asses in practice every time.

My muscles were certainly protesting all the contortions I'd put them through this morning. The throb in my right knee told me I'd gone too far in trying to prove myself to my new team. I needed to save that shit for game nights. My body took every opportunity to remind me that I wasn't a young man by hockey standards anymore.

The deep ache had me reaching one hand down to press on my thigh under the table, seeking some sort of relief.

I lamented not taking some acetaminophen before leaving the locker room. Not that it did much for me, but some days, it could take the edge off the worst of the pain. I wouldn't allow myself to take anything stronger.

"No worries, man. Campbell here just asked how you are settling in. Can't be easy after so many years in Vancouver." Michaels didn't seem to mind filling me in.

"Can't say that I expected a trade this late in my career. After a dozen years with the Frost, I thought I'd do the impossible and stay there until I had to think about the dreaded R-word."

Not too many players wanted to even think about retiring. And I certainly didn't either.

Pain, however, had a way of forcing a person to consider things they never wanted to. The sliding scale of discomfort to stabbing pain was my daily reminder that the choice to begin the next stage of my life might be taken out of my hands at any moment.

Even though I'd known for a year that I'd need knee surgery, I was no closer to figuring out what was next for me.

Money aside, I'd literally only ever been good at hockey. What if there wasn't another dream for me to chase out there? What if I never found something I could be passionate about?

I'd tied my identity to hockey since my mid-teens. Who was I without it?

The thunk of an arm across my back jolted me out of my existential crisis. Campbell, the more tactile of the two, gripped my shoulder and gave me a hard pat on the bicep.

"You'da missed out on our sparkling personalities, then. What a loss that would have been."

Michaels reached around my back to give his alternate captain an affectionate shove. Campbell let his arm drop.

"Man, way to ruin a moment. I'm trying to be all supportive and shit here. Can't you pretend to be serious for a minute?"

Rubbing his arm as if Michaels had really hurt him, Campbell gave him an exaggerated pout.

"Aw, Cap, I was bein' serious. Who would want to miss out on all this?" He gestured to all of himself.

The warmth of his slight Southern accent was contagious. A small smile formed on my lips before I could stop it. God knows it didn't seem like Campbell needed any encouragement in the joker department.

"Nah, it's all good, guys. I was too comfortable in Vancouver. It's not a bad thing to shake things up. My game's going to be better for it." The words were ash on my tongue. I struggled to imagine successfully integrating myself with the Tempests.

"Shit, Yao. Your game gets much better and we'll lose you to another trade before the end of the season. It was a stroke of lightning that management got you in the first place," Campbell chuckled, knocking my arm gently with his elbow.

Nodding my thanks, I couldn't lie. I didn't mind his praise. Coming from a damn good player, it meant something, especially since a constant undercurrent of worry had plagued me all of last season.

Until I figured out what I wanted to happen next, I couldn't bear the sense of purpose I'd found in hockey being ripped away from me.

"Yeah, also, Campbell doesn't like anyone to take the attention off him. He's a bit precious that way." The captain's shoulders shook with laughter at his friend's expense.

It was clear that these two had a strong bond. It took a bit of the pressure off my chest to know that they could have this after only a few years. It boded well for the rest of the team being welcoming too.

"Alright. Enough of the support shit talk. Tell us, Yao, you got a girl back in Vancouver? Or San Jose—that's where you're from, right? Or a guy, maybe? Both? I'm definitely down for hearing about all the kinky shit you wanna share." Campbell widened his eyes and put his chin on his fists as if I was going to spill all the information I'd never shared with the public.

"Knock it off, knucklehead." Michaels shoved Campbell behind my back again. "Not everyone wants to share their private shit in public. Nor do they use a megaphone to declare their hookups like someone else at this table."

"Yeah, Lavoie. Stop talking up your one-night stands in the locker room. Have some consideration." Campbell poked the young defenseman, who had been caught up in conversation with some of the other players across the table.

"Huh, what?" Poor guy was confused. He was also a very reserved person. Campbell was being an idiot.

"Never mind, Lavoie. Ignore this joker, we're cutting him off." Michaels gave our young teammate a reassuring nod before turning back to his alternate captain. "You shit. Don't drag innocent bystanders into your hijinks. You'll give the rookies ulcers from trying to keep up with your nonsense."

"Aw, you wound me, Captain. This is just soda. It's cheat night." He held up his glass. "Furthermore, are you referring to moi? I am the paragon of virtue on this team."

"You are the poster child of too many in-game concussions, is what you are." Michaels laughed.

"But seriously." Campbell was not deterred by our captain's interference. "You missin' someone, Yao?"

Though it took a convoluted route to get back to me, I had no problem with his original question. I taped my stick in pride colors for anyone I'd grown up with who hadn't felt welcome in a locker. And as an adult in a position of influence, I proudly wore anything related to pride for all the other kids and teens who deserved to know there were people in this league that supported them.

Thankfully, the league had allowed us to continue using Pride Tape on our sticks, having backtracked on a previous ban. Not that it would have stopped me, regardless. I'd pay a fucking fine every time.

It was nobody's business but my own. And it sure as shit wouldn't hurt to have more 2LGTBQIA+ representation in any environment, but especially ours.

I stepped down off my mental soapbox.

"Nah. I'm not seeing anyone. My life's been all about hockey for so long. It hasn't been on my radar."

They both nodded as they understood the sacrifices we all had to make. Though it certainly didn't sound like Campbell was hurting for company.

As if on cue, Campbell stood. "If you'll excuse me, gentlemen, I will be on my way to find a lovely lady to offer the pleasure of my company tonight."

Just as he made to leave the table, Michaels called out to him. "That's a pretty big call to make if you're calling anything 'pleasure' in relation to yourself. Are you sure you can put your money where your mouth is?"

Campbell, not missing a beat, whacked him upside the head in a marginally friendly manner.

"Watch me. See ya, fuckers." He gave us a backward wave as he headed over to the bar.

The captain gave me his full attention, catching me as I took a quick glance over at Indie and Andrews again. Their heads bent toward each other across the table, the conversation looking more intimate by the second.

My neck burned at being caught.

"You got something going on with Indie Layne? Because the way you're looking at her, you might start beating your chest any minute now." He eyed me carefully.

"No, man. Nothing going on with her. She's my baby sister's best friend. We kinda grew up together. She's new to the city too, and I'm just looking out for her the way I would for Emery."

His gaze lingered on the couple across the bar for a moment, as if analyzing the dynamic between them.

"Like a sister, huh? Con, I mean, Andrews is a good guy, dude. You don't have to worry there. He's as loyal as they come, with a good heart. She's in good hands with him."

He radiated skepticism at my claim of brotherly concern.

"He's just a kid, though," I growled. "I can't imagine what she sees in him."

That was a lie. Andrews was a good-looking guy, objectively, as well as from the daggers in the gazes of some of the patrons of the bar directed at Indie. He'd shown himself to be a great teammate from our interactions so far. Didn't mean I had to like him for Indie.

I didn't allow myself to admit that I would hate anyone looking at Indie that way.

Michaels's voice was low when he replied, "He's twenty-one, Yao.

Plenty old enough to know what he wants."

I forced a sip of beer down my throat. Keeping my eyes off her was becoming torture. I had to get out of here before I did something stupid like warn Andrews off her.

I had no right to interfere with her dating life. Indie wouldn't tolerate it, and Emery would seethe at my nerve. I'd just started repairing things with Emery after the trade shitshow. I couldn't risk it.

It was physically painful to turn my body in the opposite direction from them and back to the two defensemen. I asked an inane question to start them going again and let their chatter wash over me, though I couldn't help but notice the extra bit of scrutiny from the captain for the remainder of the night.

I forbade myself from looking at her anymore. Even when I saw them get up from their table in my peripheral, I kept my eyes on my teammates.

This fixation on Indie was getting out of hand.

With my future up in the air after this season, I couldn't afford to add more complications by adding Indie Layne to the mix.

I needed to keep my head—and dick—between the pipes on the ice and not on a gorgeous distraction from my past.

Eleven

INDIE

"One thousand seven hundred and seventy-six stairs Indie!" Connor mimed gasping for breath as he clutched his chest comedically. "What happened to 'piece of cake'?"

"Hey, was acting your fallback career if hockey didn't work out? You didn't actually walk any stairs at all. We both took the elevator, so what are you going on about? I didn't know you could only climb the stairs twice a year." I raised an eyebrow in question.

"But the point is you would have held me to that promise if the stairs *were* an option! I'm damn lucky that's the truth. That's the last time I agree to anything with Indie Layne without reading the fine print first." Connor, a grown man, pouted, and it was freaking adorable. Those auburn curls and blue eyes were deadly.

I held up my cocktail glass for him to "cheers" with his beer bottle. "Always read the Ts and Cs, my friend," I offered.

We both took a sip, smiling at each other. It had been a great late-afternoon outing. I got to cross something off my experience list, and Connor's easy demeanor made him good company.

Even if my legs still felt a bit like jelly after standing on the glass floor over eleven hundred feet off the ground. I had learned today that I preferred my adventures without heights. Or at least where the floor beneath me was opaque.

The smile slipped slowly off my face as I let my gaze drift down to my glass on the table. Connor was such a good guy. I felt bad that I was going to have to make it clear that we could only be friends. I wanted to feel something for him, even just for a brief Canadian hockey player fling while I was here.

Unfortunately, I'd handed off my heart to a certain goalie all those years ago and never gotten it back.

My parents having the emotional warmth of their granite countertops, I'd had no resources to repair all the cracks that had formed the moment Theo rejected me.

"Hey, Indie, look at me." He reached across the table to lightly put his hand on top of mine, respectfully withdrawing it again once I made eye contact with him.

His gorgeous face with his kind eyes looked back at me with concern. I must be tired to let my feelings show on my face. I usually had a better game than this.

"Look, it's okay. You don't need to feel bad. No hard feelings, eh?" He smiled kindly.

Why, just why, did he have to be such a sweetheart? So *nice*. So *Canadian* about everything. I didn't feel bad that nothing had developed between us after one date—especially a date that he had invited himself along on—but I was struck with more of a regretful wistfulness, wishing that I *could* feel something for him. Connor seemed like an easy person to be in a relationship with. He wouldn't be afraid to do the work to be a good boyfriend. His heart was on his sleeve.

"I'm sorry, Connor. I thought I could jump into something that

I just can't give you. It's not that I don't like you. You're wonderful. It's just…"

"You're not attracted to me either. You feel like you're dating your brother?" He chuckled.

"I don't have a brother, so I don't know about that. It's more like dating my high school best friend. But now we've gone out on a date and potentially ruined the friendship. Everything is just so *easy* between us, like we've known each other for years." I covered my face with my hands dramatically.

"The rom-coms were all lieees!" I added dramatic horror to my tone. I was keen to get away from any feelings talk.

As much as I liked Connor, I kept my secrets close to my chest. The more potential a feeling had to hurt me, the deeper I tucked it away.

Even if I was tempted to talk about Theo because this maple-syrup-flavored blip in my life would be over in mere months, I couldn't imagine admitting pining after him for more than a decade. I'd sound insane.

"Wait… What do you mean *either*?"

"You just caught on to that, eh?" He gave me another sweet smile before continuing. "Sorry, you're beautiful, of course. I had to shoot my shot. But *it* just isn't there, you know?"

As he spoke, I waved away his beautiful comment. So much emphasis had been put on me to make sure to maintain the Layne image I put little stock in someone who was just focused on my looks.

"Indie, what I mean is we just don't have that kind of chemistry. We're in the friend zone, not the 'I can't keep my eyes off you and you're on my mind all the time' thing."

He reached across and patted my hand in reassurance. He was right, of course. All I felt from his hand touching mine was a warm, comfortable feeling. It could be Emery's or Abbie's hand, with the exception of its size and callouses from his job.

I didn't feel any electricity or fireworks. I couldn't stop myself from looking over to the other side of the bar, where Theo sat with the rest of the team. I was shocked to find his eyes already focused on our table.

I shifted my gaze back to Connor, who gave me a knowing smile.

"What I am pretty sure of is that you feel that kind of obsessive feeling for someone else on the team."

He inclined his head in Theo's direction. I could deny it, but I'd been caught out. I tried to brush it off as best I could.

"It's nothing, and it's impossible anyway. He doesn't feel that way about me. We have a long history. His sister is my best friend. That's all."

"Trust me, Indie. He may not have felt the same in the past, but he's sure as shit not happy about me sitting here with me touching you if that cavern of frown lines in his forehead is any indication."

"I just can't go there, Connor." More than couldn't. I refused to allow Theo any power to hurt me again. Once had been enough.

"You may not have to. *It* might be coming for you sooner than you think," Connor's tone was cheeky.

Before I could continue, he went on, now a smaller, sadder smile on his face. "Definitely not impossible. From the way I've seen you handle Campbell like no one else has been able to, I doubt there are very many things in the world that are impossible for Indie Layne."

"Let's start over and figure out how to be friends. You'd be the first friend I have in Toronto. And I could sure use one," I offered.

I missed Abbie and Emery terribly. I hadn't realized how much I had grown to count on their presence as a comfort in my everyday life.

"Good plan. Friends it is." His shoulders relaxed as he said the words. He really was too sweet. It was clear that he'd been worried about hurting my feelings.

"I have to tell you, I'm not very good at making friends. I only have two back home. I might need some help." I dropped the volume of my voice, slightly embarrassed to admit that I didn't open myself up very often to new people.

"Years of practice over here. Gotta be good with new people when you get a whole new locker room full of them almost every hockey season." He pointed at himself. "I've got you covered."

"Okay, good. I know you grew up in Ontario. But I have literally seen nothing of Toronto other than the subway platforms and the grocery store near my apartment. And now the CN Tower. Do you think we could do the tourist thing again sometime? It'd be nice to see it with a friend."

"Remind me to show you Ste. Saint Marie on a map, babe. Then you won't feel bad for asking. I've only spent weekends here and there in Toronto before now. Let's do it."

I hoped that Connor was just one of those unusually perceptive people-watchers, like Abbie. I'd thought that I'd been good at treating Theo in a strictly professional way, not focusing on him more than any of the other guys on the team. I didn't want my inconvenient feelings broadcasted to my coworkers or, worse, Theo himself.

Connor started making a list on his phone of all the places he wanted to go in the city.

"Listen, we should start with the St. Lawrence Market. Sounds like there's a lot of good food there. They even have, ugh, kangaroo meat. Don't they know you don't eat your friends?" He wrinkled his nose.

I chanced one more look over at Theo. He was still looking in our direction, his lips pressed into a firm line.

Focused on his phone for the moment, Connor didn't notice my distraction. He continued to rattle off options as he scrolled. "Then there's Casa Loma. I wonder if it's haunted? And then maybe we should do something culture-y, like the Royal Ontario Museum. They have dinosaurs, at least, so it won't be all boring vases." He looked up at me briefly, maybe trying to read if I took his "boring vase" musing the wrong way.

"I'm game." I could only chuckle. While I could appreciate art, I, too, preferred variety if I was going to a museum.

It was a struggle to keep my concentration on Connor's growing list, my mind fixated on the man across the room. Theo could think whatever he wanted about Connor and me. The small, petty part of me I tried to keep reined in preened at the idea of Theo getting the wrong idea here.

He could be uncomfortable for a change.

The comforting feelings from my non-date with Connor didn't last. When my phone rang at 8:30 a.m. the following morning, it could only be one person.

My father.

Everyone knew my workdays were late-night affairs. He just didn't care. If he was ready to work at 5:30 a.m. San Diego time, he expected the same from everyone else. At least the time difference wasn't reversed.

Stomach clenching with the knowledge I couldn't ignore his call, I accepted the call and brought the phone to my ear. Usually I put calls on speaker because I hated talking on the phone to begin with, but the thought of my father's voice booming through my private space made me ill.

"Hello?"

"Indigo. Why haven't I heard from you?" My father had never been one for pleasantries in private. He only seemed to care about me falling in line. "Just because you are in another country doesn't mean I don't expect to be kept up to date. Tell me what they've got you doing?"

I'd assumed that when he'd asked whatever powerful friend he'd tapped to get me this job, the job description itself would have been explained to him. Or maybe he'd been so keen to force me out of my former job—since he was done "letting" me be an embarrassment by daring to be satisfied with my status quo—he'd felt that the association with the most valuable sports franchise in the NHL was sufficient to achieve his goal.

"Uh, right. Well, I am responsible for writing some of the game night social media posts during the home games. And my boss has me coordinating the players after the games for their media interviews."

"Coordinating" was a generous word for Jermaine or the team lead, Lynn, sending me to snag players after the game finished.

"Make sure you're actively seeking out every opportunity to excel. I don't want to hear through the grapevine that Gerald Layne's daughter is coasting her way through a cushy job in an attempt to catch the eye of some second-rate hockey player. It's unthinkable to imagine a match between a Layne and a *sports* star. My god." Maybe it was my imagination, but I thought I could hear the physical recoil he was experiencing in his voice.

There were so many things wrong with that statement it left me speechless.

"Anyway," he continued as if my lack of response was inconsequential, "just remember what you're there to do: learn some useful skills, impress the management, and stay out of trouble. The last thing we need is a scandal, especially in this economy."

Even though I'd flown under the radar my whole life, never once rebelling the way I'd truly wanted to, he apparently needed me to confirm I would behave myself.

"Indigo?" His tone became sharper. "I want you to think very closely about who you associate with during this next year. You are not there to socialize."

"Of course. I would never do anything to hurt your reputation, Father." Not yet, at least. He was in for a wake-up call once I was out from under his thumb and I could make my own choices.

"Good. Remember your place." He hung up without a goodbye.

Holy shit. How did he know about my non-date with Connor less than twenty-four hours later? My stomach clenched at the idea he was having me monitored by someone in the Tempests organization. He seemed to have a way of getting information so quickly that TMZ would be envious.

I'd been an idiot to think that being a couple of thousand miles away would somehow put me out of his reach. I should have known better.

Reputation was everything to my father. It was an unsettling feeling to now be the focus of his attention. Every other time he'd tried to steer me in a certain direction, my obstinance had won out, and he'd just given up on me. This persistence of his was new when it came to me.

I didn't know what he'd do next. It made me nauseous to imagine the possibilities.

He'd literally ignored me for the majority of my twenty-five-year lifespan. With the amount of disruption he'd caused in so little time, I would rather go back to being invisible to him.

All the contentment I'd been able to find since arriving in Toronto evaporated with that realization. His call took on a more sinister tone in retrospect.

It hadn't been a "checking up on me" call. It had been a warning.

Fuck. I wished I could go back to a couple of minutes ago and not answer his call. It'd been so nice just to sit with Connor last night, feeling like I'd found an ally in my temporary reality.

Now, I knew better. My father wasn't going to give me a reprieve until he had everything he wanted out of me.

Was this all about just keeping me in line for every second he could until I got my inheritance? Or was he planning something else?

Twelve

INDIE

Despite the uneasiness that haunted me through the work week, the following Saturday saw me crossing another item off my life experience list. Well, at least making a dent in my number one item. I was bringing a tiny, peach-fuzz-covered Chihuahua to my apartment. I'd wanted a dog so badly as a kid that this moment felt surreal. Not that she was my pet—something I had to keep reminding myself about—but I could pretend for a little while. I wondered how parents felt bringing babies home from the hospital. I couldn't figure out who deemed me responsible enough for this living thing. I felt underqualified. I could barely keep a cactus alive!

I was afraid to move my arms lest I drop my bundle. She was double leashed, which I appreciated. The last thing I wanted to do was lose my temporary dog.

Jermaine had been so kind to drive me out to Hamilton, just outside of Toronto, to pick up Gizmo. His wife, Amy, had tagged along for the ride and kept me entertained with little anecdotes of the places we passed on the drive. Their family's Morkie had come from the same rescue a couple of years prior.

The rescue operation was impressive. Two employees made the drive all the way from Texas to the Greater Toronto Area every month with a commercial van fitted with crates. Each with its own little rescue pup inside.

The pickup scene had been a whirlwind. I was sure that I'd listened to the answers to my list of questions, but hell if I could remember anything now that I was walking toward my apartment door.

Gizmo had been pretty quiet on the trip back. I'd read that rescue dogs take some time to decompress, so I'd just have to take it day by day.

But for now, she was all mine, a fact that was equally thrilling and intimidating.

Closing and locking the door behind me, I put her down to investigate the place. I'd already set up the pee pads, hoping her expertise in potty training prevailed.

Of the two of us, Gizmo knew more about potty training than I did at this point.

Letting her do the dog sniffing thing, I went toward the couch and sat down on the floor. I'd rolled up the existing rug, not wanting to deal with cleaning any accidents off something that wasn't mine.

I sat back to watch her before snapping a picture of her staring at her new bed with a couple of toys.

Indie

picture of Gizmo rocking a fuzzy pink sweater

Well, she's here and I have no idea what I'm doing. I hope you're happy.

Emery

OMG you actually did it! So cute!

Abbie

She is so adorable! What's she like?
Are you having fun?

Indie

So far she has slept next to me on a
blanket in my boss's car and taken about
10 steps in the apartment. Not a lot of
action yet. Why did I let you talk me into
this?

Emery

Because she's a genius! This is going
to be sooo good for you.

Abbie

Hey. Admittedly, I totally crossed the
line on filling out the application on
your behalf. But she's just so cute!
You're the one who could've said no
and didn't.

Indie

That makes me both an idiot and a
sucker.

Emery

Nooooo. It makes you a kind person
who's just a little nervous about taking
care of a pet for the first time.

At least she's not a fish. Remember
those goldfish my brothers had
growing up? Jesus, thank god Mom
had a marine biology degree with all
the chemicals and ph balance stuff it
took to take care of them. And cleaning

the tank, ewwww. (barf emoji)

Abbie

Whether you admit it or not, you like taking care of things. And Ms. I'm-going-to-run-a-non-profit, you also like helping people, as much as you don't advertise it.

Indie

So, yes. Idiot and sucker still apply.

Abbie

Keep us posted. You did so well with Mew. Maybe Gizmo can have her own Instagram account? That would be so fun! She could be a pup-fluencer.

Indie

Even "if" I liked that idea, I'd have to check what I'm allowed to post as her foster. I'm going to work on her voluntarily coming close to me first.

Abbie

I've planted the seed. You don't stand a chance with that little fashion-forward canine. No "ifs" required.

Emery

She's going to love you. Just like we do. (heart emoji)

Indie

Yeah, yeah. Me too.

Despite my flippant words, they knew just how much they meant to me, even if I couldn't say it too often. It was as if the words were locked up in my throat. We'd never said anything like that in my house growing up. I'd never outright said those words to anyone.

Looking back at Gizmo, she had made it halfway across the floor, watching me all the way. I felt my heart lighten a bit at the thought that she was reserved but not petrified.

Just as she was almost within arm's length of me, a loud thud hit the wall in the hallway just outside my apartment. The bang was followed by a low "fuck," which could only mean Theo was on the other side of my obviously not thick enough front door.

The noise sent Gizmo scuttling back to her new bed.

Great. As if having Theo across the hall and at work wasn't problematic enough, he was screwing up my first night as a dog parent.

Theo must be coming back from an extra gym session. There was no game tonight. Otherwise, I'd be at the arena running between the communications team and the media, lining up post-game interviews.

Unless he was on a date. My stomach didn't like that idea at all.

Usually, I prided myself on my independence and competency to handle anything life could throw at me. When life, however, had literally thrown Theo Yao-Miller into my path, I'd done nothing but duck for cover.

I couldn't even look at him most of the time. When I had to go into the locker room, I steadfastly kept my eyes from the far-left corner of the room where I knew his locker was.

I'd memorized the team's schedule and Theo's physiotherapy and conditioning schedule so that I could avoid being in the elevator or our hallway when he was coming home. I'd been lucky so far that he wasn't like the majority of the single guys on the team heading to the bars to wind down after home games. And definitely to hook up, if the stories I overheard in the halls of the arena were to be believed.

Under extreme duress, I could admit that I really liked the fact that Theo wasn't seeing anyone or out hooking up with randoms.

I was long past hoping for anything to happen between us. Wasn't I? My nineteen-year-old self who thought she was in love with Theo was an idiot. I cringed when I thought of that Christmas morning six years ago. How could something feel so long ago that it felt like it didn't even happen to you and simultaneously burn with the humiliation of rejection like it was yesterday?

I was usually much better at compartmentalizing than this. I couldn't stand all these murky feelings inside me. I just wanted to get on with my life, not face my past at work and at home every day.

I felt lonely in a way I believed I'd conquered when I'd come to the conclusion that I wasn't a priority in my parents' lives. I was a mere prop to drag out when it suited them, then leave the time-intensive parts to the nanny they'd hired.

The only problem being you could only pay someone to take care of your child, not love them like they needed.

Believing myself immune to this discomfort under my skin—a living, breathing entity with a mind of its own—was easier when Theo was many hours away in Vancouver. Only seeing him through the occasional social media post over the years had allowed me to keep my feelings for him packed away in the back of my mind.

Coming back to the present reality of a very small, shivering dog in my living room. I glared at my door as if I could control time and space and prevent the boom that had set her back. I tried to modulate my tone to reassure Gizmo. How one reassured a dog, I wasn't quite sure, but I hoped my tone came close to something gentle.

"It's okay, Giz. That big noise was scary, but you're okay. I promise."

She cocked her head to the side in an expression of "who, me?" It was freaking adorable. I wanted to take her picture for the bio I would need to write for her, but I was afraid to startle her again by moving too quickly.

Moments later, Gizmo bravely set off on her second attempt to conquer the great expanse of thirteen feet of bare engineered hardwood between us.

The next morning, I was up at the ungodly hour of 5:30 a.m., freezing my butt off outside the building, trying to encourage a tiny, hairless Chihuahua to do her business.

I swear to god, I'd said "go potty" so much in the last twenty-four hours that I felt like I was evicting other words from my brain as a result.

I'd turned to pleading already. So much for my no-bullshit life policy. It had taken less than eight trips into the cold before I'd been broken by the five-pound tiny Elvis-like lip curl.

"Come on, Giz. Go potty. Look. I know you're cold. But I promise today I'll get you a warmer sweater—hell, a parka. Whatever you want. Just please go potty."

It didn't help that I thought it was going to be a "quick" trip outside to do her thing when she first woke up. In another moment of great wisdom, I'd only pulled on my new Tempests hoodie that Connor had given me (with his number on it, of course). I'd accepted because it was a nice gesture and activated that petty part of me who considered wearing it to work one Friday.

Currently, the little miss in front of me stood shivering, giving me a "what the hell is this nonsense" look with one front paw lifted in the air as if she was afraid she'd freeze to the ground. Every couple of seconds, she'd lift one of her back ones too. If physics allowed, she'd have had all four feet off the ground. However, when she finally realized we weren't going in until she did her business, she gave in.

"You got a dog?" a deep voice rumbled from behind me.

No exaggeration. My soul left my body at the sound of those words coming from behind me. I could see it form a haze above me as I lay deceased on the ground.

Sorry, Giz. I won't be much of a foster mom from the afterlife.

Back in the present, I whipped around to see the last person I wanted to encounter at this moment or any other.

"Indie?" Theo tried again since I hadn't responded.

Trying to recover my voice while reattaching my soul to my body was an effort my already frozen nerves did not appreciate.

"For fuck's sake, Theo. You scared the shit out of me." I aimed a glare at him.

"Not my fault you didn't hear me walking up over your chattering teeth. Did you learn nothing from Whistler a couple years ago when you went with Emery?" He smiled irritatingly.

I narrowed my eyes at his reference to the stupid incident of we-thought-we-would-be-warm-enough on our trio's first solo getaway without adult supervision.

"How the hell do you know about that?" I narrowed my eyes at him, hoping to annoy him enough that he'd be on his way more quickly.

"I'm in the NHL, Indie. Not living under a rock. You underestimate how important it is to gather any and all intel to embarrass your siblings to use against them at a later date. Especially with the twins." He was right there. Liam and Chase were masters at chaos.

"Forget that. You still scared me. Not cool, Mr. Goalie-of-the-Year. And this is not my dog. She's my foster dog." I sniffed, both because he was annoying and the cold was causing my nose to run.

As if he had a list of ways to further infuriate me, he set his workout bag on the sidewalk and crouched down, making his imposing figure as nonthreatening as possible. He held his hand up for her doubled leashes. Still in some sort of haze, I dumbly handed them over.

"Hey, girl," he crooned. His voice took on a sweetness that set off a pang in my chest. The last time I'd heard him sound like this was when he caught me falling out of that goddamn tree when I was eight.

I didn't want to hear it now.

"Theo, what are you doing?"

"Shhh, Rocky. Let me work my magic here."

His confidence made me roll my eyes. Of course he would think that he was a dog whisperer as well as a world-class goalie.

Theo's ass was a work of art in those black sweatpants, the cherry on the top of this encounter.

But in the next moment, disbelief caused my brain synapses to misfire. Surely, Giz had not just slowly walked over to him and stood between his perfectly muscled thighs and was letting him scratch her belly.

Maybe I *had* fallen when he scared me, and all of this was a hallucination resulting from a concussion. If so, I hoped the ambulance would arrive soon.

Theo then proceeded to *pick her up* and tuck her into his coat, leaving only her small snout showing. They were a two-headed monster of cuteness.

But hell would freeze over before I let that feeling show on my face, even if it took all my willpower not to take a picture with my phone.

"Aww. You're just freezing, aren't you, girl? What a mean mommy you have, bringing you out here in the freezing cold. And she's freezing her gorgeous ass off in just a hoodie with the wrong number on it."

I crossed my arms, scowling. The involuntary shaking of my limbs may have lessened the impact of my displeasure.

"Come on, baby. Let's get you inside where it's warm." His voice was laced with honey.

He started walking toward our building's entrance, leaving me to follow.

"You're laying it on a bit thick, Theo. She'll be okay," I called out to my dog-napping neighbor.

Looking back over his shoulder, the quick flash of his grin had my breath coming up short. My cheeks heated, and it had nothing to do with the brisk wind.

"Who said I was talking to the dog?" he returned.

Thirteen

INDIE

I was beginning to see why the reporters were always keen to follow Ryan Campbell around. The assistant captain could make even the most levelheaded person's head spin.

While Connor had breezed through his feature interview the week prior, I understood why my boss had insisted I supervise when it was Campbell's turn.

He sat with a reporter from *The 49th*, a nationwide hockey magazine, in the media conference room.

I hovered at the threshold of the room, as if I could have any impact on this interview if Campbell decided to take it off the rails.

"What would you say was the biggest motivator that helped you push your hockey game to the next level?" The reporter glanced down at his notes on his tablet.

That slip of attention made him miss the smirk on Campbell's face, which he quickly schooled.

"The money. Definitely. I'm only here to make ten million," Campbell replied, tone serious.

And there he went.

Caught off guard, the reporter opened and closed his mouth a few times, which made him appear as though Campbell's answer had caused his brain to malfunction.

Perhaps I could have appreciated Campbell's sense of humor if it wasn't my job to make sure this interview reflected the image of a team that is committed to making it through the playoffs this season.

I liked to think of myself as a connoisseur of snark. Ryan Campbell was an artist. But at the moment, he was just making everyone's jobs more difficult.

"Uh, well, I've… never heard an answer put quite so… succinctly before." The reporter made a valiant attempt to steer Campbell away from the topic of money. "Most players talk about a coach or hockey hero that inspired them at a young age?" The man raised his eyebrows, eyes guileless.

"Yeah, no. It was always about getting rich for me." Campbell put a bright smile on his face as though his comments weren't completely impolite and designed to cause a reaction. "Sometimes, I'll spend a whole evening just gazing lovingly at my banking app, watching my money grow."

Campbell's response had the reporter actually choking on his own saliva.

That was it! I made my way into the room, stopping behind the reporter and putting on my most saccharine smile.

"Well, look at that, Campbell." I held up my left wrist, which was sans watch. "We've kept Grant here past your interview time. I'm pretty sure Coach needs you in his office."

My grin was all teeth now. God, I'd have to tell Jermaine this interview would need to be seriously vetted. Campbell's star power made him a fan favorite. He wouldn't even get in trouble once

Jermaine read the interview transcript. This kind of babysitting was way above my pay grade.

The only thing I had the power to do was get him out of this room ASAP.

Campbell's eyebrows raised, followed by a slow grin. He clearly enjoyed messing with people too much. I just needed to get him out of this room so I could clean up his mess.

He looked at his own watchless wrist. "You know, Indie, you're so right. I wouldn't want to keep Coach Reyes waiting. I live to serve, after all."

With the grace of a world-class athlete, he was up and halfway to the door before I realized it shouldn't have been that easy with the high level of shenanigans he seemed to appreciate.

"Honey, by the way, what time should I expect you at home?" Campbell called over his shoulder before turning his head to give me a quick glance and a wink and continued out the door.

My only consolation was that Coach Reyes had left an hour ago. *Two can play your game, Campbell.*

The reporter's gaze lasered in on my face, his former bland politeness replaced with a shrewd gleam.

"Sorry, what did you say your first name was, Ms. Layne?" He scrolled through his tablet, where he'd been making notes. "Any relation to Layne Holdings?"

Sigh. Campbell was from the East Coast; he wouldn't immediately recognize my surname. It was much easier to avoid association with my family away from the Bay Area and the West Coast in general.

There was no point in lying as a single Google search would get Grant Douglas the truth.

"Yes. You're right. That is my family's company. But you need to understand something about Ryan Campbell. That man seems to derive too much joy from pranks like his comments just now. So you can't take him seriously. He's a dedicated, elite athlete. I can guarantee you, he gives his all to the Tempests. But there isn't anything going on between us."

"Oh, I see. No problem. Off the record. Of course." Grant was nodding. As if he wouldn't tuck this little detail away and use it to his advantage at a later date.

"No, honestly." Rubbing my right temple to ease the headache that was now forming, I needed to make him understand. "When I say nothing is going on, I mean nothing. We don't play around in my family with these kinds of things. Let me be clear. Ryan Campbell was just joking. And my personal legal team would be more than pleased if any other misunderstanding were to come up in the future. Now do you see?" I kept unwavering eye contact as he processed the meaning of my words.

No longer on the offensive, Grant was starting to understand who he was dealing with. I hated to be so mercenary about it, but I could not have any whiff of controversy getting back to my father.

Whatever lesson he thought he was teaching me by demanding I come to Toronto, I needed him to continue believing that I was absorbing it into the very core of my being. I didn't want to end up in a battle for my inheritance when I wasn't sure I could win.

And if that meant Mr. Douglas here had to be scared straight, then so be it.

Clearing his throat, he took the hint and moved on. "Er, right. Ahem. You mentioned you wanted to preview the questions for Theo Yao. I assure you, they are very similar to the ones you looked over for Mr. Campbell. Is it really necessary?"

If only he knew how much more important Theo's interview was to me. Putting aside the many complications where Theo and I were concerned, it was the very least I could do for Emery to make sure her brother was well taken care of, especially when it fell under my purview at work.

"I understand. But my boss, Jermaine Kenton, you see, insists that I review all three players' questions before their interviews. I was so appreciative of you sending me Connor Andrews's list last week while I was out of the office. It's important to be able to tell Mr. Kenton that I followed his instructions to the letter. You know how this kind of thing goes, don't you? Can't let the boss down." The steel dropped from my tone into something more conciliatory.

It was more likely that Grant, here, would get whiplash from my swift change in demeanor than suddenly become my biggest fan, but Campbell had started this train wreck, and I was here to get it back on track.

I knew what I looked like, however. A young twenty-something woman in a male-dominated environment. Hopefully, in Grant's eyes, that made me nonthreatening enough that he'd somehow forget that I threatened legal action moments before.

In appealing to the idea of "jeez, aren't bosses just task masters," we might find common ground, and it would pave the way for him to hand over Theo's list of questions. Maybe I'd get lucky and he had a tyrannical editor and could sympathize with my false worries about my job security.

Whatever he saw on my face placated him enough to nod before looking down to tap out something on his tablet.

"I've just forwarded them to you. I'm going to make a quick call in the hallway. Mr. Yao isn't due for another—" Grant checked his left wrist, where he wore an actual watch. "—twenty minutes. That should give us more than enough time to make sure Mr. Kenton's requirements are satisfied."

I nodded distractedly as he stood and left the room, already opening his email to scan the interview questions.

Everything was fine until I reached the last section of questions.

-Theo, your full last name is Yao-Miller. Is there a specific reason you play only under your mother's surname? Are you trying to honor your mother or stay away from your father's standing as one of the top coaches in American College Football?

-How much did your mother's passing away affect your decision to continue to move forward after you were drafted? Weren't they within weeks of each other?

-How does your family feel about your move to Toronto? Your siblings, Emery, Chase, and Liam, how much did you see them when you were over in Vancouver compared to now?

The meaning of the words "spontaneously combust" had never been more clear to me than in this moment. I couldn't recall a time when I'd been more livid.

And that was saying something because Abbie's mother was an absolute bitch who incited my violent tendencies that I couldn't act on.

Currently, I was in a new astral plane of anger. I wasn't sure how much restraint I had if this reporter didn't back down.

How *dare* anyone even think to ask Theo these questions? In preparation for their interviews, I'd skimmed through the majority of the previous articles written about the guys, having had no experience with what should or shouldn't go into a hockey interview.

Theo never discussed his family or his personal life with the media.

Did this reporter think because they were the largest, most prestigious sports magazine in the country that he would be able to invade Theo's privacy under the guise of documenting his "legacy"? Oh no. *Think the fuck again, Grant Douglas.*

The man himself sauntered back into the room, ready to resume his line of questions. He didn't realize that the entire fabric of time and space had rearranged itself during his short phone call.

As Grant sat down before me, waking his tablet screen, he looked over at me. "Any concerns?" His tone was mild.

The out-of-line questions highlighted in black, I clicked Send to return his list to him.

"Yes. The last three. Out of the question. Those are not happening." My tone left no room for argument.

Grant's head jerked back with such force at the venom in my tone that he might need a visit to his chiropractor after our time together.

"I'm sorry, what?" Ah, the ever-present Canadian politeness. He used it now to cover what I was sure was his displeasure at a low-ranking communications employee daring to question his freedom as a journalist.

I was learning the nuances of Canadian speech now. His tone suggested he wasn't sorry at all. There was a difference between real and fake "sorrys" in this country.

"Just what I said. Theo Yao's personal life and family are off-limits. The same things you asked Andrews and Campbell are fine, but not the last section." I watched him carefully to see which direction he wanted to take this conversation: defense or offense.

"I hardly think asking some simple questions about how his mother influenced his hockey career is problematic at this point. It's been…" he said as he glanced down at his screen to scroll through his notes.

"Fourteen years." I didn't blink. If he wanted the exact days and hours, I could give him those too. Alice still made up a whole chamber of my heart, and she hadn't even been my mom. I'd just been lucky enough to be loved by her as Emery's best friend.

"Er, right. Nearly a decade and a half. Sure, I can see why it was avoided at the time. Mr. Yao was just some eighteen-year-old kid. But he's nearing the end of his career—don't you think it makes sense for him to share his thoughts with the fans? The Tempests only bought out the final year of his contract. They could extend, of course, but…"

"I'll stop you there." I'd had enough. There was no justification in existence that would change my mind, no matter what my boss or anyone else at head office said. While this was my task, Theo wouldn't be answering these questions.

"Let me put it to you this way, Grant. Your career would be safer and better off printing the completely false narrative of Ryan Campbell and I in a romantic relationship than asking Theo Yao a single question outside of his opinions on how he's liking the new team, what skills he's perfecting this year, or their chances at the Cup. You need to reference his *legacy*? Look up how many times he's won the Vezina Trophy or how much money he's raised for charity. That should cover it."

Unable to sit in this room a minute longer, I stood. As I passed by Grant, still in his chair, I looked down to give him one more warning, making sure my tone left no doubt of my intentions should he upset Theo in any way.

"Anything else goes on in the next forty-five minutes and I will personally bring you a legal shitstorm of such magnitude you'd do best to tender your resignation and file for bankruptcy upon leaving this room. And that's before I mention it to the GM and owner."

Fourteen

THEO

Crossing paths with Campbell, who wasn't supposed to be done with his interview for another several minutes, had me jolting to a stop.

I'd planned to arrive ten minutes early for my turn, keen to give Indie a break from wrangling my teammate. Campbell seemed to thrive on making trouble. Growing up, Indie could get overwhelmed when she wasn't in control of a situation. Dealing with Campbell's unpredictable nature would be like inviting squirrels high on cocaine into your home.

As we walked from opposite directions along the empty hallway in the Tempests arena, the building quiet on a non-game day, Campbell appeared too pleased with himself. From our locker room and game travel interactions over the past month, I knew his expression meant he'd created chaos for someone.

Campbell held up his fist for a greeting once we were within arm's length of each other. I tapped my knuckles against his in a distracted hello, more concerned with whatever mayhem he'd been causing.

"Hey. Headed to your interview, Yao?" He couldn't keep the humor out of his tone.

"What did you do?" I growled, finding it impossible to keep my normal cool. I didn't have it in me to fake social graces at the moment. The idea that he'd made Indie's job harder than necessary pressed all my protective buttons.

"Moi? How could you think that?" He couldn't even pretend to be offended. "Don't worry, Yao. I was just having a little fun at the reporter's expense, though it seemed like it was going to take him some time to figure out the joke. He'll get there eventually, or Layne will set him straight."

"You know she's new at her job. Why'd you have to make it harder for her? Did you even think of that?" I asked, the tension in my shoulders building until they felt like they could snap.

To his credit, an expression of regret passed over Campbell's face. Reaching up to rub the back of his neck, he looked down at the floor before meeting my eyes again, his natural charm having no effect on me. "Shit, Yao. Way to make a guy feel bad. It was just a joke. I didn't mean any harm. Gotta make this media shit pass by somehow, eh? Haven't they ever thought of asking a question that hasn't been asked a thousand times before?"

"Yeah, I get it. Nobody enjoys the media, but it's part of our contracts. So we need to just suck it up. What it doesn't mean is being a pain in the ass to the people working on our behalf." My tone left no room for argument.

"Okay, *Dad*, I get the point. No more scolding necessary." He threw his hands up in surrender.

I had a feeling that was the best I was going to get out of Campbell. Like my brothers, he loved his reputation as a prankster, so I doubted my little lesson was going to stick.

I nodded and moved around him to keep walking.

"It's a pretty nice ass, though. You can't blame me," he called out once he was a fair distance behind me.

"Campbell," I warned, stopping suddenly, and turned back.

"Oh, did you think I was talking about Layne? I meant this right here." He indicated his own backside, shit-eating grin intact.

Clearly, Campbell had my brothers' Teflon-type personality, on the surface at least. Nothing stuck for long.

Shaking my head, I pushed thoughts of Campbell aside and increased my pace toward the conference room.

It was time to get my head on straight for this interview. Though I'd done enough interviews over the years, the ones coming off the ice after a loss being my least favorite, I still owed it to the organization to be diligent with my answers.

Words like "veteran" and "legacy" didn't sit right with me. It wasn't like I needed any other reminders about how my age and a professional NHL career would soon no longer belong in the same sentence.

I wasn't sure what wisdom I had to offer future players of the game. Every season was a fresh start because nothing ever stayed the same: a new team dynamic had to be rebuilt, skills refined, and ambitions solidified.

Lost in my thoughts, I didn't hear the raised voices until I reached the threshold of the conference room, my body reeling from suddenly halting my steps.

"Just what I said. Theo Yao's personal life and family are off-limits. The same things you asked Andrews and Campbell are fine, but not the last section."

Indie's voice projected clearly out into the hall. Her words had me clenching my fists, the tension building in my shoulders again. My agent was always clear in my contracts that I didn't talk about personal stuff. So what was this?

In my fourteen-year career, I hadn't once discussed my mom's death and the devastation that followed. The memories, good and bad, were locked up securely in a vault within my mind that I rarely accessed. It was simpler that way.

Losing her had created a fissure so deep in the foundation of our family that it became a bruise that never healed. And none of us talked about it with each other.

This moment had the effect of being kicked by a steel-toe boot in that bruise. And Indie was trying to shield me from that. When I could think clearly about it, I would probably feel grateful. But not now.

Caught off guard, my ears started buzzing as the reporter spouted something about his questions being justified until the sound of my pulse beating my ears was all I could hear. My breathing stuttered as I tried to drag in some air. It took until Indie spoke again to wade through the fog of the shock.

"Anything else goes on in the next forty-five minutes and I will personally bring you a legal shitstorm of such magnitude you'd do best to tender your resignation and file for bankruptcy upon leaving this room. And that's before I mention it to the GM and owner."

My heart clenched hearing her defending me so vehemently with her words.

Glancing at my watch, I still had ten minutes before I was due in that room. Thoughts of arriving early evaporated from my mind. My gaze scanned the surrounding doors for a place I could use to calm down.

About twenty feet down the hallway was a maintenance closet, the door propped open with a wheeled bucket and mop. Maybe not the most pleasant space to pull myself together, but it would have to do.

Leaving the ongoing debate between Indie and the reporter

behind me, I pushed open the closet door and slipped past the cleaning equipment without messing it up. Hopefully, I could take a few minutes in here without the maintenance staff catching me.

The white-painted concrete walls blurred as I leaned against a shelf filled with bottles of chemicals.

It shouldn't be hitting me this hard after so many years.

Closing my eyes, I forced air into my lungs. The tightness in my chest resisted the expansion of my lungs.

Get a grip, Yao. You don't have time to lose your shit right now.

Maybe you should have spent more time listening to that therapist all those years ago instead of thinking you could handle it on your own.

Indie couldn't see me like this. In fact, she couldn't know that I overheard her talking to that reporter. The last thing I needed was Emery hearing that something was going on with me from her best friend.

You just keep tucking away more issues you won't discuss with your family. Where does it end?

I allowed my hands to cover my face for a moment, wishing I didn't have to face anyone right now, before raking my hands through my hair roughly.

A disheveled appearance would be the least of my worries if I couldn't pull off this interview. With my knees being a ticking time bomb, I didn't need the added pressure of management, or worse, my family, questioning my mental well-being.

"I'm just going to grab Theo from the locker room. He probably ran into one of the coaching staff on his way here." Indie's voice rang out in the hallway.

"Where are you, Theo?" she said under her breath.

I glanced at my watch. Shit, my interview was meant to start five minutes ago. So much for making a good impression on the reporter.

Hell, if I was already late, a few more minutes pulling myself together would be better than going in there still shaken.

The click of her shoes on the polished floor grew fainter as I hesitated by the door of the maintenance room. At least I would be able to avoid talking to Indie immediately after she'd defended my privacy.

With shock receding slightly, the implications of her words sunk in. The tension in my shoulders eased the more I imagined the reporter's expression after Indie was finished ripping him a new one. If they hadn't been talking about me, I'd have loved to watch her take him down a peg or twelve.

She would have been magnificent. I'd never known anyone else like her.

When was the last time someone took your side like that? She said she would personally go to bat for you, even after feeling years of hurt.

God, it was good to know someone was on my side. I was surrounded by people who saw me as a commodity they had paid for or a teammate who had the power to screw up their careers by not doing my job. Nobody was out here looking out for just Theo.

But Indie did just now. A small light flicked on in the dark part inside me. She was so much more than a beautiful, capable woman from my past. Warmth and loneliness threatened simultaneously.

Usually, I kept myself busy with extra conditioning and PT, so I didn't notice the lack of real relationships in my life. But since coming to Toronto, the chasm between me and the people who were most important to me had grown beyond just the physical miles between us.

In Vancouver, I could placate my conscience by telling myself that I would visit my siblings soon. That I would solve the lack of connection with my dad since my mom had been the natural bridge between us.

That I had time. I'd been an idiot.

What did I have going for me other than less than a year on a contract that might not be renewed?

Well, there's the woman with a heart the size of all the Great Lakes combined in this arena looking for you.

I'd given up a chance to know Indie, even as a friend, six years ago. When she ran from our kitchen that Christmas morning, I didn't chase her. Didn't try to explain that it wasn't her but our age difference and the demands of my career that made any kind of connection between us impossible.

I hadn't even allowed myself to think about it.

I couldn't fix my relationship with my family or my knees immediately, but I could get to work on repairing what I broke six years ago. And hope Indie still wanted to know me.

Our age difference didn't matter anymore. We could be friends, or more, if she was willing. There was so much about my life I couldn't control right now, but I wanted her to see *me* again. The Theo she wanted all those years ago in my kitchen.

Sliding back out of the maintenance room, I strode across the hall to get this interview over with.

I had more important things to focus on. Mainly the woman who was likely cursing my name as she searched the arena.

I couldn't wait.

Fifteen

INDIE

My role on the communications team had been wholly based in Toronto, leaving the more senior members of the team to travel with the players.

That suited me fine. I'd had enough business trips with my parents as a child to never want to stay in some random hotel for a night just to pack up again without ever seeing the city where I'd landed.

But here I was. With some awful flu virus making the rounds in the office, I was the last one standing this week. And that meant I'd been ordered to fill in for one of the team members who usually traveled with the team.

I felt horrible about leaving Gizmo, but Jermaine's wife, Amy, had offered to stay at my place with their Morkie, whom Giz adored. She'd argued that I was doing her the favor by letting her dog-sit. Since, as she put it, she'd had enough of Jermaine's "man cold."

Dog mom guilt aside, I'd boarded the bus for the ride back to the hotel where the team was staying, I kept my head bent down toward the iPad in my lap. The last thing I wanted to do was make eye contact with Theo in a confined space. I let my hair fall over my shoulders, completing my little bubble of isolation.

The overall mood of the night was subdued as the team had lost 3-2 against Montreal.

My heart clenched a little at the thought of Theo losing for the first time this season. I wondered how being a goalie factored into his sense of responsibility for game losses. People could talk all day about hockey being a team sport, but Theo seemed to give all of himself to his game. I couldn't help but think he might burden himself more than was necessary.

My throat tightened at how hard that must be.

I didn't know why I cared so much. I felt my forehead to see if I was coming down with something. Maybe that could explain the tightness in my muscles and my breathing becoming a little more difficult.

Theo was not my concern. We'd done an admirable job of being professional so far.

Professional meant that I avoided him at every possible opportunity, pre- and post-games.

Luckily, on the regular-season game nights, the media seemed to want to talk to the captain the most in terms of players, as if he had some magical insight into their current standing in the league. Then, when they wanted fodder for their social media highlights, they asked for Campbell, and he usually left them with something gossip-worthy.

And if Theo sometimes looked like he wanted to say something to me in the hallways of the arena, I'd buried my head in my tablet, pretending not to notice.

Maybe it was immature. Okay, it definitely was. But we weren't friends. *I* couldn't be friends with him.

So, really, it wasn't as if I was letting my personal issues with Theo overshadow the job I was here to do. It was just convenient to be able to avoid him as much as I had.

The problem with Theo was that he was just *so goddamn good.* It made him irresistible. He had the terrible habit of being kind, thoughtful, loyal, and caring.

Because he would cast his spell over me again before I'd even know what was happening, I couldn't risk it.

Movement in the seat beside me surprised me back into the present. I'd been thinking so intensely about Theo that I feared I'd conjured him into my orbit through thought alone.

I cast my eyes to my left, the air whooshing from my lungs in relief.

His eyes sparkling with mischief, Connor grinned his magazine cover smile at me.

"You're pretty upbeat for a guy who just lost a game, sir." I poked his rock-hard shoulder with my finger, hoping my voice sounded normal.

Ouch. Note to self. Don't risk injury. Keep hands off hockey players. They were dangerous to my health, in more ways than one.

With the inner resilience and positivity that I was learning was just a part of who he was, Connor shrugged good-naturedly.

"Ah well. Can't win 'em all, as they say." He settled back into the coach seat, resting his head against the cushion, and unsuccessfully stifled a yawn.

"Really? Just like that?" I was skeptical.

He shrugged. "No, not really. But it won't do my game any good if I'm obsessed with the last loss. Coach will torture us with endless reels of game tape and kick our asses in practice anyway. No point in borrowing trouble."

What an amazing attitude to have. I'd always had a healthy respect for all athletes, but I was learning professional athletes were just so beyond anything I could have imagined.

Between multiple games, practices, dryland training, and pre-skate conditioning, it was a wonder to me that they were even awake in their off hours.

"That's a pretty laid-back attitude for a first-year professional hockey player on a team looking to win the Cup this year."

"Yes, yes. All of that." He waved his hand in the air in general agreement with my statement. "But damn, buddy. These back-to-back away games are kicking my ass. What I wouldn't give for a night in front of the TV at my overpriced waterfront condo."

Lovely. I'd been upgraded (or downgraded—who knew?) in the Connor nickname department. We really were on our way to becoming proper friends.

"Well, old pal. Emphasizing the 'old' part. What happened to that fresh-faced young man I just proofed a magazine article about?"

He rolled his head to the side and looked at me through slitted eyes.

"You wanna go there, *Diaper Sniper*? You're the one rounding the corner on twenty-six between us. You were the one who asked me out in the first place." His tired smile turned slightly mischievous.

"*Diaper Sniper?*" I laughed. I refrained from poking him again. "You certainly rewrite history well. If you recall, you invited yourself on my afternoon escapade. Not the other way around."

"Yeah. I heard it from a teammate I had a couple years ago. He was older than you even, if you can believe it. He'd dated a fifth-year victory lapper or something while he was a first year. Er, I mean, a senior while he was a freshman in American college terminology. I thought it was a keeper." His eyes closed on another yawn. "We'll agree to disagree. Either way, it worked out great for you."

"Thank you so much for the clarification. I don't know how I would have managed without you to translate for me."

My words fell on deaf ears as the smallest snore sounded beside me. He really was exhausted.

I was worried about Giz, despite having texted Amy no less than four times in the last eighteen hours. Even though she'd provided proof-of-life photos of her curled up on the couch, sleeping happily.

Besides imagining all the new abandonment issues I was concocting on behalf of my obviously-better-adjusted-than-her-owner dog, I dreaded the idea of running into Theo at the hotel.

He hadn't been on tonight's media interview roster, having been able to glide off the ice and bypass the media while Michaels and one of the other defensemen had presented a united front against the media over tonight's loss.

The bus slowed to a stop outside the hotel, I wasn't proud of my speedy exit from my seat. I absolutely did not climb over a dozing Connor and book it into the lobby while the majority of the team paced themselves after a long night.

Of course I did. I just chose not to think about what I looked like while doing it. Luckily, Connor was a sound sleeper.

I did not have the control over my actions where Theo was concerned. I was out of my element yet again.

A quick stop at reception had my room card in my hand and into the elevator before the team made it into the lobby.

After taking a quick shower to wash off the ick of a plane ride and the adrenaline sweat from a night of media chaos at the arena, I found a text from Connor on my phone.

MVP-C

Hey buddy. You've been training extra hours I don't know about? That was some quick exit off the bus.

When had I left my phone open in his presence that he'd changed his contact name?

Indie

MVP-C, huh?

MVP-C

You know, buddy. It even rhymes so it's meant to be.

Anyways, I'm bored and so tired I can't sleep. Stupid to catch that nap on the bus. Want to come to mine and watch a movie and raid the mini bar?

The choice between sitting in this hotel room stewing over Theo versus the guaranteed good-natured distraction that was Connor Andrews was an easy one. He made it easy to come out of my natural state of isolation. Connor was just such a safe space. I hadn't realized how much I missed that with Abbie and Emery until I had it again with him.

Indie

You're on. But that doesn't sound very team nutritionist approved?

MVP-C

After all the hits I took tonight, I earned my recovery M&Ms. Room 405.

I'd changed into my pajamas after my shower. I looked down at my modal black tank and loose pants and decided the odds of seeing anyone in the hallway were slim. Unlike Connor, most of the team crashed immediately after getting into the hotel for the night. I shrugged a thin cardigan over my shoulders, just in case.

Peeking out into the hall, I made my way to Connor's room.

I definitely wasn't giving him enough time to pick the movie, or I'd probably end up watching *The Mighty Ducks* because he considered it "a classic."

Sixteen

THEO

$\mathcal{G}$etting up at 5:00 a.m. was no one's idea of a good time. A lifetime love of hockey had trained me to accept these early mornings as a necessary evil.

With last night's loss still weighing heavily on my shoulders, I dragged my ass out of bed, even though my eyes felt glued together with gravel.

Hoping the comfort of routine would shake me out of this funk, I threw on my workout clothes and left my room. I'd keep the intensity way down during my workout. It was more about having a way to clear my head.

Scrolling through my phone as I walked toward the elevator, I did not expect to run into another person at this hour. Most of my teammates would likely be starting their workout as mine ended around 6:00 a.m.

The blur of motion in my peripheral vision had me stopping just in time to avoid a collision.

A soft gasp had me looking up.

It took me a minute to realize Indie was in front of me. What was she doing in the hallway at this hour of the morning?

As I took in her appearance, my mouth hardened into a thin line. Heat simmered in my veins as I realized she was coming from that little shit's hotel room.

Fuck. First, I'd been tortured by having a front-row seat to their date in the bar. Now, I had to bear witness to a post-hookup early morning dip and dash back to her room.

This is definitely more than a hookup. You've seen proof with your own eyes. I cursed my inner voice of reason. I didn't know what felt worse: Indie and Andrews being in a relationship or just sleeping together. I hated both options with a passion.

My further survey of her state of attire just served to have jealous fury pumping through my veins. She was clearly not dressed for the day. Her paper-thin pajamas clung to the subtle curves of her body. Her sheer sweater and the tiny strap of her tank top hung off one shoulder.

Christ, she wasn't wearing a bra. I could see her nipples through the fabric draped over the swell of her breasts.

Whipping my gaze off her chest, I didn't dare look any lower on her body, afraid I'd discover a whole new selection of images to haunt me with her no doubt lack of underwear.

She turned away quickly, seeing something in my eyes she didn't want to tangle with this early. I couldn't just ignore what was right in front of my face.

"Rocky. Wait. What are you doing sneaking out of Andrews's room at 5:00 a.m.?"

I had no right to ask her that question but couldn't stop the words from tumbling from my mouth. Grinding my teeth, I forced myself to shut up before I said anything I'd regret.

She stopped her retreat and lowered her chin to her chest for a moment, taking a deep breath. Yeah, well, she could deal with the discomfort. I was already firing on all cylinders, wanting her to pay attention to *me*.

Her shoulders rose and fell with whatever reaction she was about to let loose on my ill-advised interference. Her dark hair, disheveled from sleep—thinking about anything else making her hair look that messy made my vision white out—still looked like dark streams of silk down her back.

Shifting around slightly in my direction but keeping most of her body facing away from me, she spoke in a low rasp I'd heard only once before in my life.

"Theo. What do you want?"

This was only my third morning encounter with Indie in the wee hours of the morning. The first time was in my parents' kitchen so many years ago. The last choice I made when I came upon her in such a state of undress was very different to how I would respond now.

"What do I want?" I growled.

What I wanted was an explanation. I wanted to know why she was alone in this hallway before sunrise. I wanted to know what the fuck she saw in that kid Andrews. He was not the right man for her, just barely more than a boy himself. What did he know about worshiping the ground this goddess of a woman walked on?

Mostly, I wanted to know how I could get her to feel what she felt for me six years ago.

He was probably blinded by her outer beauty, like everyone who'd ever laid eyes on her. He was way too inexperienced to understand the endless depths contained in just one of her glances.

What a goddamn waste.

"Indie." I gestured with both arms to the emptiness around us.

"You're out here practically in the middle of the night, wearing that."

This time, I gestured quickly at the tissue-thin fabric barely concealing her body from me. And any other asshole who might happen upon her in this state of undress. I had to move on from that thought quickly as I felt my knuckles pop with how tightly I was clenching them.

It was a matter of safety, for god's sake. *Yeah, you jealous fucker. Safety, sure. Green's a good color on you, man.*

Righting the sweater-wrap thing that she'd just noticed had fallen off her shoulder, she narrowed her eyes.

"It's none of your business what I do. I can be wherever the hell I want at any hour of the day. Good night. Or good morning, I guess." She crossed her arms over her chest, daring me to argue.

She spun around and started walking away from me again. Her retreat heated the emotions churning inside me further. My legs were moving, making long strides due to my height advantage and anger, before I could process the decision to go after her.

Before either of us knew it, I was right behind her when she stopped abruptly at her door.

Yeah, I'd asked the team assistant responsible for room allocations what her room number was before I got off the bus last night. I'd made some excuse about my sister wanting to call Indie about a surprise visit. I wasn't proud of the lie, but it had been out before I could stop myself.

The speed at which she'd tried to walk away from me and my determination to catch her before she unlocked her door had us both breathing hard.

"Rocky…"

She spun around and pressed herself back against her door, crossing her arms over her chest. I dared not to look away from her face now that I had her tantalizing skin within half an arm's length of my hands.

She looked up into my eyes, and I realized that I was leaning over her with my arms braced on the doorframe.

Fuck. For the life of me, my brain could not order my body to move back to give her some personal space. Not when I was the closest I'd been to her in six fucking long years. So close that I could see the goose bumps appearing on her skin. So close that I could see the flecks of golden brown in the dark shards of her eyes.

Right now, those eyes were shooting daggers at me. And shit if even her anger didn't turn me on.

"No, Theo. You don't get to call me that name as if we are old friends. We aren't. You have absolutely no say in the choices I make. So you can put all that big-brother shit away."

She thought this was some lame-ass attempt to pull the big-brother card? She couldn't be more wrong about what was going on here. There were exactly zero brotherly feelings for why I was so goddamn pissed right now.

"Baby, you aren't even in the right galaxy if you think this is me trying to protect you as my little sister's best friend."

Watching those gorgeous eyes widen in shock from my second use of that term of endearment falling from my lips had me holding back a smirk. She'd probably been forced to take etiquette lessons from birth, so getting an honest reaction out of her was a thrill.

It took all of my control not to smile. Or kiss her. Or both. Unfortunately, I didn't think either of those things would be welcome at this moment.

Leaning a little further into her space, I placed my mouth next to her ear and lowered my voice.

"Now, tell me why that asshat let you walk half-naked in the hallway alone back to your room?"

"How do you know whose room I was in?" she ground out between clenched teeth.

My proximity meant I could feel the gentle exhalations of her breaths against my neck. It also meant that her intoxicating, sweet, subtle scent was invading my senses.

"Do you think I haven't been paying attention? I know you've been seeing Andrews."

Her smaller hand appeared on my chest and pushed firmly enough to get me to look her in the eyes again. She scrutinized my face, looking for clues. She recrossed her arms, reassuming a defensive position for this battle brewing between us.

"Why the hell do you even care, Theo? It's none of your business. I'm just trying to be professional and keep my distance to make this work. I can't afford to mess up with this job." Indie sucked in a breath on the last words, her eyes widening briefly, momentarily unsure before the determined look reappeared on her face. "Whoever I choose to see on my time is none of your business."

What was going on that she was worried about messing up? I was already overstepping the line of concerned family friend, so I didn't dare ask her.

I had to swallow the growl of disagreement down my throat. Throughout my career, I'd cultivated my image as a laid-back team player kind of guy. It was a good strategy to be viewed as someone not easily rattled. It meant opponents or teammates alike were less likely to mess with me.

But five minutes on the receiving end of Indie's irritation had all my self-control unraveling. She had a way of making my blood pressure rise in a way no one else could.

"That's where you're wrong." I was taking my life in my hands, figuratively speaking—the worst Indie would do was tell me off for overstepping—telling her she was wrong about something. I barreled on before she could interrupt me.

"*You* said you decided to keep a professional distance between us. *I* never agreed to anything. And from what I see, I don't like you and Andrews together. He doesn't deserve you."

Anyone who didn't know this fiery woman the way I did would be cowering (or at least covering his or her sensitive areas) by this point. Indie's eyes had narrowed into thin slits, giving life to the expression "if looks could kill." She could be upset with me all she wanted. I'd stand firm in my resolution that she deserved better than sneaking out of some guy's room practically in the middle of the night.

Seemingly recovered from the surprise of seeing me and our physical closeness, a new emotion filled her eyes. Let's call it the I'm-about-to-mess-with-you-big-time expression. Indigo Layne did not like being told what to do. Ever. Period.

The look on her face said she was going to make me regret calling her out. A smirk formed on her lips.

"Okay, Theo. I see. Well, I'm safe and sound back at my door now, thanks to you. You can head out to what I assume was some sort of obscene professional athlete morning ritual. I've got to shower, you know, after last night. I didn't get a chance. Wouldn't want anyone on the team to smell Connor on me when we get back on the bus, right?" Her grin widened to accompany her taunting tone.

Her eyes never leaving mine, she pulled the front of one side of her sweater up to her nose and inhaled deeply. My brain could not process his scent on her skin and clothes.

Only my primal lizard brain remained. All other thoughts instantly obliterated from my mind.

When I didn't reply, having been rendered temporarily speechless, she continued.

"On the other hand, maybe I'll just get back in bed and sleep last night off. I didn't get a lot of rest, if you know what I mean." She had the audacity to wink at me, as if I wasn't holding back two hundred pounds of jealousy. "There's something to be said for wearing someone else's scent the whole next day."

"Don't play with me, Indie," I growled. I was about to burst into flames.

"What exactly are you going to do about it?" She tilted her head as if she was truly curious.

She had me there. I couldn't say what I wanted. Nothing I could say at that moment would make her dump Andrews and jump into my arms.

Jump into my arms? Where had that thought come from? Did I want a real relationship with her? Holy fuck, I did.

What I didn't want was simple: Andrews or any other asshole putting his hands on her. I knew logically I couldn't say that out loud either, so I held my tongue. Biting back my words, literally, I was sure I tasted blood.

"I'm going back to bed. See you on the bus." She gave me her back as she moved to unlock her door.

With my body and brain at a complete disconnect, she slipped through her now unlocked door, and I heard the dead bolt click before I could say anything further.

Shit. I couldn't believe her nerve. I'd always known she was a force to be reckoned with, but she'd always been quiet around me. I'd never been on the receiving end like this.

God, I loved that fire she had. Even if it meant losing this round.

Like any good competitor, I was going to have to go back to the drawing board.

I needed a new game plan where Indie was concerned. Screw the Cup. I'd spend the rest of the season playing for something much more elusive and valuable: her heart.

Seventeen

THEO

Unfortunately, my first stop back in Toronto was not Indie's front door to enact my yet-unthought-of plan to date the hell out of her.

"How's the pain been?" The question was accompanied by the sounds of paperwork being shuffled within a file folder.

Dr. Isabel Kaya, the team doctor, eyed me suspiciously. Her tone was serious but not unkind. Based on her highly respected career, first with Team Canada and now in the last decade with NHL teams across the country, she was more than capable of cutting through any bullshit a cocky hockey player might bring into her office.

"Better lately. The TENS therapy has helped." The half-truth spilled from my lips without hesitation.

I kept eye contact with her so she could see how honest I was being. It wasn't a lie. Dr. Kaya had been working with me since I joined the team on some noninvasive pain relief for my knees. It might have only made a minor difference in the pain itself, but that wasn't what she'd asked.

"Hmm, okay. Is the pain still a three out of ten most days?" She raised an eyebrow, appearing skeptical of my truthfulness.

The pain was closer to a four on a non-game day and a solid six or seven by the middle of the last period most nights.

Dr. Kaya narrowed her eyes, and she dropped her volume. "Listen, Theo, I know you're an integral part of the team's chances to make it into the postseason this year, but not at the expense of your health, okay?"

I nodded to acknowledge that I'd heard her. She was one of the good ones. In the past few months in our appointments, she'd never made me feel like a commodity or that she was putting the team's interest before mine.

"I also don't need to remind you that it is your right to seek a second opinion outside the league's medical staff. And that those results would be kept confidential without impacting your position on the team?" She eyed me carefully.

"Yep." This wasn't a road I was going down today. I also didn't mention that I'd already seen two other orthopedic surgeons back in Vancouver, and both had recommended knee surgery sooner than later.

Until I knew what I wanted for my future career-wise, I wasn't going to be put on the injured reserve if this was my last season in the league. Season-ending surgery was not on my Christmas wish list either.

Both options filled me with the same amount of dread since they both were equivalent to failure: failing my team and coaches, failing head office, who'd signed me in good faith for this season, and potentially ending a career I'd prided myself on a sour note.

"Don't worry, Doc. I'm doing okay." I gave her what I hoped was a charming wink. I didn't turn on my charm often, but I knew how to play the game when it counted. And I wanted her to sign off on me playing tonight.

"Don't think you can bat those pretty eyelashes at me and get your way," she said and laughed.

"I would never, Dr. Kaya!" I put my hand on my chest as if I was shocked by her comment.

She rolled her eyes at me and wrote something down on my chart.

"So… I'm good to go, right?" I was already sliding off the exam table and grabbing my hoodie.

Tucking the chart under her arm, she moved to the door and opened it. To our surprise, Indie was on the other side with her hand raised to knock.

"Indigo! Hello." Dr. Kaya was the first to recover, completely ignorant of the utter storm of tension that'd been brewing between Indie and me since our encounter in that hotel hallway.

Indie stepped into the room just enough to cross the threshold. She moved against the closest wall and not a step farther. It was enough room for me to leave and prevent herself from getting stuck in this room longer than necessary. Her rigid body language made it clear she wasn't here to chat.

"Hey, Dr. Kaya. Um, sorry to interrupt. I just came from a meeting with our team, and Coach Reyes asked me to come get you. He wants to triple-check with you that Andrews is safe to play tonight. He's still worried about that hit Connor took in Monday's game." Indie kept her eyes locked on Dr. Kaya.

"I'll go see him now. I swear, that man is worse than a mother hen. I can't wish he was any other way with you boys, but he drives me up the wall sometimes. I already signed off on Andrews." She gave me a warm smile as if I hadn't seen her fret about us the same way Coach did.

She tossed my chart onto her desk and headed out into the hallway, hands still in the air in good-natured frustration.

Indie made a move to sneak out the way she came but not before I had the door shut within seconds of the good doctor's exit.

"What the hell, Theo? What is with you and doorways?" The professional facade dropped as she turned her glare on me.

"If you weren't so hell-bent on hiding from me, I wouldn't have to take such drastic measures to talk to you." I shrugged, completely unrepentant. If she accidentally put herself in my orbit, I was going to use it to my advantage.

She looked like she wanted to put hands on me. The kind of hands that resulted in blood and hospital visits, not orgasms.

"Fuck off, Theo. I don't hide from anything." Her lips pressed into a tight line.

Not wanting to engage her in her clear pattern of avoidance of what was brewing between us, I took a different route.

"So Andrews, hm? Poor kid hurt his head the other night? I bet he's all better if you've been nursing him back to health." My tone was laced with false sympathy.

While I spoke, I closed the small space between us to mirror our positions from that damn hotel run-in a few days ago.

My forearms resting above her head once more, I could catch a close-up view of what my words were doing to her.

Indie was a fascinating study in contrasts. Her fierce scowl was tempered by the pinkening of her cheeks. Those who didn't know her would assume the flush was coming from anger at me, but Indie went ice-cold when pissed off. When she was angry with you, she'd either dismiss you or dismantle you piece by piece with her words.

Her beautiful skin heated, and her breathing increased, bringing my attention to the skin of her face and neck as I scrutinized her features for her real feelings for Andrews.

Her tan from the summer sun now fully faded from the dreary

fall weather's lack of sun, her skin took on a creamy, delicate tone. Her Irish heritage had her skin almost translucent it was so fine and delicate. My gaze traced the soft sweep of her skin down to the crisp collar of her blouse.

"I haven't…" she began.

I whipped my eyes back to hers. I was so distracted by her proximity I'd almost forgotten my question about her new boyfriend.

"Haven't what? That boyfriend of yours doesn't want you talking about the fact that you're dating someone on the team?" I baited her.

"Jesus Christ, Theo. Give it a rest. It's none of your business! When are you going to get that through your head? Have you taken too many hits with a puck to hear what I've been saying to you? Have you told Dr. Kaya about your selective hearing?" she asked.

She put her hands on my chest to push me away, but I just leaned further forward, capitalizing on our significant weight difference.

"No, Indie. I want to know. What's so special about this kid that you're willing to risk locker room gossip and sneak out of hotel rooms in the middle of the night?" My volume dropped with our proximity. We moved incrementally closer with each word that passed between us.

Indie's hands had grabbed handfuls of my T-shirt while I spoke. Her knuckles were white from squeezing the fabric. I could imagine she wished it was my neck.

Fists still clenched, she pushed into my chest, hard.

"Oh my god. You aren't going to let this go, are you, Theo? We're just friends, okay? I'm not seeing Connor!" She spoke through her clenched teeth.

My surprise at her admission that they weren't dating had my body surrendering to her next shove more than the momentum she caused. I staggered back a couple of steps, giving her room to throw her arms out to the side in frustration after she released my shirt.

"You're not? But what about the night at the bar? The hotel?" The images of them with their heads bent together, laughing intimately, were burned into my memory. A day didn't go by that I didn't feel the gut punch of regret of them getting together.

"We did have a drink together but decided to be friends. And for god's sake, I just fell asleep in his room watching a movie with him. Nothing has happened between us. Can you stop acting like my big brother and let it go now? I don't need you to protect me from the big, bad world. I'm more capable of protecting myself than you could possibly imagine." Her tone was defiant, determined to get me to butt out of her business.

Her arms had dropped to her side while she spoke. But now, she brought her hands up to her face, stopping only millimeters from her eyes when she remembered she was wearing makeup.

I'd seen Emery do that a time or two when she was a teenager, so I recognized the move. Emery had complained often enough about feeling pressured to wear makeup to events and then rubbing it in her eyes before regretting it because it apparently stung like a bitch. It must have been frustrating as hell.

Knowing she couldn't act on her frustration, her hands dropped to her side in temporary defeat, slapping against the side of her thighs.

"So if your curiosity is now satisfied, I've got to get ready for the game. I'm sure you have some weird pre-game ritual to do too." She waved her hand in the air like I was going to be practicing black magic and sacrificing the village goat.

My elaborate ritual included green socks for a Thursday game and my ever-present rainbow stick tape.

Without thinking, I put my hands on her upper arms to halt her movement.

"No, Indie. I'm not satisfied at all. In fact, I haven't been satisfied in weeks," I rasped.

I closed the distance between our bodies until they were flush together, my groin pressing into the firm plane of her stomach.

I slid one hand into her hair and guided her head back gently so I could see her eyes. I struggled not to be distracted by the strands of silk I'd gathered between my fingers. Jesus. Her hair was softer than I'd ever imagined.

I wanted to spend hours just gently running my fingers through it. Then, several more hours making sure it ended up in knots. But now, I need to focus on the one thing on my mind.

"The only thing I want right now is to kiss you. I sure as fuck don't think of you like a sister." I brought my other hand to the side of her face so I could brush her cheek with the pad of my thumb, keen to get as much of myself pressed against her as possible. "Are you going to let me kiss you, Indie?"

Her eyes were wide with shock and the tiniest hint of uncertainty. Could she really not see how focused I had been on her every time we were in the same space?

Pressing her lips together before taking a small, shaky breath, she whispered, "Yes."

I was on her before she could tell me all the reasons this was a bad idea.

Wrapping my other arm behind her back, I pulled her more tightly against me and took her lips with mine.

As much as I wanted to savor this second "first" kiss between us, I was out of control after weeks of hiding my jealousy while I thought she was dating my teammate.

I sucked her bottom lip into my mouth and made love to it with my tongue before I gave it a sharp nip. The twinge from my teeth had her sucking in a shocked breath and her mouth opening under mine.

I thrust my tongue into her mouth, fucking into it like I wanted to own her whole body. I consumed every plush inch of her lips and tongue as it wrestled with mine.

Holy hell. I'd never been harder in my life. My cock was pressing painfully against the zipper of my jeans.

Her hands were back on my chest, fingers digging into the meat of my pecs. I hoped she squeezed hard enough to leave fingerprints. It would be sexy as fuck to feel her marks on me while I was on the ice. I wanted to be reminded of the heady feeling of her desire every time my pads shifted while I was in goal.

It could have been minutes or an hour before I let my mouth move to her chin and neck, brushing light kisses over her skin, making her flushed skin more red with the combination of my attention and several days of scruff.

She hissed out a low sound when I latched onto her clavicle just beneath the fabric of her blouse. I nipped her skin harder than any of the previous bites, wanting her to remember this moment was real and what I wanted from her when she looked in the mirror at home tonight.

She squeezed my shoulder weakly. "Theo, we need to stop. Dr. Kaya's probably going to come back any minute."

I lifted my head to take stock of the wonderfully disheveled woman before me.

Her silky hair now slightly tangled from where my hands had been, she'd never looked more beautiful to me.

"Let me come to your place after the game tonight," I begged. For Indie Layne, I would say anything to get her to give me a chance.

I wasn't hesitating anymore now that I knew there wasn't anyone else in the picture. I was going to shoot my shot with Indie because this skyrocketing desire between us could turn into so much more.

She looked to the side as if she didn't want to see the emotions in my eyes or was hiding her true feelings in hers.

"This isn't a good idea, Theo. We can't." She kept her gaze averted.

"I want to. You want to. Please, Indie." I let the immense need coursing through me bleed into my tone.

"It would be just a physical thing." She looked up at me from under her lashes, perhaps gauging my reaction to her words.

I gently lifted her chin with the tips of my fingertips. Her lips were slightly swollen from our kisses, and goddamn if I didn't love that. If anyone paid attention when she left this room, they'd know something had happened. That illicit feeling turned me on way more than I'd been before.

"I'm not asking you for anything right now other than to see you tonight. Can I do that?" I sidestepped her comment about not wanting a relationship. Maybe she thought she wasn't ready, but I could prove her wrong by showing her how dedicated I was to the idea of us.

I brushed my thumb back and forth across her plush bottom lip, hopefully reminding her of how good what we just did felt.

She licked my thumb, turning the tables on me again.

"Okay," she whispered, the want back in her eyes.

"Thank you, baby. I'll see you later." Relief had my shoulders relaxing.

I couldn't resist one more short kiss on my way out the door. We both had a game to get ready for, and I didn't want to give her a chance to change her mind.

Tonight would be the first step in showing her how good we could be together.

Eighteen

INDIE

Theo Yao-Miler kissed me today. And it was hot as fuck.

My nineteen-year-old self was jumping up and down with joy, singing, "I knew he liked me!" over and over again on repeat in my mind.

It was like a scene from one of those high school love-story movies Abbie and Emery loved. The unrequited crush finally realizes she or he wants the main protagonist, and all of a sudden, there's this huge dopamine rush happening. That part of me that was left so crushed all those years ago wanted to run through fields of wildflowers and rainbows.

Nineteen-year-old Indie was an idiot.

Luckily, my twenty-five-year-old self could rein that shit in. Hard.

There was no way I was going to let myself fall for Theo again. I had no room in my life for romance, let alone the *Titanic*-sized baggage that came along with thinking about us in those terms.

Putting aside the question of whether it would be wrong to date my best friend's brother, years of planning since I'd learned about my inheritance were on the cusp of becoming reality. I couldn't allow myself to be distracted or swept away in everything Theo. More than that, I couldn't give my father a reason to make my life harder because I was dating a hockey player after rejecting years of potential suitors from my parents' social circle after a single date. My father would be pissed if he thought I'd been actively sabotaging his efforts to get me to marry into a worthy family.

I hadn't spent the last so many years under my parents' thumb to lose what I worked so hard for. Every time I compromised my values or held my tongue to placate their endless list of demands could be undone if I allowed feelings for Theo out from where I'd locked them away.

I'd had a single-minded focus on making a difference for kids so that they would have somewhere to turn for help. I was going to do everything in my power to make sure that as many kids as possible didn't feel utterly alone like I did because of my parents' emotional abandonment.

Even surrounded by wealth, I had been trapped without anyone I could ask for help. My parents controlled every facet of my life. Their money meant that even professionals I should have been able to turn to, when I desperately wanted to understand the feelings inside me, could be influenced to keep my parents apprised of anything I might have shared.

The fact remained that I was still stupidly attracted to Theo. I had no idea if he wanted a hookup-type situation or was looking for a relationship. At thirty-one, from what I understood from the media speculation I'd been forced to review as part of writing media releases for the team (head office was very careful about word choice, so information only came out when they wanted it to), this might be his last season. Or not. But the analysts speculated that he wouldn't stay more than a few more seasons in the NHL, especially since he'd been traded away from what he probably considered his "hometown" team since that was where his Gong Gong had watched all of his games when he'd been alive.

His life was in Vancouver, or I guess Toronto now. It didn't even matter if I liked it here, which I did; my life was in Amado. My girls were there. My professional and personal aspirations would come to fruition there.

Even with Theo within reach, I just didn't see how I could have him and make it work.

Unlocking my apartment door, I ignored the jittery feeling running through my veins.

It was like I'd mainlined espresso all day and didn't have full control over my faculties. My hands trembled as I set down my keys. My smile was a little shaky as I watched Giz tippy tap over to the door from her favorite spot in her new bed, directly next to the heating vent.

After I got her ready to go outside, Gizmo was adorable in her new red puppy parka. She sighed every time I put the matching silly "toque" I'd bought for her bald little head, making me laugh.

I had her out and around the block for a quick potty routine and back up to the apartment in record time.

I was rushing through a shower, shaving all the relevant areas before I even realized what I was doing. Nothing was going to happen—I was just buying myself a few extra minutes of sleep in the morning, that's all.

I'd barely gotten dry and dressed again before there was a soft knock on my door.

This was it. I was going be clear with Theo. We could be attracted to each other and do nothing about it. People did it all the time. We were both adults who had shown our ability to exercise discipline and restraint to get to where we were in our lives.

I took a deep breath before opening the door to see Theo staring back at me with a Cheshire cat–type grin.

"Hey, baby." His smooth, deep voice rolled over me like a physical wave. My stomach dropped with anticipation.

I would not get sucked under his spell again. I had to take back control of this runaway train we were on.

He lifted his hands as if to latch back onto me and continue where we left off this afternoon. Stepping back out of his reach, I ushered him into the apartment.

The sooner I shut this down, the sooner he would leave and I could get my head together again.

"Hi, Theo. Come in. Can I get you a drink?" When in doubt, it always worked to be polite.

I walked backward into the apartment and gestured to the couch, hoping he would take the hint and sit. I moved into the kitchen area without waiting for his response.

With a counter between us, I turned around to find him having scooped Giz up and cuddling her comfortably in one ridiculously toned arm.

I grabbed a glass to pour myself some water from the fridge dispenser. I held it up to him in question, and he just shook his head, that infuriating smile still on his gorgeous face.

Taking deliberately slow sips, I took stock of the man in front of me. Besides the tiny dog emphasizing his height and the broadness of his shoulders, the way his T-shirt hugged all those muscles he worked so hard for was nearly criminal. His nearly black hair was still damp from his post-game shower, and the scruff on his face had arousal zinging through my body.

I hadn't had time to take in all these little details this afternoon. But I realized I'd moved the hand not holding the glass up to my cheek, where I could feel some tenderness from his facial hair rubbing up against my skin. My pulse sped up with that knowledge.

Needing to break this silence between us. I spoke just to get this over with.

"Theo, what happened today can't happen again." Hopefully, the nervous rasp in my voice went unnoticed.

"Why not, Indie?" He inclined his head as if confused by the direction I had chosen.

"It's just not a good idea for so many reasons. Sex complicates everything. I can't give you what you want." I let out a deep breath. I didn't say that I was worried that physical intimacy would erase the flimsy barrier I'd put up to protect myself from falling in love with him again.

He gave Giz a quick peck on the head (shit, swoon) before setting her in the nest of blankets I'd created for her on the couch. He made his way around the counter to stand before me. He ran a searching gaze over my face. His intense focus was a direct contrast to the way he leaned his body casually against the counter.

He nodded, as if coming to some conclusion. "Hit me with 'em," he stated.

"With what exactly?" I asked.

"Hit me with all of those reasons you've got up in your head about why we can't do this." He spread out his hands in an explain-it-to-me-type gesture.

His beautiful face with its stupid model cheekbones, lush eyelashes (male DNA seemed unfairly advantaged in this way), and dark brown eyes threatened my good sense.

I *wanted* something for once. Something selfish and just mine. I'd never been allowed to want things when I was younger. My decisions were dictated by my parents' needs, which were mostly to pretend I didn't exist as anything other than a prop for when they needed to look family-friendly. I'd spent so long just saying yes to whatever was demanded of me that I'd almost completely forgotten how to *want*.

What I wanted was right in front of me. Theo. Telling me he wanted me too, in whatever capacity he did.

I wanted the ability to take a risk, not knowing the outcome. To forget about consequences and appearances for one goddamn moment.

I mirrored his stance, putting my hip against the counter. I took him up on his dare.

I held my hand up to count the reasons. He wouldn't give up until I gave him a reason to. But once he saw sense, he would walk away. It would save us both a lot of complications and potentially hurt feelings.

"One, you're Emery's brother. It's not okay to break her trust this way," I began. "Two…"

Before I realized what he had done, he'd pulled his phone from his back pocket and unlocked it, pressing a button and putting it on the counter between us.

"What are you doing?" I hissed. It was freaking 12:30 a.m.

One ring and a soft "Hello?" had my internal organs freezing solid.

"What the fuck, Theo?" I mouthed at him. He'd fucking called Emery.

"Hey, Em." He smiled in the face of my surprise.

"Theo, are you okay? Why are you calling so late, your time?" Her sweet voice seemed to echo throughout the apartment, as if suddenly eight hundred square feet had turned into a coliseum of sound.

"Don't worry, sis. Nothing happened. I just had something to ask you that couldn't wait," he explained.

"Should I be worried, Theo?" Her tone was still wary. Clearly, she was unused to Theo calling her out of the blue to ask something.

I mean, Emery, Abbie, and I would rather be eaten by dinosaurs than make a phone call, so I could understand that most of their contact happened via text.

You know, like normal people.

"Listen, Em. I want to ask Indie out on a date—" He narrowed his eyes at me as if to say, *"Look how much this isn't a problem."* "—and don't want to do it without you being okay with it first." He winked at me, as if he was the one who'd considered her feelings first.

Jerk. A handsome jerk, but still.

"Theo. I don't understand? What? You're interested in Indie? Since when?" Her questions came rushing across the line.

He didn't break eye contact as he answered her, as if he was talking to me instead.

"Since we reconnected when she started working for the Tempests. So what do you think, Em?" he pushed.

"Well, you are both adults." She chose each word slowly. "And it's not really my place to say."

Theo rolled his eyes. "Oh, come on, Em. You two have been attached at the hip since first grade. And with Abbie completing the three musketeers, you're always all up in each other's lives. Stop being polite and tell me what you think."

"Shut up. I'm not being polite." Her growl made him grin. I could still see that sibling thrill of getting under his sister's skin shining in his eyes.

She continued before he had a chance to poke her further. "Fine. Here's what I know: Indie's an adult who can make her own decisions.

So talk to her, you stupid-head. But as far as I'm concerned, I'm fine with you having a relationship with her as long as you are in it *for the right reasons*."

"And what, dear sister, are the right reasons according to you?" Theo raised an eyebrow.

Damn, was I cursed to think every move he made was sexy?

"The right reason is, you idiot, that you take care of her feelings and don't use her because you're bored or lonely or because she's familiar. If you care about her for *her* and not as just another puck bunny–type fling, then it's up to you two what you make of it." Her exasperation was clear over the phone line.

"Okay, good. Thanks, Em. I do care about her, you know." Again, his eye contact meant that he was saying the words to me, even though he was reassuring Emery.

"I know you, Theo. You're a good man. Mom would be so proud to know you. Just… don't break her heart, okay?" Emery's voice had softened again with a sadness that belied how acutely they both missed their mom.

"I'll do everything I can to avoid it. Love you, sis." His hushed tone matched hers as she echoed his words.

Ending the call, he moved a few steps closer to where I was standing. I don't think I'd moved a muscle in shock at how bold he was in just calling Emery up like that.

He'd circumvented a huge barrier in my mind, and I was scrambling internally to catch up.

The wistfulness of Emery's mention of their mom cleared from his eyes, replaced by that predatory fire that I was sure served him well on the ice.

"That's one objection down, Rocky. What else ya got?" He smirked.

Nineteen

THEO

*I*f steam could actually come out of a person's ears, I had a feeling I'd be seeing that now.

I didn't know what had possessed me to call my sister like that. If I had given even a second's worth of thought, I'd have considered how wrong that whole conversation could have gone.

Of course Emery might have strong feelings about me asking out her closest friend. But I'd needed to get through to Indie that I was serious about this, and I'd needed something shocking to make the point.

Well, the point had been made all right.

Usually, I loved watching Indie's fire come to life. The difference was I was a bystander in those cases, not the person who she might be fuming at.

She could very well tell me to go to hell since I'd called Emery without talking about it with her first.

I was putting all my eggs in one basket, and it could still go to shit on me. I had the feeling that her other reasons weren't as easily fixable as Emery being the wonderful, understanding person that I could count on her to be.

"Theo! How could you do that? You just… just called her up and said all that." She waved her hand in a circular motion in the air, gesturing to my absolute gall to call my own sister.

"Yes, baby. I did. Now, tell me what else is holding you back." I infused every bit of desire into my tone that I could.

Still on the outrage train, she continued as if she hadn't heard me.

"To just call her up, without any warning! You don't even know if I think what happened in Kaya's office was a mistake. But you just steamrolled on through." Her hands moved to emphasize her words.

I stepped closer to her until my socked toes met the edge of hers. I put my hands on her shoulders, noticing once again how fine and delicate her frame was, despite her height. How many people were fooled by her beauty and elegance to miss the steel beneath?

"Indie, look at me and listen, please," I whispered, trying to draw her focus back to just me.

My nearness seemed to calm her slightly. Her honey-brown eyes whipped to mine, widening at how close together we were now. I could smell her sweet scent and the subtle fragrance of whatever products she used to keep her skin petal soft.

"Tell me what's stopping you here, Rocky," I asked again.

With my hands on her, I could see the little jolt her nickname had as it made its way through her body. The skin I could see on her arms rose with tiny goose bumps.

My primal brain interpreted that as a sign that she wanted me, too, and hopefully wasn't too mad at me for crossing a line in her relationship with Emery.

I pulled her toward me gently, waiting to see if she would resist my touch. She didn't. So I leaned down to close the short distance and whispered in her ear.

"Tell me, baby." My hushed tone was tinged with a whiff of demand.

My lips brushed over the shell of her ear, causing us both to shudder. The mere inches between our bodies were driving me insane. I wanted to overcome all her objections and admit that she was mine.

Only mine.

Her shoulders tensed under my hands, and I braced myself for her to pull away and kick me out of her apartment.

She shocked the shit out of me by grabbing my jaw with her hands and dragging my mouth to hers.

Indie kissed me like she had thrown out whatever other fears she might have about this moment and had suddenly gone from zero to one hundred.

She sucked on my bottom lip, trying to gain entry with her sweet little tongue, causing my answering groan into her mouth.

Taking advantage of my surrender, Indie twisted and slid her tongue along mine, fucking into my mouth the way I had taken control that afternoon.

Her hands left my chin, sliding down the hard muscles of my chest and abs to reach the bottom of my T-shirt. Her lips, tongue, and teeth still attacked my mouth. I didn't dare take more than a quick sip or two of air until she had yanked my shirt up to my armpits.

Leaning forward slightly to allow her to pull the shirt over my head, I tried to get a read on her.

Her eyes were blissed-out like we'd already fucked. Her mouth and surrounding skin were swollen from my lips and stubble.

She was as sexy as fuck, but I felt a tiny tug in my gut to check in with her again.

"You sure you want this, baby?" I asked, keen to hear her give me permission.

As an answer, she whipped off her own shirt, leaving her in a simple yet sexy black lace bralette thing. The gentle swell of her tits and hard nipples exposed through the thin fabric that was clearly more about decoration than function.

"Goddamn, baby. Look at you. I want you so badly." I was so overcome by my need I could barely choke the words out.

She bit her lip, and that vicious little tug hit my gut again as she forced out what she wanted to say.

"I want you too, Theo. Obviously. But I need you to know this is all it can ever be, okay? I'm not looking for anything serious." She dragged a finger back and forth across her collarbone, hypnotizing me with her innate sensuality. "I'm leaving in nine months. We can have fun together until then, or we fuck this attraction out of us. But that's all I can offer."

Disappointment sliced straight through my chest. Why did Indie's insistence on just some fling make my heart feel like it had been filled with lead?

I wanted more from her. It was as simple as that.

I would just have to show her how good it could be between us and hope to hell that the desire she felt turned into something real.

For now, though, I didn't want to put a stop to what was happening between us. Even if she never came to feel the way I was starting to feel about her, I didn't want to waste a chance to have any part of her she was willing to share.

For now, we would do things her way.

"Okay, Rocky. I understand what you want and don't want here. You're the boss," I agreed.

Pressing a sweet kiss to her lips to seal our deal, I hoped that I could use my body to show her how much I wanted her since she wasn't ready to hear the words.

Twenty

INDIE

"*Okay, Rocky. I understand what you want and don't want here. You're the boss.*"

The boss. I could work with that.

I arched my eyebrow and started walking backward toward the bedroom.

I'd make sure the door was shut. Giz didn't need to be traumatized any further by seeing her temporary mom in a (or hopefully many) compromising position.

"Come with me." I crooked a finger, gesturing for Theo to follow me.

Theo had still not taken his eyes off me. I had to admit that level of focus was intoxicating. I'd spent so many years as an afterthought I was practically drunk on his attention alone.

After enclosing us safely in the bedroom away from little gremlin ears, I pulled Theo toward the bed.

I backed him up to the edge of my bed, sliding my hands up his smooth chest to his shoulders. Applying gentle pressure, I coaxed him into a sitting position and pushed his legs apart with mine to stand between his knees.

He was so damn sexy sitting below me, perfectly silent, waiting for my next move. I felt a surge of warmth through my chest. None of the men I had any experience with had been content to let me take the lead like this.

I loved that he gave over the reins to me thus far.

My hands still on his shoulders, I used them as leverage to bring my mouth level with his ear. His hair had grown longer in the last few months; its dark, lush waves tickled my lips as I moved to whisper to him.

"I'm the boss, huh? You really mean that, baby?" I exaggerated the endearment he'd called me a few times, needing it to have the disarming effect on him like it did me.

A legitimate shudder worked its way through his tight muscles when he heard "baby" pass my lips.

Another surge of lust and power blasted through me. The sheer intensity simultaneously rendered my body liquid and amplified my desire to take control.

"Yessss. Whatever you want, Rocky," he hissed through his teeth. It was clearly costing him something to stay still and wait for me to make the next move.

The heat of his restraint, along with the sweetness of his nickname for me, aimed to burrow deeper inside me than I was willing to let it. It was harder to push those feelings to the side than it should have been after the years of battle armor I'd equipped myself with.

I decided that thinking was going to get me into trouble, so I dove into action by whipping my soft bralette over my head.

Clearly not expecting my bold move, Theo's eyes widened as he sucked in a deep breath.

"Christ, Indie. You are gorgeous. Can I touch you?" I loved that he asked my permission.

I liked that he asked instead of just taking. To see how badly he wanted me but held himself back.

I reached down for his hands and brought them up to my breasts. "Yes. Touch me, Theo." I let some of the desperation I felt seep into my words.

I slid my hands to his wrists, wanting to keep the tether between us, to feel his movements as he was making them. I watched his face as he cupped my flesh in his hands, his focus absolute on where my skin met his calloused palms.

Fully engulfed in his grasp, I let my eyes fall shut to revel in the sensation of his touch. He brushed his thumbs back and forth across the sensitive skin on the underside of my breasts. His movements turned almost rhythmic as he then swept his thumbs over the taut points of my nipples.

"More," I breathed.

My exhalation had him squeezing my breasts in his palms. His accompanying groan was a testament to how much he loved the feel of me in his hands.

A swift pinch on my right nipple had my eyes snapping back open. Focusing on the devilry in his gaze, I watched as he stoked both our lust by giving my other nipple the same treatment. I bit my lower lip to keep from moaning at the little pinpricks and heat left behind by his fingers.

He repeated the motions with his thumbs on my sensitive skin, ending with the brief pinch on each rotation of my chest, until the nipples and areola were flushed with blood and heat.

"I want to taste you, Indie. Please." His low voice had shivers racing up my spine.

He seemed to understand how much I liked it when he asked for my consent because he didn't move to explore any other part of me without my direction.

After nodding my assent, I moved closer into his body between his legs. I let my hands drop to his shoulders, gripping the hard muscles in preparation for the onslaught of what was to come.

Keeping his eyes on mine, he lowered his mouth to my tender nipple and gave it a gentle flick of his tongue. Because of his previous attentions, even such a slight touch had my fingers digging into his firm muscles.

It was all I could do to remain standing when he sucked my nipple into his mouth fully while his tongue caressed its tip. The contrasting sensations had my lower half throbbing in anticipation. The wetness between my legs multiplied, and I pressed my thighs together in a futile attempt at relief.

"Fuck, Theo." I couldn't hold in my moan of his name. He was too intense, too good at seducing me with his hands and mouth.

A combination of rumble and groan answered my needy sound as he sucked more of my flesh into his mouth as if he was trying to consume my entire breast at once.

I moved my hands into his hair to hold him more tightly to me and reveled in the thick, soft waves. Alternating between pulling him into me and grasping the strands between my fingers, I loved the idea of him looking as messy as all the pleasure he was sending into my body.

He moved to my other breast and lavished it with the same attention as the first. The wetness left behind by his mouth, now exposed to the cool air, was a sharp contrast to the inferno of his lips and tongue, replicating the sensations on the opposite side of my body.

After floating in the sea of pleasure he was wreaking on my body, I gripped his hand and pulled his hair back gently. His lips made a loud, wet *pop* as he released my nipple.

His eyes were hazy with pleasure. I'd put money on having the same punch-drunk look on my own face.

"Lie back, please," I instructed.

Without hesitation, he treated me to a show of his powerful upper-body muscles flexing as he dragged himself backward toward the head of the bed.

His abs could have inspired a series of sculptures. Looking as hot as Theo did with his shirt off should be illegal. I wanted to trace those ridges and valleys with my tongue, maybe suck a mark or two onto his golden skin.

The hours and hours I'd spent fantasizing about Theo had nothing on the reality of him.

I crawled up the bed, moving over him until I could sit on his thighs.

Ghosting my fingers as far up his chest as I could reach and then back down to the trail of dark hair under his belly button to where it met the top of his sweatpants, I scratched my fingernails through the soft fuzz. Another deep groan was my reward.

Shit. He was so intoxicating. I kept stalling on each new part of him that I touched, getting lost in the feel of him.

I arched an eyebrow as I toyed with the waistband of his sweatpants. There was no hiding the obvious bulge pressing against the fabric.

He nodded, and I didn't hesitate to grab the fabric and tug, now impatient to bare him for my own pleasure. Because the universe seemed to be smiling upon me tonight, he'd gone commando under his sweats, and the motion of pulling them with the helpful lift of his hips had his rock-hard cock slapping against his stomach.

Jesus. I froze for a moment down by his feet after wrestling the soft fabric down his muscular legs. He was all toned muscle covered in smooth skin. He wasn't insanely bulked up like some of the guys on the team, but taking him in, I could see the lines of strength that radiated from his body.

Taking my pause as hesitation, and Theo being Theo, he was quick to reassure me.

"Hey, Indie. This only goes as far as you want it to tonight. You get me?" His tone was confident. There was no disappointment as he held my gaze, waiting for my response.

I gave him what I hoped was a feline smile. Oh, I knew just how far I wanted to go.

"Good thing I want it to go as far as it can go, then."

I made quick work of my own jeans and underwear. There would be another time for teasing while stripping off clothes.

Tonight, I wanted to get right into the good stuff. I watched him as his eyes traced my naked body, pleased with how openly he was appreciating everything on display for him.

"Christ, Indie…" My nudity had him groaning once more. "There aren't words for how incredible you look right now, baby."

I wondered if he could see the wetness on my skin between my thighs. Or feel the heat emanating from my skin at his words.

Inching back up his body, pressing as much of our skin together as possible, I settled higher than before, aiming my center right over his cock.

Neither of us could hold in our reactions when my wet, heated flesh spread over his.

The slickness and friction of where we were pressed together sparked echoes of pleasure, all centering on my clit. And I hadn't even started moving yet.

Leaning down to put my mouth on his once more, I flicked my tongue over his lips as I started sliding myself along his cock, angling my hips to catch the little nub between my folds on the head of his cock on each pass.

He met my teasing with the thrust of his tongue while lifting his own hips in return. The only sounds in the room were the wet sounds of our lips and tongues and the rustling of the sheets as our bodies moved together.

I used my hands on his pecs for leverage to push myself back into a seated position and bore down with all the force I could squeeze between my thighs.

Taking my hint, he slowed his movements as I continued rocking back and forth on his dick, chasing the orgasm that had been simmering inside me since he'd kissed me that afternoon.

"Oh, I see. My girl wants to use me as her personal sex toy. Is that it, baby? Going to rub up on me until you come?"

A shiver ran through me. Combined with the deep tenor of his voice, his filthy words had me moving faster to increase the pressure on my clit. I squeezed my eyes shut and let my head fall back as I rocked over him. The velvet yet impossible hardness of his dick made for the perfect sensation to get myself off.

"Okay, baby. You take what's yours. I can't wait to see you come."

Theo giving me the reins in this moment had my orgasm building faster than I'd ever been able to come before with a partner. Fissures and jolts of pleasure radiated from my center deep into my pelvis. God, I wasn't going to need to touch myself to get off. Just the movement of my body and his perfect hardness were going to get me there.

As the tightness and pleasure curled within me, I opened my eyes to find him watching me, his eyes hazy and mouth partially open, just as immersed in this moment as I was.

"Theo, I'm coming," I gasped out the words. The pleasure was so intense I struggled to decide whether to breathe or hold my breath.

My center contracted rhythmically, releasing hot bursts of wetness all over his cock and groin. My hips stuttered in their movements as the incredible climax fried all my nerve endings.

Not keeping the sultry atmosphere of the previous moments, I let out a laugh as I collapsed on his chest. I let my glistening forehead rest between his pecs as I tried to catch my breath.

His hands had held my thighs as I moved over him. Now, he slid one hand into the wetness where our bodies met, and he gathered the evidence of my desire on his fingers. I lifted my head again to watch him bring them to his nose before sucking two of his fingers into his mouth.

A tiny whimper escaped as I watched him taste my juices for the first time.

"Fuck, baby. You taste amazing. I can't wait to find out what we taste like together. You going to let me find that out tonight?" He cocked an eyebrow to accent his filthy question.

Dead. I was dead. He was just too goddamn sexy for words.

Twenty-One

THEO

*I*ndie was mesmerizing.

She had no idea the spell she had cast on me with her pure enjoyment of using my body to pleasure hers.

This was so different from just hooking up with someone or even the sex I'd had in a causal relationship.

This wasn't about us getting off together. It was so much more.

As she rested on my chest, the taste of her pleasure still in my mouth, I didn't give a damn that I was still rock hard and aching against her hot flesh.

If the night ended here and I could convince her to let me stay and hold her in my arms overnight, it would be enough.

It had been such a thrill to watch her take control of seducing us both I was happy to wait for her to decide what happened next.

I caressed the gentle curve of her hips and waist, enjoying the feel of her silky, soft skin under my palms while she caught her breath.

She didn't keep me waiting long before lifting her face and giving me another impish grin and pressing her heated pussy against my cock once more.

"Goddamn, Indie." The words escaped on a groan.

Biting her lip, she leaned back and took me in her hands, my shaft already slick with her come. Her grip firm but nowhere tight enough to make me come, she obviously wanted to make me beg.

And beg, I would. Happily.

"Please, baby. You feel so good, teasing me like that."

"How badly do you want to be inside me right now?" Her grip tightened on my cock as she concentrated on torturing the sensitive skin of my tip.

"I've never needed anything so badly as I want to be inside you right now, baby. Please. Put my cock into that tight heat and ride me again. You were so incredibly hot. I almost came watching you." Indie's thighs squeezed my hips at my words, shuddering with anticipation.

Moving up onto her knees to position her center over where she held my cock in her hand, she angled the tip of my cock against her pussy, rubbing me back and forth through her sopping folds.

"I want to feel you, Theo. With nothing between us." Her gaze locked on mine.

Her voice was quieter now, some of the bravado of the seductress that had taken charge this evening receding into the background. There was a hint of vulnerability there. It was the first time there had been any hesitation in her all night.

I was fully aware that making these kinds of decisions was not the smartest idea, but I wanted to feel her too. More, some caveman instinct wanted to fill her up with my come and mark her that way.

Fuck, yeah. I did. I wanted evidence of what was happening between us to mark us both.

If it had been anyone else but Indie, I would never have considered going without protection. I'd never done that, all too aware of the risks.

But in this moment, despite the powerful orgasm that we were both reminded of every time the wet sound of our movements filled her bedroom, her eyes filled with want all over again.

"I'm negative. It's been, Christ, I don't know how long since I've had sex." Shit, it'd been way more than a year. The routine team physicals were all fine.

"Me too, Theo. I'm on birth control. We're safe."

With that settled, she didn't wait to position me at her entrance and then, looking up into my eyes, sunk down on me in one swift stroke.

"God-fucking-damnit. Holy shit, baby," my voice rasped as I tried to reconcile how good she felt.

An endless stream of filth fell from my lips at the feel of her wet, tight heat completely encompassing me.

I searched her face for any discomfort from how fast she pulled me into her pussy, but she was so slick from our earlier activities she just looked blissed-out.

Squeezing her inner muscles, likely trying to push me further into oblivion, she forced more curses from my lips as she rose up until only the tip of my cock rested inside her and then thrust herself back down.

"Indie. Indie. You're driving me crazy," I whispered.

"Good," she panted, now lost in the rhythmic movements of her lower body. "Just hold on to me and let me fuck you."

Oh fuck. I might not make it through the night. She'd kill me with how good this sex was.

I decided to take her at her word. I gripped her hips in my hand, holding on firmly but letting her set the pace and intensity.

The heat of our fucking and the effort it took not to flip her over and fuck her like a wild animal had beads of sweat breaking out on my forehead, running down into my hairline.

Indie's skin was flushed with pleasure and exertion, now a rosy pink from her cheeks down to her chest.

There were too many incredible visions to feast my eyes on at once. I gorged on the slick feel of her heat on my cock as I watched the place where we were joined together. My cock was wet and shining with her arousal as she moved me in and out of her body.

I loved seeing her lose control. The walls she held so tightly around her, keeping everyone out. But here she was, present in this moment with me, our eyes locked on one another. I recognized this for the gift that it was. Indie seemed relaxed and free to take what she wanted without thinking about how she looked or how she should act.

My chest hurt with a different kind of pleasure at seeing her trust me enough to see her unguarded in this way.

I couldn't get enough of her. This connection. Us together.

It hit me like a freight train how much she meant to me. I wanted to drown her in pleasure, yes, but also keep her safe and honor that trust.

I'd just have to keep her drunk on orgasms until she let me keep her.

Now, I just needed to hold off my own orgasm until she came a second time. I was so close that I was just shy of reciting the stats from our last few games to make sure she got there.

"That's it, baby. Take what you need. Do you think you can come again?" I asked, desperate to make her feel as much pleasure as possible.

Her cheeks and chest were pink from exertion, her eyes more like melted chocolate now than their usual fierce espresso. She nodded.

"Touch yourself, Indie. Make yourself come on my cock," I demanded.

I had never been one for dirty talk, but filthy words were another thing tumbling from my mouth with Indie. I'd never been more invested in my partner's pleasure than my own. I wanted her to have everything she needed at this moment to let go.

Just as my muscles started to scream with the effort of holding back, I felt the telltale pressure of her pussy fluttering into deep contractions around me.

With a groan, my orgasm took over. I struggled to keep my eyes open as the edge of my vision blurred with the intensity of my pleasure.

I couldn't stop my hips from fucking up into her in these last few moments, keen to prolong our joint pleasure as long as possible.

The idea of fucking my come into her had that caveman part of my brain going wild, fed by the debauched sounds of our come mixing together. That thought had my cock spurting one more time with a final, nearly painful throb of pleasure.

Indie collapsed on top of me, no doubt exhausted. She'd done all the work, after all.

I gathered her in my arms, hoping she would let me hold her for a minute. I was still inside her. I didn't want to move one inch. I wanted to stay inside her warmth forever, basking in what we had just shared and keeping us locked together.

Now that we were post-sex, I didn't know how she would react. It was one thing to give in to the insane chemistry between us after months of restraint.

I also knew, practically speaking, that we had to get cleaned up at some point. Goddamn, just the thought of our combined release sliding out of her had my cock making an attempt to get hard like the dirty motherfucker he was.

Kissing the top of her head, I inhaled her sweet scent that was all Indie. Just a hint of some kind of citrus shampoo remained, but her own scent was closer to spun sugar.

"You okay, Rocky?" I spoke into her hair.

Propping her chin on her arms across my chest, she gave me the sweetest little smile. My chest throbbed with such longing I tightened my arms around her involuntarily.

I was so gone for this girl.

"Yeah, I'm good, Theo. We should get cleaned up, though." She raised her head slightly, chin jutting down between us to where we were still joined.

She pushed up off my chest, her movements had my cock sliding out of her, followed by our come.

"Fuck, baby. That's goddamn sexy," I groaned. My cock made a valiant effort to get hard at the sight.

Up on her knees, I could see our release dripping down her thighs.

"Okay, Yao. Show's over." She gave me a mock scowl.

Her talking as if we were in the locker room after a game had me busting up laughing.

Man, when had I ever gone from burning hot sex to laughter? Never, that's when.

"But it's the best show I've ever seen, sweetheart." I bit my lip, mesmerized by the evidence of our intimacy.

Her face softened from the faux scolding, she gave me a wink before turning around. I watched her walk into the bathroom, her delectable ass a view I hadn't been treated to thus far. Every inch of her did something for me.

"Aren't you going to come clean up the mess you made, Theo?" she called over her shoulder.

I'd never moved so fast in my life as I did getting my ass into that bathroom for another chance to have my hands all over her.

Maybe after we were clean, she'd let me seduce her into getting all dirty again.

Twenty-Two

INDIE

I wish I could say the following week was filled with more nights like our first, but that was sadly not the case.

After the sex that may or may not have redefined my understanding of pleasure, I'd purposefully taken our banter back to a playful place. The connection I'd felt with Theo in those moments had hit me too strongly to stay cuddled up with him a moment longer. If I wanted to keep this liaison with Theo compartmentalized as strictly a hookup, I couldn't afford to sink back into the ill-advised crush from my teenage years.

His version of help to clean up had been more making out and touching every inch of each other's skin we could reach. Eventually, I'd kicked him out to actually get clean.

By the time I'd returned to my room, Theo had passed out smack-dab in the middle of the bed. An uninvited warmth invaded my chest as I stood and watched him.

He looked so content, not to mention unreasonably sexy, that I couldn't bring myself to wake him.

I'd allowed myself one night where I didn't look too deeply at my reasons for crawling onto the sliver of mattress he wasn't occupying and covered us both with my comforter. The warmth of his body was soothing, even though my mind raced.

I'd spent the hours before dawn reminding myself why it couldn't work between us.

We were just enjoying each other while I was in Toronto. I was leaving again in a matter of months, and Theo had a contract here. It was just sex, albeit incredible sex, and that's all it could ever be.

I had plans to do some good for the people of the city I'd come to love. And even the gorgeous Theo Yao-Miller wasn't going to get in the way of that.

So by the time he woke beside me the next morning, I'd steeled myself enough to keep him at a distance. I'd sent him off to his usual morning workout with a bright smile.

That had been five days ago. The Tempests had been away for a couple of games, and we'd only exchanged a couple of texts between us in my continued effort to keep this thing out of relationship territory.

If we had a repeat of our night together, great. If it was a one-night thing, then that was fine too. I'd tell Theo the same. I was only after some simple and string-free fun.

Right, sure. Okay. Do you think you can lie to yourself so well that you might believe it?

Today was the sixth day of not seeing Theo and saw me waking up with a monster of a cold. I could admit, privately, that I hadn't been taking the best care of myself.

Breakfast was often slept through or neglected because mornings were the only time I got any decent sleep. When not desperate for an extra couple hours of sleep after rushing around behind the scenes at the Tempests games, I used the time while Giz would contentedly sleep on the couch for her routine lazy morning nap to research the endless forms and documentation I would need to start up a nonprofit. Just when I thought I'd gotten a handle on one part of the process, I'd read an article or blog about another start-up that revealed a set of regulations that I'd never considered.

Now, I was paying the price for letting stress reign supreme over my decisions.

My eyes felt gritty and glued together as I threw on whatever hoodie I'd haphazardly chucked on the couch in one of my fits of feeling overheated through the evening last night.

I was firmly in the can't-put-on-enough-blankets-to-get-warm stage phase this morning.

All the same, Giz needed a quick walk around the block. Potty time waited for no virus.

I made it down in the elevator, feeling light-headed from either the cold or sinus medicine I was using to combat some of my symptoms.

The brisk late autumn air made me cough as I followed Gizmo out the front door of the building.

I was leaning on the skinny tree in front of our building, grateful that Giz was a girl and I wouldn't be risking a potty splash zone while I let her sniff the small patch of scrubby dirt next to me.

"We have to stop meeting like this."

The rough timbre of Theo's voice floated over from somewhere behind me. I was too goddamn miserable to even be taken by surprise.

I admit that I wasn't the best patient when sick. I was used to handling this kind of stuff on my own by just staying away from everyone until I was better.

"Indie?" Theo tried again.

"Hey," I croaked. My voice was rough from disuse. I hated the sore throat portion of a cold.

I turned and saw Theo looking at me with an expression full of concern.

A glance down at Giz had her giving me some solid side-eye for not paying attention to the fact that she was done outside.

I waved my hand again in dismissal of my plight.

"It's just a cold. No big deal." I aimed for a reassuring tone.

The last thing I wanted Theo to do was feel obligated to help me. God, just the idea of being a burden to him made me nauseous.

Distracted by that mortifying thought, I stumbled on an uneven part of the sidewalk.

"Whoa, there. You are not fine. Jesus. Let me help you. Here." He put his arm around my waist to steady me.

A small, hairless bundle was placed into my hands before Theo caught me off guard by scooping me up in his arms.

I jolted with the intent to tell him to put me down, but he cut me off before I could get the words out.

"Relax, Rocky. I don't want to cop an elbow in the face this time," he said and chuckled.

He was referring to the time he caught me falling out of the tree in their backyard. Excuse me for being a child and moving my limbs while I freaked out.

"Oh, trust me, I have photographic evidence in the form of a rep division hockey card of the black eye you gave me before you calmed down. I had to lie to the team to save face. I told them I'd got it in a game of street hockey." His voice was warm with affection at the memory.

Shit. I'd spoken out loud. Defeated either by the cold or embarrassment, I let my head fall to the side so it rested against the thick fabric of his jacket. It would take too much energy to resist.

His amusement quickly turned to surprise. "It's too fucking cold to be out here in a hoodie and, Jesus, your pajamas."

"Had to take Giz out," I muttered.

"You could have let me know. I could have done that. You should be resting. When you said we couldn't see each other last night, I thought you were blowing me off." His tone held both relief and a hint of disgruntlement.

I'd told him I had a virus and didn't want to get him sick so he couldn't play. The coaches and medical team took the players' health very seriously. He could get pulled.

That thought had me stiffening. "Theo," I choked on another cough. "You shouldn't be touching me. I can't make you sick."

I'd seen how seriously all the guys took their practices, routines, and rituals. There was no room for error, let alone putting themselves in a position to be off the ice sick with a virus.

He just hummed in reply.

"Where are your keys?" Theo shifted the majority of my body weight into one of his arms, trying to find keys that weren't there, bringing his hand around my knees. He dug around into the front pocket of my hoodie until he found the small key chain I carried.

Once he got us inside, he moved straight for my bedroom. He deposited me on the bed with Giz still in my arms. Theo pulled the covers up to my waist and left the room.

"Okay, baby." He let out a breath, not mentioning anything more about my lack of proper cold-weather attire. "You two get cozy here. I'm going to get these dishes out of your way and see if you have anything to eat. We need to get you better."

Theo swept Gizmo from my arms, kissed her head gently, and popped her onto my bed with a gentleness that had a pressure growing in my chest at the sight. I couldn't blame the feeling on my cough.

"Theo, seriously. I'll be fine. You need to get out of here. You can't afford to get sick." I was torn between truly not wanting him to get sick but totally relieved at the thought of someone taking care of me for once.

He waved away my weak protest as if we weren't talking about playing professional hockey for millions of dollars a year.

Theo channeled his inner Mary Poppins as he began to pick up the random shit I'd left around my room and bedside tables. He'd started gathering up my dirty water glasses and took the bag full of tissues out of my waste bin. Turning around to look over at where I sat in my bed, still in shock that this was happening, and gave me a mischievous grin.

"Don't worry. If I get sick, I'll just blame it on Andrews." He sniggered at his own joke.

"Theo!" I tried to muster another glare. It must have been a feeble attempt, as Theo just laughed it off.

"I'm kidding." He gave me a wink.

I concluded that it wouldn't hurt to let him clean up the dishes and throw out the garbage.

I let my body lean back into my pillows, careful not to jostle the bed too much and disturb a sleeping Gizmo.

I'd just close my eyes for a minute. Then I'd remind Theo he should go.

I must have dozed off because I woke to Theo gently shaking my shoulder. He held a bowl of soup in his hand. A steaming cup of something sat on my bedside table. It was probably tea, but I'd drink anything hot at this point.

"You need to eat, baby. But first, take these." He gave me a sweet smile.

He set the soup down on the table and opened his palm to reveal some painkillers. After depositing them into my hand, he went out of the room and came back with a glass of water.

I moved my hand out from under the blanket to reach for them. I was afraid if I didn't, he'd try to feed them to me, and even worse, I'd let him.

I popped the pills in my mouth, took the glass from him as well, and swallowed them with a few sips of water.

He put his palm to my forehead, letting it rest there while he peered into my eyes.

"Hopefully, they will help bring your fever down. When was the last time you ate anything?" He took my hand in both of his, giving it a gentle squeeze as he waited for my reply.

Instinct had me about to tell him not to worry about me, but the earnestness of his expression had me holding back the words.

Of all the ways he had taken care of me today, this moment felt the most intimate. I couldn't stop the rush of emotion inside me that wanted to get used to having him care for me this way.

I couldn't afford to let him slip through the permanent crack in my heart.

Twenty-Three

THEO

Frustration and helplessness warred for the top spot inside me.

I'd nearly lost it when I saw Indie leaning miserably against the tree in front of our building. Did she even realize how cold it was outside? The stupid hoodie with the wrong jersey number (I'd make sure to fix that right away) on it and a pair of thin pajama bottoms were no match against cold autumn winds in Toronto. It might not have snowed yet, but it was still cold enough to make her sicker.

I hadn't been able to stop myself from picking her up and bringing her inside. Yeah, it might not have been my place to take over like that—I was sure she'd let me know when she was well enough to yell at me again—but no part of me could stand there and let her freeze even a minute longer.

Frustrated at myself for not pressing her when she'd said she'd come down with a cold that was "no big deal," I left her in her bed and made my way to her kitchen to look for a thermometer.

When she'd replied with short, generic texts while I was away for back-to-back series, I'd thought she was trying to give me the brush-off. She'd turned me down twice when I'd asked to see her last night and then this morning. I'd come home ready to battle my way through whatever excuses she was going to give me about keeping our connection to a "one-night thing."

Now, I knew she hadn't been lying about the cold. She'd been downplaying how unwell she felt. My chest hurt at the idea that it hadn't even occurred to her to ask for my help.

Indie wasn't alone. She had me. I was going to keep on being there for her until she understood that this was where I wanted to be.

I dug around in the kitchen for any medicine that could bring down her fever. When I found nothing in her cupboards, I nudged a couple of things aside in her purse and hit the jackpot.

Not only did I find a bottle of medicine, but a ratty old piece of paper also fell out of her wallet. Not able to overcome the impulse to read it, I scanned what looked to be a bucket-list type thing. I quickly added an item of my own at the bottom with a nearby pen before stuffing it back in her bag.

I could only hope when she found out, she would forgive me. I wanted to be the one she chose to have all those new experiences with.

When I returned to her room with some soup and medicine, Indie was in the same position as when I'd left her bedroom. She'd fallen asleep in the few minutes I'd been gone.

Gizmo, who was awake, looked at me expectantly from her dog bed. Lifting her head, she made a little huffing noise through her nose, causing one side of her lips to roll inward.

"Why didn't you tell me that she was this sick? Just because you can't talk, do you think that's a valid reason for not giving me the inside scoop?" I asked.

Giz just cocked her head at me and laid back down again with an "I can't believe how delusional these hoomans are" kind of sigh.

"You're right. It's not your job. I just wish I'd been here to take care of her sooner." I gave Giz a small stroke on her head with two of my fingers. She was such a tiny dog that I couldn't even use my whole hand to pet her. "You're a very good girl keeping Mommy company."

I shook two pills into my hand and gently pressed her shoulder to wake her up. It took a couple of soft movements of my hand, and she was squinting up at me.

"You need to eat, baby. But first, take these." I braced myself for her refusal, but she just nodded minutely, put them in her mouth after I gave them to her, and swallowed them with the glass of ice water I handed her next.

I couldn't stop myself from touching her. Truthfully, I wanted to climb in that bed with her and hold her so I could feel the second her fever started to go down and make sure she got enough sleep, but I'd taken a lot of liberties today with carrying her inside and now delivering food and medicine.

I settled for just holding her hand, hopefully reassuring her that I wanted to stay.

I didn't want her to put up any walls and throw me out for being too much. She still hadn't said anything, so I didn't know what she was thinking or how she was feeling.

"Hopefully, they will help bring your fever down. When was the last time you ate anything?" She just shrugged a reply.

"Do you think you can eat some soup?" I indicated the still-steaming bowl of canned soup that I'd heated up in her microwave.

She sat up slowly, putting her back against her headboard. "Maybe," Indie rasped. Jesus. Her voice sounded rough. I winced in sympathy.

"Okay. That's good, baby." Not waiting for her to reach for it herself, I took the bowl from her nightstand and grabbed the spoon with my other hand.

I sat down on the edge of the bed close enough to her that I could feel the heat of her thigh against my side.

"You are not going to feed me." Indie mustered what must have been her fiercest expression at the moment. I had to stop myself from chuckling because fearsome she was not. The red skin around her nose lessened the effect. It complemented her adorable scowl.

It made something inside me settle, knowing I could be here for Indie. I hoped I could give her the same feeling of comfort that my mom always gave me when I was sick.

I needed to grab her some better-quality tissues. There was nothing fun about blowing your nose with sandpaper when you felt like crap.

Everyone knew you had to get the lotion tissues when you got really sick. Those were the best. A pang of sadness hit me, remembering the way my mom would come home with her arms full of the best tissue boxes every time one of my siblings or I got sick.

She'd tuck me up on the couch, surrounded by blankets, and let me choose whatever I wanted to watch on TV for the whole day. Mom did the same thing for my siblings. It was the best medicine. Had I felt that cared for since we lost Mom?

Pushing the feeling of longing aside, I focused back on Indie, who needed me now.

"I could." I smiled, pleased at least that she had the energy to tell me off, even just a little bit. "It would be very romantic. Like a low-key picnic. Our first date."

"We are not going to have our first date with me looking like an ad asking for donations for your local hospital," Indie choked out.

I lifted a spoonful of soup out of the bowl, moving it slowly toward her.

"Theo." A warning.

"Okay, baby. You win. I won't feed you. And don't worry, I'll think of something much better for our first date." I winked at her.

"I didn't say we were going on a date, Theo." Indie took the soup bowl I placed in her hands, thankfully lifting the spoon and taking a sip.

I didn't reply right away, instead waiting for her to take a few more mouthfuls. Even if it didn't taste the best, she was eating at least.

"I distinctly heard you say we were going on a first date. I'll make you a deal. You finish that soup and try some of the gourmet toast I made. Those char marks are a sign of a culinary delicacy, by the way, and not your temperamental toaster. And I'll let you choose what we do." I grinned at her.

"You are impossible." Her voice sounded a little less strained, the soup working its magic already.

"Baby, I didn't get to where I am by sitting around and going with the flow. When I want something, I make it happen." I hoped she read my every intention in the direct stare I gave her.

"I'm not your 'baby,'" Indie muttered as she continued to eat.

"Our night together suggests otherwise. But let's not debate it now. Wouldn't want you to lose your voice, eh?"

I couldn't stop the chuckle when she stuck out her tongue at me. But she didn't stop eating until the bowl was empty. I managed to get her to take two bites of toast before her fever must have spiked again, making her drowsiness return.

I tucked her comforter back around her and made my way around to the other side of the bed. Easing myself onto the other side of the mattress, I sat against the headboard and pulled out my phone.

While she napped, I entered the list of the grocery items I was going to get delivered this afternoon so I had better options to take care of her with.

Once that was done, I fired off a quick email to team services requesting delivery of three Tempests hoodies.

This time with the right number on them. That way, even when I wasn't here to keep her warm in my arms, she'd be reminded how much I wanted her to be mine.

Twenty-Four

INDIE

Hockey players' schedules weren't for the faint of heart. Somehow, Theo had skirted catching the awful virus that kept me in bed for three days. I'd only just started feeling like myself again, knowing that I had to clarify where things stood between us, when the team set off for another set of away games.

That left us in a weird kind of limbo. I wasn't a fan of leaving things unsaid.

I had too many years being seen and not heard in my parents' circles. It wasn't the same as that sort of oppressive silence, but this time, it was a game schedule keeping me from re-establishing some boundaries with Theo.

I was grateful for his help, but I couldn't allow myself to get used to it and then have it taken away. I'd been taking care of myself since I was eighteen officially (and many years informally once my parents decided school was "too important" to drag me along as an accessory on their work trips anymore). I didn't need someone to hold my hand every time I got a little sniffle.

Wasn't it sooo nice to have someone take care of you for a change?

I shoved the traitorous voice inside my head aside. It would never have occurred to me to ask Theo for help last week, and the truth was I was still uncomfortable having accepted his help.

The cold, gray late-autumn Toronto weather seeped into my bones as I made my way to the Billings Centre, which held both head office and the main arena for the Tempests games. Even though streetcars were available to take me westward to work, there was something about the fifteen or twenty minutes of walking that helped me clear my head.

My hands buried deep in the pockets of my new wool peacoat, I felt my phone vibrate. Pulling it from my pocket, I saw the notification for my group text with Emery and Abbie.

Emery

> **How are you feeling? I hope better. That cold sounded nasty. You should come home to CA. I think some fresh Amado air would clear any lingering germs right up.**

Guilt wormed its way through my system. Even though Theo had outrageously called Emery to ask her permission to date me, it didn't feel like she took him seriously. Nor had I made any mention of even being friendly with Theo over the past month to Emery.

It was shitty of me to keep this thing I was doing with him a secret from her. I didn't think she'd care—hell, maybe she'd even be excited—but once it ran its course sooner or later, Emery would be put in the very awkward position of pointedly *not* talking about Theo in front of me for fear that she'd hurt my feelings.

My friends were absolutely my family. Emery had a family who loved her outside of me and Abbie. I didn't want to force her to pick and choose what she could share with me.

Indie

> **Ha. I wish. At least it's still above 60 there, right? It's like freaking 9C here. In the DAYTIME.**

I quickly flipped over to my trusty Weather Network internet browser bookmark to get the conversion.

Indie

> **Ugh. It's worse than I thought. That's like 48F.**

Emery

> **Brrr. All the more reason to come home. Maybe your dad has gotten over the insanity that made him think you needed to go to a whole other country to make you ambitious or whatever it was he wanted.**

I loved her trademark positivity, but short of me signing a contract with my family's empire, giving my father exactly what he wanted, there was no way I was getting to go home early.

You'd have to leave Theo then, too.

The sudden whoosh of my stomach had me seeing red. God, it was like my nineteen-year-old self had possessed some part of my brain, pushing these thoughts on me that I didn't want to deal with. They were entirely unwelcome.

Liar.

No. I would control myself and shut down weak thoughts like that. I'd only ever let my guard down once, and I'd spent those months before my twentieth birthday picking up the broken pieces of my heart. Never again.

Indie

> Yeah, sorry. It's not going to happen.
> When Gerald Layne makes up his mind,
> he doesn't bend.

Abbie

> Hey. Was just getting ready for work.
> Glad you're on the mend, Ind. What
> can we do to get your dad to let you
> come home? We missssss you. You
> also need to send us more pics of Giz.
> I'm making a Baby's First Year album.
> Congratulations Fur-Mama!

Indie

> Yeah, yeah. I can tell you're gloating from
> here. And she's five years old, Abs.

The rescue had contacted me for an update on Giz, and I just couldn't bring myself to let her go to another family. So I'd officially adopted her.

Abbie

> It's not about her age, babe. It's her
> first year in her forever home!

I could imagine Abbie waving that concern off. God, she knew how to push all my feelings buttons.

Indie

> Yep, I'm sure you were "getting ready for
> work" all right. And short of discovering
> he's been hiding a secret criminal empire
> all these years, there's nothing, babe.

I replied, shifting the conversation off my overly sentimental thoughts around finally getting a pet.

Abbie

Boo. And I was really getting ready for work. Aiden left an hour ago.

Emery

Wow.

Abbie

Wow, what?

Emery

He's sleeping in these days! Heading out at 7:00 AM is positively sloth-like for him.

Indie

Well, he does have a gooood reason to stay in bed these days, doesn't he Em?

Emery

Why, yes, he does.

Abbie

I thought we were talking about Indie. How did this become tease Abbie time?

My lips parted on a laugh, startling another pedestrian trying to pass me as I'd slowed down my pace to type.

Indie

Because it's too fun now that you are loved up in a gorgeous house with a gorgeous man. And I'm all for it, girl. For you. Not me. Give me my old apartment in downtown Amado any day. Gah. I miss walking over to the community center after work.

Emery

Oh! I meant to tell you. I stopped by there a couple weeks ago and picked up a slot to teach a drop in art class for any of the kids you were working with.

That was Emery. All goodness to the core. The muscles in my chest squeezed my heart tightly at how much I missed my volunteer tutoring shifts at Amado's central community center. I'd been working with some of the kids since I started college, and I'd had to leave them so abruptly. But of course, it was another thing my father saw as disposable in my life.

Indie

Thank you, Em. I'm sure they'll love it more than the math equations I always forced on them.

Emery

Don't for a second think that I'm going to be able to fill your shoes there. But I thought it would be good for me to remind myself that my undergraduates were once innocent. A fresh perspective and all that.

I privately wished Emery would just concentrate on creating art. She was happiest in her studio. But she wanted to be the second Professor Yao in her family, so I didn't say anything.

Abbie

OK, let's forget altruism for a second. Blah, blah good for the world and all that. You're both angels. Ind, any good inside gossip to share about those world class, not to mention

hot athletes you work with on a daily
basis? Now that neither of us are in
the main Appeal building, *nothing* ever
happens around here that's worth
mentioning.

Hoping to keep the conversation away from Theo because I didn't want to outright lie to them, and especially not to Emery, I chose the best fall guy for the job: Campbell.

Indie

Nothing huge, but Ryan Campbell, the
alternate captain and right winger, told
the largest hockey magazine in the
country that he and I were living together.

Abbie

LOL. What?!

Indie

Yep. He's from Georgia so the last name
Layne doesn't strike fear into his heart.
To be fair, he thinks I'm just another
member of his staff and he can use me in
his schemes. Which I am, except Gerald
Layne's family name isn't something he
can play around with so I had to threaten
the reporter within an inch of his life.

I wasn't going to mention what the reporter wanted to ask Theo about his and Emery's mom. That was still a barely held together wound for Emery. She didn't need to worry about the press digging into her business.

Emery

If I could admit that hockey players

> **were hot, Ryan Campbell would be top of the list. Since my brother playing hockey forced me to spend time in freezing cold arenas and outside disgusting locker rooms, I've seen the truth for myself.**

Abbie

> **I'm just over here pretending I have any idea what a right winger is. Carry on.**

Emery

> **How is Theo? I haven't heard from him since he called me a couple weeks back. How are his knees? He saw someone last year in Vancouver but never mentioned it again. Whenever I ask about it, he clams up and tells me he has to go.**

Yeah, I know. He called you from my kitchen. There was the guilt rising in my esophagus, threatening to choke me.

What could I say to her? *Gee, Emery, I think he's good after we had sex without a condom for the first time in my life, and we both came more than once. Or he stayed by my side and took care of me while I was sick.*

Yeah, right. Typing those words would happen exactly never. Both of those circumstances made this thing with Theo sound way more involved than it really was, like I trusted him a great deal.

What was the deal with his knees? It sounded like he had something significant going on, and he'd never once mentioned it.

The sting of hurt was a sign I was on the right track with my plan to set things straight with Theo once he was back in town.

This wouldn't be the first thing I kept from Emery and Abbie because I didn't want them to have to deal with my issues. And when I had to end things with Theo, they wouldn't have to worry about me.

So I kept it vague.

Indie

> I think he's OK, Em. The team's away for four days so I haven't even seen him. He's been playing better than ever, according to the coaching staff. Almost at work. Talk later xx

There. That sounded like something a friend of the family would say.

I picked up my pace, feeling colder than when I left my apartment building. Despite now being keen to get to work and distract myself with the day's tasks, I couldn't stop myself from mentally calculating how many hours were left until I saw Theo again.

Twenty-Five

THEO

I was exhausted. The team had been out of town for a longer stretch of time than usual because of the way the games were scheduled. Finishing up a series in New York before heading straight to Vancouver, I hadn't had time to register that I'd be playing my old team for the first time since the trade. Other than a quick hello from my old captain and backup goalie before the game, it was just another game with my new team but in familiar surroundings.

It made me realize that I wished I'd spent more time with my teammates socially while I'd had the chance. They were good guys, and I'd missed out on making some real friends here. The only thing I still had waiting for me in Vancouver was a storage unit full of furniture from my condo.

The major difference was the thought that crossed my mind after a particularly impressive save.

Would Indie be impressed by that? Did she see it?

No, dumbass! It takes a lot more than some athleticism to impress Indie Layne.

I kind of loved that about her. Hockey was the last reason why she'd be with me.

Getting back to the hotel was a letdown from the anticipation I'd felt earlier in the evening. I'd realized I could rid myself of this dejected feeling and get to work on Indie's bucket list at the same time. With the time difference, I had to wait for her to finish up the stats and everything else she did post-game in her role.

Grabbing my phone from the bedside table, I opened the new group chat Emery had added my brothers to. It was aptly named "Get Your Shit Together Theo & Stop Acting Like an Ass."

My siblings and I weren't known for our subtlety with each other.

Theo

Hey. I'm up in Vancouver and thinking of you guys. Wish I could stop in for a visit but we're flying back to Toronto in the early morning.

Chase

Well, well. This is new. I'm wondering what brought on this sudden need to check in on three fully grown adults.

Geez. They were good at holding a grudge. I was tempted to video call them, but none of them would have picked up. My chest burned with regret that they were still upset with me.

Liam

What's happening? I just woke up.

Theo

It's 11:30 PM

Liam

Your point? It's called a nap, bruh.

Shaking my head even though he couldn't see me, my lips formed a smile. I had no idea if he was being serious, but the details would get even more crazy if I continued down this road with him, and I wanted to catch Indie before she went to sleep.

Theo

Got it. I'm sorry I didn't reach out more when we all lived in the same time zone all these years. I didn't realize what I had taken for granted until now.

Emery

What's happening? I just woke up.

Liam

Bruh…

Chase

Ooo baby sis has jokes.

I choked out a laugh. That was new.

Emery

Obviously, this semester's undergrads have infected me with the same affliction that the twins have. Insanity.

Liam

Somebody's been watching *Bridgerton* without me.

Emery

How dare you?! I am affronted by such an outlandish accusation.

Chase

Oh yeah, she has, L.

Liam

How dare I?! What happened to "we can watch it together because it'll be cherished sibling time" and whatever else you said. I'm just there for my Kate and Anthony fix, separately.

Shit, together too. Damn, a Kathony sandwich. Delicious.

Theo

Anyone have any news from this century? The ton notwithstanding.

Chase

Look at you, T. Nobody can say you're all goalie masks and pads. So very worldly.

My eyes rolled at the jab, simultaneously releasing more tension from my shoulders. I might be incapable of getting a real answer out of the jokers, but it was reassuring to be invited back into the absurdity.

Theo

I do pull my head out of my ass occasionally, you know. It's not like the NHL runs my whole life. I'm not totally oblivious to popular culture.

Two messages buzzed at the same time.

Emery

Just 98% of it.

Liam

You should try for more than occasionally, that can't be a very

**comfortable position to hold for long.
It's gotta be killer for your neck, bruh.**

Chase was quick to chime in on Liam's line of thought.

Chase

**You're practically geriatric as a
professional hockey player. You need
to be careful about injuring yourself in
your off hours. You should listen to L.**

Goddamn. They never let up. I loved them.

Theo

**Can one of you muppets tell me
something, anything, that has actually
happened to you in the last couple
weeks?**

Chase

**I got the lead project manager role on a
new project.**

Finally!

Theo

**Congratulations, Chase. That's amazing
news!**

**But do they know they hired an infant
as a lead architect? Will you take Ted to
your meetings?**

Ted was Chase's favorite stuffed bear growing up. Emery and I
used to hide it in weird places when the twins' pranks went too far.

Chase

**Shut up. You should know better than
to bring Ted into anything.**

Liam

He definitely wraps Ted in a blanket for the bottom of his briefcase. I've seen it.

Chase

Lies! See if I bring you coffee next time you're hungover.

Emery

(good move, turning them on each other).

Theo

Other than the under-gremlins, everything OK, Em? Do you have any exhibitions coming up?

I was determined to make it home to see her next gallery showing. I'd missed the one for her master's because of the playoff schedule two years ago. This time, I would make it there to support her, even if it meant flying to and from Toronto in the same day.

The pause before her reply was longer than the other breaks in the conversation.

Emery

Nah. I don't have much of anything cohesive enough for a show. Just buckling down to get my students through the semester.

Emery had been creating less and less art. Even if I couldn't be there in person, I tried my best to keep up with her artist social media accounts.

Had Indie noticed the change in my sister?

Checking the time, I'd bet Indie was home now. I wanted to see her face before I called it quits on this day.

Theo

> **OK, let me know because I am coming to the next one. I need to go though. Early flight tomorrow.**

It was the truth. Just not all of it.

Emery

> **Not sure if the twins are arguing in their private messages now. But I can say, almost certainly on their behalf, that we love you. Take care of yourself since guys can't seem to stop hitting pucks at your head. xxx**

Theo

> **Thanks, Em. Love you all too.**

Swiping out of the chat, I hedged my bets and video called Indie. Texting wasn't enough. I wanted to see and hear her.

She just needed to pick up.

After the second ring, her lovely face appeared on my screen. Her usual subtle makeup had been washed off. She'd tied her hair up and had changed out of her work clothes into those tempting, paper-thin black tank top pajamas that I'd noticed she preferred over everything else.

Indie looked more perfect to me in these unguarded moments than any other way.

"To what do I owe this torture of a phone call? And video, Theo? Really?" Her lack of greeting might have worried some, but I'd been hungrily gobbling up every detail about her for a few months now. The first thing I saw was the smile in the corners of her mouth that she was trying to hide.

"I wanted to see you. I had to leave while you were still sick. It felt wrong, especially with the way the schedule has the team away for longer than normal." My words leaving no doubt about the fact that she mattered to me, I watched her face closely for her reaction.

Her gaze skirted to the side briefly before she looked back into her phone's camera, rolling her eyes.

"I appreciate what you did, Theo. But I *can* take care of myself, you know. I've been fine on my own for ages."

Too long. She's been doing this since she was a kid.

Knowing Indie was fiercely independent meant that I had to walk a very fine line between offering her support while trying not to be overbearing.

"I know, baby. But that doesn't mean I don't want to be there for you." I didn't want her to misunderstand me. It would just be another reason for her to keep me at a distance. And I wanted many more of the softer moments with Indie now that I'd had a small taste of her more vulnerable side.

"I'm not your baby," she replied automatically.

"I dunno about that. The way you rode me in your bed made you feel exactly like *mine*. And don't forget the way you used the length and ridges of my cock as your own personal sex toy slip n' slide," I argued, licking my lips while reliving the visual of her above me.

"Theo!" A slight pinkening of her cheeks and a sharp intake of breath contrasted her scolding tone.

Hmm. How much did Indie like dirty talk? I'd never been one to say much with other women I'd been with, often in a hurry to get off and get out.

But Indie made me want to dive into every way I could draw pleasure out of her. If I couldn't act on these urges thousands of miles away from her, I wanted her to *hear* them.

So I carried on as if she hadn't half-heartedly tried to shut me up.

There was no hint of shame in my tone as I continued.

"God, I want to do that again. And I didn't even get to taste you that time. I've had ten days of fantasies piling up in my mind. I want to take you in every position possible until we're covered in our come." I groaned, letting my head fall back for a moment while I enjoyed the visual in my mind.

When I refocused on my phone screen, her eyes were wide with surprise or shock. Maybe she hadn't done anything like this with anyone before. I sure as shit hadn't. Aside from the fact I didn't have the desire to, I could never trust the person on the other end wasn't recording my call to sell to some media outlet for a huge payout.

Trusting Indie was as easy as breathing. Well, even easier than breathing right now, considering the way she could have me panting with lust just by seeing her freshly washed face and those tiny straps of her silky tank top.

Fuck, if she *wanted* to record my voice saying dirty shit to her, I'd record an audiobook's worth of filth for her to replay. As long as she was picturing *me* wringing out the pleasure from her body, I wanted her to listen on repeat.

"Theo." Her voice came out as a whisper. She closed her eyes briefly to take a deep breath.

I used my hand not holding the phone to press against my now rock-solid length in an attempt to get some relief. I'd have to have another shower when I got off the phone with her. There was no way I could go to sleep like this.

Her gaze moved to my shoulder and down to the corner of the screen where my arm ended. She couldn't see what I was doing exactly.

"Are you touching yourself right now?" Indie's voice came out stronger, if raspier than before.

"What if I am?" I dared her.

She looked straight into the camera again.

"Show me." She grinned, her eyes sparkling with mischief.

Twenty-Six

INDIE

A jittery type of adrenaline ran through my veins. The thrill of having Theo's undivided attention transformed into white-hot lust when I saw the small movements of his shoulder and arm in the bottom corner of my screen.

I knew instantly he was touching himself. And I'd told him to show me before my brain realized what my mouth was doing.

I blamed the commentary Theo had already provided.

Where had the laid-back voyeur from our night together gone? The man who sunk deeply into his pleasure as he watched me use him to take my own.

I'd never seen Theo lose his cool. He approached our first sexual experience the way I'd witnessed his commitment to hockey over these past months. He possessed a sure, steady confidence that demonstrated he was completely present in the moment. He left no doubt about where he wanted to be, on the ice or in my bed.

I'd never felt so wanted by anyone. He was intoxicating.

Tonight, he'd unleashed a stream of dirty talk I wasn't expecting.

Hearing those words from any other man would have probably turned me off.

But Theo wasn't like any other man I'd ever met.

I stared at him through the screen, startled by the realization that I missed him more than I'd allowed myself to feel. I wanted him here in person so he could do all the things he wanted to me.

Neither of us had said anything for a moment after I made my demand, but Theo's hand had not stopped moving in the interim.

He arched an eyebrow and gave me a wry smile. "We really doing this, Rocky?"

"Why, Yao? Don't you want to?" I dared him. The truth was nerves zapped through my bloodstream at an alarming rate, turning my veins into electrical currents. I wouldn't be surprised if I could light up our apartment block by myself.

A low hum issued from his throat. I held in a grin, knowing I'd activated his professional-level competitive spirit. We had that in common, I realized. All someone needed to do was tell Theo or me what we couldn't do, and we'd jump on proving them wrong.

Did I use that to my advantage now? Absolutely. Was I ashamed of the results of my words? Absolutely not.

"Oh. I want to, baby. But it's going to be an even playing field tonight. Whatever I show you, you show me. Deal?" His dark eyes seemed intent on capturing every microexpression on my face as he waited for my answer.

There was a relief in knowing I could back out of this at any time and Theo could as well without us thinking less of each other. We were both in this for the thrill, long past the point in our lives where we had anything to prove to anyone but ourselves.

Theo was the only man on the planet I would think to do this with. He would never abuse my trust in any way, and that gave me the freedom to sink deeply into my own arousal.

"Fine. You start," I replied as if this was going to be some sort of dare. But I got wetter by the second when I thought of all the possibilities of what could fall from those perfectly formed lips of his.

I quickly swiped my thumb across the side of my mouth to make sure I wasn't drooling. My lips remained slightly parted while I got lost in the possibility of getting filthy.

Jesus. This was going to be my own private OnlyFans show.

The truth was I'd been so overwhelmed with my own arousal the first time we were together that I hadn't had a chance to appreciate Theo's body in all its glory.

Not being able to touch him was the perfect opportunity to soak up all the peaks and valleys of his body that he worked damn hard to maintain. How could I possibly do anything else but reward those efforts by ogling the shit out of his body?

"Take your shirt off, baby. That little sleep shirt drives me insane." Theo whipped his own white T-shirt off over his head, tossing it to the side out of the video frame.

I looked directly into the camera of my phone and sent him the most devilish smirk I could muster. Just because I'd agreed to play by his rules didn't mean I wasn't going to stretch his willpower until it snapped.

Gizmo was asleep in her fluffy bed on the other side of the couch. There were just some things her little subconscious should not hear, so I stood and made my way to my bedroom and shut the door behind me.

I set up the phone on my bedside table, using books to prop up my phone so that Theo could see my entire upper body down to where my butt rested on my white sheets.

"Goddamn, Rocky. When you do something, you don't do it half-assed, do you?" Theo's voice was a growl. He copied my actions and propped his own phone up to mirror the angle I was showing him. Now, I could see his ripped torso and the dark gray boxer briefs he was wearing.

His cock was already rock hard, tenting the soft fabric of his briefs obscenely. My god, the tips would be flooding in if we were recording this for public consumption.

I pulled up one side of my pajama shorts to reveal the entirety of my ass cheek to his gaze, feeling the slinky fabric slide between them. "No, I don't, but in this case, half-assed looks pretty good, am I right?"

I leaned forward to balance more on my knees and turned the bared side of my bottom toward the camera. I made sure I kept my upper body angled enough so I could see his reaction.

He did not disappoint. "Fuck me, I wish that I could take a handful of that ass right now, baby. I can't decide if I want to slide my hand under that fabric hiding your holes from me or have you sit on my face so I can bite that round peach of yours."

I sat down firmly on my heels, pressing my thighs together to stem the arousal heating my core.

"And it's still your turn, Rocky. I said take that paper-thin excuse for a shirt off. I need to see how hard your nipples are for me."

I shifted in a semicircle so I was facing the camera with the front of my body, sitting on my calves and heels.

Unraveling Theo completely was the goal here, but I couldn't stop myself from watching the screen to catch his reaction as I reached for the hem of my tank top and dragged it upward so slowly that my arms trembled slightly against the urge to rip it off and bare myself to him.

Theo caught his plush bottom lip between his teeth as his gaze tracked each inch of my skin as it was revealed. A wave of goose bumps appeared on my stomach and ribs as my apartment's drafty air brushed against my skin.

I reached the bottom of my breasts, their small curve just enough to catch the edge of the hem, and paused.

"Goddamn, baby. Stop teasing me and show me those gorgeous tits. I'm dying over here." Theo accompanied his words with a rougher stroke of his hand against his fabric-covered cock.

"Well, we can't have that, can we? Let's get your blood pumping again." My smile was feline. In contrast to my initial teasing, I yanked my tank top off to match the intensity of how he was gripping himself, the disturbance of the motion creating a little bounce of my breasts.

"Yesss… That's it. Look at those fucking perfect tits. God, I can't wait until I can fill my hands with them again." The gravel in his voice gave away how into this he was.

He pushed down against the base of his cock as if he was trying to control himself. I licked my lips as I saw a small wet spot had appeared, darkening the charcoal fabric straining against his length. My gaze refused to leave the evidence of his arousal on the screen, not wanting to miss the chance to watch it grow bigger the more he worked himself over.

Theo must have noticed my stare as I caught the moment of his chin tilting away from the screen in my peripheral vision. He stared down at the pool of precome that I was fixated on and slid his hand up from his base to grip the middle of his cock, brushing the wide pad of his thumb over the tip.

Fuck. He might have been a god of pleasure in another life. Where were these powers of seduction coming from?

And I was not immune to his seduction either. My sleep shorts still tucked up into my ass crease meant that the seams of my shorts were pressed in between my folds and taut all the way from front to back.

The roughness of the thread now stood hot and wet against my core, pumping out my own arousal as if it thought I was about to fuck him.

Sadly, lady bits, that is not on the menu for tonight. But I won't neglect you for long.

"What next?" I shifted in place to get some more friction from my heels pressing against my pajama-clad folds. He needed to continue to run this show because I was past the point where I could do anything but give him what he wanted.

"Get rid of those shorts and spread your knees further apart on the bed. I want to see your pussy while I tell you how to touch yourself."

I leaned to one side and then the other as I stripped off the final piece of clothing between Theo's eyes and the rest of my naked flesh.

"You too," I ground out, but he was already leaning back against his hotel room's headboard to rid himself of his briefs. The elastic waistband pulled his cock downward with the motion before its hardness slapped back against his abs.

Theo inched down so that he was lying on his side with his head propped up on one arm.

I wanted to lick the V starting at his hips and downward. It was a good thing I'd never gotten a look at Theo's twenty-something body when I first propositioned him almost seven years before. Nineteen-year-old Indie would not have been ready for the indecent picture of that V, his nearly black happy trail, and that impressively sized cock that I saw now.

I was so turned on I felt like I might come the second he told me to touch my clit.

He took his hard length back into his large hand and slid up and down while swiping the precome at his tip.

"Now, you're going to do exactly what I say so we can pretend I'm there fucking you in all the ways we both want me to. Okay, baby?"

I *never* liked being told what to do and hesitated out of instinct. I did like what we were doing, though. There was no reason not to sink into the intimacy of this moment, no matter who was leading the motions.

"Yes, Theo." I let my shoulders drop, and any hesitation melted away with my movement.

I was ready to give Theo the best damn orgasm of his life.

Twenty-Seven

THEO

"*Yes, Theo.*"

Thank god Indie wasn't usually agreeable because her willingness to take my direction in this moment was lethal to my sanity.

Goddamn. She was a work of art on my screen. My greedy eyes couldn't absorb all the subtle curves and dips of her body fast enough. I was a starving man suddenly presented with the feast of my dreams.

The video call forced me to savor each pixel of skin on my screen. If I were there with her in person, I would descend on her like an animal, having lost the superhuman restraint I'd held on to when I'd been in her bed.

"Put two fingers in your pussy and tell me how wet you are first. Then I want you to show me," I growled. I wanted to watch her put her hands all over herself, but I needed to know how needy she was first.

Indie lifted her hand that was resting on the bed beside her leg toward her center.

"Ah. Slower. Drag your fingers along your thigh and over your stomach as you go." The push and pull of my desperation for her had me blurting out directions.

She complied and slowed her movements. Her fingertips brushed over her outer thigh, which I knew from experience felt like silk, and then up to the crease of her hip.

I ripped my gaze from the mesmerizing sweep of her fingers as she dragged them back and forth from her hip bone to the very edge of her pelvis, never dipping down into her folds.

I mimicked the speed of her movement on my cock, making broader strokes from my base to my tip. I watched her eyes follow the motion of my hand and its vise grip on my rock-hard length.

Her breathing sped up as I swiped my thumb over the head of my cock, catching the precome that was beading from my tip. The press of my thumb on my glans as I smoothed the lubricated digit back toward my base had the corner of Indie's mouth tucking inward as if she was biting the tender skin of her cheek.

Was she holding in a sound? Or stopping herself from saying something? I wanted to find out.

I tested my theory by increasing the speed and strength of my stroke on the next upsweep of my hand. The friction of my rough palm forced another helping of precome to smear over my shaft once more.

The second my thumb made the sweeping motion, Indie's mouth opened, and a small sound issued from her throat on her exhale.

Good. I want to drive her to the brink of insanity with her pent-up desire. To push her past rational thought where her mind would be filled with images of me, of us, in this moment.

She blinked away the haze of watching me drag out my own pleasure. Her hand moved upward along her rib cage and, further up still, to the underside of her breast.

The pad of her thumb rested briefly under the swell of her breast before she used it to swipe upward, causing her small mound of flesh to bounce with the motion.

"Very naughty, baby. Did I tell you to do that?" My voice sounded hoarse as I pushed the words out.

She didn't answer me. Instead, Indie brushed her thumb and forefinger against her breast, this time circling the dark pink skin of her areola.

"Rocky…" I groaned. She was so sexy I couldn't even scold her for breaking our unspoken agreement to let me lead.

For all my years of being proud of my self-discipline, this woman could bat her eyelashes and have me following her into a burning building.

My blood thundered in my veins. The pounding of my pulse thumped so loudly inside me that I could barely hear my own breathing.

"You're driving me insane." It was clear to me she had no mercy when she responded to my plea by merely biting her plump bottom lip between her teeth and taking the tight bud of her nipple between her thumb and finger.

Then she pinched her tender skin. Hard.

"Goddamn. Fuck. Jesus." The curses streamed from my lips as I watched her ripe cherry of a nipple flash white with the rough treatment by her own hand before reddening a deeper shade than before.

I squeezed my cock at its base to hold off my orgasm. There was no way I was coming before she did. I wanted to watch her soak her hand in her own juices and imagine her stroking my cock with them after she came.

"Baby," I ground out. "Are you going to do what I asked or not? It's making me crazy not being there to take that poor, abused nipple in my mouth and soothe it."

The small hitch in her breathing told me I was getting somewhere. I pressed on, keen to get her off now, no longer content to wait after her little show of defiance.

"Maybe that little bratty move made you hotter, hm? Are you ready to show me how wet you are after proving to me that you won't follow my instructions?"

Her slow nod was accompanied by her other hand coming to her chest to join her other one. She cupped each of her small swells in her hands, rubbing her thumb gently over her nipples now. Indie's head tilted back slightly, her eyes half-closed, enjoying the sensations she was giving herself.

Or was it my eyes on her that made this so sensual for her? I wanted to watch her do this in person the next time we were together.

"I see how it is. I was stupid to think that you could behave." Her chin snapped forward, and she narrowed her eyes, looking more like the fierce woman I was used to.

I cut her off as she opened her mouth to speak, as if I hadn't noticed her wanting to tell me I was wrong. "Instead, you did what you wanted by making a show of your beautiful tits for me. Bad enough to like the little jolt you gave yourself with that pinch?"

My tone lilted up at the end of my statement, transforming it into a question. I was burning inside with what she'd say next. The thing with Indie was that I could never be totally sure what would come out of her mouth.

She stared into the camera lens now, her gaze filled with intense emotion.

"Fuck being good," she said. With those words a punch to my chest, she dropped her hands from her breasts, leaning her ass further onto her heels.

She took one hand and spread her pussy lips open with her fingers and held them open so I could see the deep pink of her wet folds. I wished there was a close-up feature on this call where I could zoom in to see her clit.

Her other hand came down, and she slipped two fingers along her slit from front to back and back again. A surge of arousal shot through me as she bore down slightly, adding pressure to her motions.

I tightened my grip on my cock, my hand having stopped moving, too captivated just watching her.

Time moved in slow motion as she dragged her fingers forward toward the camera, their wetness shining even a foot away from the camera.

"I wish I was there to taste you." The words fell from my lips as I increased my strokes on my length. The sparks that ignited low in my spine alerted me to how close I was to coming, but I wanted to watch her fall apart first.

"Me too," she whispered.

Her words were an electrical current that went straight to my cock. Nothing was as sexy to me as her wanting me in return. I was drowning in my need for her to see how special this was. How we could never reach this peak with anyone else. That the fire between us was once in a lifetime.

"Make yourself come for me. Please, Indie. I need to see it." I wasn't above begging at this point, my orgasm cresting beyond the point where I was going to be able to slow it down.

Indie seemed to be in a similar state. She let go of her folds, the voyeuristic show we'd put on for each other giving way to the primal frenzy to sate our needs, and increased the pace of her fingers.

A small moan issued from her mouth as she rocked her hips against the motions of her hands.

"Jesus Christ, Theo. I'm going to come." Her voice was breathless from exertion.

"Me too, baby," I ground out. I wanted her to know I was right there with her, every step of the way.

Despite her efforts to keep her eyes on her phone screen, her eyes half closed as the tension in her body reached its peak. Her hips stuttered as her lips parted, letting my name escape on a whisper.

"Theo."

The sound of her saying my name as her orgasm hit sent me over the edge. My hips punched upward as I fucked my fist to the sight of her body racked with pleasure. Come shot over my fist and onto my abdomen as I wrung out every last drop of pleasure that hummed in my system.

"Goddamn, baby. We need to do that again in your bedroom." I dropped down onto the hotel pillow and rolled onto my side, ignoring the mess I'd made for the moment.

Indie tipped sideways, letting her body fall onto her own pillow on a laugh.

She haphazardly reached behind her for a bed covering within reach, pulling her duvet over herself. Her body remained partially bare in some particularly tantalizing ways. I could see the lips of her pussy at the juncture of her thighs with her covering only hiding her top leg.

I must have paused with my mouth open, poised to say more, staring too long at her naked flesh. My length twitched as if it was primed for round two. Indie was a clinical strength aphrodisiac.

"See something you like, Theo?" Her orgasm had mellowed her typical snark to a drowsy, teasing-type tone.

"I like everything I see, baby." Obviously, my postorgasm haze lowered my filter. My words rang with a sincerity that communicated the depth of feelings I was holding back. I could see her expression tighten slightly with what I could guess was wariness.

"Wow. I'm impressed, Theo. We put on a pretty good show." Indie didn't acknowledge my statement, letting the subject drop, and chose instead to bring the conversation back to safer territory.

"I never doubted us, Ind. You were definitely the star tonight, though." There wasn't a situation where Indie didn't shine brighter than anyone else in the room.

Her smile softened as she snuggled further into her pillow, looking drowsy.

I glanced at the clock. Fuck. It was nearly 3:30 a.m. in Toronto— no wonder she was fading fast.

"Is Giz in bed?" I asked, not wanting her to venture outside in the dark and cold night by herself.

Indie nodded. "Yeah," she yawned her reply. "She's asleep in her bed in the living room. I'm sure she'll sneak in here any minute to steal my covers, though." Indie smiled fondly. She loved that little dog.

"Go on a date with me. I'll be home in two days, and we don't have practice on Thursday. Let me take you out, for real." I wanted to end our call with her knowing without a doubt that what just happened meant something. We were not casually hooking up.

I'd been thinking of a way to knock off some experiences on her Indie List throughout these days several days apart.

With her usual fortress of walls slightly lowered in this quiet moment between us, I needed to take my shot.

Indie looked up into the lens of her phone, giving me another soft smile.

"Okay, Theo. Yes."

Her answer had my heart beating harder than our illicit activities moments before. She was going to give us a chance.

Twenty-Eight

INDIE

"I had to tell you this, goalie, but I'm not into being blindfolded. It's just not one of my kinks. I hope it's not a deal-breaker for you," I drawled.

Theo's low chuckle followed my words. The fact that I wasn't wearing a blindfold was beside the point. For some insane reason, I'd agreed to keep my eyes closed after Theo had asked me to during the last ten minutes of our car ride to wherever this so-called "date" was taking place.

"Imagine that. Rocky Layne doesn't like to be out of control. I can't believe it." His humorous snark slithered into my heart, filling in the chasms that had lived in my chest.

He leaned down and whispered in my ear, "I'd like to think I know at least some of your kinks by now, baby. But please, do elaborate for educational purposes."

Yeah, like the little bit of voyeurism on that video call.

An inelegant snort that would have my childhood etiquette coaches expiring on the spot escaped my nose. I bumped my shoulder against his in a faux scolding.

Whoever invented feelings must have been a sadist. All this gooey warmth that swam in my veins whenever I so much as heard Theo's voice, let alone when he put his hands on me, was uncomfortable enough to make me nauseous.

It was a type of euphoric sickness that made me consider if it should be bottled and classified as an illicit drug.

How did Abbie do it all the time? She walked through life with literally every emotion plain as day on her face. I shuddered inwardly at the power of the feelings she carried so close to the surface of her skin.

Jesus Christ. A void so large that Nietzsche would have approved had lived inside me since before I hit puberty. I'd chucked so many inconvenient emotions in there over the years I was a master at feeling almost nothing. Hell, by this point, I'd probably made that dark space sentient by feeding it so many thoughts and should name it.

But here I was, not being able to go a minute without some sort of alien implantation flaring up and making me *feel things*.

My phone buzzed in my pocket with a text, interrupting my current existential crisis. It was probably my father again. So far, I'd dodged two phone calls and answered several texts with vague, unhelpful information.

I knew I was playing with fire, but I just wanted to stay in this bubble of freedom with Theo for just a little bit longer, without the problems that were waiting for me back home catching up to me.

What would it be like to be completely free of my family's demands and rules? It was a thought that came to mind more often now that Theo was in my life again.

I'll call my father tomorrow. Whatever he wants can wait another twelve hours. Just let me have this moment with Theo all to myself.

The cost of my defiance was the combination of fear and misplaced guilt that robbed me of some of the contentment I felt when I was with Theo.

The roughness of Theo's palm brushed against mine, long calloused from years of brutal hits from hockey pucks slamming his gloves against his skin.

The dry warmth of his skin said he wasn't nervous about this bloody date at all, as if it was just an everyday occurrence that he took out his sister's best friend without waiting for the bottom to fall out of this mess.

I'd grown so attuned to everything about him in such a short time. Beside me, he smelled subtly like his shower gel. I also knew if I pressed my face into his neck, I'd get a hint of the fresh, clean scent of just his skin.

Shit. I should be committed right now for waxing on about his goddamn smell.

How's convincing yourself that you're not completely obsessed with him going? Like you're not the same hopeless idiot you were at nineteen?

My inner voice was a nuisance that was getting harder and harder to ignore.

It was more inconvenient having Emery's sweet, optimistic insistence to finally go after something that made me happy.

"You do everything for everyone else, Indie. What is it that you want?" It was her eternal refrain when it came to me.

Why was everyone put out so much when I was just trying to make their lives easier?

Because you never look at what you need, girl.

I wanted to open my eyes and distract myself with something other than the sensations Theo's proximity was creating and the uncomfortable truths rolling around inside my head and heart.

"Are you sure you can't give me a clue?" I asked in my sweetest voice.

"Only a minute more. I promise, Rocky." He chuckled, not at all affected by my persuasion attempt.

He stopped for a moment, the cold, damp, late-November Toronto air weighing down the molecules surrounding us like a warning that winter was coming. He guided me to the side slightly, and I felt a blast of heat, which meant we were heading indoors. Less than a minute later, I felt a familiar chill wash over my skin, accompanied by an ever-present scent of industrial cleaners and dirty hockey gear.

My eyes flew open, and I looked at Theo's smiling face.

"You brought me to… work?" I squeaked in surprise.

I scrunched up my nose, confused.

"Baby, we're here to right a horrible oversight and check something off that list of yours at the same time." He grinned.

Shock zipped up my spine at the thought of him reading my life to-do list that lived its rumpled life in the inner pocket of whatever bag I was carrying. It was super embarrassing that he knew how much I'd missed out on in my childhood.

"When the heck did you see my list?" My cheeks heated.

It was only the deeply ingrained sense of control I'd honed through years of rigid social training throughout my childhood that stopped me from stomping my foot like a toddler. Or worse, crying from the cringe feeling of wanting so badly to be "normal" that I'd made a list to try to achieve it.

"Hey. Hey." Theo's hands gently grabbed both my shoulders, giving me a reassuring squeeze. "You don't need to be embarrassed. It fell out of your bag when I was rifling through your kitchen looking for painkillers when you were sick. I wasn't snooping… much. But I'm not sorry that I found it."

"Hmnph." I crossed my arms, not wanting to admit that I may or may not be pouting slightly. How did Theo get me to drop my guards like this?

"That list is about the most adorable thing I've ever seen in my life," Theo continued. His smile was sweet.

Apparently, I'd been having more of a moment than I thought, seeing as I hadn't noticed Theo move from my side to right in front of me.

"But… skating isn't on my list!" I blamed my slow processing of the situation on the minor humiliation I was experiencing. I may have been drunk when I wrote it back in college, but I'd read it over so many times when I was feeling down that I knew it by heart.

"It is," he argued.

"Is not," I shot back, just barely refraining from sticking out my tongue at him.

"Check again." He grinned, confident in his position. He moved his hands off my shoulders and nodded at my bag as if I didn't know the exact location of my own list.

When I didn't move, he crossed his arms and gave me a wry smile. "Humor me. Please?" His posture suggested that he would be willing to wait me out.

Geez. Maybe I was rubbing off on him or something. Why did he care about this so much?

Keen to settle this, I opened my bag and retrieved the list.

I held the familiar wrinkled paper in my hand, scanning down my handwriting until I got to number twenty-four, where the penmanship changed.

Scribbled in a different color were the words:

24. Learn to skate with the best (and hottest) teacher in the world.

My god, he'd written his own item. Gah.

I looked up under my eyelashes and gave Theo a sweet smile. "You're right. It's on there."

When I didn't say anything else, Theo tilted his head like those confused puppies that go viral on social media and smiled warily back at me.

"That's it?" he asked.

"Yep." I shrugged. Our previous interactions had him expecting more from me, as he should. I was busy cooking up a way to drive him crazy.

"Huh. Should we get this show on the road, then? We have the place to ourselves." Theo gestured to the empty arena behind him. "No one will bother us."

I straightened my shoulders slightly, now meeting his gaze full-on. "We could…" I paused. "There's just one problem." I held our eye contact for a few seconds before I looked down at the list in my hand.

His shoulders relaxed. "Baby, don't worry that you don't have skates. I ordered some for you."

Oh, you poor, sweet man. "No, Theo. It's not the skates." I brought the list back up to reading level and recited the words. "It says here, 'Learn to skate with the best (and *hottest*) teacher in the world.'"

I made a show of looking around us and widened my eyes to give off an air of complete innocence. "So when is Campbell going to get here? Or is Andrews coming?"

It took a couple of seconds for him to realize the burn I'd just given him, but then an honest-to-god growl came out of Theo's mouth. He stepped forward, gripped my waist, and tugged me until our bodies were pressed together. Taken off guard, I let him manhandle me.

He leaned down until our foreheads were pressed together and spoke his next words with his lips brushing mine on every syllable.

"No, Rocky. No one else is coming. You're mine. Haven't you figured that out yet?" Theo nipped my bottom lip before he continued. "And it's too soon to joke about any kind of shit with

Andrews, eh? I know Campbell doesn't have a chance in hell with a woman of your caliber. But I'm not ready to hear about the kid who was attractive enough to catch your eye. You feel me?"

Instead of letting me reply, he captured my lips with his. There was no slow buildup in this kiss. Theo thrust his tongue into my mouth and owned every inch he could reach. His lips were probably illegal in forty-eight of the fifty states, and that's why the NHL sent him to Canada to play. His kisses were so intoxicating that he was a matter of national security.

My hands moved up around his shoulders to grip the hair at the back of his neck. He may have caught me on the defensive with his initial attack, but I could give as good as I got.

Another growl rumbled in his throat as I tangled my tongue with his. We battled for control of the growing heat between us.

But if we didn't stop, I was going to end up fucking him against the hallway of our workplace, and that couldn't happen. And I was weak enough for him to admit that the only thing that made me pull back was the sliver of rationality around the security cameras.

Not finished yet, Theo chased after me as I withdrew from the kiss. He chose to repay me in kind by diving to one side of my neck and nipping the skin above my jugular with enough pressure that I wouldn't be surprised to find faint teeth marks in the morning when I looked in the mirror.

Theo very gently bit my chin on his way to the other side of my neck. Now, his feral kisses had mellowed to long sucks with his tongue. It felt incredible, but we should stop.

I realized that I was still pulling him closer to me with my hands at the back of his neck, so I slid them to his shoulder and rasped out his name.

He pulled back with a dazed look on his face that showed me that we'd both gone further than we intended to with our little battle of wills.

"You didn't answer me, baby. You feel me?" With his eyes more focused, a smirk formed on his mouth. He pushed his hard length against my belly button.

"I feel you, *baby*. But we can't do this here. It's my job and yours too." I reached down with one hand and gripped him over his jeans. He rutted his denim-covered cock against my hand for a second before moving back with a groan.

"Fuck, you're right. We're here for you. And I can't lie, I can't have my girlfriend out there in the world not knowing how to skate. But damn, baby. I want to take you back to your place so badly," he rasped.

Girlfriend. Did he just call me his girlfriend?

Twenty-Nine

THEO

The shock on Indie's face would have been humorous in any other circumstances. But we hadn't ever talked about what we were really doing here. I'd been chickenshit about bringing it up, not wanting to scare her off. And here I'd gone and just blurted it out like some inexperienced teenager.

But I didn't want to take it back. Being my girlfriend was just the beginning of the future I saw with Indie. So I let the words land and waited for her reaction.

Her surprise gave way to a look of uncertainty I wasn't sure I'd ever seen her wear. My heart responded to her expression by attempting to beat its way out of my chest and to lay itself at her feet.

The skittishness in her eyes did not read, "I can't wait to be Theo's girlfriend!" but more, "I'm not sure about what's happening right now?"

I'd weathered a lot of nos in my time. Indie's rejection of making our relationship official would hurt, but it was better to know now.

Her golden-brown eyes searched my face for something. I couldn't tell if she found what she was looking for, but when she took a deep breath, I steeled myself for the brush-off.

"Yes. Okay," she answered, more color pinkening her cheeks. She was adorable when she wasn't totally sure of herself.

Jesus. What a pair we made. We were thirty-one and twenty-five, respectively. Why did this make me feel like I had no idea what I was doing?

It's harder when it matters, Yao. This woman has the power to really hurt you.

I tucked that inconvenient truth away for later as her answer finally sank in. I was two-for-two tonight in taking too long to realize what she had said. I couldn't even blame hockey because I'd only had two concussions in my whole career.

"Yes?" My voice came out at half volume, as if I was about to break whatever magic spell that had made her agree.

Her smile had regained its snarky edge, and her eyes had turned sly once more. She was cooking up something I was either going to love or hate, but I was here for it either way.

You are so gone for this woman, Yao.

"Yes. I'll be your girlfriend, Theo." This time, her tone sounded sure. "I want that. But…"

I squeezed her hips gently as I mock groaned. "A catch, of course. What is the 'but' here, Ms. Layne? Other than this excellent pair of cheeks I look forward to getting better acquainted with."

I let my hands slip down to cup her ass, tugging her against me so we were pressed together, torso to thighs again.

Indie gave my hair a little pull with one of her hands. The sting just made me want to get my teeth on her again.

"Just listen, goalie. I'm saying yes, but I want you to promise me that I get to be the one who decides when we tell people about us." She narrowed her eyes in warning. "We work together. I need to clear this with Jermaine first. I don't want you going all ice Neanderthal and shouting our business to the whole locker room because you don't want anyone looking at me."

"Hey. That's offensive, baby. What's an ice Neanderthal, anyway?" I would have put my hands up in a gesture of surrender, but I couldn't make myself let go of her peach of an ass.

She let go of my hair with her right hand and brought it around and poked me on the tip of my nose like I was a misbehaving pet.

"An ice Neanderthal is a special breed of dumbass whose brain has been frozen and thus thinks with his dick instead of his head. Oh, and he also demands his female counterpart only wear his jersey number."

A chuckle rumbled in my chest. If Indie was conscious, she was keeping me on my toes. The only time my mind didn't have to race to keep up with her was when she was asleep in my arms.

"I'm pretty sure that's not a thing, Ind." The smile on my face ruined any possibility of convincing her she'd actually insulted me.

"It's a thing if I say it's a thing, Theo. And don't lie. You're more territorial than Giz, and that's what Chihuahuas are known for! First, you're all fired up about me hanging out in Connor's hotel room. Then, you steal the hoodie that he lent me and replaced it with *three* of your own. You'd love nothing more than to rub it in his face, even though he and I are just friends." She arched an eyebrow as if daring me to disagree.

"Fair." I couldn't deny her words. My lower lip might have jutted out in a slight pout at being called out on my less-than-rational behavior.

She pressed a hard kiss to my lips. "Just don't piss a circle around me, and we'll be fine. But most importantly, *I* get to be the one to tell Emery about us. No more of this calling her up out of nowhere. If you really want to make a go of this, I need to make sure my friendship with Em is okay first."

"Even though she's my sister *and* we're all adults *and* we don't actually have to justify our choices to anyone, I can agree to that." She could have asked for anything in this moment, and I would have given it to her. The reality of us being official had my chest swelling with an excitement I hadn't felt in years.

"Good. Now, you and all those 'ands' better move this date along before I change my mind on the whole girlfriend thing, hmm?" The teasing look in her eyes reassured me that we were back to our usual banter.

Her bluntness made me laugh as I moved back far enough from her too-tempting body.

"Shall we?" I held out my hand like I was some gentleman from a Regency-era TV show.

Indie rolled her eyes but still placed her hand in mine. "Yes! That's what I've been saying."

I wasted no time in entwining our fingers and led her through the hallways and into the locker room.

The smell of whatever cleaning supplies maintenance used couldn't quite cover the scent of a bunch of sweaty hockey players and their equipment and had Indie wrinkling her nose after the locker room door was shut behind us.

"Let me get you into your skates and out of here. The air is much fresher on the ice," I reassured her. No matter how many times I stepped on the ice, the cool air in my lungs never failed to wake up my mind and body.

Hockey and skating were such a huge part of my life. I wanted Indie to experience it with me rather than as a job on the sidelines merely gathering a set of data points that needed to be posted to social media.

Indie settled into my bench space. Next to her were the two pairs of skates I'd arranged for player services to leave for me.

I knelt in front of her, ignoring the small twinge in my knees from the action.

I grabbed the brand-new pair of figure skates that I'd ordered for her and undid the laces. A part of me had considered getting her hockey skates, but I'd guessed that she might prefer the toe pick and a longer blade for balance.

I looked up to see Indie watching me carefully. "Foot," I said and held up my hand to the level of her calf, a mirror image of the way I'd just asked for her hand back in the hallway.

She toed off her boots and set a socked foot in my hand.

"Thanks, Cinderella. We'll get you laced up and skating by the end of the night." I winked at her before sliding her foot into the stiff leather of the skate.

"The scent in here leaves something to be desired. But, I have to say, the view is pretty damn good." I met her gaze to see her smiling down at me.

"Like me on my knees, do you?" I cocked an eyebrow at her while I gave her skate laces a particularly forceful yank to tighten them.

"Yes, I do. As long as it's only for me." The snark in her tone melted into a seductive purr. Her eyes never left my face.

"Anytime, anyplace, baby. I could spend hours down here." I gave her one knee a soft kiss while I held her laced skate flat on the floor. The last thing I wanted was a sharp toe pick in my junk.

She leaned down in a rare moment of quiet, and I brushed my lips over hers before she sat back up again.

"Okay, Prince Charming. Chop, chop with the laces already. We haven't got all night." She winked playfully.

I laughed as I dutifully worked on her other skate, lacing it much more quickly than the first before sitting beside her to make quick work of my own skates.

"Let the embarrassment begin," she murmured as she pushed herself to standing. Her ankles promptly went askew when she tried to take her first step on the rubberized floor.

"Whoa, Gretzky. Take it easy. Let yourself get used to the feeling of the skates." My hand hovered behind her back to catch her, and I hoped she wouldn't notice.

"Am I supposed to know who that is?" Indie was half a step ahead of me as we moved toward the door, with her focused on taking careful footsteps.

Her answer had my movements stalling. "Seriously?" I was shocked. I was dating someone who hadn't heard of arguably the most famous hockey player of all time.

She turned her head so I could see her profile and stuck her tongue out at me. "I may not have known anything about hockey before coming to Toronto, but I know who Gretzky is."

Indie reached the door that led to the players' entrance to the ice and managed to pull it back without stumbling. I reached over her head and grabbed the side of the door so she wouldn't lose her balance.

She looked up into my eyes and said, "I mean, his daughter had that beautiful magazine spread for her wedding. Who wouldn't have heard of him after that?" before she ducked under my arm to get out the door.

Thirty

INDIE

The cold seeped through my jeans after landing on my ass for the third time in less than half an hour.

Who invented skating anyway? Someone just up and decided to strap knives to their boots to make an already difficult task to walk on a slippery surface even slipperier?

Ten feet away, Theo skated backward like he wasn't the biggest show-off in the universe. How dare he make skating look as easy as breathing when he did it.

"You okay, baby?" Amusement tugged at his lips; he was wise enough to keep any laughter inside. "You're getting the hang of it, I promise. You sure you don't want me to hold your hand?"

The hands that were currently holding me apart from meeting the icy, concussed fate that waited for me two feet lower? Not likely. Yeah, I should have taken him up on that hand-holding thing when we'd first stepped on the ice, but I honestly hadn't thought it would be this tricky.

"Yeah, right." I sulked, still not game to attempt to stand up.

"Well, when I first started CanSkate, the first thing they did teach us was to… fall." His infuriatingly handsome face made it hard to even pretend to be annoyed with him for very long.

Theo skated around behind me and pulled me (or scooped me; it happened with entirely too much ease) back to standing.

He held out his hand, palm up, not saying anything that would make me admit that I really did want his help. That soft, marshmallowy feeling ballooned in my chest again. It pressed up all the sharp edges of the feelings I kept buried deep.

With a sigh, I put my gloved hand in his bare one.

I wanted to distract him from my hopeless skating skills. Not being immediately good at something rankled. This kind of thing rarely happened to me. I hadn't failed so spectacularly at something since Emery tried to teach me to paint landscapes. My painting had looked more like Mr. Potato Head than a scene of mountains. I hadn't picked up a paintbrush since.

There was nothing wrong with sticking with things I was good at.

I turned my head just enough that I could look Theo in the eye. Even with him holding my hand, I didn't want to upset the gods of balance that he'd just restored by holding me steady.

There was no need to tempt chaos by doing something as crazy as… moving. Breathing seemed like a stretch at this point.

Could a bruised ass hurt when I breathed? It seemed like it.

"You learned to skate here?" I was confused. We'd both spent our childhoods in the suburbs of San Jose. I'd assumed that Theo had learned at one of the arenas in the city.

The expression in his eyes softened, but his jaw clenched minutely. He cleared his throat before speaking.

"Uh, yeah. Not here in Toronto, I mean. But Vancouver, yes." He paused on another inhale. "I don't remember exactly why, but Mom was still working jointly with the University of British Columbia, even though she'd officially left her adjunct professor position there." He rubbed the back of his head, looking a bit uncomfortable with the turn in conversation.

I didn't know if it was right or wrong to talk about his mom. I'd loved Alice too, but Emery rarely wanted to discuss her mom, and I wondered if Theo was the same. On the other hand, what if he wanted to and he never had anyone to listen before?

"I don't want to upset you, Theo. You don't have to tell me more unless… you want to?" I kept my tone soft but wanted to show him I *was* here to listen if he wanted to share with me. I looked up at him from under my eyelashes, trying to show I was paying attention but not staring at him as if he were under a spotlight.

Why the hell was it so hard to communicate sympathy-empathy-understanding-protectiveness-openness-true-interest in just a few words? There was that messy, gooey feeling again.

Theo turned his head to look me in the eye. "No, it's okay. I want to tell you."

I didn't say anything in reply, not wanting to fill the space between us with empty words. It felt surreal to have Theo being this vulnerable. I was afraid if I breathed the wrong way, I would screw up the moment.

"So, yeah. Mom was back up in Vancouver for whatever reason for a couple months, I guess? Since it was the fall and the height of Dad's football coaching season, she brought me with her, and I stayed with Gong Gong during the day while she was at work." Theo's voice was quiet; the only competing sound was the scraping of his blades on the ice.

Because, let's face it, he towed me along more than I was actually moving my feet at this point. My knees were locked straight, despite his previous reminders to keep them loose.

I'd only had the chance to meet Theo's grandfather once during a quick girls' trip with Emery and Abbie. What I did know was that he'd been Theo's biggest fan.

Theo's lips tightened briefly. "Having a three-year-old in the house full-time must have been a big change. But I never remember him getting frustrated with me. Anyway, somehow, he or Mom must have thought skating lessons would be a good activity to keep me busy. He and Por Por had emigrated to Canada before Mom was born, but neither of them had been skating before. Somehow, Gong Gong sweet-talked the instructors to let him learn along with me. I don't know if Mom ever knew about that part..." He laughed. "God, as an adult, all I can think now is we were lucky he never fell and broke his hip or something."

I squeezed his bicep that I'd been holding on to for dear life but offered him a gentle smile.

"I think it's pretty amazing that he would do that for you. From what I've seen, adults typically don't really go out of their comfort zone unless it really matters." I couldn't think of one thing my parents had ever changed with me in mind.

"And then skating lessons led to hockey the following winter." He smiled.

I left his relationship with his dad alone. There were enough difficult emotions coming to the surface for a first date.

Hell, I'd pretended to date a guy throughout my four years of college in order to keep my parents off my back, and we'd never shared a single childhood story with each other. That could have been because our parents were family friends and we'd basically lived the same life, but we'd never gotten past complimenting the other's appearance on our many "dates."

A thought leaped to the front of my mind. "Didn't your Gong Gong go to all of your home games?" I bit my bottom lip after asking, afraid I had just made Theo sadder.

He reached up with his free hand and gently tugged my lips from between my teeth, brushing his hand along my jaw on its retreat back to his side.

"Don't worry. You're not going to upset me. And to answer your question, yeah, he did. I had a standing season ticket for him from my very first game with the Frost. He even tried to make it to most of my games up in Abbotsford. I'd try to tell him that it was too far for game days, but he always said that the drive was worth it. And I'd always cook him a terrible breakfast before he drove back the next day. He never complained, and I never gave him food poisoning, so that was a win."

I laughed. "Yeah, I can't cook either. If I can't buy it precooked or eat it raw, it just doesn't happen."

"I know." Theo smiled warmly. "It's on your list."

"Ugh." I wanted to rub my face in embarrassment, but I dared not let go of the pillar of stability next to me. "I wish you hadn't seen that."

"I'm glad I did." Theo was unrepentant in his purse-sleuthing activities. "I'd go with you, you know. Somewhere we could learn not to poison people with our cooking."

The thought of Theo in an apron and an oversized chef's hat had me smiling at him in return.

"I'll think about it," I offered.

"Okay, are you ready to try this on your own again?" he asked.

I realized he'd taken us on a full loop of the rink while we'd been talking.

"No. Can't you just pull me over to the side? I bet it would be great to watch you skate from the players' bench?" I looked at him hopefully.

"Nice try. Give it one more go, and then I'll take you home, okay?" He gently detangled his arm from my death grip as he spoke.

Damn it. He didn't fall for my charm. That was the trouble with knowing someone from childhood—they knew all your tricks, even if we hadn't seen each other in years.

"Fine." I steeled myself for another fall. Trying to keep my knees from locking straight again, I pushed myself a few inches forward before looking back at Theo. "But you are taking Giz out for her walk for me when we get home." I jabbed a finger in his direction to let him know I was serious.

Unfortunately, my arm threw me off-balance, and I fell on my ass. *Again.*

"This is your fault." I glared at Theo in the mirror, switching between staring at the beginnings of a bruise that was bigger than both my hands that had started to form on the lower-right side of my ass cheek and continued around to the top side of my thigh. The dark red mark had already started to turn purple.

Theo, down to his boxers and a T-shirt, leaned against the headboard of my bed. Giz was lying next to his thigh, both having just come back from their walk while I got ready to shower. His gaze, firmly fixed on the bare skin of my ass that was revealed by my thong, darted quickly up to mine before returning to my backside.

"I'm sorry you're hurting. But as long as your beautiful ass cheeks are in front of me, I can't think of anything else but getting my hands on them." He licked his lips, and his stare became more intense.

I grabbed the sides of my thong and pulled it by the sides out and away from my bruised flesh. Just to fuck with him, I bent over almost until my fingertips touched my toes and stepped out of the flimsy black silk one foot at a time. I widened my legs when I removed the garment from each leg. I made sure to show him the full menu I had on offer. Too bad he wouldn't be dining at this restaurant tonight.

"God-fucking-damnit-shit!" The pained curses rolled off Theo's tongue like they were one word he was groaning instead of many. "Rocky, what are you doing to me?" His tone turned growly. Mmm, my favorite.

I stuck my ass out for his maximum viewing pleasure as I slowly brought myself back to standing. Once I was upright, I met his eyes in the mirror. A glance at his groin showed his dark navy boxers tenting obscenely as he gripped the base of his now rigid length over the fabric.

He reached over to my side of the bed with his free hand and put my pillow in front of Giz, who was so little that she was hidden completely.

"Jesus, Rocky. She is just a baby. We can't expose her to this kind of thing." He gestured to my now hidden pup behind the white pillow, sweeping his hand toward his erection and then to my bare ass. "Just let me put her in her bed in the living room and…"

I made an exaggerated O shape with my mouth, bringing my hands to my bra, the only remaining piece of clothing I had on. I turned to face him while reaching around behind my back to release the clasp.

The bra fell to the ground with my other clothing. Theo made another low sound in his throat and put his arms on the bed to push himself up.

"I'm just going to grab a shower. You know, get as much hot water on these sore spots as possible." I gestured to my ass. "No need to move Giz. You just relax, and I'll be back in a bit to *sleep*." I channeled my inner cartoon villain.

If he thought he was getting lucky tonight after bruise-a-palooza, he had another thing coming. As in, a matching set of blue balls. Not the kind of coming he had in mind.

A laugh escaped me when he flopped back onto the side of the bed he seemed to have claimed and earned himself a startled little growl from Giz.

I heard his petulant whisper as I crossed the threshold into the ensuite.

"Sorry, baby girl. I didn't mean to scare you. You're okay. But your mommy is super mean, did you know that?"

Thirty-One

THEO

Unfortunately, the potential of taking a cooking class together never materialized. Indie and I had managed only a handful of days and nights together, never mind knocking anything else off her list, for the remainder of the month. Never had I felt the demands of my career more than those thirty days.

Now, in mid-December, I was home for a couple of days and actually sitting in Indie's apartment in the daylight hours. It felt like a luxury.

With Gizmo on my lap (or a partial section of one thigh, for all the space she took up), I watched Indie open the blinds in her apartment with a huff.

"What's wrong, babe?" I hadn't pressed her on how hard the last month had been for her in our newly minted relationship, afraid that her answer would be that she missed me a lot less than I did her.

She glared at the window again and turned around, crossing her arms. The gray sky of the December morning framed her in its murky light.

She walked up to the counter and picked up a mug before putting it down again and pointing her finger at me.

"Here's what I want to know." Uh-oh. What had I done? I did the panic search of my brain to see if I'd annoyed her by doing any of her pet peeves recently. Towels on the floor? Nope. Spending too much money on dog toys when Giz only liked to knock over empty plastic water bottles with her paw? Nope (mostly, anyway). Toilet seat up? Nope.

"It's December in Canada, right?" I nodded, even though I wasn't following. Indie slapped her hands down on the counter. "Then, tell me. Where the hell is the snow?"

Her mouth formed an adorable little frown as she glanced out the window again. Oh, god, she was cute. My Rocky was mad because she'd expected it to be winter already.

It seemed to take her a moment to realize that her tone sounded like an eight-year-old wanting a snow day off school, and she mumbled, "Ugh. Never mind," and moved over to the coffee machine to prepare coffee I wasn't sure she wanted.

Carefully, sliding a hand under Giz, who startled at the feel of my cold hand on her peach-fuzz-covered skin, I lifted her onto a pillow before I got up to join Indie in the kitchen.

When I reached her, I pressed myself against the back of her body and wrapped my arms around her middle.

Indie so rarely gave me glimpses of her unguarded self, like she had just a moment ago. I wanted her to *want* to share more of her unfiltered thoughts with me.

I nuzzled my nose into her hair, which was still messy from our midmorning wake-up.

"You were hoping for snow, eh?" I mentally ran through her list and tried to remember if anything on it required snow.

She slowly measured out the coffee grounds and shook her head. "It's stupid. Forget I said anything."

I kissed the top of her head before gently grasping her shoulders to encourage her to turn around and look at me.

"It's not. I get it. I still remember the first big snowfall after I moved up to Abbotsford. It was enough to slow down the city for a couple days. Shoveling the driveway of the rental house I shared with a couple of teammates, though, got old pretty fast." I spoke quietly, hoping she would open up to me.

"Yeah, I guess I was thinking about how nice it would be to see why people go on and on about how great a white Christmas is. I figured, if I'm only here for the year, that was the thing I was most looking forward to." She shrugged again.

Another thing we hadn't talked about was the future. Not a single word about what would happen after this season.

How many things are you going to put off asking her about because you're afraid to hear what her answers are?

I pushed my inner Jiminy Cricket aside and focused on the problem I could solve right now: Indie was going to stay in Toronto for Christmas alone?

The thought of her being alone thousands of miles away from home was another blow. The realization was like taking a slapshot to the chest without my gear.

She didn't even sound sad about it. Just like it was a given that she wouldn't be going home or that it hadn't crossed her mind.

"Come home with me." The words were out before I thought about them.

For all I'd missed over the years, I usually made it home for Christmas Eve or Day, depending on the game schedule.

Indie had stopped coming to spend Christmas with my family

after that disaster Christmas morning when she was nineteen. In the years that followed, if the topic came up, Emery had said that Indie had other plans.

But had that been true? What if she had spent the last six Christmases *alone*?

But did I want to take my words back? No. I wanted her to come home with me, as a couple, and for her to feel the comfort she used to in my parents' house. Even if she had kept her distance over the past several years, I knew my dad and siblings still considered her part of the family.

Indie's gaze whipped to mine. "What?"

I let my hands settle on her hips. Damn, I loved the feel of this soft-as-hell pajama set now that I knew I was the only one seeing her in it. I couldn't stop my thumbs from making slow circles where they rested against her hip bones.

"You heard me, baby. Come home with me for Christmas." I held eye contact with her as I repeated my invitation.

"This isn't funny, goalie." She crossed her arms, an uneasy expression on her face. Her lips tightened into a half grimace.

Another bruise of hurt formed on my heart, for her and myself, with her defensive stance.

My first instinct was to take it personally that she thought I was the kind of guy who would joke about wanting to take her home to my family. Because that's what this would be, *me* taking her home. Not simply Emery bringing her best friend home for Christmas when Indie's parents put their careers ahead of their daughter.

This was me bringing home the woman I was falling in love with—despite her efforts to keep this relationship as something manageable in her mind—for the first time. The person I saw involved in the decisions I was soon going to have to make about my future in the NHL and elsewhere in my life.

But this was not about me. She either couldn't understand why I would seriously want her to come home with me, or it hadn't occurred to her that this was something that I would want.

Both options absolutely shredded my heart because she deserved to believe in how much she was wanted. And not just by me. She had always had a true family in Emery and Abbie. I couldn't believe that she didn't see that?

"I'm not joking." She tried to break out of the loose hold I had on her hips. I let her go, only to cage her in by moving my hands to grip the countertop behind her.

Indie huffed with frustration. "Come on, Theo. I'm serious. Move." She pressed her palms against my chest and applied a little bit of pressure, not nearly the kind of force that would dislodge the obstacle of my body in front of hers.

I leaned into her hands and brought my forehead down to hers. Her eyes closed with my movements. Good, maybe it would be easier for her to hear me if she didn't have to make eye contact.

"Come home with me. As my girlfriend. I don't want to go back without you. It's our first Christmas together." This time, my words whispered in the intimate cocoon of the short distance of my lips to hers.

"I don't understand why you are doing this." Her words were barely more than a whoosh of air, nearly inaudible. But to my ears, they roared louder than the crowds that filled the arena on game nights.

If she reached inside me, gripped my heart with both her hands, and squeezed with all her strength, she wouldn't have been able to match the crushing pressure in my chest at her question.

Fuck. What was it about her that could tear me apart so easily? How had I never seen how tender her insides were?

I needed a minute to compose myself so I wouldn't go off in a rage at the two completely useless, selfish fuckheads of flesh that she had to call her parents.

I kissed her forehead instead and let the anger at her history that I couldn't change simmer down.

"Can you look at me, Rocky?" Despite the sadness for her childhood self, whose wound was still raw inside her, my nickname for her could still bring a curve to one side of her lips.

We parted only enough to be able to see each other clearly. I let go of the counter and cupped her chin with my hands so that she wouldn't look away.

"This—us—is happening, baby. That means where I go, I want you with me whenever that is possible. You know what Christmas is like at my house. It's Emery's favorite. She goes all out every year because it's the only time she can get us all in the same room at once. It's the only time where we talk about Mom, and it's like she's..." My voice was caught in my throat with the sudden emotion. "There with us. And if you are really going to try this with me, as my girlfriend, then of course I want you there."

"You're lethal, Theo. Who could say no to that?" Her smile wobbled slightly, like her instincts wanted to hold her back from really feeling that she was wanted.

"Hopefully not you, Ind." My gaze didn't falter. I hoped she could see in my eyes that I was telling her the truth.

"Okay, but..." she started, and I groaned. Indie gave my pec a little pinch.

"Ouch! What's that for?" That shit smarted.

She rubbed the spot where she had just assaulted and looked into my eyes. "It's not my fault you can't listen."

"I can't listen! Oh, *that's* rich, baby..." I chuckled.

"Theo." She brought out the don't-fuck-with-me tone she'd used on the reporter, so I wisely shut up. "Emery doesn't know, remember? Do you recall that we agreed that I could be the one to tell her?" Indie cocked her head to the side slightly with her questions.

"Yeah, of course I do. You can. What's the problem? Just tell her." She'd need to spell it out for me. "You know what? Hold that thought. Let's sit down first."

I was done talking in the dim kitchen against a cold granite counter. I wanted my arms around her for whatever she was about to say. I'd remind her how good we felt physically together to make sure she felt how wanted she was if she was going to try to put me off.

I led her to the couch and pulled her down into my lap before she could sit on the opposite side of Giz, who was still snoring quietly in her fluffy little bed.

"Much better. I'm sorry for interrupting. What did you want to say?" I kissed her cheek and leaned back to meet her gaze again.

I knew this little maneuver was working wonderfully when the tension smoothed out of her features and her eyes softened with affection.

"What I was saying before I was so rudely interrupted—" She paused, giving me a look of playful admonishment. I widened my eyes in what I hoped resembled a look of innocence. "It's not simple just to tell Emery out of nowhere." She sighed.

I waited for her to continue, letting her put into words whatever it was that she wanted me to understand.

"My friendships with Emery and Abbie are literally all I have, Theo. Those two women are the only people I would go to war to protect." She brought one hand up to my cheek. "Until now."

I sucked in a breath at the implication of her statement. I mean, I had heard her tear that reporter a new asshole weeks ago, but she didn't know that. This was the first time she'd ever let me see a glimpse of the depth of her feelings. I wanted to tell her I'd heard her that day, but now wasn't the time.

Somewhat stunned, I could only nod in response.

"I know there's been stuff going on with Emery and your brothers. And I don't know what things are like with you and your dad. I'm not asking you to talk about it. But if you needed any of them, they would be there for you in a second. I don't have a family like that. On the other hand, I stay as fucking far away from my parents and their world as I can. So if I fuck up, it's on me. *I* handle my own shit."

She started smoothing my hair back from my forehead absently, lost in thought.

"You're right. My family are good people... But do you really think that Emery is going to mind that we're dating?" I watched her closely, keen to see any signs she was hiding anything.

"I don't *think* so," Indie admitted. "But, and it's a major but, there is a chance that she will be upset. There's a part of me that thinks she will see this as some sort of betrayal. Em was my first real friend and has been for two decades. And Theo, think about it: who's she going to ultimately side with if things go wrong?"

"You." There was no hesitation in my answer. I truly thought my sister would take Indie's side in every outcome I could imagine.

She laughed and brought her other hand up to my head so she could rub gentle circles against the skin beside my eyes while her hands threaded through my hair.

"That's a nice fantasy, goalie." She leaned down and gave me a kiss on my forehead like I was a kid who'd said something adorable. "But the hard truth is, family comes first. Hell, even with my absolute shitshow of a family, that's true. They just put the *idea* of the family name first rather than the actual people. But anyway, Emery would pick you. Then, poor Abbie would be stuck in the middle of a fight and forced to take sides. And there's nothing that girl hates more than conflict."

I wanted to say that she was more worried about hurting Emery and Abbie than herself, but I could see where she was coming from.

I also had some sense of self-preservation. Even if I thought I knew how things would turn out with Emery, there was no way to make Indie see my point of view.

It was the same reason why I never let myself get invested with my teammates in Vancouver, even after more than a decade with the Frost. Why invest in people I was just going to lose to a trade or retirement?

Yeah, and how did that work out for you? Thirty-one and just now seeing how you ensured your own loneliness all these years?

"So what do you want to do?" I wasn't sure if I was just asking about Christmas and telling Emery.

"Theo, I said I would tell Em. And I meant it. I just wasn't expecting to have a deadline put on it." I grimaced at the idea that she saw the whole thing as something that she was now being rushed into.

But would she do it if she didn't have this push? Seeing how concerned she was about the fallout, I was less certain than before I'd impulsively voiced the invitation.

She took a deep breath. "So yes, I will go home with you for Christmas. But…" She pursed her lips, considering. "I want to get a hotel room. I don't want to have this conversation with Emery over the phone. I owe it to her to look her in the eye when I tell her. The Tempests schedule gives us an extra day before Christmas Eve that we can stay over, and I can tell her."

Part of me had hoped she was going to call up Emery right this moment to get everything out in the open. But that was just me being impatient to feel more secure in our relationship. And from what Indie had said, it was the exact opposite of what she wanted and needed.

So I could continue being patient. I mirrored the way she was still holding my head by putting my hands through her hair and bringing her mouth to mine for a slow but deep kiss to seal my promise to wait for her to do things her way.

"Okay, Rocky. If that's what you want, that's what we'll do," I said after I pulled back from the kiss just long enough to let the words escape before returning my lips to hers.

Even if I'd had to collect every piece of good sense I accumulated over my entire life to navigate this conversation, her answering smile when she pulled back told me that I'd managed to say the right thing for once.

Thirty-Two

INDIE

Indie

> This was a dumb idea. I'm going to catch the next plane back after we land.

Connor

> Now that doesn't sound like the Indie I know.

Indie

> That Indie left her good sense at customs in Pearson Airport.

Connor

> If you can make a reporter piss his pants in fear and wrangle hockey players to their respective media obligations, you can talk to your friend. It'll be all good, you'll see.

Indie

> Nope. Not happening. I'm coming back

> **and I'll have Swiss Chalet for Xmas dinner.**

Connor

> **I'm beginning to think your phone has been hacked. The only fast food I've seen you consume is made with coffee beans and comes in a cup.**
>
> **TO THE HACKER OF INDIE'S PHONE—I don't make enough money to pay the ransom you are trying to extort here. You'd have better luck with Yao's account. He must be rich because he's practically geriatric after being in the league so long.**

Despite the great white shark of worry swimming in my stomach, Connor's texts had a small smile forming on my lips.

Only when I set my phone down did I feel the ache from gripping it so tightly my fingertips tingled mildly.

A warm, calloused hand enveloped mine where it now rested on my thigh, resisting the urge to fidget.

"What's got you smiling?" Theo whispered. His lips brushed my ear as they moved because he'd leaned in so close.

I held up the screen of my phone for him to read the exchange with Connor. Theo lingered in my space as he read through the texts.

"Way to throw a teammate under the bus, Andrews. What kind of loyalty is that?" He shifted back to his own side of the armrests that divided our seats.

Theo had insisted we fly business class, even though it wasn't something I did anymore because it made me feel like I was mirroring my parents' lifestyle.

He'd said he wanted me to be comfortable. For once, I didn't argue the principle of sitting in coach just because I made my decisions based on rejecting my parents' lifestyle.

Dating—whew, that was still a mind-bending concept—an NHL star came with some realities.

I'd joked that Theo Yao, the famous NHL goalie, could not be expected to fly in coach where he might be mobbed by an unknown number of rabid hockey fans, Canadian and American alike.

Plus, it meant lots more room for Gizmo's carrier, where she was currently sound asleep.

But the real reason I'd agreed was I'd noticed a few winces now and then after Theo played a particularly rough game. I'd wanted him to have the chance to recuperate as best as possible, and business class meant a lot of legroom.

I was very conscious of, ahem, the need for extra *legroom*. Theo definitely needed space for his… *large* lower appendages. I had to force myself to keep a small chuckle from escaping my mouth.

Great, not only are you an idiot for falling for him all over again, but all the sex you've been having has given you the sense of humor and maturity level of a fourteen-year-old boy.

"Baby?" Theo looked at me with a questioning gaze. He'd obviously said something I'd missed while thinking about giving up my principles to protect his *assets*.

God, his ass was a work of art too.

"Aw, Ind. It's really going to be okay. Em's not going to get mad at you, I promise. I bet, if anything, she's going to be thrilled, and then all this worry will evaporate." He moved our entwined hands from my thigh to his. I could feel the strong muscles underneath the designer black sweatpants he wore; the name of the specific sponsor was lost to the other thoughts swirling in my mind.

I needed another distraction. With my free hand, I tugged my airline-provided blanket further up and over so that it covered both our joined hands and both our laps. I leaned my head onto his shoulder, consciously ignoring the way the armrest dug into my rib cage.

Feeling unsettled was something I'd always squashed under the heel of whatever stylish shoe I happened to be wearing. I loathed the sensation of being out of control.

I gently detangled my fingers from Theo's and gripped as much of his thigh as my hand could reach, giving it a playful squeeze. "You'd bet on it, hmm?"

"For sure I would. Em will want us both to be happy." He kissed the top of my head sweetly. I *almost* felt bad for the diabolical act that was about to unfold.

"So…" I said while I dragged a finger over the soft, thick fabric of his sweats. "*What* would you bet exactly?" I tilted my head back so I could see the side of his face as I waited for him to catch on to my plan.

He glanced down at me, the side of his mouth I could see curved upward. "Like an actual bet? With stakes?"

I merely nodded, my fingertip continuing to graze his pants up toward his mid-thigh.

The competitor in him wouldn't be able to resist my challenge, and deciding the stakes would help me cope with the nerves that threatened to overwhelm me.

A quirked eyebrow completed the now intrigued expression as Theo shifted slightly in his seat to turn his head in my direction, but not enough to dislodge my head from where it leaned back against his taut shoulder muscles (nor did it stop my hand from continuing its trajectory toward its target).

"What do you have in mind?"

Taking in all his features at once was enough to scramble someone's brain if they were attracted to men. I was made of tougher stuff than most.

Goddamn, he was handsome, though.

"Whatever you want." I threw out the potentially limitless prize options to him. I returned his curious gaze with a sweet smile.

That should have raised all his alarms. But we were pretty cozy snuggled up under this blanket, and that made the anticipation of my sneak attack that much more satisfying.

His body jolted when my finger met its target. I knew I was on borrowed time with my inappropriate actions, so I was quick to add the rest of my fingers and palm to wrap around his cock.

"Rocky," he hissed but notably didn't do a damn thing to stop me. Maybe he wanted to see what I would do next.

I moved my hand up and down his length. As a man in peak physical condition, his circulation was top-tier as he immediately started to harden under my hand. I paused briefly at the tip of his length, which was now pressing upward against my hand, and rubbed my thumb over the sensitive underside of the head as much as the fabric separating our skin would allow.

"What?" I batted my eyelashes. "So what do you pick as the prize if Emery doesn't get upset about us?" His hips shifted slightly as I continued to alternate between firm and soft pressure against his fully hard appendage—that extra legroom sure came in handy. Good thing the blanket was up high enough on his chest, which gave me this room to play, or the flight attendants would be getting a show any second.

He moved as close to my ear as possible to whisper, "Can we please not say my sister's name while you have your hand on my cock?" Theo nipped the skin he'd pressed his lips against in retaliation. "Do you think I won't make you pay for this little stunt?"

This time, a laugh did break free. God, this was fun. It was easy to let go for a minute when I knew Theo would play along with whatever scheme I came up with. When was the last time I just got to enjoy something like this?

"I'm counting on it." I moved so that our lips were now pressed together. I took his bottom lip between my teeth and gave a particularly firm stroke to the rock-hard length in my hand.

He stifled his groan by pressing his lips firmly against mine and thrusting his tongue into my mouth and turned the moment from playful to hotter than hell within seconds.

There was only so far we could take this little game of arousal before a public indecency charge was added to our criminal records, and we'd hit that limit.

I pulled back to soften the kiss to little pecks and gave his cock a little "there, there" pat before I released it as an inelegant snort of laughter escaped me.

Theo grabbed my hand that had gone rogue, securing it in his once more. He gave it a warning squeeze that only made me laugh once again.

"I'm going to win this bet. And I'm going to enjoy every second of it."

I didn't mention that he hadn't set the terms yet, giving him a break because he was currently occupied with some deep breaths to relax the *largely* inconvenient situation he had going on down below.

Didn't stop him from giving me a stern look, which only served to send another sizzle of arousal through me.

I couldn't wait to see what he came up with.

Thirty-Three

INDIE

When the rideshare dropped me off in front of the familiar two-story home in Almaden Valley, for the first time in all my visits over the years, its warm stone exterior didn't spark excitement in me.

My rational brain recognized that Emery was literally the coolest, most giving person I knew.

Indie

Hey, Em. Check your porch.

Emery

I told you that you didn't need to worry about presents this year! Mailing stuff is such a pain. You shouldn't have!

Indie

Just check, okay?

Emery

Fine. Hold on.

Em's front down swung open and revealed my adorably disheveled best friend. She had blue paint on one cheek. It was watercolor, maybe, or some sort of acrylic mixture. Her hands were covered in graphite, so she added to her look when she brought her hands up to her cheeks in surprise.

"Did I break you?" My smile was timid, which was a direct contrast to the cheeky grin at surprising her any other day of our lives.

Em's giggle sounded somewhat unhinged once she got over the shock of seeing me at her door.

"I haven't slept properly in a week. Are you really here? Or am I manifesting your spirit as a distraction from my current artistic failure?" She reached out to hug me, but when her hands made it to her eye level, she discovered how dirty they were and hesitated.

"Come here." I wasn't afraid of getting dirty. Neither of us were really huggers. Emery, in particular, was very specific about that, but both our natural instincts seemed to be overridden because we'd never been separated for so long since we'd met.

This hug felt good.

"What are you doing here? Where's Gizmo?" She pulled back and held me by the shoulders. Em's brows furrowed, her eyes examining my face for clues as to why I was making this surprise appearance.

She definitely wasn't expecting me. After the third Christmas I turned her down, she'd stopped asking me to rejoin her family for the holidays. Respecting my needs, she'd never asked me why and instead just let it go.

"What's wrong?" She gave my shoulders a mild squeeze. "Did something happen? Oh my god. Are you okay? What did your parents do?" Her questions piled on top of each other so quickly that I hadn't had the chance to even answer her first one.

"Em. I'm okay. Everyone is. I have a hotel room, so Giz is chillin' out in four-star luxury right now. I just came to talk to you." I didn't mention that it was Theo who'd taken Giz in her carrier back to our hotel room with him when we'd parted at the airport.

"Yeah, sure. Come in, then." She turned to move through the threshold and then looked back when I didn't immediately follow. "You coming?"

"Yep. Can we talk somewhere private, though?" I didn't need her brothers to overhear this particular conversation.

"Tree house talk?" Em's eyebrows rose in question.

We hadn't been in her backyard tree house since we were about sixteen and Emery made us all go up there so she could tell us about having sex for the first time with her high school boyfriend.

Tree house talks were called for only the most secret and sacred reasons.

She led me around the side of the house and into the yard, where the tree house sat among the branches of the biggest tree in the yard.

"Ready?" she asked, looking back at me before she began to climb. At the top, she kind of tumbled inside, and I heard a muffled "ouch!"

"Coming? Shit, ow." Emery rubbed her forehead. "Watch your body parts when you get up here. I must have grown since the last time we used this thing. I don't remember having to bend my knees so much when I sat down."

If Emery struggled to sit at five foot four, I was going to have to crunch into a ball to fit since I was six inches taller than her.

I groaned internally, cursing the draw of the nostalgia I'd imagined was waiting for us up there. This might be one of those things that seemed like a great idea until it wasn't.

When I made it to the top, Emery had moved to the far side. There was a little bit of dirt in the corners, and the little stools and table Emery used to have were gone, but otherwise, it hadn't changed much since the three of us last squished in here at sixteen after our sophomore formal.

"So what's so important that we needed this level of secrecy?" Emery's gaze flitted all over me as if she'd find a clue somewhere on my person.

"Em. I don't know how to say this, really. But before I say it, I need to tell you how much your friendship has meant to me all these years." My eyes stung with the force of the emotions I held at bay.

Crying was not something I indulged in, but I couldn't stop my tear ducts from going rogue, threatening to blur my vision.

"Em. It's about Theo." Her eyes widened. I took a deep breath and forced the rest of the words out of my mouth. "You know how we're both in Toronto…"

Emery nodded, waiting for me to finish my thought.

"Well, we're kind of dating." I bit my lip nervously.

Her eyes remained too wide for a moment before she covered her face with her hands and pulled her knees in toward her body. She started shaking but not making any noise.

I didn't know what to do. Abbie was the cuddly one in our group. I was used to taking action. If she was upset with me, did I even have the right to comfort her?

"Em. I didn't mean to upset you," I rushed out.

Her head popped up, and she let out a peal of laughter so loud it made me afraid for the structural integrity of this twenty-year-old treehouse.

"Oh my god!" she gasped. Her shoulders shook with her laughter. "I thought… God, I thought that Theo had gotten you fired somehow and I was going to have to blacklist my most sane brother."

Stunned, I remained silent. Even if I'd been nervous, I'd known it was likely she would support me and Theo. But I hadn't expected the giggling.

Emery giggle-choked, trying to suck in more oxygen. "But you're just dating?" She managed to sound closer to her normal self. Her shoulders no longer shook.

"Just dating?" My mouth formed a shocked O. "You're not mad?" I watched her carefully, looking for any sign that she might not be telling the truth to save my feelings.

"Babe, you've always been my family." She reached out and patted my knee, giving a quick squeeze before returning it to her lap. "Also, you're an adult and can date whoever you want. So is Theo. And I love you both. Obviously, I want you both to be happy. Even if you are finding happiness with one of my idiot brothers. I'm unbelievably happy for you both! But are *you* happy? That's the most important thing here."

Filled with relief, I gave her a genuine smile.

"Yeah," I whispered, afraid that the universe might swipe it away from me if I spoke the words too loudly. "I am."

What I'd been feeling for Theo went beyond what I'd ever let myself feel before, and it was scary as fuck. It was so much easier to trust Emery and Abbie because not only did I have years of evidence that they were kind and loyal, but I'd still kept a part of myself separate all this time.

With Theo, my heart was wide open in a way that was out of my control. The same high that came with the happiness of being able to enjoy each other also came with the potential to be shoved off a cliff into a sea of heartbreak, and nobody had taught me to swim.

Emery extracted her phone from between her thigh and the wall of the tree house. She scrolled quickly and pressed a button.

"What are you doing? You're not calling Theo, are you? What are you going to say?" My questions had Emery giggling softly again.

"Calm down, Ind. I'm not calling Theo. I'm calling Abs. It's only fair she gets to find out about how Miss Love-Is-For-Idiots is just like the rest of us poor mortals. Though, I'm not gonna lie. I don't *hate* seeing you flustered. I almost want to video this moment for posterity." She grinned as the phone rang on speaker.

"Hello?" an out-of-breath Abbie answered after the fourth ring. "Emery? Is everything okay?" A few more gasps of breath accompanied her words.

"I'm fine, Abs. Everything okay on your side? I'm going to switch to video. Indie has some news." Emery pressed the video icon on her screen.

"Wait! Just give me two seconds." Emery and I stared at each other while we heard rustling and murmurs over the line.

"Oh my god. Do you think they were…" Emery's whispered, eyebrows raised.

"Were Abbie and Daddy Aiden fucking?" I winked. "Probably." Now, I was the one who was laughing. The uncertainty of the day had got to me, and I couldn't contain it anymore, especially because I could picture Aiden's grumpy face at being interrupted.

"I'm back." Abbie's face appeared on the screen. She definitely had just-fucked or just-about-to-get-to-the-fucking-part hair. Her normal long, lavender waves were frizzing out on one side more than the other, not to mention the scruff burns on her chin and neck.

"So you're having a good night." I batted my eyelashes at the screen, a Cheshire grin on my face. I couldn't help but enjoy teasing Abbie and, by extension, Aiden because they were so easy to rile up.

"Ind! You're so mean!" Emery swatted me on the shoulder closest to her. "Um, Abs. I didn't mean to, you know, interrupt your evening. You didn't need to answer if you were… busy."

"You never call, so it must be important." Abbie blushed, making it more obvious what she'd been up to just now.

In the far corner of Abbie's screen, Aiden walked by with his white dress shirt open and his own hair a mess. "Hey, Daddy!" I called out.

"Call me motherfucking 'Daddy' while you disturb my first night without overtime in weeks. I get home early, and then…" Aiden's mumbling drifted off in the background.

I cackled. "Oooo. Someone's mad. Is that going to be a good or a bad thing when we hang up, girl?"

"Shut up." Abbie stuck her tongue at me, not answering the question. But her cheeks got redder. "So what's up? And… are you two in the tree house?"

"Indie has a boyfriend!" Emery gushed. "She made me come up in the tree house because it was super-secret news, and she didn't want me screeching inside the house."

"What!" Abbie practically shouted, filling the tiny wooden box Emery and I sat in with her exclamation. "You haven't dated anyone since Wells in college! I can see why you asked for the tree house. Em, your brothers would have had a field day with this if they'd overheard you."

Oh crap. It was time to fess up.

"Er, yeah. About Wells. We didn't actually date." Twin expressions of surprise, one in person and the other on Emery's phone screen, were directed at me. "Our families kind of shoved us together. My parents were hounding me all the time to date someone of their choice, and he was the best option. We went out once, and there was nothing there. Wells came out as bisexual at the end of senior year, remember? He actually had a boyfriend since freshman year but didn't know what his stuck-up family would say." I shrugged.

"Why didn't you tell us? What about all those dates you went on?" Emery's superpower was the youngest-child pout. She was damn good at it too. It even worked on me. Looking into those big, sad eyes made me feel guilty.

"Well, um, I went to the library?" My statement ended with a questioning lilt. "I mean, earning double degrees was no joke. I got to study, and it got me out of tons of stupid fundraisers with my parents. There were so many events my parents assumed I was with Wells at a different one. Plus, it wasn't my news to share."

"That makes sense. I can't believe you kept that secret for all those years. You can trust us, you know." Abbie was quick to forgive.

"Sorry. But we got sidetracked there." Emery pointed at me with her free hand. "You are granted a temporary reprieve from the Wells thing. Abs, her fake ex isn't the real news!" She smiled wider. "It's *who* her boyfriend is that's the news. Try to guess."

"Aren't there like eight billion people in the world? How am I supposed to guess?" Abbie asked.

"It's Theo!" It was Emery's turn to shout. She was so loud that half the neighborhood knew who my boyfriend was now.

Abbie's eyes widened, and her eyebrows shot up in surprise. "You're right! That is way bigger news. Whew. Em, I'd never say this because it would have been weird before." Abbie dropped her voice to a whisper and glanced quickly at her surroundings. "Your brother is pretty damn hot."

"Sweetheart, what was that?" Aiden's voice called from another part of the house.

"Ohh, Daddy heard you, sweetheart," I teased, knowing Aiden had come a long way in being able to take a joke. With me as Abbie's friend, he'd had no choice, of course.

"Speaking of daddies, actually. Em, remind me how old Theo is?" Abbie grinned.

"He's thirty-one." She narrowed her eyes and looked between me next to her and Abbie on her screen.

"Well, that seems old enough to be a daddy, don't you think, Ind?" Abbie winked.

Emery made a fake vomiting noise, but I pretended not to hear.

"Well played, friend. You can ask him yourself next time you see him," I suggested.

"Maybe I will ask him. You'll see," Abbie insisted. She would not ask Theo. She'd burst into flames before those words would leave her lips. "We're leaving in the morning to spend Christmas with Aiden's family. Does that mean I'll miss you this trip?" Her lips turned down with her question.

"Yeah, I'm sorry, babe. Theo and I fly out on the twenty-seventh. Well, he's off to Denver for an away game, and I'm taking Giz back to Toronto."

Just then, Aiden said something in the background, but this time, we couldn't make out his words. Whatever it was, it had Abbie blushing again.

"Uh, okay. Text me. I gotta go. Love you!" With those words, she ended the call.

"I wonder if she's going to get spanked for thinking Theo is hot?" I wondered out loud.

"God, girl, your mind is filled with debauchery. Make sure you keep all those thoughts about my brother to yourself, okay? We're not *that* close." Emery scrunched her nose.

"Fair," I agreed.

Dropping her phone in her lap, Emery employed her superpower again, her eyes widening to the point she looked like an animated character. There wasn't a Disney Princess in existence that could top her sweet expression.

"Does that mean you and Theo are staying here for Christmas?"

Thirty-Four

THEO

Now is not the time to gloat over winning a stupid bet. So just keep that competitive shit under wraps. Just shut up and listen to whatever she wants to say.

Gizmo's head turned one way and then back the other as her stare followed my pacing in our hotel room.

"Listen, I'm not an idiot, okay? I know that was probably ridiculously hard for Rocky to force herself to do. I'm not even going to mention the bet. I mean, I know my sister and predicted that she wouldn't have a problem with me dating Indie. But I like my balls attached to my body, and fucking with your mommy is not on tonight's agenda."

My hands went out in front of me in a "you know what I mean?" kind of gesture. I stopped in front of Gizmo as she lay on not one but four stacked couch cushions. We'd discovered she liked the view from up high on the couch.

"Sorry for the swearing, baby girl. Though, with a mommy like yours, you'll be more fluent in profanity than any sailor, past or present." And I swear, Giz's eyebrow arched with judgment about my comments on Indie.

I flipped my hands over in a "take it easy" motion. "I'm not criticizing your mommy. It's just not my fault Indie uses profanity the way most people use punctuation."

Keeping my stare on Gizmo's face for any more objections on her part, I dropped my arms back to my side. "Where was I? Right." I started listing off the ways I could reassure Indie after her rough night.

"One, shut up and listen. Two, do not mention the bet. That was just to distract her from worrying about Emery, anyways. You're too young to know about these things." Gizmo let out a sigh.

"Three, room service or a bath?" I looked at my Chihuahua companion for her opinion. "You're right. I'll offer both. This is a very nice hotel—even if the pet damage deposit is going to be over one thousand dollars because they don't actually allow pets—that tub in the bathroom is the size of a small swimming pool. She might love it."

I moved over to the unoccupied edge of the couch, far enough away that I posed no risk to her tower of pillows, and sat down. Gizmo, confident that I was no threat to her comfortable bed, put her head down between her paws, her eyes half-closed. She was probably thrilled to have me shut up so she could catch some sleep.

I slouched further down into the couch so my head could lean on its back cushions. The reality of what Indie had done tonight started to hit me.

Jesus. She really chanced blowing up a friendship for you, *asshole.*

It didn't matter that *I* knew that Emery would be accepting of my relationship with Indie. It only mattered that Indie had been overly worried about it, no matter what her rational side said. She'd taken a huge risk for me. God, if things had turned out differently… Would Indie have been able to bear it?

My love for her grew exponentially with that realization. Without her having to say the words, her actions told me everything I needed to know about where we stood.

This was the real deal. For both of us.

It was like a physical weight pushed against my chest as I absorbed how big of a risk I'd ask Indie to take. Even during the biggest night of my life, draft night when I was eighteen, when all of us were still reeling from Mom's passing, I knew I had my dad and siblings behind me to fall back on.

My limbs sank under the weight of my actions.

The beeping sound of the hotel room door card reader drew me from my thoughts. I jumped to my feet, ready to hug the shit out of my Rocky for doing something so brave for us.

Similarly, Gizmo's little head and body popped up from her pillow. Her little tail wagged like crazy with her anticipation of her primary hooman coming home.

Not wanting to bombard Indie with questions, as that was the last thing she needed, I stood and waited as I heard her drop her bag and jacket on the front table around the corner from the living area of the hotel room.

She came into view, and I just managed to swoop down and catch Giz before she leaped off her pillow tower to see her mommy. God, this pup had no concept of her own size. She was three flipping feet or more above the marble floor of the hotel room. We didn't need a trip to the emergency vet tonight to round out the evening.

"Jesus, Giz. Do you think you're a Great Dane or something?" I admonished the vibrating ball of soft peach fuzz I held in one palm.

"Aww. Is your big, bad daddy getting my baby in trouble?" Indie smiled at Gizmo as she walked toward us.

Gizmo practically flew from my hand into Indie's chest when she got close enough, which caused Indie to rapidly rearrange her arms to secure her.

"What a little menace you are!" I wrapped both arms around Indie's waist, careful not to smoosh Giz, who was lapping up having all the attention. She promptly turned over in Indie's arms to make her status as the "little baby" complete.

"Hi." I moved my gaze from our dog to Indie's face and examined her features for signs of how she was feeling.

"Hi, goalie." She looked back at me, tired, but gave me what looked like a genuine smile.

"Let's sit. It's been a long day for you." I wrapped my arm around her shoulders to guide her to the couch. Gizmo remained content in her arms.

I quickly maneuvered myself back onto the couch and shifted so that Indie would sit on my lap rather than in the small space between me and the pile of pillows.

"Cushion tower?" She looked over at Gizmo's fortress and tucked her bare feet under the edge of the bottom pillow. Thankfully, she relaxed back into my arm that was wrapped around her waist, letting her head fall onto my shoulder.

I kissed her forehead. "Look, Gizmo demanded four pillows, okay? What am I supposed to do, refuse her the bare necessities that she needs to rest?"

The pup in question decided that we were in this cuddle pile for the long haul and started circling the divot where Indie's thigh and pelvis met. Once she plopped herself down, I brought my other hand from where it rested on the back of the couch down to pat her back with two fingers.

I felt more than heard Indie's laughter at my caving to the whims of a five-pound canine.

I hesitated to break the contentment we'd just created with them both in my lap, but my need to hear how everything had gone down won out.

If there were obstacles ahead with Indie, I wanted to know what I was up against. I shifted her closer by tightening my opposite arm around her, wanting to make it clear that she could let down her guard now that we were together.

"So, lay it on me, Rocky. How did it go?" I kept all of my initial relief and pleasure that she appeared okay, if emotionally exhausted, to myself for now.

I couldn't imagine Emery denying anyone their happiness. She was a champion at setting up random people in her life and watching them just "click" as couples. I knew she would want the same for Indie, even if she hadn't completely forgiven me for the last couple of years of keeping everyone at arm's length.

"Keen to find out how the next part of your night is going to go, babe?" Even said in jest, I wanted to wipe her mind of anything else but letting go of the stress she'd been feeling earlier.

"Ha. I'll let you in on a little secret, Rocky." I tilted my head down to speak next to her ear. "I already won the lottery the first time we kissed and every day since."

Indie shivered as my lips brushed the skin of her earlobe. I punctuated my words by pressing a soft kiss to her temple, getting a quick hit of the sweet scent of her shampoo and skin before leaning back again.

"Theo! You are not meant to be sweet right now." She swatted my arm playfully. "You're meant to be collecting your prize. Specifically, those things you texted me earlier."

My cock thought her idea was solid, and the blood flow in my body was roaring to assist, but I wasn't going to let myself get distracted. As much as my body was ready to show her how much I wanted her at any given moment, my brain pushed aside any sexy thoughts to hear what she had to say.

"My prize is sitting on my lap. So I'm doing pretty well. Seriously, Ind, tell me how it went." I gave her a gentle squeeze to urge her to keep talking.

Indie sucked in a deep breath, jostling Gizmo, who had fallen asleep almost instantly once she'd curled up—it was almost 2:00 a.m. Toronto time, after all. She snuffled a little bit with the movement of Indie's stomach.

"It was… fine." Her hesitation concerned me.

"Fine" didn't really tell me anything. Maybe I should have been the one to tell Emery to spare Indie this discomfort after all?

Before I could fall too far into the regret spiral for not sparing her from this situation, she continued.

"It really wasn't a thing. Em actually laughed." Indie shook her head as if she couldn't believe the words she was speaking. "She was happy for me—for us." Her final words came out as a whisper.

A surge of gratitude for my incredibly kindhearted sister ran through me and settled most of my worries. Having a gut feeling about Emery's reaction versus hearing it come true were totally different emotions. I was going to have to figure out how I could show my sister how important her understanding was.

Uneasy about breaking the spell of the moment, I forced the next words out of my mouth.

"How do *you* feel about the whole thing?" Indie was the queen of keeping her feelings close to her chest. Unless she was pissed off, it was hard to tell the depth of her emotions a lot of the time.

I couldn't let the subject drop without some insight into her thoughts. I wanted to be her person, in a different way than Emery and Abbie were, that she trusted with her scariest feelings. She needed to see that she could believe that I would help her carry them without demanding anything in return.

From Emery's updates, I knew Indie tended to take on the world for others. That earning the gift of having her rely on me would be something special. I wanted to be the person who helped her carry her load. And I would do just about anything to make it happen.

"I'm not sure, to be honest." She sighed, her head resting more firmly against my shoulder and her eyes shutting. "I kind of feel like I've been put through one of those pasta makers where the dough gets squished in there and then forced into a new shape."

Her head shifted slightly so her forehead was resting against the side of my neck. I waited for her to continue.

"In my head, I knew Em was going to be okay with it. She's literally the sweetest person in the entire state of California, if not the country. She'd never want either of us to deny ourselves the chance at being happy. But even knowing that, the uncertainty of messing with two decades of friendship felt much bigger than anything my brain could come up with to reassure me." She released another deep breath, like sharing her worry helped it leave her body at the same time.

As she spoke, her limbs felt like they were melting into mine. Each muscle that I hadn't even realized she'd been tensing released fiber by fiber, the toll of the situation seeming to leak out of her with each word.

There wasn't a single cell in my body that wanted to say, "I told you so." That stupid bet was just a distraction and had served its purpose. I racked my brain for the right thing to say that would show her all I cared about were her feelings right now.

"I can see how big of a risk that was now. Thank you for talking to

Emery, for both of us." My words felt too small for the significance of her choice, but it was the best I could come up with.

Indie pulled back slightly and opened her eyes. They looked clearer than before. A small smile formed on her lips.

"You're feeling really grateful, hmm?" The sly expression that she put on when she was feeling playful appeared on her face.

I bent my neck so I could reach her mouth and gave her a tender kiss. It was soft and short. I didn't want to take it any further than emphasizing how happy I was that she'd bet on us.

"Yep." I popped the *p* sound.

She raised her hand that wasn't cradling the little cinnamon bun that Giz had turned her body into and brought her fingertips to the neck of the T-shirt I was wearing, letting the tips of her index and middle finger drift back and forth under the neckline.

"So that sounds to me like you're inclined to give me anything I want at the moment, right?" Her tone was seductive.

I nodded, glad that she didn't know I was liable to give her anything she wanted at any moment.

"How about this, then… The little wager we made earlier in the day, you offer your prize to me?" The playfulness in her gaze turned heated.

My cock got right back in the game like it was the relief goalie getting called into a playoff game in overtime, thickening in my sweatpants so fast that there was no way she didn't notice.

She trailed her fingers from my throat down my chest and abs as far as she could reach before she carefully slid her hands under Gizmo. Indie stood slowly and lifted her back onto her pillow tower without startling her awake.

From her position above me, Indie arched an eyebrow when I didn't answer right away.

"Are you sure you don't just want to sleep? It's been a long day."

I scrutinized her expression, looking for a hint of uncertainty, but found none. I had to trust she knew what she wanted.

"Definitely not too tired." She held out her hand to me. There was nothing for me to do but take it and follow her into the bedroom of the suite.

Thirty-Five

INDIE

This moment was about as surreal as they came.

Having not set foot once in the Yao-Miller house since that disaster of a Christmas morning six years ago, walking toward the front door of Theo's family home felt like a pretty convincing out-of-body experience or hallucination.

Theo carried both our carry-on bags over the opposite shoulder to his hand that was currently holding mine as we walked from our rental car up their front walkway. Giz sniffed along the edge of the grass daintily, not pulling on her leash to actually step on the lawn, though. Maybe she'd forgotten the feel of grass under her paws due to living in the heart of Toronto, where concrete abounded.

Theo gave my hand a quick squeeze. "You good?" I pushed my sunglasses—god, it was good to see the sun again—up on top of my head so that he could see my eyes; our gazes locked on each other.

"Better than I thought I would be, that's for sure. It helps to have Emery on our team. And definitely less nervous than the last Christmas I was here." I winked, trying to let him know that there were no hard feelings anymore. The past was the past. We had come so far in the last several months, and this was another step forward into the life we were living now.

He brought our hands up to his mouth and kissed my knuckles. "I'm sorry again that I hurt you back then."

Unable to wave away any guilt that he still might be harboring—what with him holding on to my one hand and Giz's leash in the other—I settled for bumping my shoulder into his.

"Seriously, goalie. Even if it didn't feel like it at the time, it was bad timing for both of us." I gave him a reassuring smile. "It's much better to be here with you now."

Theo exhaled deeply, his shoulders relaxing. "Thank you, baby," he replied, his tone sounding less tense.

We'd reached the front door. Theo put down our bags to pull his house keys from his jeans pocket when the door flew open before he could fish them out.

In front of us stood a man I was 90 percent sure was Theo's brother Chase. There was always a chance it was Liam; a lone freckle under one helped me tell them apart. Either way, he was dressed as...

"Are you the flipping Elf on the Shelf?" Theo choked out, laughing. "Where in the hell did you get an adult-sized version of *that?*"

"Good to see you, bruh. I'd hug you, but you know, can't get dog fur on the outfit, huh?" Chase brushed imaginary lint off both of his shoulders. "And Abbie hooked me up. Ever since she went to Anime Expo this year, she's been going on and on about these custom costumes online."

"Gizmo's basically hairless, you dipshit." Theo let go of my hand to drag his brother into a tight hug, wrapping his arms around Chase and squeezing hard if the wheezing sounds coming out of Chase were any indication. "Good to see you, man." Theo's voice was rough with emotion.

"Hey, Chase," I said and waved with my now free hand. I was secretly pleased that I could still tell them apart.

"Well, well, well. Tell me, Indie. What kind of dirt does Theo have on you that he's conned you into pretending to be his girlfriend?" Chase moved forward out of the threshold, turning his body away from Theo as much as possible, and dropped his voice. "I told you if you needed help burying a body, Liam and I were there for you. No need to involve this guy." He jerked his thumb at Theo.

From the ground, Gizmo let out her little pre-bark "rrrruff" sound. I bent down and scooped her up in my arms.

Chase, being Chase, bent down to make eye contact with my dog and held out his right hand as if Giz were a human to shake hands with. "Pleased to meet you, Ms. Gizmo Layne-Yao-Miller. Auntie Emery tells me I'm your new uncle." He gave me and Theo a shit-disturber-type grin that let us know he was just warming up with his typical hijinks.

Gizmo batted his fingers away with her paw.

Theo didn't miss a beat. Instead of giving Chase the reaction he was clearly after, Theo picked up his line of conversation as if he expected that everyone already knew that we were seeing each other rather than the surprise I was feeling.

Hell, with this family, maybe it was to be suspected. They were all too gorgeously innocent-looking that they could crack even the toughest person wide open. It made for a wonderful combination of being exasperated that you'd spilled your secrets while simultaneously being charmed enough to forget to be mad about it.

Big business should bottle this kind of charisma.

Even at twenty-seven, Chase's innocence game was still as strong as when we were kids. It must have been genetic since they could all bend others to their will. Theo not getting ruffled by his words seemed to put Chase out.

"Fineeeeee. Be that way." Chase turned around quickly, righting the elf hat on his head that had shifted when he leaned toward Gizmo. He lifted his arm and waved us in.

"Come in. Come in. I don't know why you insisted on standing on the porch for so long." As if he wasn't the one who'd accosted us before we could set foot inside the house.

"Liam!" Chase bellowed as he rounded the corner of the foyer that led deeper into the house.

"Ugh. What's happening? I just woke up," a muffled voice answered him from somewhere inside.

"It's good to see some things don't change," Theo said quietly. He had a soft, fond smile on his face. It was though a layer of stress had just fallen off him. He shifted to give me a quick kiss on the cheek. "Are you ready for this?"

Was I ready to be back in the only place I'd ever felt truly at home? "Absolutely." I stood on my tiptoes to brush my lips over his.

At the same time, I was afraid of letting myself be too happy, though. My past experiences had conditioned me to not expect anything from anyone. So entering one of my favorite places in the world, after six years away, had me feeling vulnerable in more ways than one.

Once we were inside the threshold, Theo set our bags down by the entryway table. We followed the grumbling sounds of the two overgrown toddlers who masqueraded as adult men coming from the kitchen.

"Did not."

"Did too."

Their voices echoed all the way to the front of the house.

"What do you think they're arguing about?" I kept my voice

low. Not that I thought they could hear me as the volume of their brotherly disagreement continued to increase. Sibling fights made me very confused. It seemed like this was fun for them? I just didn't get it, but the ache inside me at being an only child made me wish that I could.

Theo, totally nonplussed by the heated voices, shrugged and said, "Siblings." (As if that explained anything to an only child!) "More than that. Twins." He jerked his thumb over his shoulder like this was just how things were.

Like me, Giz was a little put on edge with the argument happening close by. Her ears flattened as much as they could against her head to keep some of the sound out. I stroked her back over her harness, trying to soothe her. She was used to things being pretty quiet when it was just me and Theo in my apartment.

Come to think of it, when was the last time Theo slept in his own apartment? The stray thought was soon lost to a little hitch in my breath as the twins continued to argue.

He took my hand, and we made our way toward the back of the house. The Yao-Miller house wasn't a monstrosity like my parents' house, but they still had about six thousand square feet. We hadn't made it to the kitchen before I heard Emery coming down from upstairs.

"Jesus! What could they be fighting about now?" she grumbled to herself. Emery had obviously been in her studio again as she smeared white paint up her arms when she pushed her sleeves up. "Shit," she said when she realized what she had done. She held her hands slightly away from her body now that she remembered. The commotion must have interrupted her.

When she reached the bottom step, she looked up from her arms and saw me and Theo. "T! Ind! You guys are here already? I thought you weren't coming until after lunch?"

Theo wrapped his arms around my waist and gently pulled me into his side. He gave his sister the same affectionate smile that he'd aimed at Chase. "It is after lunch, Em."

"What? Shit!" She swore again. Emery hated to seem scatterbrained, but I loved that she got so involved in her art that she lost track of time.

She moved forward and raised her arms but then realized for the second time that she was covered in paint. "Rain check on the hugs."

"It's so good to see you, Em." Theo was looking at Emery like she was something precious. She was, and I loved that for her. I knew that Theo had been really trying to be more present for his siblings this past season.

A pang of homesickness hit me suddenly. I felt the same when I was tutoring kids at the community center back in Amado. Knowing that I'd helped a kid who was struggling gain some self-confidence was the best feeling in the world. God, I really missed my kids. I hoped they were doing okay with the other volunteers.

"Let's find out what all the noise is about." Theo kept his arm around me while Emery followed us into the kitchen.

She moved past us, careful not to get paint on our coats, and zeroed in on her brothers, who had yet to notice we'd entered the room. Their concentration was taken up by glaring at each other.

"What in the hell is going on now? Can't I even get one hour to work without my noise-canceling headphones while you two are home?" she admonished, but her smile lessened their effect.

Sibling stuff was sometimes confusing.

"Hey! Cut it out!" Theo's voice boomed over the bickering before it turned back into its regular deep but calm tone. "Let's not scare Indie off before dinner, okay? You don't know how hard it was to get her here."

Liam, now aware that there were three more of us in the room, looked over at Theo with keen interest. "Really, T? Tell us how *hard* it was?" Liam and Chase cackled together.

Theo just raised his middle finger at Liam without saying anything, which only made them laugh more.

"Yeah, yeah. You're hilarious, Li. I can't wait until you two idiots hit thirty. Then we'll see how hard you find it," Theo drawled.

"Ugh. You guys are disgusting. Stop talking about your dicks." Emery pushed a piece of hair that kept falling into her eyes back from her forehead. Luckily, most of the paint on her hands was starting to dry, so she didn't look totally like a skunk now… just mostly.

"Um, Em." I mimed that something was on my fingers and pointed to my head.

Her perturbed face only had the twins laughing harder. "Do you two stupid-heads even have two brain cells between you? Not everything is funny!" Her voice turned a little more shrill at the end.

"I'm going to clean up." She turned to me, her expression smoothing from irritated to pleased. "I'm so glad you're here, Ind. We'll talk in a bit, yeah?"

I nodded.

Emery paused to give Gizmo a little kiss on the head on the way out of the room and got a lick inside her nostril for her trouble. "Ugh! What was that?" Her nose wrinkled in response to Gizmo's action.

Now, it was my turn to laugh. "Um, affection?"

She pointed to Theo. "You. See if you can do something with them before Dad gets home." She jabbed a finger in Chase and Liam's direction.

Their mutual laugh-a-thon now calmed into quiet snickering every time they looked at a new way Emery had covered herself in paint.

I smiled at her as she went back toward the stairs that led to the second floor.

Theo brought my attention back to the twins. "What were you two fighting about?"

They looked at each other and replied, "I don't remember," in sync before bursting out laughing again.

"Well, I guess it wasn't too serious, then," he said, dismissing them to turn to me. "Wanna see my room?" He winked salaciously.

Thirty-Six

INDIE

Christmas morning had me awake long before dawn. I was still operating on Toronto time.

It was surprising because I'd been drowsily content for the entirety of Christmas Eve, barely able to keep my eyes open after way too many fried foods. It wasn't my fault that sweet-and-sour chicken balls were my favorite, as blasphemous as they were to proper Chinese cuisine.

Christmas Day had always been the main attraction around here, what with Joe's obligations at the college and Alice's research deadlines. It had always been Chinese food for dinner, as traditional as Alice could find in San Jose, and last night showed that the ritual continued.

There was a bittersweet tension to the dinner table by the time Joe made it home just before 6:00 p.m. He'd obviously been expecting my presence, too, since I was just one of five who got called to help with the takeout bags he brought home. He'd waited until I had my arms full to give me a side squeeze.

At six five, Joe had to lean down to give me what reminded me of a "good job, sport" kind of hug. It reminded me of when coaches congratulated their players after a good game. With the way he messed up my hair with a gentle pat on the head, I was glad he remembered I wasn't wearing a football helmet.

"Good to see you, Indie. It's been too long." He gave me a meaningful look that had my face warming slightly. Joe Miller was a pretty excellent bullshit detector. I guess he had to be with children like Chase and Liam.

"I know, Joe. I'm really glad to be here." I shrugged in a helpless you've-got-me-there kind of gesture without being completely transparent about the embarrassment that had kept me away all these years.

"Well, we're all glad to have you here. You're family, you know that." His words made my breath catch in my throat. I focused on not choking and remembering how to move air in and out of my lungs. "We all think that too."

He gave me another knowing look that dared me to disagree with him, even in my own mind. I felt so seen that I wondered if this was what it felt like when you had a parent who really saw you for who you are.

The longer he waited patiently for my response, the more I felt like I should confess that I kissed his son out of nowhere at nineteen. And maybe tried smoking a cigarette as a high school freshman during my brief grunge phase when I tried to befriend the skaters at school. Shit, maybe even my first sip of vodka from his very own liquor cabinet at sixteen that his daughter served me, followed by us refilling the bottle to its previous volume with tap water.

"Thank you, Joe. I don't... I can't say what..." My words tripped over each other.

"I understand, Indie. Don't worry." Did he? I could barely process the impact his words had on my worldview. "Let's just make sure this is back to a yearly thing, hmm? Theo is a lucky man. I'll make sure he knows it. Alice would have been thrilled." His voice became rough when he

mentioned his late wife, making my heart squeeze tightly.

I couldn't deny how incredible it felt to know that he gave me his approval before even talking to Theo about it. I heard his monthly calls with his dad, and they mostly talked sports stats and player trades.

He added one last gem before I could reply. "God knows, we're going to have to work hard enough to keep the twins from sending you screaming from the house with their shenanigans. At least Theo and Emery are here to balance things out." His voice was much quieter than before.

"I heard that!" came two deep voices simultaneously from the den. Joe hefted the biggest bag of food in his arm and cocked his eyebrow in a "see what I mean?" kind of expression.

I woke up before 5:00 a.m. Unable to go back to sleep, I stared into the darkness above me for another forty-five minutes, lying as still as possible so as not to wake Theo. Stir-crazy, I rolled out of bed as stealthily as possible. It wasn't an easy task, seeing as I was sleeping with a six-foot, built professional hockey player in his teenage double bed. There hadn't been a single moment of the night where our skin wasn't pressed against each other.

I had managed to creep downstairs without making any noise. Now, I stood in the kitchen, eyeing their fairly sophisticated coffee machine. The cupboard above it held bags of actual coffee beans. Did I have to figure out how to grind the beans before figuring out how to make the coffee brew?

I now regretted my daily choice to buy coffee on my way to work since the beginning of forever. I opened a few more cabinet doors, hoping to find some sort of pre-ground coffee. Hell, I would even take instant crystals right now.

Shit. Maybe I'll just pour six glasses of orange juice and call it a day.

I was bent over, rifling through the lower cupboards, when a deep voice had me startling.

"Rocky." Thankfully, my knees gave out in surprise rather than my head swinging upward and dropped to the floor with the grace of a tangled-up baby flamingo.

I leaned my shoulder against the frame of the cabinet and turned my head to look up at my boyfriend, who had just scared the crap out of me.

"Shit. Sorry." Theo took long strides across the kitchen, reaching out his arms to scoop me up and set me back on my feet. "I thought you heard me come down." A slightly bashful look took over his gorgeous features. His hair, now longer than his ears due to the fact that he didn't cut it during the season "for luck," was sticking up in all different directions.

I realized how lucky I felt to be the one who got to see him like this. He was about as far from the polished NHL star who held his own in post-game press conferences and interviews. My heart, recently resuscitated from its frozen state since being with Theo, warmed to the point that it sent tingles along my skin.

I shivered with the sensation. Theo, mistaking my movements for something else, gathered me into his arms, surrounding me in his gloriously warm arms and pressing me toward his chest.

"Cold, baby?" He looked down between us, gaze fixed on my usual thin tank top I wore to bed.

"Mmm. Giz?" I couldn't articulate my feelings in this moment. It was easier to let him believe I just needed some shared body heat. And I was not complaining about being surrounded by the scent of Theo's minty bodywash, leftover from his quick shower before bed, and all those rock-hard muscles he earned on and off the ice.

"She's fast asleep," Theo assured me.

Despite it being close to 6:00 a.m., a glance at the digital clock on the stove told me I'd been looking through the cupboards for longer than I thought.

"Let's get you into a hoodie." He paused, letting one of his hands drift down to tease the hem of my sleep shorts. "And definitely some pants before my family wakes up. There's no way my hooligan brothers get to see you like this." He squeezed my ass cheek possessively.

"Okay, caveman." I leaned back a bit so I could meet his gaze. "You're very lucky that—for some unexplainable reason—I find that territorial bullshit extremely hot when it comes out of your mouth."

He walked me back until my back met the counter before lifting me up to sit in front of the professional-quality coffee machine. Theo brought both hands around to the front of my body and covered the tops of my bare thighs with his fingers spread as far as they could go. He proceeded to dip his thumbs down into the crevice between my pussy and inner thighs. His firm touch swept every inch of skin he could cover with his hands as he moved them down to my knees. Once he had both my knees cradled in his palms, he firmly pushed them apart so that he could step into me, our bodies touching chests to pelvises.

"Merry Christmas, baby," he whispered against my lips.

"Merry Christmas, goalie." I smiled into his mouth, which barely grazed mine.

"I was thinking, there's something I've been meaning to correct. And now is the perfect time to do it," he said softly.

My head touched the hard cabinet behind it when I leaned back enough to see his face clearly. I had no idea what he was talking about. Unease bubbled in my stomach.

Where was he going with this? A flash of worry hit me. Was my perfect bubble with Theo about to burst with whatever he was going to say?

"Six years ago, we stood in the kitchen, and you were brave as fuck to sneak down here and wait for me, looking like a goddamn siren in that peach satin. Then you surprised the hell out of me by kissing me." He brought his hand from my knee to cup the right side of my face in his palm.

My stomach dropped for a whole different reason at his seductive words. The memory of his rejection all those years ago stung a little less with every moment we spent together.

He rubbed his thumb back and forth along my jaw. "I fucking hate that I hurt you that day. I had no idea that you had feelings for me. You have always been beyond beautiful. But I had so many firm lines drawn in my life for what I needed to do to make my hockey goals happen. At twenty-five, I was in the thick of making it to the next level."

Theo used his other hand to reach up and rub the back of his head, his lips pressed into a small grimace.

"And I was somewhat of an arrogant son of a bitch back then. I'd let the hype of being an up-and-coming star go to my head. I was never a fuckboy. But I admit to liking the attention. It was so easy to let being a hockey star distract me from really dealing with losing Mom." His Adam's apple moved with what looked like a tough swallow, like those words were physically painful to say. "You were only nineteen, and I'd always kept you firmly in Emery's best friend category in my mind…"

"It's okay. It wasn't the right time," I rushed out. It hurt me to see him struggling, and I immediately wanted to ease his discomfort. "You don't have to…"

"No. I do. Out of everyone, you need to hear this." His right hand joined his left as he held my face still so that I had no choice but to look at him. "It took me too many years to realize that I was using hockey as an escape from everything here. I'm lucky my brothers and sister are giving me a chance to make things right between us."

I kept my eyes on Theo's, wanting him to know I would listen to anything he wanted to tell me.

"I've decided I'm going to see someone about what I've been dealing with over Mom's death. You know, like a therapist. Now that we're together, it's made me want to live fully. And I can't do that until I work through all the stuff I've been trying to ignore for years." His gaze slid to the side for a second, perhaps lost in thought, before moving back to mine.

At some point, I'd unconsciously moved my hands to his waist. I gave him a squeeze of reassurance.

"That's amazing, Theo. I can't tell you how happy it makes me that you want to do this for yourself. You've already given me so much just by being back in my life," I whispered.

"I'm not going to let anything distract me from the most fearless, intelligent, and utterly gorgeous woman in front of me this time." His voice was steady.

"Theo," I whispered. Where was he going with this?

"I love you, Indie." His voice was steady and his eyes clear as he looked directly into mine.

I stopped breathing. I was certain. This was how I was going to die. Lack of oxygen from Theo Yao-Miller, my lifelong crush, saying he loved me and I forgot how to breathe in and out.

My mind raced. No one had ever said that to me before. Sure, Emery, Abbie, and I said "love you" as goodbye sometimes. But those three words had never been directed at me with the intention that Theo looked at me with right now.

I sucked in a much-needed breath, still just staring at him in shock.

"Rocky?" A little wrinkle appeared in his forehead. God, he had the audacity to be adorable by just being slightly uncertain about my reaction.

Even being equal parts thrilled and scared out of my mind by the fact that he loved me, looking at him crystallized what I'd felt in all the little moments we'd spent together since we saw each other in the hallway of our apartments: I loved him.

"Theo, I love you too." The words were out of my mouth before my mind caught up to my heart's realization. "I love you," I said again, high on the incredible intimacy of this quiet moment with him.

His eyes widened in shock, like he hadn't expected me to reciprocate his feelings or say it back to him. Until this very moment, I wasn't sure I could have either.

"You love me?" His lips broke out into the biggest grin I had ever seen him wear. It was wider than any photograph of him had ever captured—and I'd internet stalked him enough that I considered myself an expert on all Theo Yao-Miller expressions—the ones that sold millions of copies of magazines and whatever product he endorsed.

"Yes, Theo. I do. I love you." My words seemed to sink in as he surged forward and captured my mouth with his. His kiss was a feral expression of how desperate we both were from this huge emotion between us. Our tongues rubbed against each other, and we mirrored their actions by pressing our pelvises together. Both of us let out low moans as we struggled to get close enough to express the multitude of feelings we'd just experienced.

I let out a totally out-of-character tiny whimper of need as his cock hardened in his sweatpants. The two layers of thin fabric between us did little to cushion my aroused center from the rock-hard length pressed as firmly as we could manage between us.

"I JUST WANT TO SAY THAT I AM ABOUT TO WALK DOWN THE STAIRS," a voice yelled from another part of the house. My money was on Chase, who would likely be the early riser compared to Liam and his love for sleep.

Though either twin would probably delight in scaring everyone awake.

"THAT'S RIGHT. I'M HOLDING A SMALL FUR CHILD, AND I DON'T WANT HER TO SEE ANYTHING SHE SHOULDN'T. THINK OF YOUR CHILD, FOR GOD'S SAKE!"

"FIRST STEP!"

"SECOND STEP!"

Theo dropped his hands from my face, gentling our kisses enough to pull back. His shoulders dropped in resignation.

"Can't get a fucking moment's peace in this house. Doesn't even matter what time it is," Theo muttered against my lips, drawing another uncharacteristic giggle from my mouth.

Did being in love make you high? Maybe all the endorphins had rushed to my head, making me stupid. Whatever it was, I couldn't say I didn't want to bask in this sensation for days.

Preferably naked. With Theo.

"Get your ass down here, Chase! It's safe." Theo's gaze made a quick sweep of my body before he tugged his sleep shirt off and over my head, covering my sleep tank and shorts.

Chase came into the kitchen wearing pajamas and his Elf on the Shelf hat. In his arms, Giz was sporting her own smaller version with a chin strap keeping it on her head.

I arched a brow at Chase.

"What?" he said. "As if I'm going to leave out my new niece at Christmas time. I headed out to the pet store as soon as Emery told us you two were together. I'm not a monster." He shifted my fur baby so that she was more secure in his arms, even as she became less tolerant of her new hat.

I grabbed my phone off the counter to snap a picture of them.

Before the rest of the family came down, Theo adjusted his shirt so it sat evenly on my shoulders. He nodded to himself in a satisfied kind of way before he looked back up into my eyes and gave a helpless shrug of his shoulders. And here I was, amused by his well-intentioned caveman behavior again. I couldn't help as I basked in his protectiveness the same way the comforting warmth of his shirt settled over me.

I smiled at him as I rolled my eyes, letting him know he was ridiculous but that I didn't mind.

"I can't help it, baby. No one gets to see all that perfect skin but me," he rumbled.

Thirty-Seven

INDIE

After the present-opening frenzy where she'd excused herself to the peace and quiet of the living room, Giz sat in Emery's lap, being lavished with pats. She'd been rescued from the elf hat she'd been wearing earlier. It didn't seem like I was going to get much time with my own dog until we left for Toronto tomorrow.

Meanwhile, Chase and Liam were arguing over whose gift cards were whose, despite getting the identical amount from various retailers. Joe watched them argue back and forth with amusement. Were they putting on a show just for him?

Surrounded by piles of crumpled wrapping paper, I leaned into Theo's body as he thumbed through his phone. His expression was serious for the lighthearted Christmas morning we'd had so far.

"What are you looking for?" My voice was low with the din of sibling arguments in the background.

"I'm rechecking the game schedule, trying to figure out a way we could sneak back for another visit before the season ends in May, but hopefully June." His eyes focused on the screen, his forehead creased in concentration. "It's just the way the games are laid out, the ones with a little more time in between the series seem to be all on the East Coast."

He locked his phone and tossed it on the couch beside him. "Every time I come home, I remember how much I like being here. Some of the memories are hard, of course." His voice was rough with emotion, but he kept his volume almost to a whisper.

Theo looked at the mantle, where photos of his mom and the family were displayed. "When I'm not here, it's easy to put a lot of things before them." He nodded at his family. "But I've missed a hell of a lot, Rocky. There's got to be a way to get back here more. I just haven't found it yet." He rubbed his face with his hand that wasn't holding on to me.

My stomach clenched with an uncomfortable emotion, witnessing Theo struggling. I wanted him to have everything that made him happy. It rankled that I couldn't jump in and fix it for him.

As if he read my mind, Theo pulled back to meet my gaze and said, "It's not on you to make it better, Ind. It's huge that I can say aloud what's bothering me. I haven't had that in years." He nodded at the mantle again, meaning his relationship with his mom.

Against my will, my eyes started to fill and threatened to overflow. I blinked rapidly to try to clear the overwhelming warmth running through my limbs. Gah! What was he doing to me?

He brought his hand up to my chin, directing my watery gaze back to him. "It's more than enough that you're here. Having you by my side just hearing me is the biggest help, okay?"

It was all I could do to nod. I didn't trust my voice not to come out uneven, or worse, tears to start falling in earnest.

"Kids." Joe stood up and went over to a side table, where he pulled something from its drawer. "Your mom and Gong Gong would have given me hell for forgetting to give you these on Christmas. It's been years since we had the whole family together for the holiday, so this year, it feels extra important." His smile was warm but sad.

I looked at the lai see he held in his hands, my heart giving another traitorous thump. Their mom had given me my very first lai see when Emery invited me over for Chinese New Year when we were six. I still had every red envelope I'd been given in a small wooden chest I kept on my dresser.

Alice couldn't have known what it would mean to me to be included in their family traditions that first year, but she made sure I got a red envelope every year on my birthday.

He came back in front of the large sectional where we were all sitting. Joe set all but one envelope on the ottoman and stood in front of Emery, holding it out to her with both his hands.

Emery, in turn, reached up with both hands and a grin to receive it from her dad.

I surreptitiously opened my phone camera and snapped a picture of the two of them. The love they had for each other was clear in their eyes. I couldn't stop the flash of my own father in my mind and thought how many light-years away I was from the Layne family traditions.

The sweet moment was interrupted by Liam. "Hey! How come she gets her lai see first?"

Theo sighed good-naturedly beside me, his body pressing more deeply against mine as he muffled a small chuckle.

Joe didn't blink, giving Liam a quick look. "Because she's my favorite child. Obviously." He kept his expression completely deadpan as Liam's mouth formed into an O shape.

Joe kept his face neutral while Emery took her red envelope with both hands. But he didn't leave Liam hanging long before he turned and offered him a wink.

"Good one, Dad." Theo nodded and called out from beside me.

"We're just racking up the payback for all those years of pranks, Li."

Like the mature adult he was, Liam kept his attention on his dad while putting his arm up and aiming a middle finger at Theo.

Picking up another envelope from the ottoman, Joe paused in front of Liam and held it out to him. "Li, you know parents don't have favorites. Or rather, my favorite is whoever is giving me the least amount of headaches at any given moment."

Chase elbowed Liam. "Then it's really never been either of us. And he doesn't know the *half* of the shit we've pulled."

"What?" Joe's spine straightened, stopping him from leaning down to give Liam his lai see.

Liam let out a bark of laughter so loud that it startled Giz from her nap on Emery's lap. "True. They'll never actually even the score, will they?"

Chase shook his head "no" with a smile.

That seemed to be all it took to settle Liam back into his mellow mood. The rest of us received our red envelopes without any more fanfare.

Joe returned to his recliner next to the couch, and his hands suddenly looked a bit restless in his lap.

"What is it, Dad?" Emery's brow wrinkled in concern.

"God, I know you're all adults, and it should be easier to say this. But turns out it isn't." Joe's gaze landed on each of his children, still appearing hesitant. "Okay, I'm just going to come out with it… I've asked Sherri out on a date."

Sherri was their long-time next-door neighbor and family friend. She'd been the one to stay with Theo's siblings when Joe had to coach away games.

Joe's words were met with a few seconds of silence. Theo's thigh went rock hard with tension under my hand. I gently rubbed my hand back and forth across it, offering my silent support.

Once he had a chance to process the news, I would be there for him if he wanted to talk about it.

All the Yao-Miller siblings started talking at once.

"Way to go, Dad!" Theo grinned.

"Oh, Dad's going to finally get some. It's about time!" Chase said with a sleazy wink.

"That's amazing, Dad. I'm so happy for you." Though Emery aimed a reassuring smile toward her father, the slight hitch in her voice gave away her uncertainty. From experience, I knew that Emery was upset but didn't want to take away from her dad's moment.

"Is this another thing everyone knew about but me?" Liam groaned.

The Yao-Miller patriarch sagged back into his seat with relief. "Really?" he asked. "You kids are okay with this? I mean, it's happening. But I'll feel a lot better if you all are on board."

Liam, complaint forgotten, held out his fist for his dad to bump. "Go for it, Dad. You gotta keep those pipes clean, eh? All those years of no action can't be good for your prostate."

A chorus of gags and groans—including my own—rang out at Liam's statement.

"Too far, bro." Chase shoved his twin's shoulder. "*Way* too far."

Liam just shrugged, a satisfied look on his face at being back on top of this morning's shenanigans.

"What's for breakfast?" He looked around at all of us as if he hadn't just grossed us all out with his inappropriate words.

Even if food was the last thing I could think about at the moment, I was glad to be surrounded by the love this family had for each other.

I let myself picture what years of this would look like, if I could really be part of something so special.

With the din of the siblings arguing over who held the record for grossing out the family the most, I burrowed further into Theo as he debated, feeling more content than I could ever remember.

Back in Toronto a few nights later, I already wanted to be back with Theo's family.

Theo and I hadn't even considered heading out for New Year's Eve. Both of us avoided anything that had to do with over-the-top hype. And December 31 felt like the ultimate way to spend a fortune to have a crap time.

The combination of my family's name and his career made it so that neither of us had a low-key outing in years. We always had to be on guard, so it was nice just to have the time to ourselves.

"Couldn't cook that," Theo commented as we lazed on my couch with Giz. We were currently on our second season of *Somebody Feed Phil*. It had become our preferred pastime to watch chefs from all over the world make things that neither of us could ever hope to make whenever we had more than one night when Theo wasn't on the road.

We still hadn't had time to master the basics in the kitchen.

"Any resolutions, Rocky?"

My nonprofit and my list came to mind as they tended to when one calendar year ended. But for the first time, my ambitions were being balanced out by the here and now—by the man I was curled up against and had been for all these months.

I'd have to give it more consideration. It was too much for my post-Yao-Miller-Christmas-chaos brain to compute at the moment. I let those thoughts slip away as I buried my face in Theo's chest.

"Nah. Not this year." I went with the easiest answer. "What about you?"

The deliciously taut muscles in Theo's chest and abs expanded and contracted on a sigh.

"Balance," he said finally. "Not letting hockey take over everything until all I can see is the next game or the next win or getting to the playoffs." He kissed the top of my head, just brushing his lips lightly across my hair.

I smiled at the thought that we both felt the need for balance. It was amazing to be in tune that way. I hoped I gave him the steadiness that he gave me every day. But I was too chickenshit to ask him.

I opened my mouth in an attempt to be brave, but my words were cut off by the annoying-as-hell sound of my phone ringing.

My stomach flooded with unease. There was only one person I knew who would call me on New Year's Eve. Or this close to midnight any day of the year, really.

My father.

Every cell in my body begged me to ignore his call like I had done the last three times my phone rang with his number on my screen. Going to holiday parties with my mother might have kept him busy this past week, but I knew I couldn't avoid him any longer.

"Don't answer it." Theo squeezed me further into his side, as if he could insulate me from whatever had made my muscles tense.

"I have to," I whispered. I'd already taken too big of a risk putting my father off for this long.

I lifted my phone to my ear. The last thing I would ever do was let Theo hear the way my father spoke to me.

"Hello."

"Indigo. I'm not sure what you're playing at thinking that you can ignore my calls, but you're sorely mistaken." His disdain echoed down the line.

"My apologies, Father. Things have been hectic at work." I bit my lip to avoid saying all the awful words that came to mind.

"Not accepted. I run a billion-dollar corporation with a multitude of subsidiaries. My schedule is quite a bit more than 'hectic,' Indigo. But I still answer the goddamn phone when I'm expected to."

And that confirmed I had fucked up royally by putting him off for so long. My father thought profanity was vulgar and beneath him, so his use of "goddamn" signaled nothing good.

"I'm sorry." My voice was quiet, my earlier unapologetic feelings now neatly cowed.

"You're coming home. Tomorrow. Winston will meet you at the airport and bring you to my office. It's urgent." He carried on as if he hadn't heard me.

"What? Why?" The air froze in my lungs, making it hard to force out the words.

"Well, if you had answered any of my previous attempts to contact you, you would know. As it stands, I don't have the time to give you any information right now. In fact, I'm standing in the hallway of a ballroom, making this call between courses at the benefit your mother and I are sponsoring." His tone had lost the heat of his rarely revealed anger at being ignored. He was back to his normal stone-cold tone of disappointment.

I kept silent. My mind churned with possibilities for what I would be walking into tomorrow. But I knew better not to ask.

"I swear, Indigo. If you just thought of someone other than yourself for a single moment in your life, life would be much easier." With that parting thought, he hung up without a goodbye.

He was really angry with me. I couldn't understand why. It wasn't the first time I'd stretched the limit of his patience when he snapped his fingers for my obedience.

But this time seemed different in ways I couldn't define.

Thirty-Eight

THEO

"Baby?" I rubbed Indie's back gently. At some point in the short call with her father, she'd separated her body from its cozy position curled up next to me.

Now, she sat with her back straight like the manners police were due for an inspection at any moment.

Indie brought the phone down from her ear robotically. It vibrated with another notification from where she'd set it on the couch beside her.

"What's going on?" I moved from the couch to her coffee table so I could see her face. She hadn't looked at me once during or now after the call.

Indie's fair skin was now pale; all traces of the warm peach undertones that normally lit up her cheeks were gone.

"I have to pack." Her gaze darted around the room, settling on Giz for a moment when the incessant buzzing of her phone caused our little pup to shift away from the machine disturbing her sleep.

"*What?*" Giz's head popped up, ripped from her nap by my near yell.

And still, my girl didn't look at me. I took matters into my own hands, literally. I brought both my hands to her face and firmly guided her cheeks toward me to force her to fucking make eye contact.

"Tell me what's going on." I stared intently into her eyes, searching for any kind of inflection to let me in on what she was feeling.

"That was my father." Just like that, her muscles gave way like a puppet whose strings had been cut, making my hands feel like they were the only thing holding her up. "I have to fly back to San Jose in…" She picked up her phone and scrolled through the notifications. "Six hours. So yeah, I have to pack."

"I don't understand." I didn't understand anything about the moment: her total lack of emotions, the demand her father made without telling her the reasons for it, the immediate need to jump on a flight home. Not. One. Thing.

"Can you watch Giz while I'm gone?" She stood, forcing me to let go of her. She appeared like she was operating on autopilot and started listing off tasks. "I'm not sure how long it's going to be. I'll need to contact Jermaine when I get in. Hopefully, I still have a job to come back to, leaving like this."

My gut clenched. As if anything about what was about to go down was her fault. Didn't her father care that she had a life here? A job she was good at? Surely, as an all-powerful CEO, he knew you didn't behave this way as an employee.

So why was he expecting Indie to do things this way?

"Baby." She'd made her way to the threshold of her bedroom while I'd been lost in my thoughts. I crossed the space between us with long strides. "What can I do? Do you want me to go with you?"

That question had her turning back to me with wide eyes. "No. You can't. Absolutely not. I need to handle this." She turned and headed to her closet and pulled out the carry-on suitcase that we'd only just unpacked two days ago.

"Indie, please. I need you to tell me what's happening right now." I moved to take the suitcase from her hand, setting it on the ground before taking her hand in mine and leading her to the bed.

Her shoulders slumped when we sat down. A heavy feeling settled in my gut.

"So, the thing is. My grandmother left me a lot of money when she passed away, but it's been locked up in a trust until now. I've been planning for years to start a nonprofit to help kids in need." She looked down at her lap, picking at the nonexistent lint on her pants. Indie met my gaze quickly before looking at her lap again.

This was one of the few times I could ever remember Indie appearing so worried about anything.

"Baby," I said, using my free hand to reach around and tilt her chin up until I could see her eyes again. "That's incredible. I have zero doubts you can make that happen. But what does that have to do with your dad's summons just now?"

She leaned back and kissed the palm that I held against her jaw before bringing up her own hand to hold mine in place.

"My father is threatening to use his all-powerful resources to prevent me from accessing my inheritance unless I do what he wants. He's the reason I'm here in Toronto. He thought my last job wasn't prestigious enough for the daughter of Gerald Layne III," she explained.

I'd never met the man, but I already hated him. Indie was so intelligent and capable in every situation. It galled me that anyone would try to control her, but her own father doing it just confirmed what a bastard he really was.

"So, what, you're going home to see what he wants? Why wouldn't he tell you on the phone?" Worry had my throat feeling tight.

She shook her head. "I don't know. But whatever it is, I don't have a choice because if I don't do what he wants, it will only make things worse."

"Shit." There wasn't anything I could say to make it better for her.

I wanted to tell her she could give up the money. That I'd give her whatever she needed to start her nonprofit. Hell, after all these years of devoting my whole life to hockey, I had a bank account I would gladly share with her.

I didn't say any of that, though, knowing this wasn't only about the money for Indie. She'd been planning this idea for years, it sounded like. She wasn't asking me to save the day for her. Her determination to face her father showed that she was set on doing this thing on her own.

I wanted to insist that I go with her.

The thing I needed her to understand was that she could rely on me. I wanted her to lean on me in times like this. If I pushed her now, it would be all about what I needed and not her.

"Okay. I get it. But I'm so sorry that you have to go through this." I exhaled the words, trying to fight the worry flowing through my veins at all the ways this could hurt her.

It must have been the right thing to say because she turned her body toward me fully and wrapped her arms around me, letting me hold her.

I couldn't imagine having to let her go, even temporarily.

It was 5:00 a.m., and Indie left for the airport just after 2:00 a.m. After she finished packing, we just lay beside each other on her bed in silence, neither of us even attempting to sleep.

Then, her ride was suddenly downstairs, and she gave me a soft kiss goodbye before she left.

Gerald Layne worked fast. The question remained: what did he want with Indie?

Her flight was due to take off within the hour. I picked up my phone to see if she had texted from the airport.

Indie

Made it to the gate with time to spare. Hardly any lines.

Theo

I'm glad you got there safely. I'm worried about you flying by yourself on no sleep and no food. Do you have time to grab something before your flight?

Indie

Nothing's open at this hour except the newsstand. But I'm in business, so I'm sure they'll feed me something before I get there.

Theo

You sure you don't want me to hop on the next flight and follow you?

I couldn't resist offering one more time to show how serious I was about being there for her.

Indie

No. I'm sure it will be fine. Just family stuff. Need I remind you you're headed to New York tomorrow morning and you can't just skip games? I'll be back before you know it.

She was right. As much as I wanted to say "fuck it," get on a plane, and deal with the consequences of going to see her anyway, I had a contract to abide by. Not to mention teammates to set an example for.

Theo

I already know it, baby. Counting the seconds. I love you. Text me when you get there. We can videocall.

Indie

I love you too.

I'd be lying if I denied that my heart didn't beat a little harder in my chest every time she said (or typed) those words to me. It had become too much to hold them in any longer on Christmas morning. I never expected her to say them back, but goddamn, hearing her return my feelings had made me feel more alive than any other moment before it.

The proudest memory I had until Indie said she loved me was getting drafted to Vancouver. It had been bittersweet with losing Mom only months before. But I'd allowed myself to feel the happiness I knew Mom would have felt for me.

And now, Indie was slowly eclipsing all of my previous achievements simply by being by my side.

It had been three days without more than a few vague text messages assuring me that she was "fine" and not to worry about her.

Well, fuck, *I* wasn't fine, and *I* was fucking worried about her and why she'd practically gone radio silent since flying into San Jose.

I'd checked my phone incessantly all through the road trip to New York. Now, the team had just arrived back at the practice arena after a humbling loss.

Coach had let us off the hook last night, knowing we all felt like shit about our playing, but he hadn't held back once we all sat in the locker room in Toronto this afternoon. His disappointment hadn't cooled since last night, telling us all to get our heads out of our asses before we faced New York tomorrow on home ice.

Not in the mood to deal with anyone, I'd dumped my gear and was the first one out the door when Coach dismissed us.

I was heading to the truck I'd rented for the winter months when a yell of "Yao!" had me pausing midstep. Whoever called my name was going to find out pretty quick that I wasn't in a socializing mood.

"Shit. You can move when you want to, Yao. Where was that on the ice last night, eh?" Ryan Campbell's infuriatingly ever-present grin greeted me when I turned around.

"I'm not in the mood, Campbell. What do you want?" I practically growled at my alternate captain. Not a good way to build camaraderie, but I needed to get home to take care of Giz and attempt to video call Indie for the third day in a row.

"Oh, okay." Campbell put his hands up in a gesture of surrender. "Too soon. It's all still fresh from last night. I get it."

He didn't get a damn thing, but since I wasn't going to explain my personal life to anyone, least of all him, I let him think that I was upset about the team's loss.

"Get to the point, Ryan," I sighed, suddenly exhausted from the stress of the situation with Indie, the road trip, and getting my ass handed to me in goal last night. On top of all that, my knees were killing me. I should have gotten into an ice bath after the meeting, but I didn't want to deal with any of the trainers asking questions.

I might do something fucking stupid like telling them how much I hurt.

"Well, shit, man. I feel bad for ribbing you. Did you have to go and pull out the first-name business? Now I know you're really feeling it." He took off his backward cap, smoothed his hair down, and then put it back on in an uncertain gesture. "Most of the team is headed to the bar to drink away some of our sorrows. We wanted you to join us."

I looked over Campbell's shoulder, seeing members of most of the lines huddled together, ready to head out.

"Thanks for the invite. But I'm going to head home. I need a good night's sleep before tomorrow's game. I slept like shit in New York."

I didn't say it was because I'd spent every moment thinking about how Indie was faring with her family instead of getting my head and body in the zone for the game.

"Fair enough, Yao." Campbell reached out and grabbed my shoulder, offering a quick squeeze through the thick padding of my winter jacket. "See ya tomorrow."

I briefly watched him jog back to the rest of the group before I resumed my walk to my truck.

My phone buzzed in my inner coat pocket—I'd long stopped carrying it in the back pocket of my jeans during Canadian winters—and I unzipped my jacket so fast I was surprised the lining didn't tear.

"Hello?" The anticipation of hearing Indie on the other end of the line had me panting slightly.

"Theo." My stomach plummeted with disappointment when I heard my agent's voice.

"Ray. Happy New Year," I said, just to be polite. He couldn't have caught me at a worse moment.

"Same to you, Theo. Listen. Tough loss last night—not a nice way to start the new year for sure. I'm sure you're already gearing up for tomorrow's game, and I hate to put this on you now, but…" His words dropped off.

A few beats of silence followed. I waited, not interested in making small talk.

When it became clear he was waiting for me to ask him what he was referring to, I ground out a low "What is it, Ray?" to prompt him to get to the point.

"You know you're in Toronto for a year, Theo. We talked about it being a transition year, where you considered your *options*." Options was a code word for how fucked-up my knees were at any given time. "But I haven't heard any feedback from you on the new team other than when you first got there."

"It's fine," I offered, not able to get into the specifics of my experience with the Tempests right now.

"Right." He let my nonanswer go for the moment. "Well, we're only a couple months away from the trade deadline, and we need to strategize next steps, Theo. You know how it goes. There are already some whispers and some outright discussions going already."

He dropped his volume by half. "In fact, Florida's management got in touch with me about a five-year, eighteen-million-dollar contract with a no-trade clause. They have a young team, and they see you as the future captain they need to turn their guys into playoff contenders." After knowing Ray for almost fifteen years, I could easily detect the pride in his voice. He thought he was bringing me something extraordinary.

To be fair, at thirty-one, being offered a contract most often offered to twenty-five-year-olds in their prime was an astoundingly great offer.

"Let me guess. They want to know if I'm interested right away. 'Off the record,' of course. How long do I have to think about it?"

The thought of having to decide my future in the league, at this moment, sat like an anvil in my gut.

"Think about it, Theo?" Ray's voice bristled with impatience. "It's not going to get better than this. In fact, I'd say it's going to get a lot worse. With your age and, uh, other factors at play, you could see your last years in professional hockey bouncing from one team to another, each less money than the last. What is there to even think about?"

My family. My health. And most importantly, Indie.

There was a lot to consider, but I wasn't capable of explaining any of that to Ray at the moment.

"Let me get back to you, Ray. Give me a couple days." As much as I didn't want to sour the potential relationship with a new team, I couldn't give him the answer on the spot like I'd been able to do so many times over the years.

"Fine. Theo. I'll hold them off for three days. If I don't give them something positive to take to head office for the salary cap planning, they're going to move on." I respected that he didn't try to push me further right now.

"Got it, Ray. Three days." I disconnected the call as I reached my truck. I unlocked the doors and got in, immediately leaning back onto the headrest. With my eyes closed, I tried to separate all the conflicting interests, of which joining a team in Florida was no small part.

Five more years just about as far across the country from Indie as I could get.

Fuck.

Thirty-Nine

THEO

"You really pulled out all the stops tonight, Yao." Our captain held out his fist to congratulate me on a couple of tricky saves that had helped us redeem ourselves after losing the first game of the new year.

"Nah. Team effort. You know that." Sure, I'd worked harder this game than any I'd played all season, but that was because it'd been a monumental struggle to keep my focus on the ice.

"Aw, our darling goalie is so modest, isn't he, cap'n?" Campbell, who had the talent of being in everyone's face at any given time, wrapped his sweaty arm around an equally sweaty Michaels and batted his eyelashes innocently. "I'm about to cry or swoon. I can't tell which." He let out an overdramatic sigh.

"How about you shower instead, eh? You stink." Michaels elbowed his alternate captain straight in the gut, with affection.

"That is the aroma of the highest scorer in the game." Campbell added some extra Southern drawl to his normally much softer accent and stuck his nose up in the air like an affronted gentleman.

"Mmmhmm. Right. Let's leave Yao to it. You coming out tonight, old man?" Michaels's eyes glittered with amusement.

"With an invitation like that? No," I deadpanned.

The truth was, with the post-game adrenaline rapidly draining from my system, I'd be lucky to take care of Giz before falling into Indie's bed when I got home.

My heart clenched with the thought of not hearing from her at all that day. She hadn't replied to the two messages I'd sent before and after practice this morning.

"You know I'm kidding, right? You should come to the club with us. It's going to be a good night." Michaels's smile was genuine.

"Oooh, yes! You can watch all the women and men simply drop at my feet, ready to worship me. I can guarantee you'll learn a thing or twenty-seven." Campbell winked.

"If the people standing closest to you are dropping at your feet, maybe you should consider washing with soap twice in the shower now. Maybe it's your 'aroma' that's making them faint," I threw out, hoping my jab would be enough to assure them I was fine because I had no intention of hitting a club tonight.

Michaels and a couple of teammates howled with laughter. After a moment, Campbell admitted defeat in this latest battle of wits, and they headed off.

I hadn't been needed for any press tonight, so I was already showered and dressed. I threw the last couple of things into my locker, ready to head out, when a throat cleared beside me.

Andrews stood in the vacant space where the captain and alternate captain had just been.

"What?" I'd used up the last of my manners on my other teammates.

"Whoa, Oscar the Grouch. Just came over to see if you wanted to grab a beer. Something low-key, blow off some steam, you know?"

He seemed to find something about my shitty mood funny.

At least someone was having a good time tonight.

Did I want to go out with Andrews? No. Would it help to talk over stuff with someone who knew some of the pressure I was dealing with? Maybe.

Fuck it. "Yeah, fine. Let's go."

I dashed off a quick text to the emergency dog walker to ask if she could take Gizmo out since I'd be another hour or so and sent another prayer of thanks to team services for hooking me up.

A few minutes later, we ended up at the same bar where he and Indie had gone on their "date" all those months ago. The jealousy that lingered from that experience had my molars clenching briefly. Even though Indie was my girlfriend, the thought of all the little moments of the last few months slipping through my fingers made me damn glad she hadn't taken a shine to Andrews.

I must have looked extra worn-out tonight because Andrews headed straight for the bar and came back with two beers in his hands.

"Thanks." I tipped my bottle to his as he found a table in a quiet area of the bar (wisely far away from the table he'd sat at with Indie).

"So. Talk. You look like someone flushed your pet fish down the toilet. On purpose. I know Indie is seeing her family, so what gives? Trouble in paradise?" He laced his fingers together and leaned forward on the tabletop, ready to listen. "It'll help to get it off your chest."

I rubbed my eyes with the hand not holding my beer bottle. I didn't do this talking-to-my-teammates-like-friends shit.

This was a stupid idea. Just go home and get some sleep. What could you possibly say to this kid across the table that's going to help anything?

I shrugged in response to my own internal questions and rolled the bottle in my hands between my palms, watching the minuscule bubbles in the liquid make their way to the top.

"No trouble, kid. Indie's perfect," I sighed before continuing. "There's a whole storm of other bullshit that's come up that I can't untangle in my mind."

Andrews nodded encouragingly.

"I haven't heard from Indie since yesterday," I admitted. "And it's fucking with my head. I can't help wondering what's going on with her back at home and why she wouldn't be telling me anything. It's like I'm being strangled by my own imagination over here."

"I mean," Andrews began slowly, "it's possible that some bad shit is going down for her. But every moment I've spent with her makes me think she can hold her own, you know?" He grinned as if to imply, "Am I wrong?"

We both knew Indie was a force both at work and personally. More than a force.

"Yeah, you're right there. But why wouldn't she say anything to me about it?" Discomfort had infiltrated every cell in my body. Indie had opened up to me slowly but surely over the past months. It seemed like a step backward to not hear from her, especially since we'd said we loved each other.

I knew rationally that she was busy and likely overwhelmed. My heart, however, wouldn't feel right again until she told me she was okay.

"From our conversations about you," he said and waggled his eyebrows playfully. "Yep. You heard me. She respects you and your career a lot, man. God knows the entire organization has never seen someone as dedicated to his team and his game as you. It leaks out your pores. Maybe she thinks she's doing just that by handling her shit over there so you can concentrate on hockey. It's not like we have a grueling travel schedule over the next week or so, right?" He smirked.

News flash: we had a grueling schedule that was going to exhaust us all.

My mouth flattened into a grim line, which Andrews took as agreement with his statement.

"Right. So, knowing Indie, it's not like she's avoiding you, right? I mean, even if she is, it's not like you can put yourself in front of her and demand she talk to you," he said, followed by a chuckle, as if the idea was ridiculous. "Hell, we're leaving for Dallas tomorrow night."

His mention of tomorrow night's flight went right over my head. My mind focused on the idea that I catch a plane to see Indie.

Did she think she had to handle anything, big or small, on her own anymore if she didn't want to? Did she think that she needed to keep parts of her life away from me so I could concentrate on hockey?

The weight that had been sitting in my stomach all day turned into a wrecking ball.

God, I don't want her believing there is anything more important than her.

I stood abruptly, leaving my beer basically untouched. Andrews's shocked face became wary.

"Shit, Theo. What did I say? I didn't mean any offense."

I could barely hear him over the plan forming in my mind. His wide eyes watched me as I walked around the table and gave him an absent pat on the shoulder.

"You're good, kid. Thanks. You helped a lot." I tossed the words his way as I moved past where he sat, headed for the exit to the bar.

I had a Chihuahua to pick up and a plane to catch.

On the street outside the bar, I pulled up my phone and hit Ray's number. When I heard the call connect, I started speaking before he had a chance to say hello.

"Listen, Ray, I don't have long, but…" Once I started rattling off my plans, everything else just fell away.

Forty

INDIE

The thoughts in my mind had been frozen since I'd hung up with my father the night before. I wasn't sure if the previous eight hours could count as nighttime because I hadn't gotten a single second of sleep.

I'd texted Theo when we landed but had no memory of what I'd typed.

Worry and exhaustion had me in a daze as my father's driver led me to the car and helped me into the back seat.

"Miss." Winston cleared his throat in the front seat. I dragged my foggy gaze over to him. "Miss Indigo. We're here." He jutted his chin to indicate we'd stopped in front of my parents' front door.

"Oh" was all I could manage. What was my father going to say when I went inside?

He smiled kindly—for being an asshole, my father seemed to hire genuinely nice employees—and spoke softly. "Shall I get your bag? Or, erm, did you forget your toiletry bag on the plane? I could drive you to the nearest department store for replacements before you go in?"

Winston's kind offer to help me avoid this meeting for a little while longer permeated the thick wall of worry that I'd surrounded myself with. A small smile formed on my lips for the first time since I picked up my phone last night.

"No, Winston. But thank you. You're really too good to me." I patted the hand that he'd placed on the backrest of the front seat. "I'm good to go in."

"Of course, miss." He nodded and got out of the driver's seat as if he hadn't just offered to help me run away.

He ushered me into the front hall, where Angelina gathered me in her arms for a quick kiss on my cheek. "My girl. Good to see you." Her greeting was warm, but her expression was strained. "I've been told to take you directly to his office, I'm afraid." Her smile dimmed.

"I'll go." Before she could argue, I'd given her hand a squeeze and headed down the long hallway to my father's office.

I paused in front of my father's imposing office door, my knuckles poised to knock. I took a deep breath and tried to convince myself yet again that just because this was an unusual meeting request, it didn't mean it was going to be as bad as I was imagining.

Right before I knocked, I heard muffled voices coming from inside the office. My spirits rose for a second at the thought that he was dealing with something important and my conversation with him would be cut short.

I rapped my knuckles on the door gently and was granted entrance with my father's deep voice calling out, "Come in."

I pushed open the door and stepped right into the middle of his conversation with a youngish man in a designer suit. It was draped over his body too perfectly to be anything but custom.

If he was in a meeting, why had he let me in?

"Ah, Indigo. Yes. Come sit down." My father stood momentarily, obeying social niceties before waving me to the other empty chair in front of his desk.

I jerked my gaze away from the stranger, hoping my father was going to explain what was going on here.

I could have given Pinocchio a run for his money with the woodenness of my steps. Each joint and ligament worked against one another as I forced myself to take a seat.

"Hello, Father. I hope you are well." The well-trained social robot had taken over my mouth with the appearance of this man beside me.

"Yes, quite. Thank you. Let me introduce you, Julian." He'd turned his head toward the man in question, and I mimicked his movement. "Julian Fairbank, this is my daughter, Indigo."

My eyes were trained on Julian as he smoothed his suit over his abdomen, half getting out of his chair and offering me his hand. Without my conscious direction, my hand met his halfway, and the soft, dry skin of his palm touched mine briefly in a polite squeeze.

"Lovely to meet you, Indigo. Both of our fathers have told me so much about you." His smile was perfectly practiced, so I couldn't tell what he really thought behind the calm stare he was aiming my way.

Since I hadn't heard a damn thing about him before, I offered a simple "thank you" in reply.

"Julian and I were just speaking about the very important fundraisers happening this week. And, well, with his father, Robert, announcing his bid for the Senate next month, we all thought it was time I introduced you two." My father's eyes took on a hard glint, a severe warning against saying anything out of line.

"Congratulations. What an exciting time for your family" was the best I could offer. My gaze darted between the two men, desperate to figure out what was going on here.

Julian nodded his thanks while my father continued speaking. "So here's the itinerary for this week. You will dine out Friday evening, just the two of you, followed by brunch with Robert and Elise and your mother and I on Sunday. There is one nonprofit benefit on Tuesday evening in San Francisco, which we will all attend. And we'll finish out the week with your father's campaign fundraiser on Friday evening, Julian." My father gave the other man a confident smile.

"Sounds right to me, Gerald." His self-assured tone matched my father's.

It was clear that nothing was expected of me in this exchange because neither man spared me a glance until Julian stood. Had I been called home just to stand here as a prop? Neither my father nor Julian seemed inclined to enlighten me as to why I had to stand here feeling off-balance while they kept me out of the loop.

"Well, I wish I didn't have to rush off so soon after we've been introduced, but I have a full day at the office with clients who can't be put off, unfortunately."

My father and I both followed suit, rising from our seats.

"Of course, Julian. A distinguished corporate lawyer such as yourself knows too well how business never waits for any of us." My father chuckled like these easygoing chats were somehow a natural part of his personality and not some act.

The men shook hands, and Julian turned to focus exclusively on me. His gaze moved from my face, doing a brief sweep of my body, before he shook my hand again.

"I am really looking forward to getting to know you better in the coming days, Indigo." A bit of heat slid into the controlled, confident expression in his eyes.

Ick. It was not that he was bad-looking at all, but I had absolutely no interest in any of the hidden implications of his statement.

"Nice to meet you as well, Julian." Politeness was the only thing on my menu this morning.

I sat back down while my father walked Julian to the door of his office and shut it behind him. He made his way back behind his desk with measured steps.

He took his seat once more and shuffled some of the piles of paperwork on his desk from one side to another while I waited silently.

I'd never been so shocked in my entire life. My mind raced to catch up with the implications of what had just happened.

He picked up a page, scanned it, and then put it down again. He repeated the action three times before he acknowledged I was still in the room.

As much as I wanted to light every solitary piece of paper and the wood of his desk on fire for putting me through the last ten minutes, I held my tongue. I was smarter to figure out his angle first.

He would see my anger as some childish tantrum rather than true outrage at his absolute audacity to spring this meeting on me.

"So that went well." He took a sip of the coffee on his desk and eyed me over the rim of the cup, assessing. "I've known Julian's father since college. A brilliant man with a doting, supportive wife. Couldn't ask for a better family. Julian is an excellent choice." He set his cup back down, still staring at me intently.

"Excuse me, Father." My voice was rough from the inferno raging inside me and from sitting like a bloody statue while the two men talked around me. "Could you just clarify *what* Julian is an excellent choice for?"

He wasn't suggesting… He couldn't be… Bile rose in my throat. I swallowed hastily to regain control of the urge to be sick.

"Indigo, you are many things. Impulsive, yes. Immature, yes. Naïve, definitely. But stupid, absolutely not. Julian is the ideal candidate for a husband."

I was going to vomit. Had I walked onto the set of *Bridgerton* unknowingly? A Brontë novel movie adaptation? Was he going to start spouting off about dowries and maidenheads next?

"Marriage? I don't want to get married." The thought of marrying someone—in this case, Julian Fairbank—for political or business reasons made me want to flee the country. Hell, maybe the continent.

Time to brush up on that high school French, girl. You can change your name and never have to deal with any of this. Would Theo consider running away to Paris with me?

"Of course marriage," he snapped. "You're twenty-five years old, directionless, and a Layne!" A vein in his forehead became raised with how hard he was frowning.

"I'm not directionless. I have huge plans to start a nonprofit. I've been planning it for years."

An inheritance that was still eight months away.

"See!" He slapped his palm on his desk angrily. "That is what I'm talking about. You are so naïve that you think you can make all these unrealistic dreams come true just because you like the idea of something. The Layne family donates millions of dollars to charities every year. We do not *run* them." His last words came out on a sneer.

"Aligning ourselves with other well-placed families through marriage is the way to maintain our place in the world. To maintain the status and influence our family has achieved for generations." His eyes locked on mine. "Now, it is your turn to do your duty to this family. You've spent years messing around, achieving nothing while pursuing your little tutoring hobby in Amado. And I've allowed it. It's time to grow up and live up to the responsibilities of this family's legacy. Beyond doing it for your inheritance, as your family, you simply owe us this loyalty."

"But…" My mind was reeling after having my lifestyle and goals completely shredded with a few harsh words. Did he really think so little of me that he hadn't actually *cared* what I'd done with my life these last several years?

"No 'buts,' Indigo. You will go out with Julian two evenings from now. You will summon every ounce of propriety and charm you can excavate from your upbringing, and you will wow him. You will show him how lucky he is to be in the presence of a Layne. And you will reinforce his wise decision to follow me and his father's directions regarding this match. Or you will regret it, I guarantee you. My assistant will contact you with the details of your reservation. Now, go."

His eyes narrowed when he looked at me, and he used his free hand to point at his door.

Forty-One

INDIE

*I*t was almost as if I was outside my body as my limbs moved out the door and shut it behind me. I still couldn't believe what had just happened. My father had made it sound like a done deal.

A suffocating feeling in my chest formed. My dreams of making an important impact with my nonprofit plan felt further away than ever. What would it mean if I couldn't help people the way I always wanted to? What if I couldn't get out of this?

And Theo. My heart squeezed painfully. Everything we had was so far removed from the reality I faced.

"Indigo?" Julian's quiet whisper ripped me from my mental haze.

"Um, I'm sorry, you were saying?" I hadn't heard a word anyone said since we'd sat down at the brunch table.

A tolerant, possibly sympathetic, smile formed on his lips. "Never mind. It wasn't important. Let's talk about you. You've let me go on and on about work all week, and I realize we've hardly scratched the surface of what makes Indigo Layne tick."

There will be no scratching of any kind, buddy.

I was still reeling from the fact that I was sitting at this table at all, surrounded by both sets of parents, who were all too happy to ignore how freaking insane this entire situation was.

I'd mistakenly called my mother after I'd left my father's office several mornings ago.

"My god, Indigo. You interrupted my partners' meeting for this? *Since you never call, I thought it was something important, like you or your father were in the hospital or something. I don't know what you are going on about here. This is how things happen in our world. Do you think good matches just happen at random? These types of things take careful planning and care. Honestly, you should be grateful."*

"But…" I began.

"I don't have time for this. If you insist on belaboring the point, we can do that when you're not costing me one thousand dollars an hour."

As I glanced at my parents across the table, so united in their goal of this merger, it was all too easy to picture myself and Julian in their place in twenty-five years. Would there be any shred of myself left in that future?

It would have been easier to get up and storm out of here if Julian had been an asshole. He wasn't. He was polite and seemingly respectful. He didn't talk over me. There was even a chance he seemed a smidgen less arrogant than the average twenty-something male in my parents' social circles. He was also classically handsome and well-dressed.

I bet my parents liked him so much they wished they could just swap kids with the Fairbanks rather than deal with all the fuss of a wedding.

"Uh, well, I've spent the last few years figuring out what I wanted to do. Not very interesting at all. I really want to hear more about the intellectual property case you mentioned." I arranged my facial features in an expression that hopefully appeared genuine.

"I see what you're doing here." Julian winked conspiratorially. "But you don't need to worry. I was already interested before we even met this week."

Barf. He thought I was fawning all over him to charm him in some way. Before I could consider a polite response, my phone buzzed from where I'd slid it between my leg and the chair.

"Um, would you excuse me for a moment? I just need a quick moment in the ladies' room."

"Of course." Julian, with his perfectly molded etiquette, half stood as I got out of my chair.

Once I was safely around a corner at the back of the restaurant, I unlocked my phone.

Theo

Hey baby, I've been thinking about you non-stop. I have to admit I'm getting a little worried. I don't like that you're out there on your own and I still don't really understand what's going on. I'm glad you're staying at the house, though.

I'd been staying in the Yao-Miller guest room all week. Emery had jumped at the chance to spend more time together so unexpectedly soon with us having left just last week.

Indie

I'm fine. Like I said, boring family stuff. It's almost over and I'll see you soon.

> **Just out to brunch with my parents. Text you later? Love you.**

Theo

I miss you. Love you.

I hoped and prayed that I would be able to weasel my way out of this marriage problem with limited drama.

For now, I had to survive the rest of this meal.

When I arrived back at Emery's house, I was shocked to find Abbie and Emery sitting at the Yao-Millers' kitchen table with three iced coffees in the middle of the table.

"Hi! Look who's here!" Emery bounced a little in her seat.

"Hey, girl, what are you doing here! I thought you were spending this week down in LA with Aiden's family?" I was surprised but thrilled to see Abbie, who'd been with Aiden's family over Christmas. They weren't supposed to be back yet.

Abbie stood for a quick hug after I reached the chair next to her.

"Something came up, and we're back a bit early. I missed you so much." She reached for my hand that rested on the table, giving it a quick squeeze.

Emery smiled happily at having all of us in the same room again. We'd all taken this for granted, being in the same city for so long, that moments like these had become precious.

"It sucks that you had to cut your visit short. Though I am really happy to see you." I gave her a wide grin. "But I have to ask, I thought you had sworn off iced coffee for good?"

A mishap with an iced coffee during a team meeting had landed

Abbie a promotion… and a boyfriend last spring.

"Well…" She toyed with the straw in her cup, a blush pinkening her cheeks. "Since it brought me the love of my life, I'd have to say it's forgiven."

As the other half of the reason for said mishap, I raised my eyebrows. "Oh! Does that mean *I* get some credit for your current heart-shaped pupils?"

It was true. Abbie had consistently looked more content and a hell of a lot more loved up since being with Aiden.

Emery stood quickly and went to the kitchen counter, returning with a… meat tenderizer and a cutting board??

"Um…" I looked between them. Abbie also stared at the kitchen utensil.

"This meeting will now come to order." Emery used the mallet to gently tap the cutting board and then held it in her fist, resting the handle's end on the table.

"I'm so confused. What are we meeting about?" I frowned. "And why do you need a weapon for it?"

"This is not a weapon. It's a gavel," Emery replied.

Abbie reached over and gently encouraged Emery to put down the steampunk justice mallet. "Em. We get it, sweetie. We're going to be serious here."

Emery pouted a little but released her accessory. She looked over at Abbie and nodded.

"So, despite that start," Abbie began while Emery huffed, "this is a bit of an intervention. For you, Indie. But in a we-love-you-so-much kind of way."

I laughed. "An intervention for what?"

"This whole arranged-marriage business your stupid father is trying to pull!" The words burst from Emery's mouth, her volume at least double that of Abbie's.

"What? Nobody's getting married here. I'm just biding my time until I can think of a way out of it that will make my father think it was his idea." I shrugged, not mentioning my last few sleepless nights where I came up with exactly zero plans.

"That! That's what I'm talking about!" Emery jabbed her finger into the table for emphasis. "You're about to bide your time into an engagement if you're not careful."

I sighed. Emery was right. I needed help, and here were the two women I respected and valued most in the world.

"You're right." I nodded at Emery. "Can you help me figure out how to handle this?"

Twin expressions of surprise looked back at me.

"Oh my god. Do you know that this is the first time you've ever asked me for anything? I love you so much, Ind. Thank you for letting us be there for you the way you've been there for us all these years." Abbie's eyes welled with tears.

Whoa. A tidal wave of emotion washed over me. I'd never wanted to ask for anything because I hated feeling like a burden. I'd always believed that it was my responsibility to take care of the few people I loved without asking for anything in return. I thought that's what being a good friend meant.

Had I denied them the ability to reciprocate their support by pretending I could handle everything on my own?

"It's not that we think you need the help, babe," Emery added. "But why should you have to do everything by yourself? We're here for you. You've got Theo now. Hell, my entire family loves you like you're our own. We're going to have your back.

"Speaking of Theo, what does he have to say about this mess?" Abbie injected quietly, her gaze sympathetic. They know me well enough to guess I haven't told Theo anything.

Shit. That worry about being a burden was just popping up all over the place.

"That too!" Emery pointed at both Abbie and me this time. "It's not like I'm rushing to call him up and spill all your secrets. But that brother of mine—my nicest brother, as you know—is in love with you. He's all the way in Toronto moping around your apartment with only a small, practically hairless pup for a companion, not knowing what to think."

I threw up my hands in front of me as if I could stop the correctness of their words before the sounds reached me. Unfortunately, physics didn't work that way, and I heard them loud and clear.

"Actually, he's on his way to Dallas tonight. So he'll be moping there, if he is at all. And Giz will be with my boss and his wife. But fine, you're right. He doesn't know. But he would be on the next plane out here beating his perfectly muscled caveman chest if he heard what my father was up to."

"So?" Emery said, angling her head inquisitively.

"*So* he has this little hiccup called the contract he signed with the Tempests, and he's not allowed to miss games. I don't want him making any decisions that will affect his career based on me. It's his dream, and I refuse to put him in a situation where he might make a choice he will later regret." My traitorous eyes were slightly blurry as they filled.

"That's really sweet, Ind." Abbie reached across the table once more and turned her palm up, letting it sit between us. She knew I didn't always want the touchy-feely kind of comfort, but I placed my hand over hers, taking her up on her offer this time. "And you know how much I hate saying anything you don't want to hear, but are you worried that he would choose you over his career and then regret it?"

"Of course he'd choose you!" Emery's tone left no room for doubt. "And he wouldn't regret it. He's lucky to be with you. And he knows that."

"But what if he didn't? I don't think I could handle that for the second time." My voice was quiet.

"What do you mean, second time?" Emery's gaze sharpened.

"I kind of kissed him on Christmas when we were nineteen." I let go of Abbie's hand, covering my face. "I'm sorry. I shouldn't have. Nothing happened."

"This calls for the gavel." Emery picked up the utensil and banged it on the cutting board. "So that"—she pointed with the mace-like cooking tool—"is why you stopped coming to stay for the holidays since then?"

I dropped my arms to the table and nodded, now worried I'd have a second Yao-Miller sibling upset with me.

"Aw. That's really beautiful. You took a chance at love." Abbie's smile was dreamy.

"Yeah, and got my heart beat into submission with the equivalent of that thing." I pointed at the meat mallet. "That took me *years* to get past. Now that Theo and I are together, I can't do anything that will force him to choose between the things he wants."

"Girl, we're going to have to have regular tree house meetings when you get home again. You are just full of secrets, aren't you?" Emery joked, thankfully lightening the mood a little.

"I promise, you know my only two now. Pretending to date Wells in college when I was really studying in the library on weekends and the Theo kiss. That's it, Your Honor." I lifted my right hand as if swearing to my statement.

"Fine. But seriously, you aren't going to sit back and let this archaic setup your father is arranging get in the way of your relationship with

Theo, are you? You love him." She gently put the mallet down again.

"How do you know I love him?" I had barely admitted it to Theo. I hadn't been brave enough to tell my friends how deeply I was invested in my relationship.

"If you think a single thing is a secret in this house, you're dreaming, my friend. The twins and I were sitting at the top of the staircase while you and Theo exchanged 'I love yous' on Christmas morning. Chase had a bag of treats, keeping Giz quiet." She grinned while Abbie broke out in giggles.

Embarrassed, I actually blushed for the first time in forever. My cheeks heated, and little prickles formed at the back of my neck as I thought about the three of them, plus dog, eavesdropping on the most important moment of my life.

"You guys are the *worst*! I'm not even sure I can be associated with you anymore." My tone was horrified, but I was only half-mad.

"Welcome to the family!" Emery cheers'd me with her ice coffee cup. "Plenty more privacy invasions where that came from." She grinned.

"Not that that wasn't the best thing I've heard all year," Abbie laughed, as if it wasn't like less than a week into the new year, "but to bring us back to the task at hand. I hate to push you on this, but I don't think you can sit on this thing your father is trying to do. You might lose Theo in the process. Is your inheritance really worth that?" Her expression had lost all its mirth.

"No," I answered immediately and then gasped. Shit! I hadn't even had to think about it. Theo was more important than any previous dream, I realized. A life with him was my new dream.

"But what about all the kids I could help? If not me, then who?" My heart felt heavy with selfishness in choosing love over making a difference to the kids I'd witnessed needing more help.

"Does it have to be all or nothing?" Emery asked, settling her elbows on the table and propping her chin on her hands. "You've been a volunteer tutor since high school. What is the best thing about that?"

"That's easy. Seeing a kid break through an obstacle that they thought they couldn't." My reply was instantaneous.

Emery nodded. "So is dumping ten million dollars into this huge undertaking the only way to help kids do that? What about teaching?"

"Yes!" Abbie practically vibrated in her seat. "You would be an amazing teacher! You're sooo patient with the kids. Not to mention, you have that effortless 'cool' factor that kids just eat up. Just by being yourself."

"Teaching?" I hadn't ever considered it before. Something warm expanded in my chest, relaxing my tense muscles and allowing my breath to come a little easier.

What was I really trying to prove by being so stuck on this one idea? Did I really need my inheritance to make a difference?

You're trying to prove you're not your parents while still trying to impress them at the same time.

Oh god, I was, wasn't I? That thought made me sick. My parents didn't even care about doing good in the world. They used charities as tax write-offs. It stung more than a little that even after a lifetime of never being there for me, I still secretly hoped for their approval.

And now, they wanted to use me as a tool to further their ambitions with Robert Fairbank's senate campaign.

"Shit, you're right." I scrubbed my face with my hands. "I gotta go. I need to confront my father and tell him that there is no way in hell that I'm going along with this any longer. What was I thinking this week?"

Abbie gave me a soft smile. "It's pretty hard to say no to our parents, even when they haven't treated us well. My therapist says it is totally natural to still want their approval. But I think you've found something you want more than that now, right?"

I nodded, unlocking my phone to order a rideshare. I had to deal with this right now.

She was right. I wanted Theo more than anything.

I let myself into my parents' house, pleased that they hadn't changed the codes. I didn't feel the need to give my father any warning of my arrival.

There was no stopping me now that I was sure of what I wanted. I didn't stop to knock on his office door, knowing he'd be working since it was early evening.

The sound of the door had him looking up from his computer, an annoyed frown on his face.

"Indigo. What are you doing here?" He leaned back in his chair, his arms crossed.

"I'm not doing it," I spat out angrily.

I could feel my heartbeat in my throat, almost like I could choke on it. Not once in my life had I talked back to my father. First, I kept myself under the radar so that I could survive unnoticed until I was old enough to move out on my own. And for the last seven years, I'd sat in this office four times a year, letting him criticize even the most inconsequential things in my life.

But I was done.

"What exactly aren't you doing?" His tone was sharp, warning me to tone down my attitude.

"I'm not going along with this insane scheme of yours to gain political favors. I won't be seeing Julian again. Hell, you probably sent me to Toronto just so I wouldn't hear any of the gossip about

this so-called engagement you cooked up with Julian's family."
I crossed my arms and stared back at him, letting my feelings of
distaste and betrayal bleed into my expression.

"Indigo, I do not have time for you to have a tantrum. You will
be at that fundraiser in two days. Then, once you finish out your
contract in Toronto, you'll attend any other function Julian requires
you at, period. Our family will be joined with the Fairbanks."

Before I could answer, a soft knock sounded against the office door.

"What now?" my father called out.

The door opened just enough for Angelina to pop her head in.
"Excuse me, Mr. Layne. There is a gentleman here…"

The door was pushed open all the way before I could process who
was behind it.

Theo. I couldn't believe it. Was he appearing before my eyes
because I'd missed him so much that I was imagining things now?

"Theo?" I whispered. "How?"

He made his way into the room, ignoring my father completely,
before gathering me into a tight hug.

"Emery. I came straight from the airport," he explained.

"Thank you." I squeezed him back.

"Rocky." He spoke quietly into my ear, his lips sending shivers
through my body from where they grazed my skin. "You don't need
me here. But I had to be. I'm always going to have your back. Please
don't leave me in the dark again." His tone was rough with emotion.

"I'm sorry. I didn't know what to do, but I do now. Wait for me?"
I moved my hands to his jaw so that I could bring his mouth to
mine for a soft kiss.

"Always." He leaned back to offer me a wink.

"Excuse me. Who the hell are you?" My father stood behind his
desk now, incensed.

Shit. I had totally forgotten where we were for a second. Such was the power of Theo Yao-Miller's spell.

"I'm here for Indie," Theo stated.

Theo stepped back from me, mouthing, "You got this," and went to lean against the wall by the now closed office door, crossing his arms over his chest. Gone was the soft side of Theo that he only showed around me and his family. Instead, the formidable competitor who was used to eighty-mile-an-hour pucks flying in his direction stared my father down.

"This is Theo. My boyfriend. Who I'm in love with." I raised my chin defiantly.

"Love? You're joking," my father scoffed. "You think that changes anything? It doesn't. You will go through with this engagement to unite our family with the Fairbanks."

A choking sound came from behind me. I chanced a glance back at Theo, whose eyebrows were aiming for his hairline, his face a picture of shock but not anger.

"Sorry," I mouthed, putting all the emotions I felt for Theo into my gaze, hoping he would understand I was about to get us out of here.

I turned back to my father and opened my mouth to speak, but he cut me off.

"If you and Julian want to discuss matters"—he flipped a dismissive hand at Theo—"then that is your business. But you will live up to the expectations of this family."

"No," I said, not backing down.

"Do I really have to go through all the ways I can make your life difficult in getting your inheritance you want so badly? Julian is even willing to humor your altruistic tendencies." He spoke like wanting to help people was a disease I was afflicted with.

"Julian won't have to put up with anything. He can find himself some other woman whose goals are similar to his." My father opened his mouth to speak, but I kept talking. "You can keep my fucking inheritance. I don't want it anymore. Is that what you want to hear? You don't even give a damn about me—you never have. You don't even care about the money; it's just a tool you used to keep me under your thumb all these years. Well, I'm done. If you want to make it difficult for me to access my inheritance, be my guest and call my lawyer directly. I'm done with this family, the Layne name, and you."

When he didn't respond right away, his face beet red in anger or shock, I knew I'd gotten my point across.

I turned and walked to his office door, offering my hand to Theo, who thankfully took it.

As we crossed the threshold of his office, I tossed the final words I would probably ever speak to him over my shoulder. "Goodbye, Father. I hope the ten million was worth it. Good luck explaining everything to the Fairbanks."

Not that I thought he would miss me or feel a real loss at my departure from their lives, but I had to remind him one last time that it was his own choices that brought us here.

Let him be the one to clear up the shitshow he'd created.

Forty-Two

INDIE

The adrenaline faded as Theo drove us back to his family's house. The anger I'd used to get through standing up to my father left me hollow and exhausted. But the accompanying relief was so profound it confirmed how right my choice was. I was finally free, for the first time in my life, to choose what to do next without the impossible weight of my parents' demands.

For the first several minutes of the ride, neither of us spoke. The knots in my stomach reformed when I thought about how I had kept all of the events of this past week from Theo.

"I'm sorry," I said, turning in my seat to look at his profile in the driver's seat. "It wasn't that I was hiding this mess my parents roped me into before I could process it…"

"Rocky." His expression was calm when he looked at me quickly before returning his eyes to the road. "Let's talk at the house, okay? We're almost there."

"Okay," I replied quietly, looking down at my hands in my lap. It was fair to give Theo some time to process the shitshow he'd just witnessed in my father's office.

Hell, I'd just done the one thing I'd feared all my life: taking a direct stand against my parents' orders.

So I could certainly give Theo a few minutes with his thoughts.

As if to reassure me, Theo reached across the console to take my hand in his. He interlaced his fingers with mine, leaving our joined hands resting on my lap. A surge of relief and gratitude washed over me.

We would be okay. Theo was the only one I wanted by my side as I took on this next stage of my life.

Emery's suggestion of teaching surfaced in my thoughts. The more the idea rattled around in my mind, the happier I felt. With the right qualifications, I could live anywhere while doing something that I loved and mattered to me.

And Theo. Most importantly, I wouldn't have to leave Theo. Even if my father decided to go to his contact in the Tempests' head office to get me fired, making my life difficult like he promised, I had more than enough savings to stay in Toronto until I could work out some sort of visa.

Before I knew it, we'd arrived back at the Yao-Miller house. Theo guided me into the house before whisking me into his arms as soon as the front door closed behind us. Even caught off guard, my legs had wrapped themselves around his waist automatically.

He pressed me into the back of the now closed front door and brought our foreheads together, searching my face with concern.

"Are you okay? That was a hell of a moment you just had." That his first words were asking about my feelings had me melting into his arms.

I trusted him to hold me up.

"Yeah. I just blew up my life, didn't I?" I buried my face against his neck, calmed by the scent of his skin.

"Look at me, Rocky." He spoke his request against my hair.

As much as I wanted to stay fused with him forever, I knew I owed him an explanation for what he'd heard my father say. I lifted my head so that I could see his face once more.

"An engagement? Is he insane?" Theo growled.

"I should have cut ties with my father when he sprung this absurd plan on me when I arrived. I was just so caught off guard and felt so trapped all of a sudden, I couldn't think straight." I kept my gaze steady on his, hoping he could see how sorry I was.

"Baby. First of all, you're mine," he growled, the caveman persona making its reappearance. "There is no fucking way some rich douchebag is going to come between us. I know you."

He punctuated his words by capturing my mouth in a filthy kiss before pulling back with a nip to my bottom lip.

"God, you're delicious." His tone was gravelly with lust. "Definitely more of that later. But please promise me that we're going to lean on each other from now on. I know it's so hard when you've taken care of everyone, including me, before yourself. But I need us to be partners, okay?"

My eyes widened in surprise. "What do you mean 'taken care of you'?" What was he talking about?

"I heard you that day, sweetheart. Remember when you ripped that reporter a new one over his questions about my mom?" His expression brimmed with affection.

"Oh. That." My cheeks heated, slightly embarrassed at how intensely I'd gone after the reporter. But who was I kidding. This was Theo. I'd do it again and again.

"That was the moment I started falling in love with you. Even if it took me some time to realize what I was feeling. You stood up for me, even when things were a mess between us. No one in my life has had my back like that for a long time, Ind. It meant everything to me in that moment. Now, *you* mean everything to me. But more importantly, for what I think is the first time, you put yourself first today. You stood up against your father's bullshit manipulation and took your life back, Rocky. I'm so proud of you." His beaming smile blurred as my eyes filled.

I was so overwhelmed by the last part of what he said I couldn't address it right now. But there were things I absolutely knew to be true that I could share with him.

"You're everything to me too, Theo. And yes, I'm going to do my best from here on out to be your partner and let you in. I know I'm going to make mistakes, though. Can you be patient with me as I figure it out?" It was a struggle to keep eye contact when I wanted to hide from my own vulnerability.

"Considering I plan on spending forever with you, baby, I can definitely promise to do everything I can to honor your trust," he said and grinned.

A few tears escaped my eyes at his declaration. I quickly swept them away. He shifted me in his arms, and I realized that we'd just had this whole conversation with him holding me up.

I wiggled my body until he set me down with a chuckle.

"Wait! Don't you have to be in Dallas in, like, eight hours?" My brain caught up to reality in this moment. Shit! What was he even doing here? He wasn't allowed to miss games.

"I couldn't wait to see you. I've felt wrong all week without you in Toronto. I know hockey made it impossible for me to be here with you the whole time, but next time something happens and you need to be somewhere, I'm coming with you. Where you go, I go, from now on, okay?" He wrapped his arms around my waist as if he couldn't bear any space between us.

I lifted my face to his for a kiss that quickly turned heated again. After a few minutes of making out like teenagers after curfew against the front door, he pulled back, both of us breathless.

"I'll take that as a yes. Now, tell me the rest," he demanded.

"Okay, okay! Can we at least move out of the front foyer for this?" I squeezed his forearms where my hands rested.

Theo grunted before he picked me up again, carried me into the kitchen, and deposited me on the counter.

"Yeah, it's absolutely insane. Apparently, I was naïve in thinking this kind of thing didn't happen anymore, but my parents insisted. They wanted a connection with this Fairbanks family. They'd tried setting me up multiple times before, but I never expected anything like this. I guess I'd underestimated how far they would go to get what they wanted." I leaned back against the cabinet door behind me and waited for Theo's reaction.

"Let me get this straight. Your parents wanted you to marry some stranger sooner than later, but you potentially chucked your inheritance—which now makes a lot of sense when you talked about your nonprofit idea—literally in their faces and walked away from your family and what was rightfully owed to you for… us?" Theo's eyes started welling up in the corners. He tried to blink rapidly to clear it but kept his watery gaze on me.

"For us. For you. And for me." I wiped the errant tear that rolled down his cheek with my thumb before I kissed the path where it had trailed over his skin. "The life we're building together, be it in Toronto or wherever your contract is next year, that's what's most important to me. To be free of all of the stuff from my childhood that I've always hated and make choices about what's best for us and myself."

"Holy shit. We're really doing this." Theo's smile was as bright as I'd ever seen it. "Fuck, ten million dollars, really?" He scrunched his nose.

I got it. I really did. It was a lifetime's worth of money.

"Yes. Don't tell anyone, but I have ten million reasons right here worth infinitely more." I brought my hand between our bodies and pressed it against his heart. "There is no contest, goalie. You win every time."

"You have turned into your own worst nightmare right here, Rocky. We might as well be writing billboard messages to each other at this point." Theo kissed me sweetly.

I gave him a faux annoyed look. "But your secret is safe with me," he promised.

It was true. For Theo, I was a not-so-secret marshmallow on the inside.

"And about next season, I'm hoping we'll be spending it in Amado." His gaze held mine.

"What? What about your contract in Toronto? Are you okay? Is it your knees? Why did you pick me up if you're hurt?" Worry raced through me that something had happened that no one had told me about.

"Easy, baby. I'm fine. I've got a bit of a long story for you too, but the gist is that I told my agent that this season is my last." Theo's face was the picture of calm.

"What? Why?" He was giving it all up? Oh god, did he think I didn't want him to play anymore?

"I can see you freaking out." He squeezed my waist in reassurance. "Like you, Ind, I've realized I have new dreams. I've loved playing professional hockey, but I'm at a point where for the first time in a long time, I have so much more than hockey going for me. I want to spend my time living rather than keeping up with a grind that left me constantly nursing injuries and separated from those I love most."

I slumped in his arms in relief but couldn't stop myself from saying, "Because you know that I'd go anywhere with you. You don't have to retire to make me happy. I want you to have your dreams."

"You are my dream now, baby. Buying a house together and building a life with Giz. The best part is that we can do that from Amado, which I know you miss, and I can make up for all the years I've missed with my family." He brought his hands from my body to my cheeks so that I had to really look into his eyes.

His expression was confident and happy. He really wanted this.

"Okay, Theo. Let's do it. I love you."

"I love you too, Ind." He kissed me quickly before he pulled back to make eye contact once more. "And, baby?"

"Yes?" He leaned forward again so that I spoke the word against his lips.

"The only person you'll be marrying one day is me."

Epilogue

INDIE

MAY

The hum inside the Billings Centre was electric. It was game six for the Tempests against Boston, and Toronto was down three games to two. They had to win tonight, or they wouldn't move forward into the second round of the playoffs.

My seatmate's focus, however, was not on the nail-biting pressure facing the Tempests tonight.

Abbie's jaw had dropped with one glance at the ice when we'd arrived early to make sure we had everything ready for when Theo's family got here.

I leaned toward her, putting a finger underneath her chin to gently close her mouth as she watched the teams' warm-ups.

"Careful. Aiden's going to come back with your drink and find you ogling the hockey players," I teased.

Her gaze flipped to mine for a second before being drawn back to the ice.

"Indie." Her voice was a strained whisper. Abbie pressed her shoulder into mine as she spoke out of one corner of her mouth. "You never told me anything about the warm-ups." She choked on the last word.

I laughed at her reaction to the more—ahem—enthralling nature of some of the players' pre-game stretches. Currently, a couple of Boston's players were working through some vigorous hip rolls and lower-body stretches.

"Jesus. It's worth the price of admission alone just to see them warm up." The words slipped from Abbie's lips before she quickly slapped her hand over her mouth in embarrassment.

"What's worth the price of admission?" a deep voice came from behind us.

The pink blush that decorated her cheeks as she watched the players thrust their hips toward the ice spread like wildfire over her cheeks and neck at the sound of her boyfriend Aiden's words.

"Oh! Nothing." She cleared her throat before offering Aiden a sweet smile.

Aiden, having forgone his usual bespoke suit for the occasion, still looked ready to take on a boardroom in a cashmere sweater and perfectly pressed black slacks.

A glance at the ice had a hum emanating from his mouth, "I have an idea of what you two were just talking about." He reached our row, moving to stand beside Abbie and handing her the soda he'd gone to the concession stands for. He leaned into her space. "As long as you remember you're mine, sweetheart," he spoke into her ear.

Standing so close to Abbie's other side meant I felt the shiver that ran through her with his words. Those professional hockey players on the ice were a momentary blip in Abbie's thoughts, judging by the adoring gaze she gave Aiden.

Before I could tease either of them, a commotion came from the other side of the row. The Yao-Miller family had arrived.

"Excuse me, pardon me. Just going to sit and watch my brother play a very important game. It's a surprise, you see. He doesn't know we're coming." Chase spoke animatedly to the couple that he was about to climb over to get to our seats.

"Chase! They don't need your whole life story. We're never going to get to our seats if you keep talking. We're already running late as it is." Emery's voice rose from behind her brother. "Sorry about him."

After successfully making it into our row, Chase offered me a side hug before Emery pushed him out of the way so she could take the seat beside me.

Their dad, Joe, mouthed, "Thank you for this," over his bickering children's heads, giving me a warm smile. I grinned back at him. I was overjoyed to have them here on Theo's behalf.

"Sorry we're late. You have no idea what it takes to wrangle the twins to get somewhere on time. Even from a hotel steps away from the arena." Emery rolled her eyes as she jerked a thumb in Chase and Liam's direction.

"Hey! I resent that completely correct accusation." Liam leaned around Chase to offer Emery an unconvincing glare.

"Yeah. We had to get our signs ready," argued Chase. He unfolded the posterboard from under his arm. It read, "Wash your socks, Yao! I can smell you from here!" complete with blue and gold glitter that flaked off every time he moved the sign.

"You are not holding that up." I narrowed my eyes at him. Nothing was going to mess up this game for Theo. It was the only game I could make everyone's schedules work out, and the hockey gods had blessed my plan to make sure Theo's whole family was together.

"I thought you might say that." Chase winked and nudged Liam to open his sign. "So we made another boring, sentimental one."

Liam revealed a similarly glitter-tastic poster, except this one had the words "We're proud of you, bruh! Yao's our hero!"

"Good." I nodded. "You can hold up that one."

Emery jumped in to change the subject, elbowing me gently in the arm. "Do you think Theo's going to be surprised? Are you sure he doesn't know we're coming?" She bounced a bit on her toes. The excitement in the arena was contagious, and besides, there was nothing Theo's siblings loved more than taking each other by surprise.

"Definitely. Aiden bought these tickets. He's expecting me and you to be sitting over on that side." I pointed across the ice to another section of glass-side seats nearest to the goal. "And he has no idea that your dad, Chase, and Liam were able to get the time off."

While Emery and Liam had some flexibility with their jobs, it wasn't the case for the whole family.

Once Theo told his family he was retiring, Chase had volunteered to let one of his co-leads take on the big project his architecture firm was working on this spring so that he'd have more freedom to come to Theo's games. And for the first time in his career, Joe had left the SJSU football team in the hands of his assistant coach for a handful of games in order to be here.

My eyes threatened to fill every time I thought about them coming together for Theo. I swiped a finger under each eye just in case any rogue tears threatened to escape.

I'd worn waterproof eye makeup for a reason.

"Aw. You're such a softie now, Ind. I love it," Abbie said fondly.

"Am not," I argued half-heartedly. I totally was. And I didn't even mind anymore.

Even though I couldn't see Theo's face through his goalie mask when he'd come on the ice during the pre-game program, I knew he'd been thrilled. Last night, I'd texted Michaels to point Theo in our direction before the game started.

Instead of skating straight to goal, Theo made his way over to the glass and pointed his stick at me with a nod.

Now, hours later, after a nail-biting game, Joe and I made our way toward the locker room. I hoped that having his family here to celebrate him would ease the sting of the Tempests' loss.

As we rounded the final corner toward the locker room, Joe stopped short.

"Indie, I know you must be anxious to make sure Theo's okay, but do you mind if I go ahead and have a quick word with him first? I don't want to spoil your moment." Joe's usual calm was punctuated with a quick roll of his shoulders. He glanced toward the door where the players would exit from.

Knowing how much Theo had always wished his dad had made it to more of his hockey games over the years, there was no way I was going to stand in the way of their father-son moment, especially with Joe initiating it.

Theo and I had all the moments in the world ahead of us.

"Of course, Joe." I offered him a soft smile. "I can…" I gestured around the corner, offering to give them total privacy.

"No need. You're welcome to stay. I only want to make sure Theo hears what I have to say before we rejoin the family and the chaos begins again. And before he comes out here, I want to thank you, Indie. Not just for now but for making my son so obviously happy all these months. I haven't seen this kind of joy in him since before we lost Alice." His jaw tightened briefly mentioning his wife's name, but the tension around his eyes smoothed once he took a deep breath.

"He makes me really happy too." My voice wobbled on the few

words I could force out.

"I do hope you'll consider calling me 'Dad,' you know, when the time comes?" He winked before moving to wait just outside the locker room door.

I couldn't do anything except lean against the opposite wall, a ripple of surprised pleasure lingering in the wake of Joe's words.

It was several minutes after the majority of players had already left until Theo emerged.

Thankfully, the hallway had quieted, giving Theo and his dad a moment together without his teammates vying for his attention.

Despite the team's loss, Theo grinned when he saw us both waiting for him.

"Hey, Rocky. Hi, Dad." He sounded tired but happy. As much as I wanted to jump into his arms and celebrate his last game with him, I nodded toward Joe.

Joe pulled Theo into his arms for a tight hug. He murmured something quietly into Theo's ear before releasing him.

Joe kept a hand on Theo's shoulder, his gaze steady on his son.

"I want you to know how proud I am, and have always been, of all you have accomplished in your career, Theo. I know for a fact that all my players over the years probably got tired of me bragging about my talented, dedicated son." Theo's mouth opened in shock, but no words emerged before he closed it again. Joe gave his shoulder an affectionate squeeze before continuing. "One of my biggest regrets has been that you might have believed that I didn't support your hockey dreams."

Theo swallowed deeply, hesitating.

"You mean you wouldn't rather I played football?" he said quietly.

"Never," Joe insisted, his tone sad. "I should have made myself clear when you started out, but I loved that your mom went all in with you on your dream. I wanted you two to have that bond since lord knows she had zero interest in football despite marrying a college football coach." He chuckled warmly with the memory before sobering once more.

"I'm sorry, Theo." He brought his other hand up to Theo's shoulder, looking directly into his eyes. "I'm just as proud of you today, retiring as one of the top goalies in the league, as I was the day your Gong Gong first put you onto the ice in your brand-new skates. I have that very moment framed on my office shelf. It was always one of our favorite photos. Your mom was so happy when you were happy, T. Now that you've found love yourself"—he turned his head to smile at me—"and are moving home again, I hope you'll give me a chance to be more present in this next stage of your life."

Theo threw his arms around his dad in response. "Thank you, Dad. I want that too." His voice was thick with emotion.

Joe gave Theo a kiss on the top of his head before pulling back. "I will see you both shortly. I'm going to make sure your siblings have behaved since I left them."

"Thank you, Joe." I tried and failed to hide the tremor in my voice after being allowed to share in such an important moment.

I moved toward them to hug Joe as he took his leave. Being part of the Yao-Miller family felt tangible to me now. I wouldn't take this gift for granted.

Then, it was just Theo and me.

Before we left the arena to celebrate with our family, I had one more surprise for him.

I wrapped my arms around his neck, bringing our mouths together for a kiss. Theo deepened the kiss, his hair still damp from his shower when I wove my fingers into it.

Moments later, I pulled back and linked my hands behind Theo's neck. His hands remained on my hips, giving me a squeeze where they rested underneath his jersey I wore.

"How do you feel, baby?" I tilted my head back to make sure I could see his whole face.

"God. Ten minutes ago, I would have said tired, proud, and sad that we lost tonight. It feels right, you know? I gave this team my all for this last season, and I'm leaving with no regrets. But then my dad goes and says all that? Shit. It's like a weight I didn't know I was carrying lifted off my shoulders." A deep sigh accompanied his words.

"He's proud of me, Rocky. He told his players about me," Theo whispered, a few tears running down his cheeks. "All these years, he's…" His eyes closed, letting more wetness escape, unable to finish his thought.

I moved one hand from behind his neck to gently wipe them away.

"Yes. All these years, he's been proud of you. I could see it in the way he watched you tonight. Like he couldn't look away from you for a second or he'd miss something." I gave him a watery smile. "I'm sorry the team didn't win tonight, Theo. You deserved to make it all the way to the Cup."

"I'm not, baby. I'm winning at life right now. I don't need a trophy to show me how lucky I am. I've got everything I need right here in my arms." He kissed my lips softly before continuing. "And I have all the most important people in the world to me in one place tonight because the love of my life surprised me by getting my whole family here to see me play my last game."

"You deserve to be celebrated, Theo. And I have one more surprise before we head back to my place." I stepped back, pulling up the jersey I wore to the waistband of my jeans.

"Rocky…" He looked around us and up at the ceiling for cameras. "What are you doing?"

"Giving you your surprise, goalie." I flipped the button on my jeans, giving me just enough room to expose my hip area. "Look." I jutted my chin down.

Always protective of me, Theo closed the short distance between our bodies, using his height and bulk to hide me from anyone who might walk by.

I moved the fabric further away from my skin so Theo could see his surprise.

About two inches inward from my hip bone was Theo's jersey number, an eighty-eight stylishly tattooed where only he'd ever get to see.

"Fuck me, Rocky." He ran the tip of his index finger over the healed skin, making me shiver.

"We'll get to that later, if you're up for it, goalie," I teased.

Unable to take his eyes, or finger, off his surprise, he didn't look up even as he started to harden against my opposite thigh.

"Oh, I'm up for it. I've never seen anything so sexy in my fucking life, baby. Well, this tattoo and everything else about you, that is. Thank you." I grinned at his enthusiasm.

After one last swipe of his finger against my skin, he buttoned my jeans and pulled the fabric of the jersey from my hand so it covered my waist once again.

His gaze met mine, shining with more love and sexy promises than I'd ever dared hope for. And now this kind, loyal, and gorgeous man was mine.

"Ready to go?" I asked.

"More than ready, baby." Theo wrapped his arm around my waist as we walked toward the players' exit. "I can't wait to get back to Amado with you and start our life together there."

"Me too." I raised my hand to his chin, turning it so that I could look into his eyes. "I love you, Theo."

"I love you too, Rocky." Theo kissed my temple. "See what I mean? What's one fleeting moment holding a trophy over my head when I have a million more like this to look forward to with you."

Acknowledgements

Thank you to my whole family for putting up with the fact that my most productive writing hours are the least convenient family-related hours of any given day.

My biggest thank-you has to go to my husband, for the second time. Thank you for continuing to encourage me during the difficult stages of the writing process and for being so supportive even though I haven't let you read this book yet!

And to you, my readers. Thank you for taking a chance on Indie and Theo's love story. Indie is fierce and independent as a result of her childhood. My favorite thing about Theo is that he is her number one fan in every situation. She never has to shrink herself to keep Theo's love. They are true equals. I hope Indie's fearlessness in standing up for her loved ones, and finally, herself in the end, felt as empowering to read as it was for me to write it. I'm so grateful to you for reading!

I hope you'll join me for Emery's book which will release in 2025!

About the Author

VIOLET K. AVERY has been a fan of all genres of romance since she picked up her very first romance novel at the age of sixteen. It was like a whole world opened up before her and she hasn't looked back since. While her professional background is in education, writing a novel has been a lifelong dream.

Her characters deal with real issues and difficult emotions. Their HEAs are a celebration of how far they've come as individuals and as partners.

When Violet's not writing, she's spending time with her family and cleaning up the latest chaos created by their two adorable rescue dogs.

Violet lives in Ontario, Canada.

Let's Connect!

Want to talk about all the bookish things?
I'D LOVE TO HEAR FROM YOU!

EMAIL: info@violetkavery.com

WEBSITE: www.violetkavery.com

INSTAGRAM: www.instagram.com/violetkavery.author

TIKTOK: www.tiktok.com/@violetkavery.auth

FACEBOOK: www.facebook.com/profile.
php?id=61560409499379